W9-BRO-081

Strongholds of the 10/40 Window

*Intercessor's Guide
to the World's Least
Evangelized Nations*

Strongholds
of the
10/40
Window

Edited by

George Otis, Jr.

with Mark Brockman

YWAM
P U B L I S H I N G
A Ministry Of Youth With A Mission
P.O. Box 55787, Seattle, WA 98155

YWAM Publishing is the publishing ministry of Youth With A Mission. Youth With A Mission (YWAM) is an international missionary organization of Christians from many denominations dedicated to presenting Jesus Christ to this generation. To this end, YWAM has focused it's efforts in three main areas: 1) Training and equipping believers for their part in fulfilling the Great Commission (Matthew 28.19). 2) Personal evangelism. 3) Mercy ministry (medical and relief work).

For a free catalog of books and materials write or call:
    YWAM Publishing
    P.O. BOX 55787, SEATTLE, WA 98155
    (206)771-1153 OR (800) 922-2143

George Otis, Jr., Executive Editor
Mark Brockman, Managing Editor
Charlie Sturges, Associate Editor
Michael McCausland, Production Manager

Contributing Writers:

Mark Brockman
Thomas Combrink
Matthew Hand
Brian F. O'Connell
George Otis, Jr.
Charlie and Barb Sturges

STRONGHOLDS OF THE 10/40 WINDOW
Copyright © 1995
The Sentinel Group

Published by YWAM Publishing
a ministry of Youth With A Mission
P.O. Box 55787
Seattle, WA 98155

All rights Reserved. No part of this book may be reproduced in any form without permission in writing from the publisher, except in the case of brief quotations embodied in critical articles or reviews.

ISBN 0-927545-86-1

Printed in the United States of America.

Acknowledgments

The Sentinel Group gratefully acknowledges the contributions of the following individuals to the completion of this book:

Jim Alexander of Mission to Unreached People for his firsthand information on events in Nepal.

Scott Anderson for his willingness to share his wealth of research and firsthand experience in Nepal.

Howard and Jo-Ann Brant of SIM International for checking the reliability of a vast amount of information on countries where SIM works.

Darrell Dorr of Frontiers for providing valuable contacts for information and photographs.

Pastor Bill Ilnisky and the Des Plaines Publishing Trust for their help with field research and product design.

Harold and Joanne Kent, without whose help this book would never be in print.

Peter Lee of Cornerstone Ministries for hard to find information on North Korea.

Dr. Ananda Perera of the International Theological Seminary for his insights on Sri Lanka.

Frank Stookey for freely giving of his knowledge of Saudi Arabia.

Warren Walsh, Tom Bragg and those at Youth With A Mission Publishing who believed in this project.

Cliff Westergren of the Christian and Missionary Alliance for graciously and carefully checking the manuscripts of many Asian countries.

Jim Ziervogel of the Institute of Chinese Studies for his useful comments on China and Taiwan.

A number of other individuals who have made equally valuable contributions, but who wish to remain anonymous due to the sensitive nature of their work.

A Note From
The Sentinel Group

*E*very effort has been made to insure the factual accuracy of this book. Statistical information is presented principally as a means of comparison and should not always be regarded as authoritative. Updated information is most welcome and will be incorporated into the continuing research of The Sentinel Group.

Foreword

While precise statistics are hard to come by, reliable estimates suggest that the ranks of committed global intercessors have grown dramatically in recent years. At least one researcher, Dr. David Barrett, speculates that the number of weekly prayer meetings being held worldwide may now exceed 10 million. And while it is safe to assume that a majority of these are primarily concerned with issues close to home, at least 160 million participants (according to Barrett) have trained their sights on world evangelization.

Along with this numerical growth has come a voracious appetite for information. People don't just want to pray, they want to pray intelligently. They want to ensure that their prayers will have a genuine impact on the spiritual battle raging over specific communities and people groups. To accomplish this, they understand, requires accurate targeting coordinates.

In short, detailed information is valuable to intercessors because it leads to fervency—and it is the fervent prayer of righteous men and women that avails much. Consumed with the details of a case, intercessors are able to sustain their vigil before the Throne of Grace; to shoulder up out of the depths that which they so passionately desire to see.

What is the 10/40 Window?

The following profiles represent a fresh attempt to supply the kind of specificity that intercessors want - and need. Used alongside quality resources like Patrick Johnstone's Operation World, this collection will undoubtedly help to fill in some of the informational gaps that exist relative to spiritually strategic peoples, places, obstacles and trends within the 10/40 Window (the area from 10° to 40° north of the equator, stretching from West Africa to Japan).

In compiling information for this intercessory handbook, we have tried to consider themes and categories that are often overlooked. While some of these inclusions - such as religious festivals and pilgrimages - may seem unusual, their relevance should not be underestimated. It has been widely reported, for example, that spiritual oppression and persecution tend to increase markedly during, and immediately following, religious celebratory rituals. These events may also be viewed as seasons of spiritual negotiation during which contemporary generations reaffirm ancient pacts with the spirit world originally entered into by their ancestors.

Why have we focused our attention on the 10/40 Window? Because from the days of the earliest migrations out of Babel, no other geographic corridor has contained such a profound concentration of spiritual darkness. The ancient roots of Babylon, Egypt and Ephesus have never been fully plucked up, and their legacy continues to do violence to the original design and purposes of God. With its teeming population centers daily attracting the attention of demonic powers, the 10/40 Window represents a crucial focal point for missions minded intercessors.

What are "strongholds"?

It is important as well that we understand the true nature of spiritual strongholds. While it is easy to assume that they are idolatrous sites or perhaps even demons themselves, the truth is they are neither. Rather, spiritual strongholds are the invisible structures of thought and authority that are erected through the combined agency of demonic influence and human will. In this sense they are not demons, but the place from which demons operate.

Although the 10/40 Window is littered with an astonishing diversity of natural and man-made sacred sites, these sites are not strongholds but portals to the Other Side. The stronghold is not the door, but the imaginary edifice to which the door leads. Such sites have been included in this book because they are important points of contact with the spirit world; strategic places where people go expecting to receive spiritual revelation. As such, they are targetable elements in the Enemy's deceptive web.

Finally, it is useful to note that genuine spiritual strongholds are possessed with both a defensive and an offensive character. The practical effect of this fact is that they will simultaneously resist light and export darkness. It is always both - never just one or the other.

The good news is that God's people have begun to take the challenges of the 10/40 Window seriously. Starting with the October 1993 "Praying Through the Window" campaign in which some 20-30 million intercessors committed themselves to a month of focused prayer and fasting, unified prayer efforts for this needy area have grown exponentially. The happy result of this fresh attention has been a steady stream of reports attesting to a wide variety of divine initiatives and evangelistic breakthroughs.

It is our intention at The Sentinel Group to update the information in this prayer guide on a regular basis. This will be accomplished by maintaining at least fifteen separate databases that will be fed by an international network of dedicated watchmen and women, and by field research carried out by our own staff.

Although my own name appears on the cover of this book, it is important to acknowledge the fact that a majority of the profiles were researched and written by others. I want to thank each of them for their outstanding contributions.

George Otis, Jr.

Contents

Afghanistan

During more than a decade of unrelenting war, Afghanistan has become known as "the Lebanon of Central Asia." In December 1979 the Soviet Union invaded the country to prop up its shaky communist regime, and the resulting exodus of refugees to Pakistan fueled a protracted turf war between local warlords, which escalated into a brutal civil war after the Soviets withdrew.

Invasions and tribal wars are a part of the history of this turbulent land, but what is different about the current civil strife is the fact that the warfare now taking place is between guerrilla factions representing different Islamic ideals. Afghans are now killing each other in the name of God, ironically continuing the destruction of the nation they are trying to rebuild.

Landlocked Afghanistan is one of the world's least developed countries, with 80 percent of the population living in rural poverty, partly as a result of geographic isolation. The Hindu Kush mountains form a formidable barrier, making Afghanistan a mountainous fortress situated between Central Asia and the Indian subcontinent. A majority of Afghanistan's people actually live outside the war zone as refugees in neighboring countries, especially Pakistan. Severe wartime isolation, combined with the Soviet's brutal scorched earth policy, as well as sabotage and fierce fighting between the warring factions of the mujahidin (holy warriors), has destroyed most of the nation's already poor infrastructure. The countryside is littered with live land mines, and many people, including numerous children, continue to suffer horrible maiming and death from stepping on these explosive booby traps.

Basic Facts

Location:
West Asia

Neighboring Countries:
Iran, Turkmenistan, Uzbekistan, Tajikistan, Pakistan, China

Population:
23,141,000

Capital City:
Kabul

Major Cities:
Herat, Qandahar, Ghanzi, Charikar, Baghlan

Government:
Chaotic; Islamic republic besieged by opposing internal forces

Leader:
President Burhanuddin Rabbani

Major Religions:
Islam

Historical Background

The history of this portion of Central Asia can best be described as a constant cycle of invasion and conquest by neighboring nations and kingdoms. The Hindu Kush mountain passes of Afghanistan have long been an established trade and invasion route between Central Asia and the fertile plains of India.

During the 19th century, Afghanistan was profoundly influenced by European nations, as British power expanded north from India and Russia moved into Central Asia. The country became the playground for the "great game," an intelligence operation played out between the agents of Britain and Russia.

The final phase of this game resulted in the massive invasion and occupation by Soviet troops in 1979. However, they ran into the brick-wall determination of the fierce mujahidin fighters, as well as Afghanistan's uncompromising terrain. Moscow conceded defeat in 1990 in what turned out to be the USSR's "Vietnam," and pulled back some 150,000 troops, leaving the country in the hands of at least five guerrilla factions, who celebrated their victory by fighting among themselves, thus prolonging the national misery.

Unreached Peoples

Afghanistan's patchwork of cultures is a reflection of its turbulent history. The largest group are the Pushtun, a semi-nomadic people divided between Pakistan and Afghanistan. They live by a severe code of honor embracing the following tenets: hospitality, bravery, chivalry, persistence, self-defense and revenge. This "right to revenge" has led to the ongoing blood feuds between clans and has created an opening for a spirit of violence, which certainly characterizes the country. While almost all Pushtun are Sunni Muslim adherents, they are strongly influenced by folk Islam, a mixture of Islam and animistic practices.

The Tajiks, who live in the northeastern part of the country, supported the Tajik rebellion in Turkmenistan. General Dostam, the Tajik warlord, openly sided with Tajiks in Turkmenistan by supplying them with heavy armaments and troops. The Tajik advances however, were repelled by Soviet troops. Tajiks on both sides of the border have not been reached with the gospel.

Afghan Uzbeks are native Turkish speakers and identify closely with Uzbeks living in Uzbekistan, a republic of the former Soviet Union. They are predominantly Sunni Muslim and are heavily influenced by shamanism.

Spiritual Competition

While the dominant social and political role of Islam comes as no surprise, the influence of pre-Islamic religions in Afghanistan is noteworthy. The nation's complex cultural mix has influenced day-to-day religious practices, with influences from Zoroastrianism (the religion of ancient Persia) and shamanism evident. Despite this strange mixture, significant aid from both Saudi Arabia and Iran has been channeled to the mujahidin, who have embarked on a mission to turn Afghanistan into a strictly Islamic country. There is also a powerful spirit of violence and barbarism present, which has held the nation in its grip for decades, if not centuries.

The country has always been resistant to Christianity. The only church known to have been built in Afghanistan was erected by missionaries in the 1960s, but it was bulldozed to the ground by the government several years later. However, there are now several thousand Afghan believers, despite the fact that the government has prohibited Muslim evangelism for many years. These believers are the fruit of the fervent prayers of God's people, the blood of Afghan martyrs, the sacrifices of early missionaries, and the servant hearts of modern tent-makers.

Noteworthy Trends

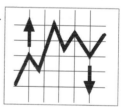

The new government of the Islamic State of Afghanistan is trying unsuccessfully to carve out a lasting peace between its own warring factions. Deep ethnic divisions between north and south, hidden during the Soviet invasion, have once again surfaced. Since both groups are bound by cultural rules concerning tribal fighting, the repetitive cycle of cease-fire, truce and revenge may continue indefinitely. This prompted ex-president Najibullah to remark "What then? Who will rule the cemeteries?"

Kabul, the capital city, has been reduced to rubble by rocket bombardments, and many of the inhabitants were forced to flee to Pakistan. Opposition forces led by radical fundamentalist Gulbudin Hekmattar have fought the government to a stalemate, with little relief in sight. Neither side appears strong enough to win the civil war. A further sinister development has been the increased drug trade by the mujahidin to finance their weapons purchases.

The misery of the Afghan people has been great, leaving some of those who have suffered at the hands of their own "brothers" to doubt the value of Islam. One Afghan told BBC radio bitterly that he wanted to leave Afghanistan and go away, "anywhere where I won't have to hear the sound of the Azan (Muslim call to prayer)."

National Prayer Concerns

Obstacles to Ministry
Pray about these challenging circumstances:
•Damaged Infrastructure
Continued war makes travel/communication difficult
•Islamic Extremism
Forces of Gulbudin Hekmattar want Islamic state
•Evangelization of Muslims Outlawed
Severe repercussions for Afghans that convert
•Few Trained National Leaders
No Bible school programs to prepare disciplers

Spiritual Power Points
Pray over these influential locations:
•Pakistani Border Region
Stronghold of fanatical Hezb-i-Islami sect
•Majid-i-Jami and Gazargah (Herat)
Spectacular mosque and ancient Sufi monastery/tomb
•Mosque of the Sacred Cloak (Kandahar)
Houses a cloak thought to have belonged to Muhammad
•Shrine of Ali (Mazir-i-Sharif)
Also called the Blue Mosque - the country's most sacred Islamic shrine

Festivals and Pilgrimages
Pray during these spiritual events:
•Ramadan & Eid al-Fitr (Varies: '96 = Jan/Feb)
Month of fasting and prayer followed by two day feast
•Navrouz Festival (March)
New Year celebration with pre-Islamic roots
•Ashura (Varies: '96 = May)
Shiite passion play celebrating Hussein's martyrdom
•Mawlid an-Nabi (Varies: '96 = July)
Celebrations honoring Muhammad's birthday

Albania

Albania was the last bastion of Communism in Europe. A Stalinist state ruled by the iron fist of the brutal dictator Enver Hoxha, Albania was so paranoid and xenophobic that it was the only nation in the world to deny international airline flights permission to overfly its airspace. After the other Marxist governments in Eastern Europe fell like dominoes, Albania's leaders tried to hold out, but the writing on the wall was all too clear, and the tyrannical regime finally collapsed in 1991.

Albania is a Balkan country located on the east side of the Adriatic Sea. A very mountainous land, its name is derived from the rugged topography, as Albania can be translated as "sons of eagles." Its location on a major Roman military and trade route called the Via Ignatia made it the center of many battles, and the country has a history of being conquered and re-conquered. It is the only country in Europe where most of the population is Muslim, due to the fact that the Turkish Ottoman Empire ruled Albania for more that 500 years. The apostle Paul first preached the gospel here, but Islam and Communism reduced the church to minority status; Albania is about 18% Christian, mostly Orthodox and Catholic. The country is presently open for gospel work, and Western Christians have entered the country without difficulty. But Albania's transition to a Western style democracy has not been easy. After the downfall of Communism hundreds of thousands of its citizens attempted to flee the country via boat to Italy, but most were forcibly returned. Without question it is the least developed and poorest country in Europe, with a population that suffers from deep psychological and spiritual wounds.

Basic Facts

Location:
Southern Europe

Capital City:
Tiranë

Leader:
Premier Alexander Meksi

Neighboring Countries:
*Greece, Yugoslavia,
Macedonia, Italy*

Major Cities:
Durres, Viore

Major Religions:
*atheism, Islam,
Christianity*

Population:
3,521,000

Government:
Democracy

Historical Background

Albanians are an Indo-European people who settled on the northwest part of the Balkan peninsula around 1000 BC; in antiquity the land was known as Illyricum. At the height of their expansion, the Illyrians extended their borders from the Danube River in central Europe to northern Greece and westward into Italy. It is surprising that despite the powerful nations around it, the country never lost its own cultural identity. The Illyrian language was spoken throughout the area in the centuries after Christ, but by the 7th century most of the surrounding provinces were taken over by the Byzantine Empire and Slavic culture and language became dominant. Albania thus remained as the lone descendant of the ancient Illyrians.

The most notable spiritual event in the history of this land is that most of its citizens were forced to become Muslim after the conquest by the Ottoman Turks in 1500. During this time many Turkish Muslims from the Bektashi sect (a Sufi sect of mystical Islam) were banished to Albania. As a result, even though most people are considered Sunni Muslims, over 200,000 are still Bektashi. Albania became a Communist state after World War II, but remained outside of the Soviet-controlled East Bloc.

Unreached Peoples

Because Albania was a rigid and extremely repressive Communist nation for almost 50 years, most of the population is unevangelized and thus unreached. The nation was almost completely cut off from the rest of the world during this time, making it a place where there has been little spiritual seed sown; in fact, there were few nations on earth more hostile to the Church. Catholic priests were executed for such acts as baptizing a baby in the home of the parents. However, since the fall of the Marxist regime in 1991 many Christian groups and evangelical organizations have begun to send workers to Albania.

In pre-Communist days, Albania had the largest Muslim population in Europe, about 70%. Exactly what that percentage is today may be difficult to determine. Some suggest a figure as low as 20%, while others think the number to be closer to 50 or 55%. The Greek Orthodox and Roman Catholic populations were estimated at 20% and 10% respectively in the pre-Communist era, but now the number is less than 20% combined. At the present time Albania can be considered an atheistic or agnostic state with a predominantly Muslim heritage. Within this Muslim population most loosely identify with their Sunni heritage.

Spiritual Competition

$\mathcal{J}$f the psychological and social situation is any indication of the spiritual state of the nation, it seems obvious that there is a spiritual battle in the nation at this time. Religious freedom has become a major issue, as Muslims from Turkey and the Mideast are mounting an offensive to restore Islam in the shattered country. The Catholic and Orthodox minorities are adverse to foreign Protestants entering the country, although there has been a significant increase of evangelical ministries despite this adversity.

Like other Eastern European countries, Albania is spiritually hungry, but the big question is who will be feeding them and what will they be eating. As in many of the destitute nations of the former East Bloc, hopes revolve around the powerful seduction of Western materialism rather than the search for spiritual truth. There is an ever-present danger that the desperate Albanians will confuse the Western Christian community with the materialist ideals that they yearn to attain. The spiritual battle in Albania is not only against the enticements of counterfeit religions and materialism, but against general confusion and desperation, as the Church seeks to reach them with the gospel.

Noteworthy Trends

$\mathcal{J}$n 1992 a newly elected government took control in Albania. Although their grip on power has been tentative, they have managed to stop much of the rioting that bordered on outright anarchy the previous year, but the country remains dangerous and unstable. Albania is still the most underdeveloped country in Europe, although its excellent location, good climate, and wealth of natural resources, coupled with the newfound freedoms of its citizens, should speed its development. An influx of foreign investment is needed to draw Albania into the global network of trade and social exchange.

The Church in Albania was freed from decades of brutal persecution after the Communist regime fell from power, and the Christian community is steadily growing. It will be instructive to watch the impact that the renewed church will have on its Muslim neighbors, and to what extent these Muslims are willing to consider a Christian alternative. In this respect, Albania may provide an interesting and strategic case study, for the country's Muslim majority is nominal and searching, and much more open to the claims of Christ than other Islamic populations around the world. Moreover, it is imperative that Christians act immediately, since foreign Muslim operatives are already hard at work to make Islam dominant in this needy land.

National Prayer Concerns

Obstacles to Ministry

Pray about these challenging circumstances:

•Possible Curbs on Religious Freedom
New constitution may discriminate against Christianity
•Severe Poverty and Unemployment
Poor economic conditions are breeding crime
•Lack of Albanian Christian Literature
Few foreign workers are fluent in the Albanian language
•Islamic Revival
Many Albanians are returning to their Islamic roots

Spiritual Power Points

Pray over these influential locations:

•Mosque of Ethem Bey (Tirane)
Most significant Islamic center in the country
•Bektashi Tekke (Kruje)
Ancient worship center of Islamic mystic sect
•Mirahorit Mosque (Korce)
Oldest mosque in Albania; revived pilgrimage site
•City of Gjirokaster
Ancient religious city; birthplace of the former dictator Enver Hoxha

Festivals and Pilgrimages

Pray during these spiritual events:

•Ramadan & Eid al-Fitr (Varies: '96 = Jan/Feb)
Month of fasting and prayer followed by two day feast
•Islamic New Year Celebrations (Varies: '96 = May)
Commemorates hegira
•Gjirokaster Festival (Every Five Years in July)
Promotes traditional Albanian folk culture
•Pilgrimage to Mirahorit Mosque (All Year)
Revived pilgrimage especially during Islamic celebrations

Algeria

Algeria, an ancient land that was once home to St. Augustine, the most influential of the early church fathers, is now close to civil war. The second largest country in Africa, it is dominated by mountains and deserts, with 90% of the population living on the narrow but fertile coastal plain. The country has moved from a shaky peace to bloody civil hostility as the result of virtual warfare between the military government and various Islamic fundamentalist political parties. More than 3,000 people have lost their lives in the last three years, as a result of bombings and executions by the Islamic militants, and brutal reprisals by the military. Military and police personnel have borne the brunt of the attacks, but lately the fundamentalist groups have also begun to target intellectuals and foreigners.

Following Algeria's successful war of independence against France in 1962, the country became a model for revolutionary movements around the world, including the Palestine Liberation Organization. Natural bounties of oil and gas have enabled Algeria to develop economically and to export its own peculiar brand of Islamic socialism.

After the initial oil boom of the 70s, Algeria has had to deal with a growing foreign debt and numerous failed economic experiments. This has resulted in an unemployment crisis for the nation's young, who comprise more than 50% of the population. These masses have eagerly listened to the voice of the radical Islamic movements calling for the overthrow of the government. Thus the government which was recently praised as an anti-Western and anti colonial model by the Arab world has now become a symbol of corruption and repression.

Basic Facts

Location:
North Africa

Capital City:
Algiers

Leader:
President Limine Zeroual

Neighboring Countries:
Morocco, Mauritania, Mali, Niger, Libya, Tunisia

Major Cities:
Wahran, Qacentina

Major Religions:
Islam

Population:
29,306,000

Government:
Military

Historical Background

Like many Islamic lands around the Mediterranean, Algeria had a strong Christian presence in the first seven centuries after Christ. However, the church grew weaker and weaker in North Africa and the Middle East, and was not prepared for the onslaught of Muhammad's armies, which easily suppressed Christianity.

When Islam began to spread out from the Arabian Peninsula in the 7th century, it first expanded eastward and then west to North Africa. The native Berber population effectively resisted the Ummayad Arab invaders for 15 years before they were brought into the Islamic fold. The Kabyle and other Berber groups of the Atlas mountains still speak their own language and are resistant to the government's program of Arabization.

From the early 1600s, Algeria and many other Mediterranean nations saw an extended period of Turkish domination under the Ottoman Empire, which shaped some of its institutions. By the late 1800's France occupied Algeria, and the capital, Algiers, was the administrative center of France's North African holdings. Algeria only won its freedom from France in 1962 after a long, protracted and often brutal war that cost the lives of an estimated 250,000 Algerians and French national settlers.

Unreached Peoples

The majority of Algerians are descended from a mixture of the native Berbers and Arabs. However, there are four and one-half million Algerians who still consider themselves to be pure Berbers. The Berbers have adopted the form of Islam but tend not to be bound by its legal essence and are therefore more open; there are now a substantial number of Berber believers in the Kabyle tribe.

The Mzabis are a group of 80,000 located deep in the Sahara desert in the region of a dry river bed called the Wadi Mzab. They are known for their industrious and disciplined lives, meticulously watering their elaborate network of palm groves and gardens by hand. The Mzabis fled to the Sahara because of persecution and consequently now consider themselves distinct from both Arabs and other Berbers. There are no known believers among these isolated people.

Algeria's Ahaggar Mountain Tauregs are relatives of the nomadic Tauregs found in Niger, Sudan, Chad and Mali. They are recognized by their distinctive headgear - the men are veiled, while the women are not, contrary to Islamic custom. The Taureg are also distinct because of their loose relationship with Islam and the fact that women have a prominent role in their society. Evangelistic work has been difficult with these nomadic people, but there are a handful of Taureg believers in Chad and Mali. There are 76,000 Tauregs in Algeria and possibly 900,000 in all of North Africa.

Spiritual Competition

Shock waves spread across North Africa when the fundamentalist Islamic Salvation Front (FIS) emerged victorious in Algeria's first round of free multi-party elections in 1991. The government canceled the second round, a move that enraged the FIS and set off the current violent confrontation. Experts predict that the surging Islamic movement will be unstoppable. The fundamentalists are inspired and supported by Iran, and also receive financial aid from Saudi Arabia. The formation of the FIS is unique since it is a Sunni Muslim movement with Shiite backing. Many view this alignment as proof of the Khomeini revolution's power to cross the traditional divide between Sunni and Shiite Muslims, and Iran is widely admired throughout Algeria.

A North African expert has remarked that the Islamic political groups do not usually have clear economic or political goals. Leaders often respond to probing questions by answering "Islam Al-Hal," a vague slogan meaning "Islam is the solution." Grinding poverty and government oppression and corruption have fueled the fundamentalist movement throughout the Mideast. Algeria's situation holds many parallels to Tunisia, Morocco, Egypt and Jordan, whose governments are also sitting on Islamic fundamentalist powder kegs, though none of those groups are as large or powerful as Algeria's radicals. Many fear that a civil war in Algeria and the increase of Islamic fundamentalist uprisings will be the pattern for many Muslim countries with secular governments.

Noteworthy Trends

Amnesty International reports that since the imposition of martial law in 1991, more than 9,000 activists have been held in detention camps, and torture has become routine. Hundreds of police and army officers have also been killed, and random acts of violence continue unabated. Some of the violence appears to be aimed at making Algerians toe the radical Islamic line. A case in point was the murder of two teenage girls who were killed for not wearing veils. Algeria's future looks bleak indeed, with many predicting all-out civil war in the near future.

Tough government counter-measures have only hardened attitudes, giving fundamentalists more desire to overthrow the regime. If the FIS succeeds, they are likely to establish an Islamic state under Shariah law. This would be a major blow to the emerging church in Algeria, which already suffers severe restraints. Many Christian workers see 1993 as the year when the window of opportunity began to close. However, there may be an increased potential to reach Algerians with the gospel in other countries, especially France, which has a large Algerian population. The inevitable turmoil caused by the current strife and possible civil war will result in further opportunities to work with refugees, and the church should begin to prepare for this new opportunity.

National Prayer Concerns

Obstacles to Ministry

Pray about these challenging circumstances:

• Growing Islamic Fundamentalism
Fundamentalist strength checked only by martial law
• Lingering Resentment of Colonial Past
Many carry bitter memories of French "Christian" rule
• Inadequate Church Facilities
No official churches; only small home fellowships
• Prohibition of Christian Missionaries
Little outside help and few mature national leaders

Spiritual Power Points

Pray over these influential locations:

• Tassili-n-Ajjer (Central Sahara)
Eerie site of ancient animist tribal paintings
• Sidi Abderrahman Mosque (Algiers)
Oldest mosque in country; important pilgrimage site
• Tomb of Qba Ibn Nafaa
Algeria's oldest Muslim shrine
• City of Ghardaia
Desert sanctuary of fundamentalist Ibadite sect

Festivals and Pilgrimages

Pray during these spiritual events:

• Tamanrasset (December/January)
Islamic folklore festival
• Ramadan & Eid al-Fitr (Varies: '96 = Jan/Feb)
Month of fasting and prayer followed by two day feast
• Eid al-Adha (Varies: '96 = April)
Feast of Sacrifice; coincides with culmination of Hadj
• Pilgrimage to Sidi Bou Mediene (All Year)
Visits to Tlemcen's most famous Islamic shrine

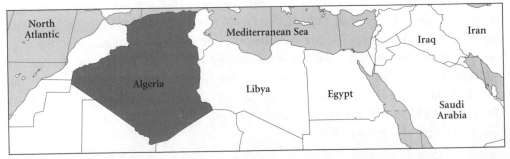

Azerbaijan

Azerbaijan and its Turkish-speaking people derive their name from the words azer, meaning "fire," and beijan, meaning "guardian." The appellation is a perpetual reminder of the days when sacred oil fires blazed on the Aspheron Peninsula, a petroleum-rich protrusion on the western shore of the Caspian Sea.

By the 1920's, the Azerbaijanis were the most advanced Turkic people of the so-called Northern Tier. Within a short time their country became the world's largest oil producer—and a shining source of pride. Unfortunately, seventy years of Soviet rule also brought nightmarish pollution and economic mismanagement. Now free of Soviet rule, the Azerbaijanis are hoping to restore their former glory by forging economic and spiritual links with ethnic cousins scattered throughout Central Asia.

Although Azerbaijan is a small country, few areas of the world can match its geographical variety. From low lying semi-desert plains along the Caspian Sea coast, the terrain ascends steadily to over 14,500 feet. In the north, the Greater Caucasus Mountains divide the country from neighboring Georgia; in the south, the Talysh mountain range provides a thick curtain between Azerbaijan and Iran. In the center of the country the Araks and Kura Rivers water fruitful orchards along with rich tea and cotton plantations.

As for Azerbaijan's broiling conflict with Christian Armenia, perhaps Illona Turanszky put it best: "Here in Transcaucasia's high mountain region, Christianity and Islam met; the hat and the fez, the low-cut dress and the veiled face. They met, but never mingled."

Basic Facts

Location:
*Central Asia
(Transcaucasia)*

Neighboring Countries:
*Iran, Armenia, Georgia,
Russia, Turkmenistan*
Population:
7,642,000

Capital City:
Baku

Major Cities:
*Kirovabad, Sumgait,
Kuba, Mingechaur*

Government:
Republic

Leader:
President Geidar Aliev

Major Religions:
Islam, atheism, animism

Historical Background

With a recorded history dating back to the days of Noah, the Caucasus region, not surprisingly, hosts a remarkable collection of memories and cultures. The earliest inhabitants of the southeastern plains and valleys that comprise Azerbaijan were a nomadic branch of Indo-Iranian peoples. Impressed by the smokeless flames that burned perpetually on the surface of local hillsides (actually natural gas fields), pagan temples were erected to honor the gods of this sacred landscape. Soon Persian Zoroastrianism mingled with the pagan rites of fire worship.

Azerbaijan's introduction to Islam came in the 8th century when Arab invaders galloped into the area with their fine horses and gleaming scimitars. If the Arab's religion took root, however, their language and culture did not. These would instead come as the legacy of Oguz Turkish tribes who swept in from Central Asia in 1090. In the early 1500's Shiite Islam was birthed under the Azerbaijani Safavids, becoming the primary religion not only of Azerbaijan but of neighboring Iran as well. After being razed by the scorched-earth Mongols in the 13th century, the area became the object of a power rivalry between Persia, Russia and Turkey – a condition that persists to this day.

Unreached Peoples

The Azerbaijanis, representing more than 80% of the republic's population, are by far the largest unreached group confronting mission workers. The vast majority are Muslims, with about two-thirds of these adhering to Shiism. As of mid 1993, only about 50 Azerbaijani Christians were known to exist inside the country. There are no Azerbaijani churches.

While the largely urbanized Azerbaijanis have lost many of the tribal distinctions that were once characteristic of their culture, the estimated 20,000 Talysh people who live in the mountains along the Iranian border have not. Speaking their own distinctive language, the rural Talysh are reputed to be the most fervently religious people in Azerbaijan. They are almost entirely unreached.

Among Azerbaijan's other significant non-Slavic minorities, only the Lezgin and Armenians have been Christianized. The rest, including the Avars, Kurds and Tatars, are almost entirely made up of unreached Muslims. Unfortunately, the Scriptures have yet to be translated into several of the country's minority languages. Other challenges include inhospitable terrain, suspicion of foreigners, and the ongoing military conflict with neighboring Armenia.

Spiritual Competition

$\mathcal{A}$ major concern for Christian workers and intercessors has to be the strength of Islam in Azerbaijan. Even under the most severe Soviet restrictions there were over 1,000 clandestine prayer houses. Today, with these restrictions removed and Christianity associated with the Orthodoxy of arch-rival Armenia, Islam has prospered even further.

The Shiite regime in Iran has worked especially hard to encourage fundamentalist thinking and practice in Azerbaijan. From 1986 to 1987 alone, Iran invested a total of nearly $10 million to produce special religious audio and videotapes for use inside Azerbaijan. Radio broadcasts have been stepped up as well – and the tactic seems to be working. In early 1990, for example, Azerbaijani Muslims gathered along the Iranian border to voice their support for the Khomeini Revolution. The Azerbaijani Shiites have resumed intense celebrations during Ashura to honor the virtues of martyrdom.

Folk Islam is also strong in Azerbaijan, a fact underscored by the more than 300 active pilgrimage sites in the country. The popularity of these pilgrimage sites along with the fervent celebration of the pre-Islamic Newroz feast is indicative of the continuing vitality of pre-Islamic spiritual forces.

Noteworthy Trends

$\mathcal{W}$hile Azerbaijan emerged from the breakup of the Soviet Union with several advantages – including strong cultural ties with Turkey, religious and familial ties to Iran, and substantial natural resources – there have been serious problems as well. Not the least of these are political instability, economic stagnation, and the need to clean up severe pollution created by Soviet era quota-driven development. In order to deal with these and other problems, Azerbaijan has increasingly turned to foreign experts.

This "help wanted" atmosphere has presented abundant opportunities for tentmaker missionaries; and while few Christians have yet ventured forth to take advantage of them, other forces – including Mormons, Muslims and materialists – have not been so slow to respond.

Another serious concern is the dislocation that has been caused by the nation's war with Armenia. Besides producing thousands of refugees, and blocking gospel access to certain areas of the country, there is also the potential for this conflict to escalate out of control. Already the Turkish government has massed troops on its border with Armenia after the latter proposed annexing the Azerbaijani enclave of Nakhichevan.

National Prayer Concerns

Obstacles to Ministry

Pray about these challenging circumstances:

•Shortage of Tentmaker Missionaries
Few skilled Christians have applied for positions in area
•War with Armenia
Continuing conflict has cost lives and retarded travel
•Christian Emigration
Many Slavic and Armenian Christians have left the country
•Growing Islamic Extremism
Iranian-influenced groups are calling for Sharia law

Spiritual Power Points

Pray over these influential locations:

•Adjarbek Mosque (Baku)
Important Shiite worship center
•Mazar of Hayy-Imam (Kirovabad)
Shiite holy shrine and pilgrimage site
•Atechghiakh Fire Temple (Sourakhany District)
Animist fire worship-ritual site in temple courtyard
•Muslim Board for the Transcaucasia (Baku)
Regional center for Islamic planning, study and outreach

Festivals and Pilgrimages

Pray during these spiritual events:

•Ramadan & Eid al-Fitr (Varies: '96 = Jan/Feb)
Month of fasting and prayer followed by two day feast
•Ashura (Varies: '96 = May)
Shiite passion play celebrating Hussein's martyrdom
•Pilgrimage to Zarrabi Madrasah (All Year)
Revered and recently restored 17th century monument
•Pilgrimage to the Tomb of Khizir Zindeh (All Year)
Saint associated with the search for the spring of eternal life

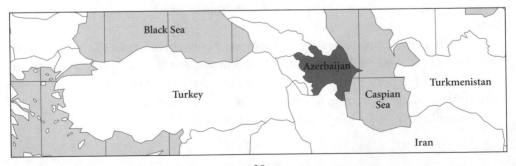

28

Bahrain

*O*n most world maps, the nation of Bahrain is represented by little more than a dot. Yet, in spite of its size – some would say because of it – this tiny, sun-soaked archipelago in the Persian Gulf has one of highest population densities in the Middle East. And while it is easy to wonder why so many people would be attracted to a small island beset by scant rainfall and blazing summer temperatures, Bahrain's natural springs have made it a place of fertile refuge for at least three millennia.

Educated Bahrainis like to compare their country to the southeast Asian nation of Singapore. The association is fitting not only in geographic terms, but also in the sense that both nations have striven to transform themselves into service centers of international renown. In the case of Bahrain, this strategy has been driven largely by the knowledge that its declining oil reserves are due to run out completely by the end of this decade.

Given its position between two of the world's most orthodox Islamic states (Saudi Arabia and Iran), it may be that Bahrain's most remarkable characteristic is its relative socio-political freedom. The fact that alcohol is sold openly, and that women can work, dress and conduct themselves in a manner forbidden in neighboring countries has made the island a magnet. In fact, a causeway connecting Bahrain to the Arabian mainland routinely channels thousands of pleasure-seeking Saudis onto Bahrain's liberal soil. Fortunately, this freedom is also manifest on the spiritual plane as is evidenced by an emerging national church and several high-profile Christian institutions.

Basic Facts

Location:
Middle East (Persian Gulf)

Neighboring Countries:
Saudi Arabia, Qatar, Iran

Population:
601,000

Capital City:
Al Manama

Major Cities:
Isa Town, Al Muharraq, Sitra

Government:
Emirate (Monarchy)

Leader:
Emir Isa bin Sulman al-Khalifa

Major Religions:
Islam

Historical Background

The first inhabitants of Bahrain were part of the ancient—and almost fabled—Dilmun civilization. While the precise origin of these peoples remains obscured in the mists of history, there is some evidence that they entered the region from the direction of South Asia. What is clear is the fact that ancient pagan ritual sites have been found on the island that include stocks and basins for animal sacrifice.

While Bahrain has been Arab and Muslim since the Islamic conquest of the 7th century, it was in the 10th century that the island saw the founding of an unusual Islamic socialist society. The architects of this community were the Qarmations—members of a splinter Islamic sect related to the Fatimid Shiites of North Africa. Controversial from the beginning (their detractors falsely accused them of sharing spouses in common), the Qarmations found Bahrain to be a safe haven in which they could develop their radical society.

In 1783, a family of puritanical Sunni Arabs from central Arabia—the Khalifas—sailed into Bahrain and took control of the island. After years of war, piracy and slavery, Bahrain became a British protectorate in the mid 1800's. During this period, Bahrain became the first nation in the Gulf to discover oil.

Unreached Peoples

Today, nearly 70% of Bahrain's indigenous population base is comprised of Shiite Muslims. Often identified with the poorest social classes, the Shiite community represents by far the most sizable evangelistic challenge in the nation. Although many Shiites maintain households in Manama and al-Muharraq town, they also comprise the bulk of Bahrain's rural populace. Although some are said to resent the ruling Khalifa clan, the Emir himself is well liked, and has fed the perception of accessibility by taking occasional walks on the beach with his subjects. Sunni Muslims, who represent just over 20% of the nation's Islamic population, tend to be better represented in ruling political and commercial circles. Most are urbanites.

This leaves the foreign community. In addition to Saudis, Lebanese, Egyptians and Palestinians (the ranks of the latter were thinned out following the Gulf War), the country also maintains a fairly sizable non-Arab population (about 25-28%). The vast majority of these are guest workers from Iran, Pakistan and India. While most are Muslim, about half of the Indian workers profess Hinduism. Among the Korean, African and Filipino communities, on the other hand, there are a significant number of Christian believers who meet regularly for fellowship and Bible study.

Spiritual Competition

While folk superstitions persist in Bahrain—and may be seen in such practices as the wearing of amulets and ritual bathing in sacred springs (there are several on the island)—the main competition facing the gospel comes in a more orthodox package. Though socio-political strictures are comparatively relaxed in Bahrain, Islam is still the dominant force in both the government and society at large. In addition to zealous Wahhabite influences from neighboring Saudi Arabia, there are also regular overtures from Shiite Iran.

The Iranians have long considered Bahrain to be a natural extension of their Persian domain. In fact, even after Bahrain's declaration of independence in 1971, the Iranian parliament continued to maintain a desk for "the Province of Bahrain." The affinity is not simply political; there are strong religious links between the two nations. Today, Bahrain is the only Gulf state where the Shiite festival of Ashura is widely celebrated.

Shiite religious life on this small island nation still revolves around local communes known as ma'atam; and familial and communal loyalty is a powerful deterrent to change. The general sense in Bahrain today is that personal freedom exists in proportion to one's personal discretion.

Noteworthy Trends

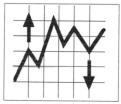

The recent Gulf War led the ruling Khalifa family to tighten its relationship with the United States. It even dropped long standing objections to the establishment of a permanent U.S. base in the region, opening the door for the relocation of the U.S. Central Command from Florida to Bahrain. At the same time, however, the pragmatic Khalifas have also been urging a speedy rehabilitation of Iraq and the immediate establishment of normalized relations. This betrays their fear of Iranian influence in the Gulf. A strong Iraq is seen as an important counterweight to the newly aggressive Iran.

Bahrain is only beginning to grapple with the consequences of losing its oil reserves. For the first time in modern history, young Bahrainis must face the future without the certainty of getting a job that they really like. So far the country's industrial diversification program has shored up the economy in the face of not only declining oil reserves but also big setbacks in the banking service sector.

While discreet Christian worship and witness have been tolerated in Bahrain for some time, the number of indigenous believers has remained static. If the national church is to grow, evangelistic boldness is a must.

National Prayer Concerns

Obstacles to Ministry

Pray about these challenging circumstances:

•Lack of Indigenous Christian Leadership
Very few trained and motivated Bahraini leaders exist
•Cultural Pressures
Family ostracism is a major block for Muslim converts
•Lack of Privacy
Life on this small island is lived in a fishbowl
•Prevalence of Materialism
Many citizens are concerned only with the good life

Spiritual Power Points

Pray over these influential locations:

•Beit al-Quran (Manama)
Regional center for Islamic study and outreach
•Ain Adhari (Virgin's Pool)
Sacred spring believed to have healing powers
•Barbar & Diraz (Al Budayyi Area)
Ancient ritual sacrifice and temple complex
•Al Fateh Islamic Center (West Manama)
Religious complex including largest mosque in country

Festivals and Pilgrimages

Pray during these spiritual events:

•Ramadan & Eid al-Fitr (Varies: '96 = Jan/Feb)
Month of fasting and prayer followed by two day feast
•Ashura (Varies: '96 = May)
Shiite passion play celebrating Hussein's martyrdom
•Pilgrimage to Tomb of Nabih Saleh (All Year)
Veneration of Islamic saint buried on island
•Ain Adhari Pilgrimages (All Year)
Practice of folk Muslims seeking healing and blessing

Bangladesh

A weary traveler once remarked that "Bangladesh is not a nice place to visit, and I certainly wouldn't want to live there." Perhaps his tired cynicism is a bit harsh, for the country has a rich culture as well as some beautiful tropical beaches and rustic scenery. However, Bangladesh is poverty-stricken, overpopulated and under-employed, and is frequently devastated by annual visitations of floods, cyclones and typhoons of epic proportions; in 1970 a single storm claimed 300,000 lives. The story of Bangladesh has been one of extremes: of turmoil and peace, prosperity and destitution, mirroring the natural cycles of tropical calms, floods and cyclones. It has thrived under the refinements of an ancient culture and suffered under the ravages of particularly brutal civil war.

Located at the mouth of the Ganges River on the Bay of Bengal and stretching north almost to the foothills of the Himalayas, this region of the Indian subcontinent is the land gateway to Burma and the Far East. This position has assured its place in the cultural, political and religious conflicts of the subcontinent through the centuries.

Bangladesh has a booming population of 132 million people, most of whom are Muslim, and about 50 percent are under the age of 16. These teeming shores make Bangladesh the second most densely populated nation in the world after Singapore, which is a small city-state. The country is predominantly rural, with only 13 percent living in urban areas, and most of the people live in the low-lying delta region. With an annual per capita income of $150, Bangladesh is also one of the world's poorest countries, with most people involved in subsistence agriculture.

Basic Facts

Location:
South Asia

Neighboring Countries:
India, Nepal,
Myanmar (Burma)

Population:
132,219,000

Capital City:
Dhaka

Major Cities:
Chittagong, Khulna

Government:
Parliamentary Democracy

Leader:
Prime Minister
Khaleda Zia

Major Religions:
Islam, Hinduism

Historical Background

Throughout its tumultuous history Bangladesh, or Bengal, has known civil strife, suffered invasion upon invasion and witnessed the rise and fall of mighty empires. It has benefited from the trade and culture brought from foreign lands and been subject to the introduction of new religions. The earliest history of Bengal is relatively obscure, but in the 3rd century the region was part of the Buddhist Mauryan Empire. By the 8th century AD Buddhism was in decline and Hinduism was experiencing a resurgence. Both Buddhists and Hindus were overcome by the flood of Muslim invaders, and Islam has remained the dominant culture through the years. The British East India company represented Britain in Bengal and India before the British annexed the entire subcontinent in the 19th century.

Modern Bangladesh is twice born - once as East Pakistan in 1947 during the partition from British India and again in the savage war of independence from Pakistan in 1971. The country was taken over by Pakistan, and for nine months the Pakistani army committed atrocities against Bangladesh, possibly killing a million people, but eventually they were forced to surrender to intervening forces from India. On December 16, 1971 Bangladesh was born as the world's 139th nation.

Unreached Peoples

The ethnic makeup of Bangladesh is surprisingly homogeneous, with native Bengalis comprising over 97 percent of the population. Bengali is the official language and is a unifying factor between the Hindus and Muslims. The language has a rich literary tradition of poetry and song. Rabindranath Tagore, who won the Nobel Prize for literature is the most well known Bengali writer in the West.

The remaining three percent of Bangladesh's population is comprised of over 30 tribal groups of which the Chamka, Mogh and Santal are the largest. These tribes are typically concentrated in the wooded Chittagong Hill Tracts, and in the region near Cox's Bazaar along the Myanmar border. There have been substantial numbers of conversions among eight of the smaller tribes, some of whom are now well over 50% Christian.

Other significant minorities are the Bihari of north India, who are non-Bengali Urdu-speaking Muslims who fled to Bangladesh in 1947. These stateless people live in large refugee camps on the border with India and are seeking to emigrate to Pakistan. Another refugee group are the 200,000 Rohingya Muslims who fled government persecution in Myanmar in 1978 and 1992.

Spiritual Competition

Bangladesh was a secular state until 1988, when the government declared Islam the state religion. This decree has had the result of further increasing the tension between Muslims and the followers of other religions. Islam has not always dominated the culture of Bangladesh, and was preceded by Buddhism and Hinduism, which still have many adherents in the country. About 85 percent of the population is Muslim, making Bangladesh the second-largest Islamic country in the world after Indonesia.

The content and the social structure of Islam has been strongly influenced by Hinduism. In the rural areas the practice of Islam has increasingly become a mixture of Islam and Hinduism, although Hindus have come under pressure from Muslim militants, and reciprocal agitation by Hindu nationalists in India have also caused some concerns for Muslims in Bangladesh. Proselytizing is permitted under the constitution but Christian missionaries are closely regulated. In some areas thousands of both Hindus and Muslims have come to Christ, and the growth of the church is heartening, but the sheer numbers of people still to be reached makes Bangladesh a daunting mission field. Relief and development affords an open door for Christian missions to work in the country.

Noteworthy Trends

Born in turmoil, war and poverty and subject to the ravages of natural disaster, Bangladesh is bravely struggling to keep up with its neighbor India. Corruption and political instability as well as assassinations and 18 coups have marred the years since Bangladesh was freed from the oppressive hand of Pakistan. A nine year military dictatorship ended in 1991 with the restoration of democracy and the election of a government led by a woman, the prime minister Khaleda Zia. Militant Islam is starting to rear its head in Bangladesh, and an incident in 1994 attracted international attention when a prominent woman writer made disparaging comments about the prophet Muhammad, and was forced to flee the country to save her life.

The cruelty of Pakistan's repression of another Muslim nation in the 1971 war temporarily weakened Bangladeshi loyalty to Islam, and resulted in opportunities for the gospel. The harvest in Bangladesh has been good in comparison to other Muslim countries, and Bangladeshi converts are not afraid to share their newfound joy with their extended families. However, this is still an Islamic society, and prayer is needed for the protection of these converts as they face ostracism and hostility.

National Prayer Concerns

Obstacles to Ministry
Pray about these challenging circumstances:
•Tendency toward Christo-Islamic Syncretism
Brought on by faulty contextualized approaches to evangelism
•Inadequate Leadership Training Programs
Christian training materials have been late in coming
•Severe Poverty
Christian workers face great misery with few resources
•Lack of Christian Boldness
Church leaders are easily intimidated by the government

Spiritual Power Points
Pray over these influential locations:
•Temple of Wrath (Natore)
Dedicated to Radha, consort of Krishna
•Mausoleum of Ghiazzuddin Azam Shah (Sonargaon)
Major Islamic pilgrimage site
•Somapuri Vihara (Pahaur)
Largest Buddhist monastery south of the Himalayas
•City of Bagerhat
360 mosques are dedicated here to Khan Jahan Ali

Festivals and Pilgrimages
Pray during these spiritual events:
•Ramadan & Eid al-Fitr (Varies: '96 = Jan/Feb)
Month of fasting and prayer followed by two day feast
•Durga Puga (October)
Birthday of Durga, wife of Hindu god Shiva
•Mawlid an-Nabi(October)
Celebrations honoring Muhammad's birthday
•Jagannath Festival
Celebrations honoring Hindu god Jagannath in Dhamrai

Benin

A small wedge-shaped country on the Bight of West Africa, Benin is the original source of the dark voodoo religion. This blood-soaked land has a history replete with slavery and human sacrifice, and it is difficult to think of any single nation that has had so strong a negative spiritual impact as small Benin. A long time exporter of spirit worship, idolatrous fetishism and voodoo, Benin is a country languishing in primitive and fearful spiritual bondage; lives held captive to the elemental spirits of the air are everywhere in evidence in this poverty-stricken nation. Animism and ancestor worship so define the culture that even Catholics, who comprise the largest Christian group, will often rush out of mass to perform their sacrifices at family altars.

This steamy tropical country is classified as one of the least developed nations in the world by the International Monetary Fund and the World Bank. Over 80 percent of the population is involved in subsistence agriculture on very poor soil. After independence from France in 1960, Benin became a political puppet show of almost comic proportions. In a nine year span the country experienced four successful military coups, nine changes of government and five different constitutions. The land is divided into three distinct geographical regions: the coastal belt with sandy beaches and lush lagoons, a clay soil belt in the center of the country, and the Atakora mountains which rise up from the rain forests on the northwestern border.

Basic Facts

Location:
West Africa

Neighboring Countries:
Togo, Burkina Faso,
Niger, Nigeria

Population:
5,573,000

Capital City:
Porto-Novo

Major Cities:
Cotonou, Parakou, Abomey

Government:
Democracy

Leader:
President Nicephone Soglo

Major Religions:
African traditional
religions, Christianity,
Islam

Historical Background

The most important time in the history of Benin is the period identified with the Kingdom of Dahomey, which flourished from 1600-1900 and was founded by King Guezo, using an army of trained women. This was the beginning of the bloodthirsty and dominant Dahomey Empire, which was built on the principles of the divine worship of the ancestral spirits of the king and ruthless expansionism. These conquests of neighboring lands provided the king with slaves to sell and human sacrifices for the veneration of the ancestors and other daily rituals requiring sacrifices. The Kings wielded total control over their subjects, and an old Dahomian saying illustrates this: "My head belongs to the king, not to myself; if he pleases to send for it, I am ready to resign it."

After the nine years of instability following independence from France, Dahomey was ruled for the next 17 years by Mathhieu Kerekou, who came to power in a military coup. Kerekou established disastrous Marxist policies, to the extent that the nation became known as "the Cuba of West Africa." Economic and moral decay coupled with total bankruptcy forced Kerekou to throw Marxist ideals out the window and allow multi-party elections, which he lost to a former dissident.

Unreached Peoples

Benin's population of 5.6 million is a mosaic of 52 distinct ethnic tribes. These 52 groups are dominated by four principal tribes, the Fon, Yoruba, Bariba and the Adja. There is considerable cultural diversity among the various ethnic groups comprising Benin's population. The Fula farmers of the north are Muslim relatives of the Fulani traders who dominate the northern areas of Nigeria and Burkina Faso.

The Fon or Dahomey are the people group that have had the strongest influence upon the nation. The Fon, who are the descendants of the Dahomey Empire, are proud of their heritage and are known as the most devoted fetish worshipers in West Africa. Each Fon homestead has an "asen house" where iron altars or "asen" are housed, as a point of contact and communication with their ancestors. The Fon believe that the ancestors actually take up residence on these altars and there can be consulted about family matters. While a majority of the Fon are dominated by the worship of ancestors and fetishes, there has been some movement toward the Christian faith among these people. Pray for the establishment and continued boldness of Fon believers as they face persecution and occult activity directed at them by the fetish priests of their own tribe.

Spiritual Competition

The leading spiritual force in Benin today is the indigenous religion of voodoo. The spirit of voodoo was spread from Benin via the slave trade to Haiti where it has virtually claimed the nation, and to Brazil where it is known as Santeria and Umbanda. Benin is regarded by many to be the least evangelized non-Muslim country south of the Sahara. The spiritual state of the nation and its closed attitude to the gospel are the direct result of the impact of voodoo, fetishism, and spirit worship and the effects of past human sacrifices by the kings of the Dahomian Empire.

The role of human sacrifice in the history of Benin cannot be underestimated. Ancient Dahomian Kings would sacrifice prisoners of war, slaves and criminals to their ancestors. The royal throne of King Guezo was mounted upon the skulls of four enemy kings so that he could flaunt his dominion over them. In Abomey, the royal capital, the asen house where the spirits of the royal ancestors are venerated has eight inch thick walls built out of clay which is mixed with human blood instead of water.

Noteworthy Trends

Benin, which is now taking faltering steps towards democracy, has many hurdles to face. The economy is a shambles, and civil servants and teachers are often not paid for months at a time. Human rights abuses which were widespread in the Kerekou era have subsided, but the press is not totally free. Another area of concern for the nation is the political instability of its neighbors; coups in Nigeria and Togo have lead to a mass of refugees seeking asylum in this already crowded land.

The country is trying to make itself attractive to tourists. The port of Ouidah, the slave trading center of the 17th century, has actually billed itself as the "cradle of voodoo" and is the site of the International Vodun Festival. Like many struggling African states, Benin stands at a crossroads in its history, with half of the population below the age of 15. Much prayer is needed for those who believe, and that God would continue to prosper his church in this small but spiritually significant nation. Pray that instead of the being known as the "cradle of voodoo" Benin may soon be known as a source of light.

National Prayer Concerns

Obstacles to Ministry
Pray about these challenging circumstances:
•Prevalence of Witchcraft and Voodoo
Country is a haven for sorcerers and snake worshipers
•Disheveled Economic System
Years of Marxist incompetence has impoverished the land
•Syncretistic Tendencies in Church
Animistic practices still evident in some churches
•Deep Ethnic Divisions
Tensions between northern and southern tribes for cultural and political reasons

Spiritual Power Points
Pray over these influential locations:
•Abomey Region
Location of fetish temples, voodoo activities
•Muslim Towns
Parakou, Kandi, Malanville, Djougou, Porto Novo
•City of Ouidah
Major hub for voodoo and snake cults
•Grande Marche de Dantokpa
Market for fetishes and religious paraphernalia

Festivals and Pilgrimages
Pray during these spiritual events:
•Ramadan & Eid al-Fitr (Varies: '96 = Jan/Feb)
Month of fasting and prayer followed by two day feast
•Tabaski/Eid al-Kabir (Varies: '96 = April)
Islamic sacrificial feast; most important in West Africa
•Festival at Ondo's Shrine
Celebrations of the animist Yoruba people
•Voodoo Ceremonies (Yearly)
5-day events involve dancing and sacrifices to god Ia

Bhutan

Situated high in the Himalayan Mountains of Asia, the tiny kingdom of Bhutan represents one of the world's most remote and spiritually darkened lands. About the same size as Denmark, the secluded country unfolds over sloping terrain which descends from sacred glacier-laden peaks to leech-infested jungles along its southern perimeter with India's Assam Province. Thimpu, the nation's exotic capital perched at an altitude of 8,400 feet (2550 meters), claims a stable population of only 15,000. The majority of Bhutan's 700,000 or so citizens (plus an additional 800,000 non citizens) prefer to live in the country's fertile central valleys. Frequent, violent thunderstorms give the country its magical nickname: "Land of the Thunder Dragon."

In reality the kingdom of Bhutan is a 20th century monarchy caught in a medieval time warp. 85% of the population is rural based, only a few valleys have electricity, and the government still rules from a fortress. There is also but one plane in the national airline. Cloistered in its mountain sanctuary, Bhutan has marched to the beat of its own drummer for centuries. Forbidden to all foreigners until 1974, the country is still not thrilled with the idea of strangers trekking through its winding valleys and streets (the latter were finally paved in 1968). In 1990, ostensibly to shield his culture from outside influences, Bhutan's King Jigme Wangchuk initiated tougher restrictions on tourist visas to further assure the kingdom's isolation.

Sandwiched between two giant neighbors, China and India, and rendered inaccessible by the razor peaks of the Himalayas, Bhutan could easily be the Land that Time (but not God) Forgot.

Basic Facts

Location:
South Central Asia

Neighboring Countries:
India, China
(Tibetan Autonomous Region)

Population:
671,000

Capital City:
Thimpu

Major Cities:
Paro, Bumthang, Puntsholing, Tashigang

Government:
Constitutional Monarchy

Leader:
King Jigme Singye Wangchuk

Major Religions:
Tibetan (Lamaistic) Buddhism, Bonism, Hinduism

Historical Background

Bhutan's spiritual umbilical cord is attached, both historically and theologically, to Tibet. In 747 AD, according to ancient Bhutanese scripture, a Tibetan religious leader rode into Bhutan on a flying tiger and defeated the demon spirits that were obstructing the spread of Buddhism. While the flying tiger may have been somewhat suspect, the man, at least, was real. As the original architect of Bhutan's Buddhist world view, Padmasambhava, or the Guru Rimpoche, has become almost as highly esteemed as the Buddha himself.

Before the advent of Buddhism, the dominant religious force in Bhutan was an esoteric form of spirit worship known as Bon. Rather than replacing Bon, however, Buddhism readily absorbed its magic rituals. Even today the idea of malevolent and protective deities is widespread. Dhomtsham, the protective deity over the capital of Thimpu, was reportedly consecrated by a Tibetan monk named Nima in the 11th century. In 1616, another Tibetan lama, Ngawang Namgyal, united the country around the Kagyupa sect of Tibetan Buddhism which is now the national religion. The current hereditary monarchy began in 1907, partly as an offshoot of a British expedition which passed through Bhutan enroute to Lhasa. Serfdom was not officially abolished until 1956.

Unreached Peoples

The Drukpa, who are the majority people of Bhutan, are composed of two main groups, the Nyalongs and the Sharchops. The Nyalongs in the West are descendants of the Tibetans and speak Dzongkha, while the Sharchops in the East are the original inhabitants of the land and speak Sharchopkha. The Drukpas dominate the government and are devoted followers of Tibetan Buddhism. Their whitewashed masonry and solid wooden homes are typically accessible only to those who are willing to walk along steep, rocky trails. Very few Drukpa have ever heard the gospel; fewer still have become Christians.

The superstitious and semi-nomadic Brokpas represent another challenge. Living in the isolated Sakteng Valley on the nation's eastern border, they are as apt to consult village shamans and exorcists as they are Buddhist clergy. Other isolated minorities include the Gakhis and Makheps.

In fact, the only people whom the gospel has touched in any notable fashion are the Nepalese living in the southern lowlands. Even here, however, the need is enormous. Discriminated against by the government, most have retained their Hindu beliefs.

Spiritual Competition

Lamaistic Buddhism is the state religion, and all government workers must take an oath which affirms their allegiance to "One Nation, One King, One Religion." Public worship, evangelism and proselytization by any other faith is illegal. The Je Khenpo, a national religious leader considered to be equal in rank with the king, maintains a headquarters in the same facility as the national political administration.

In addition to its repudiation of a personal God, Tibetan Buddhism is steeped in animism and the occult. Demons—and not just imaginary ones—have become as familiar to the religion's practitioners as cliff-hugging monasteries, prayer flags and prayer wheels. Every night throughout the kingdom hundreds of Buddhists practice a ritual known as the Mystic Banquet. In this gruesome rite, demons are invited to feed on their bodies which have been dismembered through intense visualization techniques. Some are lost in the process to a condition known as "religious madness."

Astrology also plays an important role in the lives of many Bhutanese, and government subsidized astrologers operate in virtually every village in the country. A five year course is offered at the Astrological Institute for aspiring seers.

Noteworthy Trends

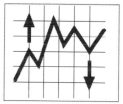

Despite the fact that Bhutan is one of the least developed nations in the world – infant mortality is very high and literacy is only about 30%—Christians tentmakers involved in medical, agricultural and educational projects are rapidly being phased out. In addition, a number of small hospitals run by missionaries have been nationalized. From the government's perspective, the situation is clear: Christianity is a Western institution that represents a potential threat to the country's Buddhist establishment.

Another disturbing trend has been the recent large-scale deportations of ethnic Nepalis who could not prove they were in the country prior to 1959. The deportations, which began in 1989, have meant that many of Bhutan's Nepali Christians—the largest group of believers in the country—have become refugees in Nepal. Already this backdoor ethnic cleansing has led to some unfortunate bloodshed. And while there are at least several hundred believers of Nepali descent still in the country, most of them live in the southern frontier area from which they are forbidden to move.

The good news is that new intercessory prayer efforts and evangelistic radio programs are beginning to target Bhutan.

National Prayer Concerns

Obstacles to Ministry

Pray about these challenging circumstances:

•Overt Curbs on Religious Freedom
It is currently illegal to preach the gospel or convert to Christianity
•Lack of Christian Literature
Very little is available in the official Dzongkha language
•Official Xenophobia
The result is severely limited tourism and a phase-out of existing Christian tentmakers
•Demonic Influences
Demonic bondage is powerful and widespread; government subsidized astrologers operate in every town

Spiritual Power Points

Pray over these influential locations:

•Chang Ganka Monastery (Thimpu)
Consecration site of Thimpu's ruling deity
•Tiger's Nest (Paro Area)
High, cliff-hugging Buddhist meditation center
•Burning Lake (Bumthang)
Meditation site associated with 15th century saint
•Tashichho Dzong (Thimpu)
Spiritual and political center; seat of Je Khenpo (nation's top lama)

Festivals and Pilgrimages

Pray during these spiritual events:

•Birthday of Guru Rinpoche (June/July)
Celebration of Buddhist patron saint Padmasambhava
•Thimpu Tsechu (October)
One of many regional Tibetan Buddhist mask dances
•Buddha's Descent From Heaven (October/November)
Time for virtuous deeds and temple worship
•Pilgrimages to Meditation Sites (All Year)
Key sites include Mt. Chomolhari & Taktsang complex

Brunei

Brunei is one of the world's newest and smallest countries, but it is also one of the richest. Fattened by large offshore oil and gas reserves, the country has the second-highest per capita income in the world. Little Brunei Darussalam ("Abode of Peace") is also a tightly controlled Muslim nation; the present sultan, whose theocratic rule is absolute, is the 29th in his line.

Brunei is a spot of land made up of two coast-and-jungle enclaves on the north coast of Borneo. Once inhabited by head-hunting tribes, today's modern cities give little evidence of the primitive past.

Despite its size (about the same area as Delaware), state construction is done on a grand scale. The airport is suitable for a country perhaps ten times the size of Brunei. Public buildings are ostentatious in proportion, and the sultan's recently constructed palace is already in the Guinness Book of Records for its nearly 1,800 rooms. Perhaps this is to be expected, for the Sultan is the world's wealthiest man.

Apart from the capital and a few other coastal towns, Brunei is mainly a sparsely populated rain forest. The country has a large expatriate community which is dominated by American and European "orang puteh" (white men), who run the oil business. Because of the high standard of living and exotic climate, Brunei is often considered a desirable post in a tropical paradise.

The British held Brunei along with the Malay Peninsula for over 100 years, and only granted the colony its independence in 1984. It is said that Brunei remained British as long as it did simply because it enjoyed the comforts and amenities of the crown, and saw little advantage in becoming independent.

Basic Facts

Location:
Southeast Asia

Neighboring Countries:
Malaysia, Indonesia

Population:
301,000

Capital City:
Bandar Seri Begawan

Major Cities:
Seria, Kuala Belait

Government:
Independent Sultanate

Leader:
Sultan Hadji Hassanal Bolkiah Mu'izzaddin Waddaulah

Major Religions:
Islam, Chinese religions, Christianity

Historical Background

Although it is a newly independent oil-rich nation, Brunei is not really among the nouveau riche; in fact it is not such a new country at all. When Magellan's ships visited Brunei in 1521, they found the Muslim sultan's court to be the most impressive among all those they encountered on their journey. Brunei was then still at the zenith of its power, ruling Borneo and much of the Philippines with an economy based on commerce, and with trading partners ranging from the Middle East to India to the coast of China.

Hinduism appears to have influenced early Brunei, as the legend of the origin of Brunei's royal line closely parallels Hindu mythology. Because of this similarity, Brunei's sultans have been and to some extent still are perceived as possessing magical powers. Because the scribes of the royal court used bark paper which did not stand the test of time in a humid tropical climate, it is not clear exactly when Islam was introduced to Brunei, but by the 16th century Islam was firmly entrenched as the royal religion. The nation's modern history has been similar to that of other Muslim petro-kingdoms - a rapid rise from colonial obscurity to a level of wealth and technology that would have been unthinkable a few short generations ago.

Unreached Peoples

The Brunei Malays, who comprise about 65% of the population, are staunchly Muslim. They have ruled Brunei for most of its known history, and maintain a discreet but effective force of security police. No evangelism is permitted among Muslims and there are no known believers who have come from this community. However, they are doing quite well at propagating their own faith, as there is a steady stream of converts to Islam from among the tribal and immigrant communities. Islam is the state religion and great pride is taken by those who have made the pilgrimage to Mecca.

The Chinese account for about 20% of the population and are involved in trade and business. The majority of these are permanent residents, and most are stateless. It is nearly impossible for the Chinese to obtain citizenship and they are thereby excluded from certain privileges such as free medical care. The government allows local Christians to evangelize non-Muslims and thus far the most significant response has been among the Chinese. However, as is typical elsewhere, Brunei's Chinese are often caught up with material concerns which keeps them preoccupied and makes them somewhat resistant to the gospel.

Spiritual Competition

$\mathcal{A}$s mentioned, Islam is the official religion and the sultan is the guardian of the faith. The Omar Ali Saifuddin mosque is the tallest building in the capital and the spiritual vortex of Islam in Brunei. Some travelers consider it one of the most impressive buildings in all of Asia. Freedom of worship is guaranteed for followers of other religions, but in practice this freedom is limited and closely monitored. The Ministry of Religious Affairs is an arm of state security, and makes arrests for religious offenses, censors the media and disseminates information on Islam, among other activities. It is not uncommon for Muslims who drink in public or unmarried couples who get too close to each other on a park bench to be arrested. Even foreigners working in Brunei feel the presence of the religious police and some have been deported for various infractions.

While Islam is the religion of most of the indigenous people in the country, it is heavily intertwined with animistic beliefs and appeasement of the spirit world, as well as placation of "other beings" who are neither human nor animal, but nonetheless real to Brunei Malays. This traditional belief system is a carry-over from the time when many of the tribal peoples were head hunters. A crude commemorative shrine near Kuala Bulai exhibits a wooden display case full of skulls which was left by these people.

Noteworthy Trends

$\mathcal{T}$he sultan has become increasingly devout, emphasizing the importance of the Malay Muslim monarchy, a gesture designed to insure his continued rule as absolute and uncontested spiritual and temporal sovereign. In the process, Islamic conservatives have gained the upper hand in government, and their influence has been growing. This has been worrisome to many, especially the Chinese, who have been steadily leaving the country.

Anything viewed as a threat to Islam or critical of the government is quickly suppressed. In 1962 the current Sultan's father experimented with democracy under British oversight, only to declare an awkward state of emergency when the election did not turn out in his favor. Although the state of emergency has never been canceled, observers both inside and outside Brunei consider the current regime to be relatively benevolent.

The expatriate oil workers and businessmen are allowed freedom of worship, and St. Andrew's Anglican Church in the capital dates back many years to British rule. However, any attempt to evangelize Brunei Malays will result in trouble if not expulsion. Moreover, most of the population is quite content with their smugly comfortable Muslim lifestyle, which accounts for the almost total disinterest in Christianity. Much prayer and a creative, tactful approach is needed to form a spiritual bridge from the foreign Christians to the native Muslims.

National Prayer Concerns

Obstacles to Ministry
Pray about these challenging circumstances:
•Legal Prohibitions on Evangelizing Muslims
Proselytizing Muslims can result in jail or deportation
•Lack of Christian Boldness
Many believers have adopted laissez fare attitudes
•Prevalence of Materialism
Many citizens are concerned only with the good life
•Printing Restrictions
All printing in Brunei is regulated by the government

Spiritual Power Points
Pray over these influential locations:
•Omar Ali Saifuddin Mosque (Bandar Seri Begawan)
Nation's dominant Islamic center
•Royal Ceremonial Hall (Lapau)
Site where traditional and religious events are held
•Kampung Ayer
Ancient and sacred cluster of 28 water villages
•Tomb of Sultan Bolkiah (Bandar Seri Begawan)
Mausoleum of former revered leader of Brunei

Festivals and Pilgrimages
Pray during these spiritual events:
•Ramadan & Hari Raya Puasa (Varies: '96 = Jan/Feb)
Month of fasting and prayer followed by two day feast
•Chinese New Year (January/February)
Includes special rituals with "kitchen god" idols
•Isra Dan Mi Raj (Varies: '96 = April)
Special events celebrating Muhammad's Ascension
•Mawlid an-Nabi (Varies: '96 = July)
Celebrations honoring Muhammad's birthday

Burkina Faso

The name Burkina Faso means "Land of Incorruptible Men." However, given the overwhelming presence of bizarre spiritism, demonized rituals and occult secret societies, this would appear to be somewhat of a misnomer, to say the least. Situated in the heart of West Africa, landlocked Burkina Faso is so dominated by idolatry that it successfully resisted the onslaught of Islam in the 17th century, and is one of the few nations in Africa where native animism is still the major religion. As a result, traditional religion and superstition influence every facet of life.

Burkina Faso is dominated in the north by the semi-arid Sahel (Arabic for "shore of the desert"), where herding animals is the traditional livelihood. The central grassland with its red termite mounds is the most heavily populated region of the country. The humid south, crisscrossed by the three Volta rivers (Red, Black and White), is almost uninhabited despite fertile soils, because of the constant presence of disease, especially river blindness and deadly sleeping sickness.

The Burkinabe, as the people of Burkina Faso call themselves, cling tenaciously to a difficult existence in a very inhospitable environment. Drought and famine are frequent visitors to this poverty-stricken land; a third of the nation's livestock was lost in the drought of the 1970s. Because of this, it is not surprising that animism permeates the lives of the Burkinabe, who turn to the spirits to strike a bargain for existence in the hostile land.

Basic Facts

Location:
West Africa

Neighboring Countries:
Mali, Niger, Benin,
Togo, Ghana, Côte d'Ivoire
Population:
10,382,000

Capital City:
Ouagadougou

Major Cities:
Bobo-Dioulasso,
Koudougou, Ouahigouya,
Banfora

Government:
Military

Leader:
President
Captain Blaise Compore

Major Religions:
African traditional
religions, Islam,
Christianity

Historical Background

The origins of the Burkinabe are lost in time, but Arab historians say that the ancestry of the West African peoples is linked to Kush, the grandson of Noah, who migrated with many people from the Nile toward the setting of the sun. The earliest known inhabitants of the region were the Bobo, Lobi, and Gurunsi, all tribes practicing forms of animism in which spirits and ancestors are worshipped.

Burkina Faso was influenced by neighboring African empires who ruled over the region from about 300 AD. The Mossi, who ruled in the 15th century, were able to repel invasions by neighboring Muslim tribes, the Songhai and Fulani, thereby keeping the area under the influence of animism.

Political turmoil has dominated the nation since independence from France in 1960. In 1983, Captain Sankara deposed the government in a coup and established a populist revolutionary government, whose rallying cry was "two meals and clean water." While extremely popular with the people, Sankara antagonized the landlords of Burkina Faso and was himself deposed.

Unreached Peoples

The prevalent animistic practices dominate the lives and rituals of the major tribes, the Bobo and the Mossi. Nowhere is this more apparent than in the creation of larger-than-life-size masks of birds and animals. The Bobo believe that the spirits of their ancestors find peace in animal bodies, and each mask is said to house one or more spirits or powers. Although a significant Christian movement is taking place among the Bobo, the vast majority are still trapped in the darkness of the spirit world.

The 175,000 member Lobi tribe keep ancestor figures on the clan altars, relating to these figures as if they were real people, even making sacrifices of chickens and goats to them in order to solicit their help. Miniature ancestor figures are used as charms or amulets and kept close at hand. Most of the Lobi are unevangelized and can see no exit from the unrelenting cycle of spirit bondage.

Spiritual Competition

Nearly 75 percent of the Burkinabe are animistic, stubbornly clinging to the ways of their forefathers. The dark secrets of animism, often accompanied by overt demonization, are a formidable obstacle to the gospel. Although about five percent of the people consider themselves Protestant, and a further 14 percent claim to be Roman Catholic, syncretism, resulting from failure to break with the old ways, plagues the church.

While Islam was not able to dominate Burkina Faso in the middle ages, its influence has increased dramatically since 1900. Approximately 48 percent of the population now claim to be Muslim, although most of these are really animists. Strong political ties with Libya have strengthened the Islamic influence in the north. A majority of the Burkinabe practice folk Islam, with its use of charms, amulets and veneration of saints.

The type of shamanistic bondage to spirits found in Burkina Faso is very powerful, but it is also very crude. Moreover, the great weakness of spiritistic animism is that it binds people out of psycho-spiritual fear, and fear is a condition that the gospel directly addresses. Presented with a clear vision of the power of the cross over these elemental spirits, many animists will gladly embrace Jesus.

Noteworthy Trends

The disastrous Sahel droughts of the 1970s provided an opening for Christian aid and relief organizations to work in the country. The government is favorably disposed toward Christian relief efforts in this needy land. Due to the dire economic circumstances in the country, over 1 million Burkinabe have migrated to other lands in search of work. The emigration of active men from the community has caused severe problems, such as family breakdown, economic stagnation and social upheaval.

Political instability is also the norm in Burkina Faso, with six coups since independence in 1960. The 1983 coup brought in a left wing revolutionary regime which had the enthusiastic support of urban young people. By 1987 the revolution had failed to bring about change, and its leader, President Sankara, was assassinated by his closest associate, Captain Blaise Compore. The assassination of Sankara and Compore's rise to power has left the country in a serious malaise. The youth are now frustrated and disillusioned, with poor prospects for employment and advancement. Pray that this disillusionment may help to create an atmosphere of openness to the light of Christ, which is desperately needed in this land of abiding spiritual darkness.

National Prayer Concerns

Obstacles to Ministry

Pray about these challenging circumstances:

•Prevalence of Occult Practices

As elsewhere in West Africa, animism is widespread

•Political Confusion

A serious malaise has set in; government seems to lack direction

•Growing Muslim Population

As their numbers increase Muslims are becoming active

•Economic Fragmentation

This is coupled with massive internal migration

Spiritual Power Points

Pray over these influential locations:

•Crocodile Lake (Ouagadougou)

Sacred site where homage is paid to the crocodile

•Ouagadougou Mosque

Primary mosque in capital city

•Sacred Fish Pond (Dafra)

At this site fish are venerated

•Gaoua Town

Spiritual center of the traditionalist Lobi people

Festivals and Pilgrimages

Pray during these spiritual events:

•Fete des Masques

Festival with dancing and children being violently whipped

•Dodo Masqurade (March)

Mossi male-only tribal celebration with ritual dancing

•Tabaski/Eid al-Kabir (Varies: '96 = April)

Islamic sacrificial feast; most important in West Africa

•Dyoro Initiation (Every Seven Years)

Lobi animist initiation rites teaching taboos, etc. to boys

Cambodia

The ruins of the mysterious temple grounds of Angkor Wat, a sprawling architectural jewel in the midst of the steamy jungle, as well as a quaint and somewhat exotic tropical Asian culture once made Cambodia a charming tourist destination. However, it is now best known as the home of the "killing fields," where over two million Cambodians were brutally murdered by the fanatical Khmer Rouge government of Pol Pot during a four year period from 1975 to 1979.

The forced evacuation of all cities and towns to concentration camps, the savage killing of former military and civilian leaders as well as those who were wealthy or educated, has left the country in a degraded, primitive state, with one of the poorest economies in the world. The task of rebuilding following the Khmer Rouge holocaust and the Vietnamese occupation (1979-1989) demonstrates how easy it is to destroy a nation and how difficult it can be to restore it, a lesson that the world is learning over and over again in the twentieth century.

A quarter century of war and genocide has left a horrible mark on this once placid country. Many who have survived the horror of Pol Pot's camps have permanent emotional scars, and the nation is still in psycho-spiritual bondage to the spirits of demonic violence that have rent the nation asunder. Since the occupying Vietnamese pulled out of Cambodia in 1989, there have been intermittent skirmishes by rival groups, including the murderous Khmer Rouge, who could conceivably take over the country again. During the 1993 UN-supervised elections the royal line was reestablished when Prince Norodom Sihanouk's party won, but corruption and violence marked the electoral run-up, and the nation could disintegrate into chaos and civil war once again.

Basic Facts

Location:
Southeast Asia

Capital City:
Phnom Penh

Leader:
King Norodom Sihanouk

Neighboring Countries:
Thailand, Laos, Vietnam

Major Cities:
Battambang, Siemreap

Major Religions:
Buddhism, animism

Population:
9,205,000

Government:
Socialist Parliamentary Democracy

Historical Background

$\mathcal{E}$arly in the ninth century AD at Phnom Kulen, King Jayavarman II performed the first devaraja ceremony in the region, thus establishing his rule over the Khmer people. This was to become the Kingdom of Angkor and later the country of Cambodia. During the elaborate ceremony, presided over by a Brahman priest, divine status was bestowed on the king by Shiva, the Hindu god of creation and destruction. So began the royal patronage of Shiva which continued through the reenactment of the ceremony by each successive ruler until Prince Norodom Sihanouk was ousted in 1970.

According to Hindu legend, Shiva is the ultimate agent of chaos, who, at the end of each eon, dances gleefully as the universe is destroyed. Allegiance to this deadly god has proven costly for Cambodia. Until French colonial rule in 1863, Thailand and Vietnam took turns invading Cambodia. The Japanese occupied the country during World War II, followed by prolonged civil strife and involvement in the Vietnam War, finally culminating in the reign of terror of the Khmer Rouge, which resulted in some of the worst carnage in history. As one Western writer observed, "Like Shiva on a rampage, the Khmer Rouge seemed to prefer destruction and chaos..."

Unreached Peoples

$\mathcal{T}$he Cambodian people, known as the Khmer, make up about 85% of the population, and are still largely unreached even though growing churches are being planted among them. Centuries of allegiance to Hinduism, followed by Buddhism and interwoven with strong animistic beliefs, have kept the Khmer blinded to the truth. Little impact was made by the Roman Catholics who began work in 1660 or by the Protestants, who started in 1923. However, about 1970 a spiritual awakening began. Although the seeds of this awakening were brutally snuffed out by the Khmer Rouge in 1975, they sprang to life among Cambodian refugees in various nations.

The minority Cham Muslims can be divided into two groups: the traditionalists and the orthodox. The traditionalists, while acknowledging Allah as the all-powerful god, also recognize other non-Islamic deities. They rely heavily on magic and sorcery, show little interest in pilgrimage to Mecca and the daily prayers, but do celebrate many Muslim festivals and rituals. The orthodox Cham send pilgrims to Mecca, and generally practice a "purer" form of Islam. Only a few Christians are reported among the Cham.

Spiritual Competition

After the decline of Hinduism and the abandonment of Angkor Wat in the 15th century, Buddhism has been the dominant religion of Cambodia. The Khmer, who are the majority people, practice a form of Buddhism which is heavily animistic. They believe in a host of spirit beings which sometimes need to be placated through a medium or shaman. Under the Khmer Rouge, 90% of the monks were killed, but there has been a Buddhist revival in recent years, as the country has tried to regain some sense of national pride and cohesion.

Buddhism (and Hinduism before it), has been an integral part of the inauguration rituals of each succeeding ruler of Cambodia since the ninth century. Due to a history of encroachment by foreign powers, anything foreign has usually been viewed as a threat, including Christianity. While the number of Christians has grown steadily in recent years, Cambodian identity is still wrapped up in its Buddhist heritage and Christians are viewed as second-class citizens. It is still too soon to know the long-term attitude of the government, but it is encouraging that Christianity has again been legalized.

Noteworthy Trends

The ravages of war, the devastation of the Khmer Rouge and general social disruption have helped bring about an openness to the gospel, which actually began shortly after Prince Sihanouk was deposed in 1970. His ouster marked the end of a chain of national leaders who had enacted the devaraja ceremony, perhaps breaking the bondage to Shiva and opening the way for a move of the Holy Spirit. In the refugee camps of Thailand, large numbers of despairing Cambodians turned to Christ. Many Christians have returned to the country to share their faith, and there are now 5-6,000 believers meeting in over 100 church groups all over the country. These numbers were unheard of prior to 1970, when there were only 600 Christians in the entire country.

An incident in November 1994 may indicate some trouble ahead for the church. A foreign evangelist and his team were forced to flee Phnom Penh and cut short a five day crusade after angry crowds gathered and denounced the evangelist because expected miraculous healings had not occurred. Following this incident there were a number of negative news articles about Christianity. Prayer is needed for the young church to overcome such misunderstandings, as well as for increased sensitivity on the part of Western missionaries who may not fully understand the culture.

National Prayer Concerns

Obstacles to Ministry
Pray about these challenging circumstances:
• Khmer Rouge Agitation
Genocidal group seeking return to power through force
• Lack of Trained National Leaders
Exacerbated by shortage of Christian resource materials
• Hostility of Buddhist Establishment
Many Buddhist leaders would like Christianity banned
• Travel Dangers
Many areas of the country are still mined and patrolled

Spiritual Power Points
Pray over these influential locations:
• Phnom Kulen
Site of ancient pyramidal temples and initiation of national pact with Shiva
• Angkor Temples (Tonle Sap)
World renowned 72 temple complex
• Wat Phnom (Phnom Penh)
Primary Buddhist temple in the capital city
• Dangrek Mountains
Stronghold of the murderous Khmer Rouge

Festivals and Pilgrimages
Pray during these spiritual events:
• Magha Puja Festival (February)
Similar to All Saints Day celebration
• Visakha Festival (May/June)
Celebrates birth, enlightenment and death of Buddha
• Wan Atthami (June)
Celebration commemorating Buddha's cremation
• Kathina Ceremonies (October/November)
Monastic retreat season

Chad

Chad is a relatively barren, landlocked and isolated country in north-central Africa. Like so many other African countries, this poor nation has been smitten by the modern plagues of civil war and famine. Providence appears to have turned its back on this land, as Lake Chad, which is the world's 11th largest lake, is drying up, and the country suffers from periodic plagues of locusts. Famine caused by the great Sahelian droughts, and suffering intensified by civil war since the early '70s have taken their toll in this historical crossroads of northern Africa.

Chad is a nation divided along geographic, climactic and ethnic lines. The mountainous desert north is home to Arab Muslim desert dwellers. The arid central plains and the fertile lowlands of the extreme south are home to the predominantly animist and Christian Bantu. These crosscurrents of the north and south, resulting in a clash of Muslim, animist and Christian cultures, have left a deep scar and many hostilities among the people of this land.

Possibly the worst wound in Chad comes from slave raids carried out by Muslim kingdoms in the north on the peoples of the south. So devastating were these raids that a French observer in the 19th century estimated that for each slave in the market, ten had been killed. The resulting hatred that exists between the north and the south was summed up by an Udeme man, who remembered the slave raids: "The Wandala (slavers) are clever. They bought our iron, then used it to make the shackles that they held us with..." It is no wonder that French colonizers were welcomed as liberators by the southerners in 1910.

Basic Facts

Location:
North-Central Africa

Neighboring Countries:
Libya, Niger, Nigeria, Cameroon, Central African Republic, Sudan

Population:
6,447,000

Capital City:
N'Djamena

Major Cities:
Moundo, Abéché, Sarh

Government:
Republic

Leader:
Colonel Idriss Deby

Major Religions:
Islam, African traditional religions, Christianity

Historical Background

$\mathcal{C}$had has a very rich and ancient history. The first records of human habitation go back 2,000 years, when the Sao people migrated from Egypt. Settling on the shores of Lake Chad, their villages later became brick walled cities, and the area then became the intersection for two caravan routes trading in minerals and slaves, which brought new cultures and influences into Chad.

The French forced the villagers to grow cotton as a cash crop by introducing a head tax which had to be paid in cash. Forcing the south to produce crops for artificially lowered prices backfired, and soon the southerners began to hate their French "liberators" with as much passion as the northerners.

The post-independence history of Chad is tumultuous and tragic, as the country has been ravaged by civil war for 25 years. Successive regimes were propped up by French and U.S. aid as warlords fought across the devastated country. Manpower was so short in the civil war of the '80s that eleven and twelve year-olds were conscripted for the warlords' armies. Deep feelings of hatred were exacerbated when ex-president Habre ordered the gratuitous murder of 300 political prisoners the day before he fled the capital of N'Djamena.

Unreached Peoples

$\mathcal{G}$eographic variation, as well as ethnic and linguistic diversity and religious differences have presented serious obstacles to nation-building in Chad. With three of Africa's four major language groups represented within its borders, Chad's people do not share broad cultural characteristics, as do the Bantu peoples of eastern and southern Africa.

The people of Chad speak more than 100 different languages and divide themselves into many ethnic groups. Chad's languages fall into ten major divisions, each of which belongs to either the Nilo-Saharan, Afro-Asiatic, or Congo-Kordofanian language families. Among the Nilo-Saharan speakers of the north, the Teda form one of the largest groups. About one-third of the Teda are nomadic, while the remainder are semi-nomadic, moving from pasture to pasture during eight months and returning to permanent villages during the rains. Arabic predominates among the Afro-Asiatic languages and there are about thirty different dialects of Arabic in Chad. The Awlad Sulayman tribe originally moved to Chad from Libya in the nineteenth century; most of these Arabs are herders or farmers. The Fulani are representative of the Congo-Kordofanian languages but are not as numerous in Chad as they are in other west and central African countries. Many Fulani are fervent Muslims and often serve as teachers of the Koran.

Spiritual Competition

The separation of religion from society in Chad represents a false dichotomy, for they are perceived as two sides of the same coin. Three religious traditions exist in Chad—traditional African religions (animism), Islam and Christianity. Both Chadian Islam and Christianity retain some aspects of pre-Christian animism.

Traditional animistic religion is practiced by approximately 35 percent of Chadians, many of whom are nominally Christian or Muslim. Animists in Chad regard the world as a complex system of relationships among people, living and dead, interacting with animals, plants, and natural and supernatural phenomena. Ancestors play an important role in the traditional religions, where they are thought to span the gap between the supernatural and natural worlds. Among the more centralized tribal societies of Chad, the chieftains are frequently associated with divine power.

To appease traditionalists, ex-president Tobalbaye forced southern males to participate in the harsh physical and psychological yondo initiation rites, making them compulsory for any non-Muslim seeking admission to the civil service, government, or higher ranks of the military. In the early '70s hundreds of Christians were martyred for refusing to partake in rites that were anti-Christian.

Noteworthy Trends

Ethnic disputes have continued to hamper the government of Chad, even though President Idriss Deby has established a council that includes ministers from different tribes. According to Amnesty International, "Traditional ethnic conflict, intensified by colonial intervention, has resulted in the emergence of warlords who have capitalized on regional divisions and traditional conflict." The current wave of ethnic slaughter, with over 800 civilians killed in a ten month span, comes hard on the heels of Habre's eight-year dictatorship, which claimed more than 40,000 lives. Once again Chad is faced with the miseries of drought and famine with the shadow of potential civil war looming over the troubled land.

The rise of Islamic fundamentalism has also affected Chad, supported by Libya, Kuwait and Saudi Arabia. The church, which enjoyed rapid growth in the '60s and '70s, experienced severe repression at the hands of southerners and growth slowed in the '80s due to nominalism, lack of teaching and legalism, which sapped the inner life of the church while war, famine and poverty hampered evangelistic outreach. There is an increased interest to evangelize the Muslims in the north, and prayer is needed for revival in the church so that it will reach out to its Muslim and animist neighbors.

National Prayer Concerns

Obstacles to Ministry
Pray about these challenging circumstances:
• Political Instability
Frequent civil war since independence in 1960
• Muslim Opposition
Strongest in the north
• Syncretism in Churches
Old animistic beliefs continue among many Christians
• Lack of Trained Christian Leadership
War has hindered much training

Spiritual Power Points
Pray over these influential locations:
• Grand Mosque (N'Djamena)
Center of Islamic activity in the capital
• Sarh (Southern Chad)
Sara people brutally interned here during construction of Congo railroad
• Abéché
Islamic center in eastern Chad
• Fada
Oasis town in northern Chad with ancient grottos and cave paintings

Festivals and Pilgrimages
Pray during these spiritual events:
• Ramadan & Eid al-Fitr (Varies, '96 = Jan/Feb)
Month of fasting and prayer followed by two day feast
• Tabaski (Eid al-Kabir) (Varies, '96 = April)
Islamic sacrificial feast; most important in West Africa
• Mawlid an-Nabi (Varies, '96 = July)
Celebrations honoring Muhammad's birthday
• Eid al-Adha (Varies, '96 = April)
Feast of Sacrifice; coincides with culmination of Hadj

China (PRC)

The mere mention of the name "China" conjures up many images: the Great Wall, a sophisticated ancient civilization, marvelous art, Confucius, pampered emperors, silk, tea and savory food. Of course, there is also a darker side—Mao's purges, the Long March, the Cultural Revolution and Tiananmen Square. Whatever comes to mind has probably existed—at some time, in some way, somewhere within the borders of the enigmatic People's Republic of China, the world's most populous country.

The teeming cities of Shanghai, Guangzhou (Canton) and Beijing stand in stark contrast to the vast grasslands of Inner Mongolia and the barren deserts of Qinghai and Xinjiang provinces. Brilliant scholars, award-winning scientists, Olympic gold medalists, simple peasants, common workers and party functionaries all combine to make up the fantastic mosaic of China. Dominated by the ethnic Han majority, there are 55 officially recognized minorities making up China's 1.2 billion people.

If human history continues well into the 21st century, China may become the world's dominant nation. The Chinese are by nature hard and determined workers, and their long and difficult history has taught them to be long-suffering and ingenious. Fueled by unlimited manpower, a newfound zeal to enter the global marketplace and a worldwide network of wealthy "overseas Chinese" (the code name for the large diaspora population), this is a nation where the future is already reaching critical mass. The biggest question mark is the political outcome of the current turmoil. With the passing of Deng Xiaoping, the power struggle concerning the form and function of the increasingly paranoid Communist regime remains an intriguing subject.

Basic Facts

Location:
East Asia

Neighboring Countries:
Russia, Mongolia, Kazakhstan, Kyrgyzstan, Tajikistan, Afghanistan, Pakistan, India, Nepal, Bhutan, Myanmar, Laos, Vietnam, Taiwan, North Korea

Population:
1,214,221,000

Capital City:
Beijing

Major Cities:
Shanghai, Tianjin, Guangzhou, Shenyang, Wuhan

Government:
Communist state

Leader:
Currently in transition

Major Religions:
atheism, Confucianism, Buddhism, Taoism

Historical Background

 $\mathcal{E}$ arliest Chinese history records a supreme deity known as Shang Di, who possessed some similarities to the God of Israel. This was the name that missionaries used for God, in an attempt to make Christianity more understandable to a people already suspicious of anything foreign. The first missionaries arrived in 635. These Christians were Nestorians from the Mideast, and established at least eleven churches, even managing to penetrate the imperial court. Unfortunately, they eventually disappeared and the reason for their demise seems to have perished with them.

China's recent history began in 1949, when Mao established The People's Republic of China after a long guerrilla campaign. Most foreigners were subsequently expelled, including missionaries. Most corruption was wiped out, and women gained a new status in society, but the disastrous "Great Leap Forward" begun in 1958 brought about mass starvation, and ten years of the "Great Proletarian Cultural Revolution" (1966-76) destroyed the economy and created widespread fear and terror. With the death of Mao in 1976, a more moderate economic course was taken, although the regime remained repressive. It is estimated that Mao's many purges and ongoing consolidation of power cost at least 35 million Chinese lives, leaving a psychological and spiritual pall hanging over the country that remains to this day.

Unreached Peoples

 $\mathcal{T}$ he Zhuang are China's largest minority (16 million people), and one of the largest language groups in the world with no scripture, no gospel recordings and no Christian radio broadcasts in their own language. A tribal people who love festival singing and dancing, the Zhuang are indigenous to southern China. The Zhuang easily assimilated Chinese customs and today are almost indistinguishable from the majority Han. Most Zhuang are polytheistic, animist and Taoist.

The Muslim Hui are a virtually invisible minority in China. Descended from Arab and Persian traders who came across on the Silk Road, they are scattered all over the country. The highest concentration live in China's arid Northwest. The Hui dress, speak and look like the majority Han, although the men can sometimes be distinguished by their round white caps. Many young Hui do not follow Islam, but keep only family traditions.

The real unreached people of China are the ordinary citizens of all ethnic groups who have been subjected to two powerful forms of spiritual deception: traditional Chinese folk religion, which is fearful and superstitious, and Communist atheism; both of these belief systems are powerful forms of bondage.

Spiritual Competition

The old-line Marxist stand against religion still prevails in China, and it may be intensifying due to fear on the part of party officials who observed the role of the Church in the overthrow of Communism in Eastern Europe. While the church in China has suffered greatly at the hands of the government, the efforts to stop the Church have been unsuccessful. In 1949, at the time of the Communist takeover, there were less than one million followers of Christ in all of China. By 1992, that number was about 30 million and growing.

The seeds planted by missionaries in the 19th and 20th centuries has borne amazing fruit in the years since World War II. Under the bleak hopelessness of Communism, the people have been very receptive to the gospel despite the risks. Moreover, the Chinese seem to have a good intuitive understanding of biblical Christianity, generally rejecting liberal theology for what it is—just another form of humanistic philosophy. Despite this progress, the ancient Chinese folk religions continue to dominate among the common people. A haphazard combination of Buddhism, Confucianism, primitive animism and ancestor veneration, these practices are essentially an attempt to control demonic forces, but in reality the demons end up controlling the practitioners.

Noteworthy Trends

In the summer of 1989 China dominated international news as thousands of students demonstrated for democracy in Tiananmen Square and were then brutally suppressed and massacred by government troops. In the years following the incident, the government has gradually tightened political control throughout the country. As a result, Christians have faced increasing persecution, including raids on house churches, and those engaged in unregistered religious activities have suffered arrest, torture, and even death. Most of the growth of Chinese Christianity has been through the underground house church movement; while this is certainly encouraging, there is a great lack of trained pastors, which has resulted in many strange teachings and heresies.

While government opposition and persecution of the Church has been devastating, especially in terms of leadership training, there is a potent new foe which has begun to flex its muscles: materialism. Rampant materialism figures to provide the stiffest test yet for the church in China and could be more deadly than guns and bullets. Economic reforms are moving China toward a more market-oriented economy, resulting in a tidal wave of materialism, and people are now in a virtual frenzy to make money. It remains to be seen how the Church will weather this present storm and how unbelievers will respond.

National Prayer Concerns

Obstacles to Ministry
Pray about these challenging circumstances:
• Persecution of House Church Movement
Communist authorities frequently raid home meetings
•Atheistic Educational System
Presents students with distorted view of religion
• Shortage of Trained National Leaders
Lack of theological training increases possibility of heresy
• Prohibitions on Evangelism
Witnessing to youth under 18 is strictly outlawed

Spiritual Power Points
Pray over these influential locations:
• Emei Shan, Jiuhua Shan, Putuo Shan, Tai Shan and Wutai Shan
China's five sacred mountains; active pilgrimage sites
• Altar of the Earth to Temple of Heaven (Beijing)
Powerful North-South axis of capital city includes Tiananmen Square, Mao's Mausoleum
• Temple & Forest of Confucius (Qufu, Shandong Province)
Site of tomb of Confucius, the advocate of filial piety which encourages ancestor worship
• Longmen Caves & Shaolin Monastery (West of Zhengzhou)
Major Buddhist pilgrimage and meditation sites

Festivals and Pilgrimages
Pray during these spiritual events:
• Chinese New Year (January/February)
Includes special rituals with "kitchen god" idols
• The Lantern Festival (January/February)
Ends New Year festivities; spirits believed to fly home
•Pilgrimage to Tai Shan (Mostly March & April)
Ancient tradition for Taoists, Buddhists and Confucianists
• Hungry Ghosts Festival (August)
Celebration with mixture of Buddhist and Taoist beliefs

China (Taiwan)

Taiwan is the distilled essence of China. Members of most of Mainland China's ethnic groups have migrated to the island nation, giving the visitor a total cultural immersion experience. If you like Chinese atmosphere and food, you'll love Taiwan. One of Asia's economic "little dragons" (the others being South Korea, Singapore and Hong Kong), Taiwan catapulted into international economic importance in a scant 40 years. Having one of the world's most dynamic export-oriented economies, this island is no longer considered part of the third world, but rather a "newly industrialized country."

Although the Republic of China (Taiwan) and the People's Republic of China (the mainland) disagree on many points, they do have one common view: that Taiwan is a province of China. Their point of contention is the matter of which government is the rightful ruler of China; each claims sovereignty over the other while conceding that they do not currently administer the other. Taiwan's national assembly includes representatives for all the provinces of the mainland, and population figures on both sides of the Formosa Straits reflect a combined total. Domestic weather reports on the mainland always include Taipei along with all the other provincial capitals, and the national railway schedule of the PRC actually lists Taiwan, although without an actual time schedule.

Rugged mountains cover the eastern two-thirds of the island, with some of the world's highest cliffs dropping abruptly into the Pacific Ocean. When Portuguese sailors first saw the lush West coast, they called it Ilha Formosa (beautiful island), a name that lived on for centuries. The economic boom and high population density have created several smoggy urban centers, but forest-covered mountains and unspoiled beaches are still in abundance. Taipei is a teeming Chinese city, caught halfway between the past and present. Ancient temples and makeshift food stalls stand beside high rise buildings and modern shopping malls.

Basic Facts

Location:
East Asia

Neighboring Countries:
People's Republic of China

Population:
21,507,000

Capital City:
Taipei

Major Cities:
Kaohsiung, Taichung, Tainan

Government:
Republic

Leader:
President Lee Teng Hui

Major Religions:
Chinese traditional religions (Taoism and Buddhism mixed with Chinese folk religion), Christianity

Historical Background

According to Chinese legend, dragons frolicking off the coast eons ago stirred up the sea bottom and created the island of Taiwan. Apart from such tales, there is no real history of Taiwan until the 17th century. The aboriginal inhabitants of that day are the ancestors of today's tribal people.

In 1622 the Dutch began to colonize the island, and in 1627 the first Dutch missionary arrived. From the beginning, missionary efforts were directed toward the tribal people, but for unknown reasons no concerted efforts were made to evangelize the Chinese living on the island. By 1650 there were over 7,000 baptized believers. In 1662 the Chinese pirate Koxinga drove out the Dutch and sought to obliterate all foreign influence, including Christianity. However, fifty years later Jesuit missionaries visiting the island found aborigines who abhorred idol worship, had faith in a triune God, and knew the ritual of baptism.

From 1683 to 1859, the Chinese-controlled island was closed to missionary activity, and Protestant missions did not reenter until 1865. Japan took control of Taiwan in 1895 and expelled all missionaries in 1940. When missionaries returned after the war, they found an active Christian church among one of the tribes, which has since resulted in all ten tribes embracing Christianity.

Unreached Peoples

The great unreached people group of Taiwan is the common Chinese people of both Taiwanese and "mainlander" background. The Taiwanese are people who have been on the island for about 300 years, their ancestors having migrated from Fujian Province in Southeastern China. They speak the Minnan dialect, which is different from standard Mandarin Chinese. Comprising about 75% of the population, they are concentrated mostly in the fertile plain along the west coast. Due to early missions emphasis on the tribal peoples, and later efforts directed toward the mainlanders, the Taiwanese seemingly haven't received as much missionary attention as their numbers deserve.

The mainlanders came from different provinces of China, but did not arrive in large numbers until 1948-49. At that time, Chiang Kai Shek and about 1.5 million of his Kuomintang supporters fled to Taiwan after being defeated by the communist forces. They established their capital-in-exile at Taipei, where many of the mainlanders settled. Due to the very difficult circumstances surrounding their arrival on the island, it was a fertile mission field, and many responded positively to the message of Christ. Although constituting only 15% of the population, they have controlled the government since their arrival.

Spiritual Competition

Taiwan is a secular state with freedom of religion. Most of the inhabitants still adhere to a combination of Chinese folk religions, a way of life handed down from one generation to the next. The actual practice of most people is a fusion of Confucianism and ancestor worship, permeated with Taoist elements, and often placed in a semi-Buddhist framework. A high degree of superstition is involved, as exemplified by the uniquely Chinese concept of feng shui, which often dictates the placement of doors, the location of a building, or where a family will build their home. Chinese folk religion, found among Chinese throughout the world, is a subtle yet powerful form of spiritual bondage. Small altars devoted to departed ancestors and gods can be found in many shops and homes, and most of these people's lives are controlled in varying degrees by obligations to the dead or fear of elemental spirits.

Many young people have given up the ways of the past and are either non-religious or vaguely superstitious. In a fast-paced and competitive society, the vicious trap of materialism has dulled spiritual sensitivity and interest to the point where most people are apathetic toward Christ. Taiwan has become very prosperous in the last decade, and the spirit of materialism and the desire to make money are the driving psychological and spiritual forces at work in the nation today.

Noteworthy Trends

Since its arrival in 1949, the Kuomintang Party (KMT) has maintained control of Taiwan. The avowed goal of the KMT has been to reassert its authority over all of China. However, despite years of rhetoric by Taiwan's politicians, the average citizen has little interest in retaking the mainland, and likewise there is no attraction to the communist system. Economic prosperity has spawned a certain satisfaction with the political status quo. But the difficulties of visiting and communicating with family across the straits, a desire to have more freedom to travel, and to have easier access to mainland markets has increased pressure to begin serious negotiations with the People's Republic. Relaxed relations are a likely short-term outcome and reunification looms as a long-range future prospect.

The relative apathy of Taiwanese toward the gospel is in stark contrast to the warm reception of those on the mainland. However, materialism has already begun to control the People's Republic, and needs no further encouragement. Although the simple faith of mainland Christians has been an inspiration worldwide, they are in dire need of theological training, which could be supplied from Taiwan if there is a further opening between the two countries.

National Prayer Concerns

Obstacles to Ministry
Pray about these challenging circumstances:
• Strength of Traditional Religions
Confucianism, Taoism and Buddhism predominate
• Growing Materialist Influence
Many Taiwanese are caught up in pursuit of wealth
•Long Dependence on Foreign Church Resources
Severe lack of national pastors is but one result
• Successful Cults
Many have joined the True Jesus Church and Mormons

Spiritual Power Points
Pray over these influential locations:
• Temple of Matsu (Lukang)
Pilgrimage site honoring patroness of the Taiwanese and protectress of seafarers
• Tsu Shih Temple (Sanhsia)
Recently renovated; significant Buddhist temple
• Foukuang Shan Monastery
Buddhist center with university
• Long Shan Temple (Taipei)
Major Buddhist and ancestor worship center

Festivals and Pilgrimages
Pray during these spiritual events:
• Chinese New Year (January /February)
Includes special rituals with "kitchen god" idols
• Lantern Festival (January/February)
Ends New Year festivities; spirits believed to fly home
• Birthday of Matsu (Varies according to lunar calendar)
Thousands make pilgrimage to her temple in Lukang
• Dragon Boat Festival (June)
Honors death of Chuh Yuan & White Snake legend

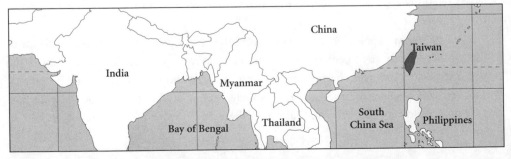

Djibouti

Welcome to Djibouti. As you leave the airport on a summer day, the temperature is 115 degrees with high humidity. On your way into the capital, appropriately named Djibouti-Ville, you pass through the suburbs - row upon row of ramshackle tin huts, baking in the desert sun. The great majority of the people don't work, and can be seen strolling between the huts, clad in brightly colored clothes.

Little Djibouti, a postage stamp-sized country wedged between Ethiopia and Somalia, has no natural resources and has been independent only since 1977. A former colony of France, it is still kept on a leash, with some 4,000 French soldiers stationed there, including the famed Foreign Legion. Generous amounts of aid, as well as French food and wine, are pumped in from Europe to stabilize the local economy and shore up the troops.

Djibouti is also considered one of the hottest countries on the globe, with temperatures sometimes hitting 140 degrees in the interior. It is one of the poorest as well, with an average income of about $475. With no industry and virtually no agriculture, Djibouti must rely on the service sector for its business. Supplying and catering to the French army comprises a substantial portion of the wages in the city, and other businesses have developed around the airport, the good deep-water harbor, and the rail line into Ethiopia. Like all of its neighbors, Djibouti is embroiled in ethnic conflict. The dominant Somali Issas are highly resented by the ethnic Ethiopian Afars, who have commenced a civil war to redress their grievances.

Basic Facts

Location:
East Africa

Neighboring Countries:
Eritrea, Ethiopia,
Somalia, Yemen

Population:
473,000

Capital City:
Djibouti

Major Cities:
Ali-Sabieh, Dikhil,
Obock, Tadjoura

Government:
Republic

Leader:
President
Hassan Gouled Aptifdon

Major Religions:
Islam

Historical Background

The Afars and the Issas have inhabited the Horn of Africa for thousands of years. The Somalis converted to Islam during the ninth and tenth centuries; since then Islam has been an integral part of their culture. The Afars, who are also Muslims and long-time residents of the area, have never acknowledged the borders between Ethiopia and Djibouti. The Afars are divided into four sultanates, two in Djibouti and two in Ethiopia.

The French originally used the port of Djibouti as a refueling station for their ships. France established an interest in colonizing the region during the "rush for Africa," when European powers expanded their spheres of influence, which took place around the middle of the last century. Ethnic tensions have never been far below the surface in Djibouti, as the Issas have always tried to dominate the area, even in colonial days, but the Afars were able to distance the republic from Somalia by changing its name to the "French Territory of the Afars and the Issas." This kept the two groups at bay until independence from France was obtained in 1977, when ethnic Somalis again wanted to align the new nation more closely with Somalia.

Unreached Peoples

Djibouti has a population of approximately 473,000, with slightly more Issas than Afars. The President is an Issa who has surrounded himself with many of his clan members, who hold significant positions of power in the government. The Somalis also dominate the civil service, police and military forces of the nation. This imbalance of power has left lingering resentments among the Afars.

The Afars, who have their ethnic roots to the north, have more in common with Ethiopia and Eritrea, where other Afars are found. The Issa-dominated government has been slow to recognize the needs of the Afars and this has led to a large scale Afar insurgency in the northern part of the country. Both Afar and Issa claim a tradition of individuality and independence, which are cornerstones of their nomadic past.

There are approximately 45,000 refugees in Djibouti, having fled wars in Ethiopia, Somalia and Eritrea. The refugees live in four camps in the desert or in the slum townships surrounding the capital. The government wants to repatriate the refugees and has stepped up these efforts, resulting in even more hardship for those who do not wish to leave.

Spiritual Competition

$\mathcal{E}$ntrenched Islam is the major stumbling block to the propagation of the gospel in Djibouti. Both the Issas and Afars have a strong Muslim heritage dating back over 1,000 years, with both their national and tribal identities strongly linked to Islam. Many Djiboutians were nominal Muslims, but an upsurge of fundamentalism from Saudi Arabia has lead to the foundation of a Saudi-sponsored institute for Islamic studies in the capital.

Extremely high unemployment (up to 80%) is another major problem that impacts the spiritual temperament of Djibouti. The country is almost totally dependent on outside aid for the sustenance of its citizens and for development funds. This unhealthy situation has possibly intensified the addiction of a large portion of the population to khat, a narcotic leaf imported by air from Ethiopia and Yemen. Khat is Djibouti's third largest import and many workers spend almost half of their income on this drug, which also causes physical and social problems.

There is a fledgling church in Djibouti with a majority of ethnic Somalis. There is more spiritual movement among the Ethiopian refugees, where there are about 200 believers. The tough security police in Djibouti are mainly responsible for the persecution of indigenous believers and have been implicated in the death of one local church leader.

Noteworthy Trends

$\mathcal{T}$he next few years are crucial for the survival of the nation of Djibouti. Caught between anarchy in Somalia and considerable uncertainty in Ethiopia, the country's future is mirrored in the present situation of its southern neighbor Somalia. Djibouti will either find a way to reconcile its ethnic tensions or run the risk of anarchy and further bloodshed. The French and other aid donors have been pressuring the government to make democratic reforms after attempted coups and the Afar insurgency in the north. The Afar rebellion against the Issa-controlled government stopped for elections in 1992, but was resumed after the balloting failed to effect changes. The resulting military mobilization has devastated Djibouti's economy, and maintaining the army on a war footing has accounted for about 35% of the government's expenditures.

Djibouti is attempting to renovate its port and to become less dependent on foreign aid. The rail line from Djibouti to Addis Ababa still remains the only land route between Ethiopia and the sea. Prayer is needed for national stability and for the 25 missionaries who labor under oppressive physical conditions in a land that continues to show resistance to the gospel.

National Prayer Concerns

Obstacles to Ministry
Pray about these challenging circumstances:
• Persecution of Muslim Converts
Djiboutian converts have been beaten and imprisoned
• Growing Islamic Fundamentalism
Sudan and Saudi Arabia are exerting growing influence
• Lack of Privacy
Little goes on in this tiny state without police knowledge
• Few Indigenous Churches
Only a handful of small house fellowships exist

Spiritual Power Points
Pray over these influential locations:
• Altixad School (Djibouti City)
Islamic Brotherhood training center
• Jamac Mosque (Djibouti City)
Major Islamic worship center in heart of the capital
• Almadars (Various Locations)
Islamic house schools meeting weekly in each village
• National Police Headquarters (Djibouti City)
Interrogation and prison site for several Christians

Festivals and Pilgrimages
Pray during these spiritual events:
• Ramadan & Eid al-Fitr (Varies: '96 = Jan/Feb)
Month of fasting and prayer followed by two day feast
• Leilat al Meiraj Festival (Varies: '96 = April)
Special events celebrating Muhammad's ascension
• Ashura (Varies: '96 = May)
Shiite passion play celebrating Hussein's martyrdom
• Mawlid an-Nabi (Varies: '96 = July)
Celebrations honoring Muhammad's birthday

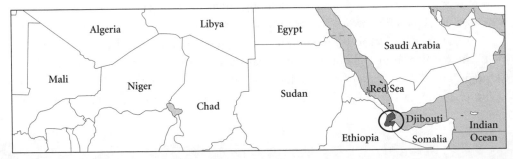

Egypt

Renowned as the land of the Pharaohs and their magnificent Pyramids, Egypt is also noteworthy as the ancient home of the Hebrew children. It is the land from which the Messiah Himself was beckoned: "Out of Egypt I called my Son." Years after its days as a key player in Biblical history, Egypt has once again found itself on the center of the Middle Eastern stage. The most populous, and arguably the most influential nation within the Arab world, Egypt is a study in contrasts. While harboring some of the region's most volatile Muslim extremists (including those with ties to the World Trade Center bombing), it is also the first Arab nation to enter into a peace accord with Israel. Besides hosting a growing fundamentalist movement, it is also home to the largest number of Christians in the Middle East.

Located at the southeastern end of the Mediterranean, the country is bordered by Libya on the west and Israel on the east. Topographically it is marked by the Nile river, which, along with the Gulf of Suez, separates the bulk of the country from the Sinai Peninsula. A millennia-old life source, the Nile leads a narrow march of green through large tracts of uninhabitable desert. Cairo, the capital, is a huge megalopolis of over 15 million people. Though reports vary on the exact numbers, the country is made up of mostly Sunni Muslims (82-85%) and Coptic Christians (15-17%). Cairo is also home to Al Azar University, one of the oldest and most influential Islamic universities in the world.

Basic Facts

Location:
Middle East/North Africa

Neighboring Countries:
Israel, Libya, Sudan,
Saudi Arabia, Jordan

Population:
60,470,000

Capital City:
Cairo

Major Cities:
Alexandria, Al-Mahallah,
Giza, Port Said, Suez

Government:
Republic

Leader:
President Mohammed
Hosni Mubarak

Major Religions:
Islam, Coptic Christianity

Historical Background

$\mathcal{E}$arly Egyptians were known to have worshipped a pantheon of gods, most of these relating somehow or another to the sun and fertility. The Egyptians were not Arabs and had a distinct language and culture.

Egypt witnessed large-scale conversions during the second and third centuries AD. After major disputes with Constantinople, however, the Egyptians separated themselves from the Church and formed a new Coptic order. When Muslim forces arrived in 640, the Christians in Egypt literally handed over the government of their country without a fight.

The rise of Cairo as the Egyptian political and spiritual center did not occur until the late 10th century, when the Fatimids moved their capital from Tunisia. The Fatimids soon turned Cairo into an Islamic center rivaling Baghdad. During this time they founded Al Azar University which, to this day, remains a major Islamic institution.

In 1928, a young schoolteacher by the name of Hassan al-Banna established the Muslim Brotherhood, the first of a new generation of Islamic fundamentalist organizations. In the '70s and '80s, other radical groups grew up around local leaders.

Unreached Peoples

$\mathcal{T}$hough not traditionally an Arab country, Egypt is now almost 99% Arab. Even so, most major publications still distinguish between Egyptian Arabs, who account for about 86% of the population, and other Arabs. These other "semi-Arab" groups include Nubians, Bedouins and Berbers—each consisting of 2-3% of the total population.

Just how these groups break down religiously is difficult to assess. Some say the Muslims represent 92% of the population, while others insist the number is closer to 82%. The remainder would be mostly Coptic Catholic and Protestant, with the Catholics being numerically the dominant of the two.

Some of the more challenging unreached groups are the Nubians and Siwa Berbers (many of whom live in desert areas where the gospel is not preached) and uprooted peasants trying to eke out a living in urban slums. Many of the latter have proven to be ripe fruit for the country's Islamic fundamentalist organizations.

While the potential evangelistic force in Egypt is substantial when compared to other Middle Eastern nations, religious barriers and latent fears have yet to be fully overcome.

Spiritual Competition

Without a doubt, the most formidable external threat facing the church in Egypt is Islamic fundamentalism. In addition to attracting thousands of urban and rural poor with a message that reaffirms the faith's solidarity with the oppressed, Islamic militants have launched hundreds of violent attacks on churches and foreign tourists in recent years.

Besides the demolition of churches—some of which the government will not allow to be rebuilt – Christians have faced other forms of Muslim harassment ranging from taunts to outright murder. Outside of Cairo, two of the areas hardest hit by the fundamentalists have been Alexandria and Asyut.

A large percentage of Egypt's Muslim population also favors the introduction of Sharia (Islamic Law). This poses an immense threat to the growing Christian community and should be made a matter of urgent prayer.

Another concern is the lingering, and in some quarters growing, influence of early Egyptian paganism. In addition to making pilgrimages to such sites as the Temple of Osiris, Heliopolis and the Pyramids, a large number of Egyptians still court and fend off spirits through various types of folk rituals.

Noteworthy Trends

Although Egypt emerged from the Gulf War with new authority in the Middle East, Islamic fundamentalism began to severely test the Mubarak government in late 1992. A communiqué issued by the outlawed Gamma al Islamiyya warned investors to liquidate their Egyptian holdings or risk "legitimate retribution." They also urged all foreign governments to get their citizens out of the country "for the sake of their lives." This followed months of verbal warfare between Cairo and Tehran, with the former complaining that Iran was behind several of the more notorious extremist groups in Egypt.

At the same time, the government has made a serious attempt to blunt the influence of domestic fundamentalists by cracking down on Christians. Even today, many Catholics and Protestants are being held in Egyptian prisons on the flimsiest of charges.

There is, however, some good news in all of this. Despite this persecution—some would say because of it – a modest but genuine revival has been occurring within the Coptic Church. In some instances, traditionally negative attitudes toward Muslim evangelism have been changing. Accordingly, many Muslims are coming to Christ; some in response to miracles.

National Prayer Concerns

Obstacles to Ministry
Pray about these challenging circumstances:
• Lack of Consensus Over Muslim Evangelism
Some traditional and evangelical churches are hesitant about outreach to Muslims
• Islamic Perceptions of Christianity
Muslims associate Christianity with Coptic nominalism or Western culture
• Growing Pressure from Islamic Fundamentalists
Churches have been damaged and believers beaten and murdered
• Government Policy Affected by Politics
Christians have been arrested and imprisoned on flimsy charges to placate fundamentalists

Spiritual Power Points
Pray over these influential locations:
• Karnak (Luxor)
Main center of Amun worship in ancient Egypt
• Al Azar University (Cairo)
Renowned center for study of Islamic doctrine and politics
• Mosque and Schools of Sultan Hassan (Cairo)
Schools teach the doctrines of the four Islamic sects
• Great Pyramid of Cheops (Giza)
This symbol of Egypt's spiritual past serves as a magnet for international mystics

Festivals and Pilgrimages
Pray during these spiritual events:
• Ramadan & Eid al-Fitr (Varies: '96 = Jan/Feb)
Month of fasting and prayer followed by two day feast
• Mawlid an-Nabi (Varies: '96 = July)
Celebrations honoring Muhammad's birthday
• Pilgrimage to Ra's al-Husayn (All Year)
Mausoleum in Cairo where Husayn's head is buried
• Pilgrimage to the Temple of Osiris (All Year)
Shrine to Osiris, ancient and venerable god of the dead

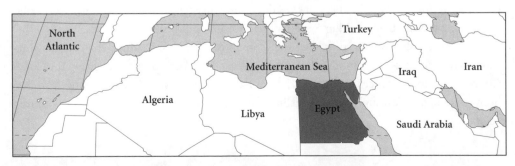

Eritrea

$\mathcal{E}$ritrea, a little-known East African country, is the last colony to gain independence, becoming Africa's 52nd nation on April 27, 1993. The Eritrean people voted unanimously (99.8%) for separation from Ethiopia and the creation of a free Eritrea. The plebiscite ended a fierce 30-year war by Eritrean insurgents, who fought the large Ethiopian army to a standstill, eventually driving them out of the country with almost no outside help.

Located on the Red Sea across from the Arabian peninsula, the country is about the size of Pennsylvania and contains rugged mountains reaching 10,000 feet in the south-central highlands. In the west are plains, crossed by rivers and fertile valleys, while the coastline is a shrub-strewn desert.

The long Eritrean struggle was often ignored by the West and has never been a "fashionable" war; the Wall Street Journal called it "A Bargain Basement War," in which almost a third of the 100,000 fighters were women. Alone and without foreign aid they fought a protracted guerrilla war using captured arms. At one point 70% of the population was dependent on food aid from abroad, and one million refugees fled. With the fall of Ethiopia's Marxist dictator Mengistu Haile Mariam, the country was able to free itself and realize their dream of a free Eritrea. After the declaration of independence people flooded the streets of the capital Asmara waving green leaves as symbols of victory. In contemplating the future, one women remarked, "The future looks very bright. We have each other."

Basic Facts

Location:
East Africa

Neighboring Countries:
Ethiopia, Djibouti, Sudan, Yemen

Population:
3,677,000

Capital City:
Asmara

Major Cities:
Massawa, Assab

Government:
Secular state under a transitional constitution

Leader:
President Issaias Afwerki

Major Religions:
Christianity; Islam

Historical Background

*E*ritrea first entered the modern arena as an Italian colony between 1889 and 1941. The region was used as a staging ground for many Allied and American operations in the Middle East during the Second World War. After the Allies freed the country from the Italians, the British and the United Nations relinquished control of it to form a loose federation with its southern neighbor, Ethiopia. This resolution ignored Eritrea's desire for independence and sowed the seeds of war. An armed struggle for independence began in 1961 after years of peaceful protest against Ethiopian violations of Eritrea's rights, which had produced no improvement in the deteriorating situation.

During the civil war the Eritreans suffered from severe droughts, which resulted in the flight of almost one-third of their population to camps in Sudan and elsewhere. The Eritreans suffered greatly at the hands of the Ethiopian security forces, and agriculture declined as farmland was neglected; severe deforestation has also resulted. The civil war ended in 1991 when occupying Ethiopian military forces, demoralized and confused by the fall of their Marxist government to rebels, fled the country under pressure from the Eritrean People's Liberation Front (EPLF).

Unreached Peoples

*E*ritrea contains at least nine people groups, with those of Semitic origin comprising some 70% of the population. The major peoples within this group are the 1.9 million Tigrinya, who are mostly Christian. Other Semitic people groups are the Tigre, Mensa and Arabs, who are predominantly Sunni Muslims. There is however, a minority Christian presence among the Mensa people.

People of East African Cushitic extraction comprise the only other large group in Eritrea. Among them the largest are the 300,000 Afars, who are also found in the tiny neighboring nation of Djibouti. Other members of this ethnic block are the Saho and the Beja; all three of these peoples are predominantly Muslim, and there is little Christian outreach into their communities.

Another smaller group are the Nilo-Sudanic peoples, who have more in common with ethnic groups in the Nile valley of Sudan. These tribes are the Kunama and the Nara; the latter are predominantly Muslim and are considered unreached, while the Kunama have a Christian minority. A veteran missionary who spent ten years in Eritrea believes that despite the fact that almost half of the population is considered Christian, much of the country is still unevangelized.

Spiritual Competition

$\mathcal{E}$ritrea is a secular state under a transitional constitution that allows freedom of religion. The country has slightly more Muslims than Christians. The Tigrinya people are mostly Orthodox (40%) with the remainder belonging to either the Coptic-Catholic or Protestant denominations. The Eritrean church was refined through the long civil war and the despotic and cruel Marxist military regime of Ethiopia, and the Coptic, Orthodox and evangelical Christians have drawn together in fellowship as a result of their years of suffering.

The Tigre-speaking Muslims dominate the northern area of the country. While there is a Bible translation in Tigre, there are few committed Christians. The Beja, Afar, Nara and Saho people, who are also Muslim, have no known churches or existing outreach among them. The Red Sea coast area and the cities of Massawa and Assab are strongholds of Islam. There is a strong push by Sudanese-inspired Muslim radicals to push Islam to political ascendancy, but so far the government has been very careful to balance Christianity and Islam. The government is very wary of allowing fundamentalist Muslims to de-stabilize their new nation.

Noteworthy Trends

$\mathcal{E}$ritrea has become one of the bright hopes in Africa, a continent often characterized by corruption, mismanagement and tribal warfare. A proud and independent people, the Eritreans are true survivors and the country suffers little sectarian strife. The main threat to political and spiritual stability of the country lies in Islamic aspirations for power. Traditionally, Christians and Muslims have coexisted well, with their mutual struggle for independence forming a bond of respect that transcended religion.

The grass roots political process in Eritrea is laying a foundation for democratic freedoms. President Issaias Afwerki has proven to be a fair, no-nonsense leader who is strongly committed to bolstering the educational system, and the new government is looking to the 75,000 Eritreans who live abroad to help with the rebuilding of the nation. The people have a strong national consciousness, internal stability and a will to make things work. An Asmara shopkeeper said, "This may be a paradox, but after 30 years of war we may be the most stable country in the region." Pray that Eritrea's internal peace is maintained so that the proclamation of the gospel may go forth unhindered.

National Prayer Concerns

Obstacles to Ministry

Pray about these challenging circumstances:

• Islamic Extremism
Radical Islamic elements pushing for political ascendancy
• Lack of Trained Christian Leadership
All areas of ministry lack training and skills
• Damaged Infrastructure
30 years of war have made travel and communication difficult
• Potential Ethnic/Religious Divisions
Factions which united to secure independence may polarize during peace

Spiritual Power Points

Pray over these influential locations:

• Anwar Mosque (Asmara)
Largest Islamic worship center in capital
• Roman Catholic Cathedral (Asmara)
Some tension between Protestants and Catholics
• Eritrean Orthodox Churches and Monasteries
Similar problems with Protestants and Catholics
• War Museum (Asmara)
Stirs up animosity of the past

Festivals and Pilgrimages

Pray during these spiritual events:

• Ramadan & Eid al-Fitr (Varies: '96 = Jan/Feb)
Month of fasting and prayer followed by two day feast
• Eid al-Adha (Varies: '96 = April)
Feast of Sacrifice: coincides with culmination of Hadj
• Mawlid an-Nabi (Varies: '96 = July)
Celebrations honoring Muhammad's birthday
• Timqat (Second Week of January)
Cultic celebration of Jesus' baptism

Ethiopia

$\mathcal{E}$thiopia is the only continuously independent country in Africa. Mentioned over 60 times in the Bible, it has existed for almost 3,000 years and has a history that is intertwined with Israel and the Jewish people. It is the ancestral home of the only tribe of black Jews, the Falashas, most of whom were airlifted to Israel in a rescue operation in the 1980s.

The best known reference to the country in the Bible is the account of Philip's witness to the Ethiopian eunuch in Acts 8:26-40. In the fourth century it became one of the first nations to embrace Christianity, and the Ethiopian Orthodox Church remains the faith of the majority of its citizens.

Ethiopia was in isolation for centuries and used to be called the "Hidden Empire," which led to the development of a distinct and noble culture with a sense of history, setting it apart from the more primitive tribalism of much of Africa. Located on the edge of sub-Saharan Africa, Ethiopia now lies in the "trouble belt" of war and famine. Sandwiched between turbulent Sudan, which is currently embroiled in a protracted and bitter civil war, and Somalia, the basket case ex-country administered by the UN. Ethiopia is now land-locked, as the coastal province of Eritrea won its independence in 1993.

Ethiopia's ancient kingdom disintegrated in 1974 with the deposing of the regal emperor Haile Selassie, who was taken to prison in the back seat of a VW beetle and executed. The country then suffered under the brutal rule of a Soviet-backed Marxist regime until 1991, which almost ruined the nation. Today this proud land is one of the poorest countries in the world.

Basic Facts

Location:
East Africa

Capital City:
Addis Ababa

Leader:
President Meles Zenawi

Neighboring Countries:
Sudan, Kenya, Somalia, Djibouti, Eritrea

Major Cities:
Dire Dawa, Nazret

Major Religions:
Orthodox Christianity, Islam

Population:
52,569,000

Government:
Transitional military rule

Historical Background

$\mathcal{A}$mong all the sub-Saharan African nations, Ethiopia and Sudan are the only countries that can trace their history back to antiquity. Ancient Egyptian pharaohs called Ethiopia Punt, meaning "land of God." There were powerful dynasties which ruled from Ethiopia: The Sabeans were the most dominant pre-Christian kingdom, while the Axumites were the principal kingdom of the Christian era. Even today Axum remains the spiritual and religious center of the country, including a significant Falashan Jewish presence. At various points in history parts of the population were converted to Judaism, mainly through Jews who came from Yemen, across the Red Sea.

Menelik I, the founder of the first Ethiopian empire, was according to some traditions the son of King Solomon and the Queen of Sheba, and legend holds that his line remained unbroken until the last emperor, Haile Selassie. In the first centuries after Christ, large numbers of the Jewish population were converted to Christianity, but remained Jewish in their worship and culture. Meccan Muslims arrived in the 7th century, but it wasn't until the Fatimid invasion in the 14th century that Islam arrived in force. Nonetheless, Ethiopia remains one of the few Christian nations outside of Western Europe that did not fall to Islam.

Unreached Peoples

$\mathcal{E}$thiopia is a land so full of cultural and linguistic diversity that it has been referred to by some as "a museum of peoples." Muslims, numbering around 17 million or 35% of the total population, undoubtedly comprise the bulk of the unreached people in Ethiopia. The most significant Muslim strongholds are in the north and southeastern areas of the country. In the north are the Muslim Tigre, Beja, Baraya, Afar and Arab peoples, plus the unreached Muslims of Wallo province. Together these Muslim groups comprise a majority of 65% of the total population of that region. In the southeastern provinces of Harar and Bale there are large numbers of Muslims in an area with little gospel witness.

Since Ethiopia borders central Africa, there are still a fairly large number of animistic tribes, numbering around five million, or 10% of the population. These live in the far south and southwestern portions of the country. In addition, it is difficult to ascertain what proportion of those who consider themselves members of the Ethiopian Orthodox Church are severely compromised by syncretism or nominalism.

Spiritual Competition

*E*thiopia's location on the Red Sea made it a focus during the Cold War for both Soviet and American interests. However, as a result of the collapse of the Soviet Union, the battle lines are being re-drawn by spiritual forces, pitting Islam against the church throughout Africa. Two prominent Muslim power points in the country are the Shrine of Sheik Hussayn and the Grand Mosque in Addis Ababa, which testify to the growing influence of Islam. Sudan has also been intensifying efforts to export its brand of Muslim socialism to Ethiopia through financial aid and business dealings. Iran also funds Islamic projects such as new mosques, and even supplies money to bribe converts. Muslims were not persecuted as severely as the Christians were under the Marxists, and have emerged in a strengthened position.

The church in Ethiopia needs healing. Seventeen years of harsh repression have left it exhausted and reeling. There is also resentment among the Orthodox at the recent expansion of the Protestant evangelical churches. This schism is potentially serious and weakens the church in its ability to counter a more homogeneous and aggressive Muslim advance. Much prayer is needed for the unity, strength and vision of the Ethiopian church.

Noteworthy Trends

*A*fter the fall of the Marxist regime in May of 1991, the country has been led by a "transitional government" of ex-guerrillas. They have begun some democratic and private market reforms that have helped to stabilize ethnic tensions and the floundering economy, but free elections have yet to be held. The ancient kingdom is now dead, and national unity is lacking. A worst-case scenario forecasts the breakup of Ethiopia into smaller ethnic states, as occurred with Eritrea's recent secession.

On the positive side, the evangelical church is experiencing a tremendous period of growth, especially in urban areas. One church in Addis Ababa reports a weekly attendance that approaches 5,000. The Orthodox church, which enjoyed a comfortable status as the state church prior to 1974, is also experiencing some renewal. Since 1991 missionaries have been allowed to return, bringing much-needed aid and education.

A significant event now making international headlines is the genocide trial of some 3,400 former Marxist officials who are believed responsible for the torture and murder of more than 100,000 of their countrymen. It is the first time since the Nuremberg war crimes trials in 1946 that such proceedings have been carried out against a defeated regime.

National Prayer Concerns

Obstacles to Ministry

Pray about these challenging circumstances:

• Rapid Growth of Islam
Rural mosques are springing up everywhere
• Increasing Tribalism
Fresh sense of ethnic separation is tearing at the country
• Antagonism of Ethiopian Orthodox Church
Orthodox leaders have had evangelicals beaten
• Low Literacy Rate
This has reduced impact of Scriptures in some areas

Spiritual Power Points

Pray over these influential locations:

• Monastery of Lalebila (Axum)
Ethiopian Orthodox pilgrimage site similar to Lourdes
• Menilik Mausoleum (Addis Ababa)
Burial site of former emperor
• Shrine of Sheik Hussein
Tomb of an Islamic saint; pilgrimage site for folk Muslims
• Grand Mosque (Addis Ababa)
Largest and most influential mosque in the country

Festivals and Pilgrimages

Pray during these spiritual events:

• Ramadan & Eid al-Fitr (Varies: '96 = Jan/Feb)
Month of fasting and prayer followed by two day feast
• Eid al-Adha (Varies: '96 = April)
Feast of Sacrifice; coincides with culmination of Hadj
• Maskal Festival (September)
Ancient Christo-Pagan festival celebrating Spring
• Seged Festival (November)
Commemoration of the dead by the Falashi people

Gambia

The tiny West African nation of Gambia is a geographic oddity, a country that is no more than a wide river bank, a populated strip built up on both sides of the Gambia River and entirely surrounded by its larger neighbor, Senegal. Gambia was described by a former British colonial governor as a "geographical and economic absurdity," and current observers have called Gambia, "a hot dog in a Senegalese roll." Up until 1981, this little African country had no army, and its image of peace enhanced its attractiveness abroad, giving it the rather misleading nickname "the Switzerland of Africa." This status changed in the aftermath of a coup that year, which led to a failed attempt to form a confederation with Senegal; another coup was carried out by Lieutenant Yahya Jammehon and other junior officers on the 26th of August 1994.

Founded in 1588, Gambia has the dubious distinction of being Britain's first overseas colony, and is a fine example of colonial meddling in Africa. The country is only 10 kilometers at its narrowest point and 58 kilometers at its widest, running for about 320 kilometers along the Gambia River. Peanuts are the staple crop, with 75 percent of the population engaged in subsistence agriculture. Tourists are attracted by good beaches on the Atlantic, as well as lush tropical forests with abundant wildlife. North Americans may be familiar with Gambia as the country where the late author of Roots, Alex Haley, found his ancestor Kunte Kinte. Along with the entire west coast of Africa, Gambia shares a sad legacy of enforced slavery, which has left an indelible scar on the psyche and social fabric of these nations.

Basic Facts

Location:
West Africa

Neighboring Countries:
Senegal

Population:
983,000

Capital City:
Banjul

Major Cities:
Georgetown, Bakau, Kombo

Government:
In transition (constitution suspended due to recent coup)

Leader:
Lieutenant Yahya Jammehon

Major Religions:
Islam, African traditional religions

Historical Background

The first non-African peoples to visit the region of Gambia were the ancient Phoenicians, who were following trade routes around Africa in search of ivory and gold. Gambia was populated as the result of both voluntary and involuntary migrations over some two thousand years. The first major thrust of peoples into the region came from the Kingdom of Songhai, a great Muslim city state located in present-day Mali. This kingdom dominated the trans-Saharan trade routes from Morocco to the coast of West Africa, but the influence of the empire had decreased by the 16th century.

The Muslim-dominated trading kingdoms were eventually replaced by the Portuguese, who gained the upper hand by controlling the maritime trade routes. When the Portuguese arrived at the delta of the Gambia River, the area was then under the control of the Kingdom of Mali. In 1588 the Portuguese sold the trading rights on the Gambia River to the English, who dominated the region until independence. In the 17th and 18th centuries the region was the focus of a power struggle between Britain and France for supremacy over the barbaric but lucrative slave trade.

Unreached Peoples

Over 25 ethnic groups live side by side in Gambia, with a minimum of inter-tribal friction, each preserving its own language and traditions. The Mandingo are the largest tribe and comprise approximately 40 percent of Gambia's population of 983,000. These predominantly Muslim people are found throughout the country and constitute the western extension of their tribe, which can be found throughout West Africa. The Mandingo social structure centers around the griots, who are traditional bards and oral historians who keep the history of the families alive in song and folk tales.

The next largest ethnic group are the wide-ranging Fula, who are concentrated in the east. They are related by language and family ties to the Fulani shepherds who are found throughout West Africa and as far east as the Sudan. These strongly Muslim people have lately started to show an interest in the gospel, with some conversions. Prayer is needed for continued momentum and a strong Christian movement among these strategic people. The Wolof and the Jola, who are a mixture of Mandingo, Fula and Berber stock, are the other principal people groups of Gambia.

Spiritual Competition

Approximately 85% of the population are Sunni Muslim, but this was not always so. Islam first came to the West Coast of Africa through the efforts of Arab merchants and traveling teachers in the 12th century. However, it was not until the Soninke-Marabout wars in the mid-1850s that most of the population was converted to Islam. Most of the major tribes are entirely Muslim, but the Jolas still follow traditional African beliefs.

These early animistic practices are centered about an idol called a jalang, which can take the form of a snake, tree or other objects. Sacrifices are made to the jalang, which looks after the family, makes decisions for it, and even brings evil if shown disrespect. Marabouts, the wandering Islamic holy men, were also welcomed in Gambia for their magical powers and their ability to make amulets containing verses of the Quran. The mystical Sufi brotherhoods are also a potent spiritual and economic force in the country and are linked to the orders found in surrounding Senegal. Islam in Gambia is mixed with animistic beliefs, the worship of saints, and witchcraft. Christians are estimated to constitute less than four percent of the population.

Noteworthy Trends

Since independence in 1965 Gambia has had the appearance of a true democracy. However, the government of ex-president Sir Dawda Jawara was in fact a de facto one-party state that controlled access to political power. The past president has been accused of benign neglect of his countrymen, failing to build even a single new hospital in 30 years. More telling than the lack of hospital facilities, and likely to affect the course of the country for generations, is the deposed president's failure to build a university, or even a single new high school.

The Gambian way is to leave things to fate, which does not bode well for their future. A former government minister summed up the current situation in Gambia for the New York Times, sounding as if the nation were in a stupor: "We had elections every five years; it seems that was the legacy. It seems clear that we could have done a lot better. All that we can do now is pray that these young fellows will know what to do." This attitude is largely due to the popular notion of predestination in a country that is 95% Muslim. However, there is freedom of religion and a small but growing evangelical movement in Gambia.

Obstacles to Ministry

Pray about these challenging circumstances:

• Nominalism in Churches
Christians are often little credit to the gospel
• Growing Influence of Islam
Some elements desire an Islamic state
• Association of Christianity with White Colonialism
Makes it an undesirable foreign religion
• Political Uncertainty
August 1994 military coup may affect missions and religious freedom

Spiritual Power Points

Pray over these influential locations:

• Grand Mosque (Banjul)
Center of Islamic worship in capital
• Fort James
Former major slave transshipment center
• Wrestling Arenas (Many Villages)
Competitors rely heavily on magic charms
• Stone Circles (Wassu Area)
Occult ritual burial grounds

Festivals and Pilgrimages

Pray during these spiritual events:

• Ramadan & Eid al-Fitr (Varies: '96 = Jan/Feb)
Month of fasting and prayer followed by two day feast
• Tabaski (Eid al-Kabir) (Varies: '96 = April)
Islamic sacrificial feast; most important in West Africa
• Mawlid an-Nabi (Varies: '96 = July)
Celebrations honoring Muhammad's birthday
• Eid al-Adha (Varies: '96 = April)
Feast of Sacrifice; coincides with culmination of Hadj

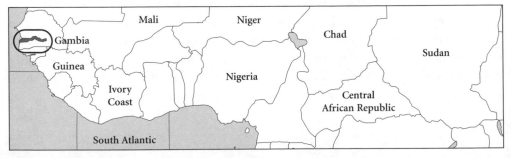

Guinea

Guinea is an impoverished state in a rich land. It is a country of great contrasts, with physical beauty to spare: tree-covered uplands, steaming mangrove swamps and a cool mountainous interior provide great variety. Apart from beauty, Guinea also possesses great natural wealth, and was one of Africa's most prosperous colonies under the French.

All this changed however, under the leadership of the strongman Sekou Toure, who followed his own peculiar brand of socialism. His independence slogan, "We prefer poverty in freedom to riches in slavery" turned out to be all too true. Toure threw out most missionaries and embarked on a series of disastrous programs until his death in 1984.

Economically, Guinea is a typical African nation - largely undeveloped, with about 80% of the population engaged in rural subsistence farming. Many of these farmers and herders migrate during the wet and dry seasons, even across national borders. Adult literacy is below the average for West Africa.

The overthrow of Toure's government after his death has started the nation down the slow path to national recovery and healing. Missionaries are once again welcome and there is a measure of freedom for the church in comparison with other Muslim-dominated lands. The French Catholic presence has remained strong over the years as a result of high quality education provided by the mission schools, which have educated many of the country's leaders.

However, despite years of Catholic influence and effort, Guinea is still regarded by many as one of the least evangelized nations in Africa. This is due in part to the twin pillars of animism and Islam, which have shaped the nation's spiritual formation.

Basic Facts

Location:
West Africa

Neighboring Countries:
Guinea-Bissau, Senegal, Mali, Côte d'Ivoire, Liberia

Population:
7,807,000

Capital City:
Conakry

Major Cities:
N'Zerekore, Kankan, Labe, Siguiri

Government:
Republic

Leader:
President Brigadier General Lansana Conte

Major Religions:
Islam, African traditional religions

Historical Background

While Guinea's historic roots can be traced to the great trading kingdoms of the Sahel, especially Ghana and Mali, it is the specter of slavery that overshadows the history of Africa's west coast. The area was a center of the slave trade, with the first evidence of organized slavery dating back to the early seventh century. In the fifteenth century Guinea contributed about one third of the slaves from the African continent. The conversion to Islam by the Sahelian princes in the seventeenth century provided a convenient justification for fighting neighboring tribes. Islamic holy wars in the Fouta Djallon highlands served to preserve the practice, as captives were sold into slavery.

The first known Christian missionaries were French Catholics, who settled on the coast prior to formal annexation by the Europeans, but later were heavily identified with the colonial enterprise. Another influence from this period was the introduction of freemasonry, and Guinea became a veritable hotbed for this activity in the early 1900's. French freemasonry generally has more ties to the occult than other varieties of freemasonry, and the package seems to have tied in well with the pre-existing secret societies.

Unreached Peoples

The Baga, who were the earliest inhabitants of Guinea, are known for their two-meter high python helmet sculptures, and the use of giant Nimba fertility goddess masks, one of the largest, bulkiest, and heaviest masks used anywhere. Mission work among the Baga is in progress, with at least 150 believers in 1993, out of a total of 32,000.

The Mande, a trading people who moved into Guinea, were well known for their "power associations" - secret societies designed to preserve Mande culture and trade routes. The power associations were formed around metal smiths due to their mysterious ability to work with iron, a skill not known to the common people, as well as their magical powers. Metal smiths supposedly had the ability to make potent amulets and effect a variety of cures.

The power associations had a shadowy, ultra-secretive inner circle that was reputed to possess "much high magic," and its membership was limited to leaders of the lodges. The python is a symbol among the Mande as well, widely associated with animistic rites and the power associations. There are now some Christians among various Mande people groups, but more laborers are needed among this tribe, who have largely turned to Islam.

Spiritual Competition

Guinea is a secular state, with a tolerant stance toward Christianity, despite the fact that the country is predominantly Muslim. This tolerance was recently reaffirmed by the president, who changed the Ministry of Islamic Affairs to the Ministry of Religious Affairs. While there is no official prohibition against evangelism, social pressure from family and friends prevents many people from learning about Christ.

A revival of interest in fetishism, animism and occult practices in Guinea is sending many people spiraling deeper into darkness and despair. Even Islam has not escaped the prevailing spirit of animism unscathed, as traditional beliefs have become mixed with orthodox Islam.

The government's show of force against Christianity following independence helped Islam and animism solidify their positions in Guinea. Even the well-established Catholics have had their share of difficulties, such as having their schools nationalized in 1961 and their missionaries expelled (along with almost all others) in 1967. Despite having relatively few converts to show for all their labor since the late 1800's, they are nonetheless well respected for their significant contributions to education and social and economic development. It is this fact which is at least partially responsible for the current official toleration of Christian witness.

Noteworthy Trends

The death of Sekou Toure in 1984 and his replacement by Lansana Conte was a watershed in the modern history of the country. The change was marked by a shift from isolationism, Marxism and Islamization to greater openness to the West, as well as religious tolerance. The devastated economy has picked up, basic freedoms have been restored, and the transition to civilian rule has been promised by the military government. In an environment of revitalization, people are more open to change, and this may be a window of opportunity for the gospel.

The political situation however, remains uncertain. Violent clashes motivated by political and religious differences have become more common. Some Muslims oppose Conte's tolerant approach to Christianity and would like to see greater privileges and influence for Muslims.

Despite the political uncertainty, as well as the lack of a major spiritual breakthrough, the Christian mission force has been slowly increasing in this land of rugged living conditions, great beauty and poverty of spirit. Pray that by the turn of the century Guinea is no longer one of Africa's least evangelized countries.

National Prayer Concerns

Obstacles to Ministry
Pray about these challenging circumstances:
• Small Indigenous Church
Guinea has long been one of Africa's least evangelized nations
• Lack of Christian Literature
Little translation work and only one Christian bookstore
• Strong Muslim Influence
About three-quarters of all Guineans are Muslim
• Severe Poverty
Country has yet to recover from reign of Sekou Toure

Spiritual Power Points
Pray over these influential locations:
• Jugunko (Fouta Djalon Highlands)
Historic Muslim retreat center established by Al Hadj
• Grand Mosque (Conakry)
Main Islamic worship center in capital
• City of Kankan
Stronghold of Manika Muslims; site of largest mosque
• La Dame de Mali (Mali Area)
Legendary rock formation in the Fouta Djalon

Festivals and Pilgrimages
Pray during these spiritual events:
• Ramadan & Eid al-Fitr (Varies: '96 = Jan/Feb)
Month of fasting and prayer followed by two day feast
• Tabaski/Eid al-Kabir (Varies: '96 = April)
Islamic sacrificial feast; most important in West Africa
• Mawlid an-Nabi (Varies: '96 = July)
Celebrations honoring Muhammad's birthday
• Quinzaine Artistique (Autumn)
Islamic and animist folklore festival

Guinea-Bissau

Guinea-Bissau is a little-known West African country with a tragic link to America. For thousands of slaves sent to sweat and die in the plantations of the New World, the swampy coast and beaches of Guinea-Bissau were the last sight of their African home. The effect of the slave trade on West Africa was devastating, with an estimated one-fourth of the population forcibly sold into slavery. The impact of slavery and colonial exploitation are still felt in the region to this day, like an ancient curse that still hangs over this impoverished and spiritually darkened area of West Africa.

A country with a population of many ethnic groups, Guinea-Bissau was under Portuguese control for 400 years, a turbulent time that ended in 1974 when Portugal was forced to give up its colonial claim, leaving behind only a language and a carnival. The pre-Lenten Catholic carnival was a good party tradition that the natives carried on, but the Europeans did nothing to help the colony to its feet when they left. Twenty years of independence without armed conflicts or natural calamities has not helped the country to advance economically or politically, and it remains a stagnant African backwater.

Guinea-Bissau has promising potential as a rich agricultural land with good mineral deposits, yet it is ranked as one of the poorest nations on the continent. Rivers provide the primary means of access to the low lying swampy interior of the country. Approximately 95% of the population live in rural areas and are engaged in farming.

Basic Facts

Location:
West Africa

Neighboring Countries:
Guinea, Senegal

Population:
1,150,000

Capital City:
Bissau

Major Cities:
Bafatá, Bolama, Buba

Government:
One party military rule

Leader:
President Joao Vieira

Major Religions:
African traditional religions, Islam

Historical Background

*U*nlike today, seaports were of little value in ancient West Africa, where the major trade routes were overland to North Africa and the Middle East. The kingdoms which controlled these trade routes were centered inland and were the chief political powers of the day. For more than a thousand years the coast of Guinea-Bissau has been occupied by iron-using farmers. With the breakup of the ancient Ghanaian empire, displaced peoples sought refuge near the coast, and later the region was drawn loosely under the influence of the Malian empire. The peoples who settled on the coast were later caught up in the slave trade.

Portugal had to relinquish control of its first colony because of a successful guerrilla war of liberation, a war which succeeded in part due to the heavy-handed actions of the Portuguese military. The Marxist government formed by the guerrillas had close ties to the island nation of Cape Verde, which lies several hundred miles offshore in the Atlantic. All hopes of unification with the islands were dashed after the president of Guinea Bissau was ousted in a coup by Joao Vieira in 1975. A major result of the coup was the expulsion of the mixed blood Cape Verde civil servants and technicians, and their replacement with Africans. Since 1992 President Vieira has been pressed to allow multi-party political reform and is moving very slowly in that direction.

Unreached Peoples

*T*he population is comprised of some 23 separate ethnic groups with close ties to larger populations in Ghana and Senegal. The Fulani and Mandinga, who are Muslim farmers and traders, are the dominant tribes of the interior. The Fulani, who have recently responded to the gospel, are spread throughout West Africa and a breakthrough among them could have a far-reaching impact.

The 250,000 Balanta are the largest and most widespread people group in the country. They are fiercely independent, and during the war provided the majority of the guerrilla forces. The church is stronger among the Balanta than among most other people groups, but the majority continue to follow traditional animistic religions.

The impact of traditional religion on the culture is very powerful, as illustrated by the practices of the people of the Bijagos Archipelago, a group of coastal islands. Because of obsessive superstitions involving spirits, the dead are transported by canoe to a spirit island where they are buried. The families are obligated to make regular trips to the spirit island with supplies to nourish the dead.

Spiritual Competition

Islam claims about 44% of the population, with most adherents belonging to either the Tijaniyah or Quadiriya brotherhoods. Interestingly, the Catholic Portuguese supported the expansion of Islam to help counteract the influence of nationalist leaders. Since independence, the government has joined the Islamic Conference and receives aid from Saudi Arabia and Kuwait. As is the case in most tribal societies, local Islam is heavily interlaced with traditional religious beliefs and practice, resulting in a highly syncretistic variety of folk Islam.

These traditional religions are the predominant spiritual force in Guinea-Bissau. Almost half of the population openly follow traditional religious practices, such as worshipping ancestors, fearing and appeasing spirits, and observing occult rituals. The impact of traditional religion is further strengthened by those who practice it under the veneer of Islam or Christianity. Traditional beliefs are strongest among the coastal Balanta and other West Atlantic peoples.

The history of the church in Guinea-Bissau is closely associated with Catholicism brought by Portuguese priests who arrived with colonial trading companies. Their influence was largely confined to the expatriate European population, with little impact on the local people. Until the 20th century, Catholics were the only Christian missionaries allowed in the country.

Noteworthy Trends

The political and economic future of Guinea-Bissau looks bleak, with little respite in sight. The promised and long-awaited transition to multi-party democracy will not be sufficient to solve the nation's ills. The economic situation is bad, with barter often replacing hard currency in the teeming markets of the capital, Bissau. Public health continues to be miserable, with an adult life expectancy of 42 years, and 45 percent of the children dying before the age of five. Much of this dismal situation can be traced back to the forcible expulsion of thousands of mixed race administrative staff, both civil servants and skilled workers, who came from Cape Verde.

Recently municipal workers and teachers in Bissau concluded a 200 day strike against the government for failure to pay back wages. Teacher's salaries are now being supplemented by aid payments from Europe. However, from a Christian perspective, the situation may never have been more encouraging. Since 1990 additional Christian mission agencies have been allowed in the country for the first time since 1939. More workers are desperately needed to take advantage of the opportunities in this poor nation which is only now becoming open to the gospel.

National Prayer Concerns

Obstacles to Ministry
Pray about these challenging circumstances:
• Growing Islamic Influence
40 percent of populace is Muslim; mostly upcountry
• Widespread Animism in Coastal Region
Fetishes, mask dances and ancestor worship
• Severe Poverty and Health Problems
45 percent of children die before the age of five
• Social Ostracism of Believers
Believers are often persecuted by heathen relatives

Spiritual Power Points
Pray over these influential locations:
• Bijagos Archipelago
Center of animist superstition and immorality
• Curadores (Bissau)
Healing houses operated by witch doctors
• City of Bafata
Popular venue for animist dancing with rope and bells
• Avenue de Cintura Mosque (Bissau)
Major mosque in capital city

Festivals and Pilgrimages
Pray during these spiritual events:
• Ramadan & Eid al-Fitr (Varies: '96 = Jan/Feb)
Month of fasting and prayer followed by two day feast
• Carnival (February/March)
Multi-day events including animist mask dances
• Tabaski/Eid al-Kabir (Varies: '96 = April)
Islamic sacrificial feast; most important in West Africa
• Nourishing the Dead (All Year)
Family visits to spirit island in Bijagos Archipelago

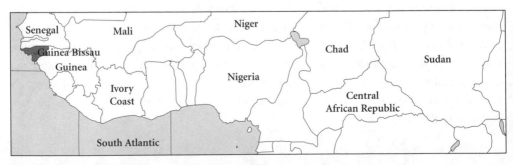

India

The Ganges River, the heart and soul of India and essence of the nation's being, flows from the western Himalayas to the Bay of Bengal, and is the most sacred place in the world for Hindus. Considered a living water deity by many, the Ganges' muddy, littered and disease-filled waters could hardly be thought to possess any cleansing value, yet millions of Hindus make annual pilgrimages to bathe and wallow in it for spiritual purification. Perhaps the British saw the significance of the sacred rivers when they gave the country its current name, deriving from the Sanskrit word sindhu, meaning river, which was originally applied to the Indus River.

A cacophony of bizarre beliefs, practices, rituals, and festivals make India a bewildering maze of religious experience. India is the birthplace of two of the world's great religions, Hinduism and Buddhism. Two other religions, Jainism and Sikhism, were also born here and are largely confined to the subcontinent. In addition, Christianity, Islam, Zoroastrianism, and even Judaism have also taken root in India. As bewildering as the religious landscape may be, the ethnic diversity is perhaps the most complex in Asia.

India is second in the world to China in terms of population. While most of the people still live in rural areas, there are more than 60 cities with populations over 300,000. Places such as Bombay, Delhi, and Calcutta are well known for their teeming millions, many of whom are slum dwellers, living in squalor that most Westerners would have to see to believe. However, almost two-thirds of the rural population still reside in their native districts because of deep-rooted ties to land and community.

Basic Facts

Location:
South Asia

Neighboring Countries:
China, Nepal, Bhutan, Myanmar, Bangladesh

Population:
904,800,000

Capital City:
New Delhi

Major Cities:
Calcutta, Bombay, Madras, Bangalore, Hyderabad

Government:
Federal Republic

Leader:
Prime Minister P.V. Narashima Rao

Major Religions:
Hinduism, Islam

Historical Background

$\mathcal{A}$ highly developed civilization existed in the Indus Valley (now part of Pakistan) from about 2300 to 1750 BC. The Aryans arrived from the northwest between 2000 and 1000 BC, introducing the Sanskrit language, the Vedic (Hindu) religion, and the caste system. In the 6th century BC, Buddhism and Jainism arose as reform movements of Hinduism. King Ashoka, a famous ruler of the Mauryan empire during the golden age of Buddhism (321-185 BC), sent out many missionary monks and was known for spreading Buddhism throughout much of Asia, and even influenced the pagan spirituality of the eastern Mediterranean.

According to tradition, Christianity was first brought to India by the Apostle Thomas, and Indian Christians generally accept this as historical fact. In any case, it was certainly established by about 350, giving India one of the longest surviving Christian heritages outside of the Middle East.

Muslim invasions began about the year 1000 and Muslim political control lasted until the late 1700s, but never replaced Hinduism as the major religion. Modern missions began to arrive on the coattails of the colonial powers, particularly the English and the British East India Company, who gained control of India in the late 1700s.

Unreached Peoples

There are an estimated 3,000 major ethnic groups (castes and tribes) in the country, with only 22 of them having a significant Christian minority. A further 50 groups have only a small Christian population. The continuing need for cross-cultural evangelism is staggering. The higher castes in particular have shown little response to the gospel.

The 88 million Muslims are probably more accessible for Christian witness here than in any other country on earth. Although the number of Muslims was significantly reduced when Pakistan and Bangladesh were partitioned off as independent Muslim states, Islam is still the second largest religion in India. Outreach to them is difficult and often costly, but there are several Indian missionary societies specifically dedicated to this task. There seems to be a marginally greater responsiveness now than in the past.

With 75% of the population living in rural areas, there are approximately 600,000 villages in this vast and overpopulated country. Very few have Christian congregations, and in north India there may be only one church for every 2,000 villages. Comparatively little indigenous missionary effort has been focused on the major task of reaching those in the countryside.

Spiritual Competition

Although India is a secular state that grants freedom to all religions to practice and propagate their faith, in reality there is strong pressure from Hindu militants to limit that freedom. Millions of Harijans (outcasts or untouchables) have turned to Buddhism, Christianity and Islam to escape the oppressive caste system, and this has angered Hindu militants. Violence against religious minorities, persecution of Christians, discriminatory legislation in several states and the forcible conversion of tribal people to Hinduism has resulted.

Hinduism is far from a monolithic entity. Its various sects often appear to be distinct religions, tied together only by belief in reincarnation, the veneration of cows and the caste system. This variation gives it a broad base of appeal, not only in India, but also in Western countries where the philosophical and mystical aspects are attracting growing interest.

The caste system itself poses a major challenge for the Church. The low social origin of most Christians can create a problem for higher caste Hindus who are otherwise attracted to the gospel, and continued castism among Christians can likewise repel Harijans.

Noteworthy Trends

One of the truly exciting missions movements of this century is taking place in India. The almost incomprehensible task of evangelizing the multiplied millions of unreached people in thousands of distinct ethnic groups is great. However, God has been raising up a growing army of Indian missionaries to take up the challenge of evangelizing this vast nation. This is particularly significant because there has been a rapid reduction in the number of foreign missionaries, as visas have been severely restricted since 1984. So far, the growth of Indian missionaries has exceeded the decline in foreign workers. In addition to missionaries, the Indian church has produced a number of outstanding and mature Christian leaders of international stature. They have made vital contributions not only to the evangelization of India, but also to such international cooperative efforts as Lausanne II and the Asian Missions Congress.

However, the Indian church in general suffers from two major problems, which are concerns for prayer. One is the influence of liberal universalist theology in the mainline Protestant and Catholic churches, and the other is nominalism. Despite the crop of dynamic new evangelists, the vast majority of India's church members have no vision for the evangelization of their country.

National Prayer Concerns

Obstacles to Ministry
Pray about these challenging circumstances:
• Hindu Fundamentalism
Churches have been burned; re-conversion efforts abound
• Enormous Population Base
India will soon overtake China as world's most populous nation
• Religious Diversity
Hindus, Sikhs, Muslims, Jains, Buddhists and Zoroastrians
• Severe Poverty
India's cities teem with untold suffering and despair

Spiritual Power Points
Pray over these influential locations:
• City of Varanasi
Earthly abode of the Hindu god Shiva; most sacred Hindu pilgrimage site
• Prasanthi Nilayam
Spiritual community of Indian power guru Sai Baba
• Nechung & Namgyal Monasteries
Residence, temple and oracle room of the Dalai Lama
• Golden Temple (Amritsar)
Holy shrine of the Sikh faith

Festivals and Pilgrimages
Pray during these spiritual events:
• Holi Festival (March)
Spring "oneness" festival; often abusive in cities
• Karttika Purnima (November)
Vishnu bath festival celebrated in over 100 locations
• Pancakrosi Yatra Pilgrimage (All Year)
108 shrine Hindu pilgrimage route near Varanasi
• Kumbha Mela Festival (Every 3 Years)
Hindu bathing festival celebrated by rotation at four sacred places

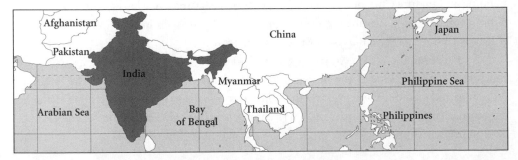

Indonesia

$\mathcal{A}$ fascinating tropical country with a unique and exotic culture, Indonesia is scattered like a strings of jewels thrown into a coral sea. The 13,667 islands of the Indonesian archipelago stretch across a vast area between the Southeast Asian mainland, the Philippines, and Australia. Not only the largest archipelago nation, it is also the fourth largest country in the world by population. It is one of the most highly volcanic regions in the world, with more than 100 active volcanoes. Only about 1,000 of the islands are inhabited, and most of the population is concentrated on three large islands, Sumatra, Java, and Celebes, and on part of two other islands—Borneo and New Guinea. Java is one of the most densely populated parts of Southeast Asia, with more than half of Indonesia's people.

The nation straddles the Equator and has some of the world's last great rain forests, which are sadly being depleted by slash-and-burn agriculture; its climate is tropical throughout the year. Because of its equatorial location, Indonesia has no seasons, and the days and nights are always about twelve hours long.

Indonesia has more Muslims than any other country in the world. Over 80% of the population are considered Muslim according to government statistics, although they follow a mix of animist, Hindu and Muslim beliefs and rituals. More than 300 different ethnic groups, the majority of which derive from Malay stock, are scattered throughout the islands. Many live in modern cities, but most are in rural areas where they are engaged in agriculture. In Irian Jaya and Kalimantan there are many primitive tribes, some of which still practice cannibalism.

Basic Facts

Location:
Southeast Asia

Capital City:
Jakarta

Leader:
President Suharto

Neighboring Countries:
Singapore, Malaysia,
Papua New Guinea,
Australia

Major Cities:
Surabaya, Bandung,
Medan, Semarang

Major Religions:
Islam, Christianity,
Hinduism, animism

Population:
195,623,000

Government:
Independent Republic

Historical Background

The earliest Indonesians were probably migrants from South Asia and followed a form of spirit worship. Hinduism was introduced from India in the first century AD, with Buddhism following later. The two greatest early empires were the Buddhist kingdom of Sri Vijaya which arose on Sumatra by 600, and the Hindu kingdom of Majapahit which came to power in the 1300s on Java.

Islam spread along the maritime trade routes, and by 1500 most Indonesians had become Muslims, with many of the Hindus having fled to Bali. In the 16th century Islam became the state religion and was superimposed on the mixture of Hinduism, Buddhism and indigenous animist beliefs. Thus it became a peculiar Indonesian hybrid religion which is common in much of the country today.

Nestorian Christianity first arrived in the seventh century, possibly continuing for hundreds of years until the Portuguese arrived in 1511 and the Roman Catholic Church began its work. St. Francis Xavier played a key role in the Catholic Church's endeavor. Protestant missions arrived with the Dutch in 1605, who controlled Indonesia until the Japanese invaded during World War II. With the Netherlands in shambles after the war, Indonesia proclaimed its independence in 1945, and finally freed itself from foreign domination after some 400 years.

Unreached Peoples

One of the largest non-Christian people groups in the world is found in Indonesia. The 30 million Sundanese of West Java are staunchly Muslim, although they have underlying animistic beliefs, and the old Sundanese religion still prevails in some areas. There are a few Sundanese Christians, but they tend to be nominal and culturally isolated from the Muslim majority. Converts to Christianity can be sure of persecution, and therefore many have no interest in evangelism. Christian outreach is being directed toward these people, but the task is difficult and must be handled with utmost discretion.

The people of Bali are predominantly Hindu, in contrast to the Muslim majority in most of the country. The island itself is a favorite tourist destination, with over a million visitors annually. Part of the attraction is the mystique created by the exotic landscape and the ancient shrines and temples, as well as the cultural and religious practices of the people. In reality the Balinese live in a spiritual nether world - stories of demonic manifestations and occult practices are legendary and well-documented. The cost of discipleship is high for the Balinese, who face ostracism and persecution from family and friends if they convert and turn away from their former way of life.

Spiritual Competition

$\mathcal{I}$ndonesia has an interesting provision in the preamble of its constitution which calls for all Indonesians to believe in one supreme God. It doesn't matter which one—Allah, Buddha, Vishnu, Jesus, or whoever, as long as a person is not an atheist. This is the first principle of what is called Pancasila, the constitutional principles by which the country is ruled. All faiths, including Christianity, are accepted as long as they have a supreme God. Even Hinduism and Buddhism are included in this category due to their long history in the country.

Pancasila is designed to keep political peace among the various competing religions, and also serves as an effective antidote to evangelism. Needless to say, it is useful in consolidating Muslim power, which has been the dominant and stabilizing influence in the government. Because of the sheer numbers of Muslims and their political strength, they have a definite advantage and are often able to limit Christian expansion. Nonetheless, Christians enjoy considerable freedoms compared to other Muslim nations.

Animism, although discouraged by the government, is an active force throughout the islands and especially among the primitive tribes. As alluded to earlier, animism was the earliest religion among the peoples of Indonesia and still provides the core of many people's beliefs.

Noteworthy Trends

$\mathcal{S}$ince 1945, when then President Sukarno first expounded the Pancasila, the Indonesian government has pursued a course designed to bring unity in the midst of the extreme diversity. In 1998, incumbent President Suharto is widely expected to relinquish office. Already rival groups have begun maneuvering to strengthen their positions. One such group is the Muslim Intellectual's Association. While they are not a Muslim extremist group, the potential for increased Muslim influence in government may not bode well for Christians. An opposing faction is the military which has moved back into civilian politics and has a pan-religious approach to government. The military continues to hold substantial political power.

The church in Indonesia is one of the strongest and fastest growing in Asia (some experts believe the country is actually 25% Christian, but the government will not confirm this), and it faces stiff opposition from growing Islamic militancy. Missionary visas are almost phased out, but there is an open door for university professors, English teachers, and businessmen. With the world's fourth largest population and booming economy, Indonesia is a critically strategic nation for the church in Asia. No amount of prayer, energy, or money will be wasted on this country, which is truly on the razor's edge of contemporary missions.

National Prayer Concerns

Obstacles to Ministry

Pray about these challenging circumstances:

• Huge Muslim Population

Indonesia is the largest Islamic nation in the world

• Animism, Idolatry and Christian Syncretism

Especially on the islands of Bali, Sumba and Flores

• Reduction in Missionary Visas

Foreign Christian missionaries are being phased out

• Geographic Complications

The country is spread out over more than 13,500 islands

Spiritual Power Points

Pray over these influential locations:

• Borobudur (Java)

Major Buddhist temple modeling mythical Mt. Meru

• Mt. Gunung Agung (Bali)

Most actively worshiped mountain in Indonesia

• Mt. Bromo (Java)

Volcano through which spirits of dead pass to paradise

• Pura Besakih (Bali)

Hindu "Mother Temple;" host to Eka Dasa Rudra

Festivals and Pilgrimages

Pray during these spiritual events:

• Ramadan & Eid al-Fitr (Varies: '96 = Jan/Feb)

Month of fasting and prayer followed by two day feast

• Bhatara Turun Kabeh (April)

"The god's descend all together" festival in Bali

• Waisak Day (May)

Annual Buddhist ceremony at Borobudur & Mendut

• Eka Dasa Rudra (Generally every 100 years)

Elaborate multi-month Hindu festival held in Bali

Iran

Iran is an ancient montage of divergent cultures and languages contained by the frontiers of mountain and desert which have defined its borders for thousands of years. This cross pollination has produced a rich culture, one that is largely responsible for giving order and stability to the Muslim world, especially in the early days of Islamic development. Iran (formerly known as Persia) provided the bureaucratic know-how and a systematized language for the inexperienced Arab invaders.

Needless to say, this same diversity of peoples has at times led to conflict and disarray. However, strong spiritual beliefs have long been the key to Iranian unity and strength. This was recently manifest when the Ayatollah Khomeini led the restless Iranian populace in a spiritual revolution that rocked the world in 1979. Many Western experts doubted the Iranian revolution's ability to weather the hardships brought on by the revolution itself and the debilitating eight year war with Iraq. That it has succeeded even after the death of Khomeini is an indication that the revolution is now firmly rooted and entrenched.

Much of the current turmoil in the Mideast is directly traceable to Iran. The Khomeini regime's virulent outbursts against the "Great Satan" of America, as well as its contempt for European Christendom in general have been both the spark and the flame of the current worldwide pan-Islamic resurgence. Iran has managed to convince a large part of the Muslim world that the U.S. and Western Europe are engaged in a systematic and orchestrated destruction of Islam; the fact that this is highly unlikely and without evidence is of little concern to the Islamic masses that have embraced Iran's fiery rhetoric.

Basic Facts

Location:
Middle East

Neighboring Countries:
Iraq, Afghanistan, Turkey, Armenia, Azerbaijan, Turkmenistan

Population:
64,525,000

Capital City:
Tehran

Major Cities:
Esfahan, Mashhad, Tabriz, Shiraz

Government:
Islamic Republic

Leader:
Ali Akbar Hashemi Rafsanjani

Major Religions:
Islam

Historical Background

Persia has been a major power since its victory over the Babylonians in the sixth century BC. The Persians adopted the Zoroastrian religion of their allies, the Medes, and upon entering Babylon found that they had some beliefs in common with the Jews who were held captive there. God used the Persians to restore Israel and assist in the rebuilding of the temple; some prophecies even picture the Persian King Cyrus as a benevolent hero.

The Persians resisted Greek and Roman influence and maintained their Zoroastrian religion and culture right up until the battle of Qadisiyah in 637 AD. After this crushing defeat at the hands of the Arab Muslims, Persia seemed to go into shock. It was not until an Azeri Turk named Ismail entered the scene in 1501 that Persia's national pride was fully restored. He entered the Iranian city of Tabriz and declared that Shiite Islam would be the new Persian empire's religion. Despite the fact that Ismail was a foreigner and most Persians were of the rival Sunni sect, his Shiites took complete control of Iran in less than ten years. His Safavid Empire dominated the country for the next 450 years, culminating in the modern Shiite Islamic Republic.

Unreached Peoples

The Turkish Azeri nation, located in Iran's northwest frontier bordering Turkey and the old USSR, is Iran's largest minority. As mentioned, the Azeris introduced Shiism to Iran as a national religion, and today they are divided into several tribes. The Shahsevan, a semi-nomadic tribal group, is composed of 300,000 people; like their cousins, the Avshar and Kajar tribes, the Shahsevan are famous for their colorful and valuable kilim carpets.

There are about five million Kurds living in Iran. These often persecuted people are one of the largest unreached groups in the world. Descended from the ancient Medes, they inhabit a land they call Kurdistan, which in reality exists only in the hearts and minds of the Kurds. If it were to be drawn on a map, Kurdistan would cover parts of Iran, Iraq, Turkey, Syria and the Caucasus, where the Kurds have dwelled for many centuries. Their rich spiritual heritage also includes being the descendants of the New Testament Magi who visited the baby Jesus. The Kurds have been disappointed by their recent flirtation with various spiritual and economic ideologies, and many Kurds are now actively seeking an alternative to the Islamic faith and would welcome the opportunity to hear Christian teaching.

Spiritual Competition

Shiism's main appeal seems to be its anti-establishment ideals. Historically, Shiism has been embraced by people who are marginalized and locked out of the corridors of power in the Islamic world. Iranian Shiism sprang forth from the fanatical devotion of 15th and 16th century Sufis (Muslim mystics) who lived in the mountainous northwest near the modern Turkish and Russian borders. This early movement incorporated many animist practices into its anti-establishment Islamic theology, venerating sacred stones and trees, and relying heavily on the use of amulets and spells. Their spiritual life was centered on allegiance to holy men and saints, which is common in central and south Asian Islam.

When Ismail the Azeri declared Shiism the state religion of all Iran in 1501, the leaders of his new empire had to import the theology and methodology of the Shiites from what was the real Shiite stronghold of the time, southern Lebanon. The brief period it took for it to spread across Iran is an example of Shiism's broad appeal to its constituents, the disenfranchised common people. Today, Shiism again seeks out the poor, using them as its power base in a bid to recover the entire Muslim world.

Noteworthy Trends

Surprisingly, businessmen still view Iran's economy as a good investment. The nation is now soliciting foreign funds, and the upgrading of its military arsenal is a high priority. The CIA reports that Iran has all the components required for the construction of two to three nuclear weapons. Indeed, this is a major worry for the West. Having neutralized Iraq's nuclear threat in the Gulf War, the Allies now face a similar and potentially more dangerous threat in Iran before the decade is out. During the last year, the country has shifted its emphasis from Shiite revival and has begun to recruit, encourage and arm extremists from the mainstream Sunni Muslim world. Iran is almost certainly the major single sponsor of global terrorism, and is able to finance these sinister activities by its sale of oil—often to the same nations it targets.

Ironically, one positive development since the revolution has been church growth among nominal Muslims. Many who became discouraged with Islam after it was revealed to them in its "pure form" by Khomeini's ruthless police state are now turning to the Church. Iran is a nation ripe and ready for the truth of the gospel, and prevailing prayer may well make the difference.

Obstacles to Ministry

Pray about these challenging circumstances:

• Muslim Evangelism Strictly Forbidden
Witnessing to Muslims can result in severe punishment
• Few Cross-Cultural Mission Opportunities
Fundamentalist regime has poor relations with the West
• Christians Facing Harsh New Persecution
Imprisonment, torture and executions have been reported
• Extensive System of Police Informers
Many purists are members of neighborhood "komitehs"

Spiritual Power Points

Pray over these influential locations:

• Behesht-i-Zahra (Martyrs Cemetery)
Site of Khomeini's tomb and "blood" fountain
• City of Qom
Holy Shiite city hosting key theological seminaries
• Mount Demavend
Cosmic mountain of Zoroastrian mythology
• Taleghani Center
Islamic terrorism and missionary command post

Festivals and Pilgrimages

Pray during these spiritual events:

• Ramadan & Eid al-Fitr (Varies: '96 = Jan/Feb)
Month of fasting and prayer followed by two day feast
• Ashura (Varies: '96 = May)
Shiite passion play celebrating Hussein's martyrdom
• The Six Gahambars (Events Held Throughout Year)
Chain of festivals honoring immortals of Zoroastrianism
• Pilgrimage to Behesht-i-Zahra (All Year)
Site of Khomeini's tomb and massive Martyrs' Cemetery

Iraq

Historians depict the area between Iraq's Tigris and Euphrates rivers as the birthplace of civilization. The world's first cities, governments, legal codes, written languages and international communication systems all found their start here in the "land between the rivers." Mesopotamia's seminal impact on the development of the modern world can be judged by the attitudes of the empires of Assyria, Babylon, Persia and Greece; each of these reckoned that control of the Sumerian heartland was necessary to rule the world. Biblical accounts imply that Iraq may be the headquarters of something beyond the conquests of men: Nimrod, Babel, Ur, and Babylon are some of the most obvious names associating Iraqi territory with the real "Mother of all Battles"—the global spiritual war for the lives of peoples and nations.

Doubly blessed with oil and water, modern Iraq could have been among the most prosperous states in the Middle East. Its leaders, however, had higher priorities than increasing the standard of living. Seemingly energized by the demonic forces of yesteryear, their insatiable thirst for greater power and influence has only been satisfied by an unending flow of blood from the Iraqi people. The Gulf War is only the latest in a long series of horrors that have befallen this ancient nation. Saddam Hussein's purposeful rebuilding of the pagan and demonic ruins of Babylon is no coincidence - it is the deliberate expression of a direct and tangible connection from one despotic and murderous regime to another. The fact that thousands of years separate these dark kingdoms matter little to the timeless spirits who have ruled this land with a blood lust since the dawn of history.

Basic Facts

Location:
Middle East

Neighboring Countries:
Iran, Jordan, Syria, Turkey, Kuwait, Saudi Arabia

Population:
22,411,000

Capital City:
Baghdad

Major Cities:
Basra, Mosul

Government:
Republic

Leader:
President Saddam Hussein At-Tikriti

Major Religions:
Islam

Historical Background

As the cradle of civilization, Iraq has repeatedly been the location for watershed events in human history. Not the least of these was the emergence of the pagan pantheon upon which the cults of Egypt, Greece and Rome were based. Even now it is not hard to see the continuity between the Babylonian religions of old and the rise of militant Islam, right down to the modern identification with these supernatural forces in Saddam's Arab Republic.

One striking example is the battle of Qadisiyah (637 AD), a battle that is unrivaled in importance to the Islamic world. It was the real breakthrough for Islam in which the Persian Empire was defeated, ushering in Islam's golden age. Qadisiyah was a defining event for the Islamic world as a whole, and a point when many Christians and Jews began to capitulate to Muslim sovereignty throughout the Mediterranean.

The division between the two branches of Islam also occurred in Iraq shortly after Qadisiyah, due to a dispute over the rightful successors of Muhammad. Thus both major divisions of Islam, Sunni and Shia, were born on Iraqi soil. Part of the Ottoman Turkish Empire for centuries, Iraq's modern boundaries were drawn by the Europeans after the First World War.

Unreached Peoples

Iraq's Kurds came to the world's attention at the end of the Gulf War when hundreds of thousands of them were stranded as refugees on Iraq's northern mountainous borders. The Kurds make up 23% of Iraq's total population, and have repeatedly pressed the Iraqi government for political autonomy, which has often led them into armed rebellion. Although some mission work was started here in the early 1900's, very little progress was made because of the constantly shifting political environment of this area. Some spiritual ground was broken however, with the founding of a Lutheran church in the Kurdish city of Erbil.

The Kurds had already endured tremendous physical hardship before the Gulf War. Saddam Hussein's government systematically destroyed 3,500 Kurdish villages over the past twenty years, using chemical warfare and massive firepower. The Kurds are now under UN protection but the situation is still very difficult for them. They are cut off from essential supplies by an embargo from Iraq, so that all goods must enter the Kurdish region from Turkey, a country that is very unfriendly to Kurdish aspirations. Although they are Muslim, the Kurds "hold their Islam loosely," and a serious effort is now underway to plant a viable church among them.

Spiritual Competition

The powerful spiritual forces active in Iraq reveal themselves in many disguises. Arab nationalism and Islamic fundamentalism are the most influential. The Iraqi government has methodically cultivated and affirmed its origins in the religious cults of ancient Babylon by "resurrecting" pagan festival sites and actually reinstating modern Arab versions of many Babylonian pilgrimages, which are blatant affirmations of the gods of the past.

At times the various extremes of Iraqi polity seem to conflict, but they are all undeniably flowing in the same direction. Saddam's heavy handed regime has empowered one segment of Iraqi society (the ruling Baath party) and brutally suppressed the other (the Shiites). In these two rival confessions lay the main obstacles to the gospel. Baath Arab nationalism is a mystical glorification of the Arab ethnic identity, and is in every respect a religious belief. The rival Shiite religion thrives on rejection and persecution, and has therefore been decidedly strengthened by Baath oppression. Given these conditions, it is surprising to find that the Iraqi church has been allowed considerable freedoms, partly due the fact that Saddam likes to encourage certain minorities for political reasons. The country is about 3% Christian, mostly Orthodox, but the Protestant church is growing.

Noteworthy Trends

In the minds of many Iraqis, the chief result of the Gulf War has been to save the wealthy and corrupt Kuwait regime on the one hand and to punish the already poor peoples of Iraq on the other. Disenfranchised Arabs everywhere sympathize with Saddam's regime for this reason, even though they personally dislike him. The Arab proverb "Me and my brothers against my cousins, me and my cousins against the world" best summarizes the situation in Iraq today. Many Arab countries, including Gulf states like Bahrain, are urging a speedy restoration of ties to Iraq in order to form a united Arab alliance against the increasingly powerful Iranians, with whom Iraq fought a long and very bloody war in the 1980s.

On the positive side, the opening of Iraq to foreign humanitarian aid has presented some new openings for the gospel and converts have been reported as a result of Christian involvement in various aid programs. Many Kurds in Iraq are already fed up with what they view as an "Arab" religion, and are making inquiries into Christianity. Sooner or later Saddam will fall, and Iraq's future direction will then be fiercely contested by the West, The Iranians, the surrounding Arab nations and internal forces.

Obstacles to Ministry
Pray about these challenging circumstances:
• De Facto Political Fragmentation
Northern Kurdistan has been cut off from rest of Iraq
• Large Shiite Population in South
Centered around holy cities of Najaf and Karbala
• Active and Brutal Secret Police
Fear has spread through church and society at large
• Lack of Christian Literature
Global sanctions and internal policies have cut supplies

Spiritual Power Points
Pray over these influential locations:
• Nippur
Ancient religious center of Sumerian civilization
• Lalish & The Sinjar Hills
Community of Yezhidi devil worshippers
• Babylon
Ancient center of idolatry rebuilt by Saddam Hussein
• City of Karbala
Holy city at the center of Shiite martyrdom fervor

Festivals and Pilgrimages
Pray during these spiritual events:
• Ramadan & Eid al-Fitr (Varies: '96 = Jan/Feb)
Month of fasting and prayer followed by two day feast
• Pilgrimage to the Tomb of Hussein (June)
Homage at revered shrine of Shiite martyr
• Ashura (Varies: '96 = May)
Shiite passion play celebrating Hussein's martyrdom
• Feast of the Assembly (October)
Principal festival of Yezhidi devil worshipers

Israel

"Mount Zion, the joy of the whole earth," exclaimed the psalmist in reference to Jerusalem. Three thousand years later, this ancient Middle Eastern city remains beloved by millions and is still at the center of world attention, as well as being a holy city for three faiths, Judaism, Christianity and Islam.

However, Jerusalem is also the capital of the nation of Israel, a fiercely independent country that has become a homeland for the world's Jews, who have returned after 1,900 years of wandering and persecution. As such, it has become the flashpoint for one of the most problematic and protracted political slugfests of the twentieth century: the battle for Palestine between the Jews and Arabs, which has resulted in five fierce wars since Israel's founding in 1948, as both sides lay claim to the land.

Modern Israel is a fascinating country, pulsing with life and energy not only from unfolding events, but also from the past - visitors to this storied land cannot help but feel the ghostly momentum of the historical process that has shaped this place, which has long been at the center of the human drama. Jericho, the oldest continuously inhabited city in the world, lies just to the east of Jerusalem, which itself is over 3,000 years old. Today Israel is a modern technological state with a relatively high standard of living, and its citizens have transformed the desert into a bountiful garden through intensive agriculture. Despite its small size and the ever-present political and military tension, Israel is a beautiful country, cradled on the west by the Mediterranean, and on the south by the Red Sea, with fertile Galilee and Mt. Hermon in the north and the fabled Jordan River and the Dead Sea lying to the east.

Basic Facts

Location:
Middle East

Neighboring Countries:
Egypt, Jordan, Syria,
Lebanon

Population:
7,000,000

Capital City:
Jerusalem

Major Cities:
Tel Aviv-Yafo, Haifa

Government:
Parliamentary Democracy

Leader:
Yitzhak Rabin

Major Religions:
Judaism, Islam

Historical Background

$\mathcal{A}$s most Christians know from reading the Bible, God's covenant with the human race was first made with the Jewish people through Abraham, probably about 2,000 BC. The checkered and fickle history of the Israelites is duly recorded in Scripture, and their wayward ways finally resulted in divine judgment and the destruction of the nation. In a lament over Jerusalem, Jesus predicted that "not one stone would be left standing upon another," a prophecy that was fulfilled four decades later when the Romans razed the city, destroying the temple and forcing the Jews to flee to the corners of the earth. The people kept their religion, language and customs alive during this scattering among the nations, known as the Diaspora.

Israel itself was inhabited by a variety of peoples over the centuries, each leaving behind their own peculiar imprint, but there has always been a Jewish presence in the land. European Jews often suffered persecution, culminating with the Holocaust in World War II. After the war, many sought refuge in Palestine, where the Zionist movement had established a Jewish homeland. This created resentment among the Palestinian Arabs, and when Israel became independent in 1948 it was immediately attacked by Arab armies. The Israelis successfully pushed out the invaders, resulting in the current deadlock.

Unreached Peoples

$\mathcal{J}$ews account for about 82% of the population, but they are hardly a monolithic group. In the last 50 years, the people of the Diaspora have poured back into Israel, coming from over 100 nations. The Jews are sharply divided by theology and culture; the Orthodox believers still observe the Old Testament law and await the messiah. The liberal Reformed Jews are unconcerned about such matters and are often agnostic and secular. Evangelical missions to the Jews have resulted in about 100,000 conversions worldwide since the turn of the century, but most Jews are highly resistant to the gospel because of their historical mistreatment by the Church. This sad persecution of the Jewish people by Christians has created enormous cultural, social and emotional taboos that keep a Jew from coming to faith. As a result of the heavy anti-Christian bias and propaganda that most Jews grow up with, they cannot listen to the gospel with an open mind.

Palestinian Muslims make up about 12% of the population. Their story is a sad one, as they are pawns of international politics caught between the Israelis and their Arab kinsmen, and many live in exile and poverty. Fifty years ago the Arab population was 30% Christian, but most of these have emigrated to other countries.

Spiritual Competition

Lhere is a resurgence of Orthodox and funda-
mentalist Judaism that has attracted some who were raised in a more
liberal or secular lifestyle. In other branches of Judaism there are
strong occult movements. The Kabala, which is a part of much
Western occult thought, is a medieval Jewish philosophy. There are a
number of strongholds in the land where much occultism is practiced. The city of Safad is
the major Kabalistic center in the country, although this form of mysticism is practiced
everywhere. The Jewish communities that came from North Africa have a superstitious tradition that mingles occult Islam with Judaism. There are also devoted followers of various
Rabbis who claim to have powers of healing and gifts of divination.

The Israeli government, as well as the Orthodox, have targeted the Jewish believers
in Israel, who are believed to number about 5,000. Although they have no legal standing and
cannot immigrate into the country, there are over 40 messianic assemblies, which are monitored by the police. An important thing to remember about the Jewish holy days, which are
observed in Israel, is that they are biblically mandated. Because of this, these feasts should be
the focus of prayer, so that the true significance of these days might become known to the
Jewish people.

Noteworthy Trends

Lhere is now once again a living Jewish church in
Israel. Congregations are composed of both Jews and Gentiles and
some have Arab members; many new converts are former Soviet citizens. Recent court cases have ruled that Messianic Jews are not Jewish
according to the laws of the State of Israel, and the whole question has
received much publicity and has even found some sympathy among a segment of the population.

Muslim Arabs in the Holy Land are divided between two groups. The Israeli Arabs
are citizens of Israel. The second group, the stateless Palestinians, are those who live under
Israeli administrative rule in the West Bank and Gaza strip. Shiite Islam, which always
appeals to the underdogs of Islam, is now a potent and widespread movement, exercising a
great deal of leverage through Iran's support of radical elements among the Palestinians.

Because of Israel's extraordinary political and religious importance, as well as being
the focal point of God's redemptive work in the world, the nation needs fervent and frequent
prayer focused on its many problems, needs and hopes. The countdown to the year 2000 will
bring increased opposition to the peace process and those who support it. May God's kingdom come, that Jerusalem might again be the joy of whole earth.

National Prayer Concerns

Obstacles to Ministry
Pray about these challenging circumstances:
• Deep Anti-Christian Attitudes
Due to historical persecution of the Jewish people by the Church
• Jewish Believers Considered Unpatriotic
Seen as betraying country and heritage, going over to the "enemy" camp
• Ancient Prayer "Brichat Ha Minim"
Recited daily, curses Jewish believers to death, excommunicates them from family of Israel
• "Veil" on the Jewish Heart
Jewish people blinded by unbelief (for the sake of the Gentiles according to Romans 11)

Spiritual Power Points
Pray over these influential locations:
• Temple Mount (Jerusalem)
Now occupied by Dome of the Rock & Al Aqsa Mosque, third holiest shrine of Islam,
it is still revered and regarded by Jews as future site of the temple
• Western (Wailing) Wall (Jerusalem)
Focal point of Jewish prayer and pilgrimage for 2,000 years
• Golgotha & Mount of Olives (Jerusalem)
Site of the crucifixion and Jesus' last hours on earth
• Safad & Netivot
Centers of Jewish mysticism and occultism

Festivals and Pilgrimages
Pray during these spiritual events:
Pray that the spiritual significance of these days would touch the hearts
of the Jewish people and direct them to their Messiah:
• Yom Kippur (September/October)
Day of Atonement, the time to "get things right" with God and man
• Sukkot, Simhat Torah (September/October)
Feast of Tabernacles; many scholars believe Jesus was born during this time
• Passover (Spring)
The Passover service foretells Jesus' death, burial and resurrection
• Shavuot (50 days after Passover)
Pentecost, the giving of the Law and the coming of the Holy Spirit

Japan

In the imagination of many Westerners, the land of the rising sun casts a serene glow. The symmetrical cone of Mt. Fuji levitating above the clouds; crimson tori shrines silently guarding the rocky coastline; office workers strolling through tranquil bonsai gardens accented by stone lanterns and multicolored carp. Others see a precisely choreographed society highlighted by geishas, samurais and bowing salesmen. The images are correct, but only partly so.

In reality, modern Japan has become a jumble of contrasts and contradictions. Among other things, it is a land whose lovely gardens are increasingly found in the midst of cacophonous urban gridlock. Real estate is now so scarce that Japan's citizens, who are very wealthy by world standards, are routinely forced into shoebox-sized urban living quarters. Straitlaced social traditions are rapidly giving way to the likes of McDonald's hamburgers, karaoke sing-alongs, Disneyland and punk hairdos. Even the well-worn spiritual paths are changing, as ancient Shinto and Buddhist beliefs are amalgamated into hundreds of home-grown "new religions" such as Sokka Gakkai and Agon-Shu.

Unfortunately, one thing that has not changed in modern Japan is the country's traditional resistance to the gospel, even though missionaries of many stripes have taken up the challenge of spreading the good news throughout Japan's islands. With a Christian population of 1-2%, the nation remains one of the more unresponsive mission fields in the world. In the years after World War II there was a national crisis of faith, as traditional Shintoism lost much of its force in the shattered nation. Despite initial response to the gospel in the late '40s, Japan soon found a new religion to salve its wounds: international business.

Basic Facts

Location:
East Asia

Neighboring Countries
Russia, South Korea,
China, Taiwan

Population:
126,319,000

Capital City:
Tokyo

Major Cities:
Osaka, Yokohama, Nagoya,
Kyoto, Kobe, Sapporo

Government:
Parliamentary Democracy
with a Constitutional
Monarchy

Leader:
Prime Minister
Kiichi Miyazawa,
Emperor Akihito

Major Religions:
Shintoism, Buddhism,
Japanese New Religions

Historical Background

According to legend, the nation was founded by the emperor Jimmu, a direct descendant of the sun goddess, who has long been the principal deity in the Japanese pantheon. About 400 AD the imperial court adopted the Chinese writing system and Buddhism was introduced two centuries later, forming strong cultural links with China. From the 8th through the 19th centuries, Japan was ruled by feudal military governors known as shoguns.

In 1542 the first contact with the West occurred when an off-course Portuguese ship landed by accident. Soon traders from other European nations arrived, followed by a number of Roman Catholic missionaries. The introduction of Christianity soon resulted in a xenophobic reaction, and in the 17th century all foreigners were expelled and Japan had virtually no contact with the outside world until 1854, when American Commodore Matthew Perry sailed into Tokyo Bay. This renewed contact with the West profoundly altered Japanese society, as feudalism was abolished and a Western constitution and legal system was established. By 1920 Japan was one of the most powerful military-industrial nations in the world, and the country soon became intoxicated with militant patriotism fueled by a fanatical military; this aggressive expansionist surge finally ended with Japan's crushing defeat in 1945.

Unreached Peoples

Japan is ethnically homogeneous, with 99% of the population considered Japanese, although there are three subgroups, the Eta, the Ryukyuan, and the Okinawan. The Eta, with a population of 2.5 million, are the largest distinct people group in the country, and are largely unevangelized, with no Christian outreach targeting them. The descendants of outcasts and slaves, the Eta still suffer considerable discrimination within the subtle layers of Japanese culture, and many of them have embraced Sokka Gakkai.

Undoubtedly the most unique group are the Ainu people, who live on the northern island of Hokkaido. Racially distinct from the rest of the Japanese, the Ainu are the original inhabitants of Japan, and few Christians are known to exist among them. There is also a substantial Korean community, largely descended from the workers brought to the country after the Japanese army annexed Korea in 1910. While the Koreans may look like native Japanese, they are easily distinguishable by their family names, and are often treated as second-class citizens. Missionaries have planted over 70 churches among them, reflecting the historical openness of these people to the gospel. Unfortunately, the Korean community is sharply divided in its loyalties between North and South Korea.

Spiritual Competition

*O*n the surface, Japan appears to be an ultra-modern secular state that worships only international business and technology. However, beneath this futuristic cover, Japan is a boiling pot of occult superstition and ancient religious practices.

The homegrown religion is called Shinto, a polytheistic combination of legend, intricate ritual, ancestor veneration and spiritism. Shinto is the Japanese equivalent of the better known Chinese "folk religion," and holds that the world is essentially a spiritual place, with many thousands of gods (kami) animating the realm of nature. Ancestors are honored and appeased through various rituals to insure that they will not turn into nasty or malevolent spirits. Shinto reached its peak during World War II when Emperor Hirohito was regarded as a living deity who would lead Japan to victory; his renunciation of this divine status, combined with the devastating military defeat, shocked and stupefied the nation. Buddhism is also prominent in Japan and usually overlaps with Shinto, although Buddhist and Shinto priests perform different rites. The country has recently witnessed the explosive growth of hundreds of new religions, which are usually offshoots of the traditional religions, often with an added New Age twist.

Noteworthy Trends

*J*apan's national psyche suffered a hammer blow in the wake of the disastrous 1995 Kobe earthquake, which destroyed one of the nation's most beautiful and prosperous cities, and proved that technology is no match for the dreaded tremblors that have been shaking the island nation with brutal regularity. Residents of the vast Tokyo-Yokohama urban sprawl are deeply concerned that a similar quake could kill thousands more and paralyze the country.

Japan also must tread lightly in international affairs. Many deep scars remain throughout Asia as a result of Japanese aggression during the war, which is compounded by envy on the part of other nations. Many Asians also feel that the Japanese have never admitted full responsibility for most of the brutal acts perpetrated during that time. This tension is increased by the fact that Japan has little in the way of natural resources and is dependent on imports of raw materials and foreign oil to fuel its hard-charging economy. Hence Japan must play a game of diplomatic touch-and-go lest it offend the rest of the world. The ongoing trade rift with the U.S. is perhaps the most visible sign of this delicate problem. Japan has long been resistant to the gospel, and prevailing prayer would seem to be the best antidote for this proud nation's spiritual ills.

National Prayer Concerns

Obstacles to Ministry

Pray about these challenging circumstances:

• Power of Tradition and "Group Think"
Strong pressure to conform to societal expectations
• Pervasive Influence of Superstition
Society has active relationship with the spirit world
• Rapid Growth of Japanese New Religions
Hundreds of new groups have millions of members
• Few Trained Christian Lay Leaders
Preaching and evangelism seen as domain of clergy

Spiritual Power Points

Pray over these influential locations:

• Taiseki-ji Temple
Head temple of Nichiren Shoshu/Sokka Gakkai sect
• Mts. Fuji, Haguro, Ontake, Tateyama & Osorezon
Divine dwelling places and major pilgrimage sites
• Imperial Palace (Tokyo)
Abode of Emperor Akihito
• 88 Places of Shikoku and 33 Places of Western Provinces
Recognized pilgrimage routes of ascetic shamans

Festivals and Pilgrimages

Pray during these spiritual events:

• Nehan & Hana Matsuri (February & April)
Ritual celebration of Buddha's birth & death
• Mountain Pilgrimages (Spring & Summer)
Spirit petition pilgrimages to sacred Japanese peaks
• Gion Matsuri (Summer)
Shinto protection processionals centered in Kyoto
• Obon Festival (August)
Nationwide honoring of returned ancestral spirits

Jordan

Jordan is a relative newcomer to the community of nations. Very little could be said about Jordan between its days of fame as the Old Testament kingdom of Moab and its 20th century incarnation as a prefabricated Arab kingdom. Although this area was occasionally the site of influential cities, including what is today's capital of Amman and the beautiful ruins of Petra, the idea of a national entity east of the Jordan River was unheard of before 1918. Jordan is a "developing country" in the most literal sense.

The mostly barren land of Jordan is bereft of natural resources, a Middle Eastern Arab kingdom with no oil to lubricate its economy. Since the birth of Israel in 1948, the country has been defined and shaped not by an internal identity but by outside forces. The country's foundations were laid in response to European incursions upon the Arab world, and Jordan was created as a nation largely in reaction to the establishment of the Jewish homeland in Palestine. Its original name, "Trans-Jordan," or the country "across the Jordan River" is suggestive of this reality. The many elements which make up King Hussein's constituency all vie with one another to impress their own characteristics upon the emerging national identity.

At times these opposing forces have led to strife and confusion, particularly with regard to the Palestinian refugees who settled there after Israel's surprising thrashing of the Arab armies in the 1948 war of independence. Their tenure as second-class citizens has been made worse by three successive Arab military defeats at the hand of the Israelis, and simmering hostility between the Jordanian government and the Palestinians.

Basic Facts

Location:
Middle East

Capital City:
Amman

Leader:
King Hussein I

Neighboring Countries
Israel, Saudi Arabia, Iraq, Syria

Major Cities:
az-Zarqa, Irbid

Government:
Constitutional Monarchy

Major Religions:
Islam, Christianity

Population:
3,813,000

Historical Background

ordan's capital of Amman can trace its name back to Biblical Ammon. Together with Moab and Edom, Ammon was an important player in the unfolding of Israel's history. Their role as the antagonists in the "affair of Peor" (Numbers 21-24) is the most striking example. But apart from these biblical references, there is not much record of Jordan's distant past.

As mentioned, Jordan does not reappear as a place of historical significance until the turn of the century. During the First World War, Hussein of Mecca (a direct descendant of Muhammad) helped the allies' efforts to drive the Ottoman Turks out of the Middle East. Hussein's cooperation was given in exchange for promises that the Arabs would be given sovereignty at the end of the war. However, France's occupation of Syria and Lebanon ended his dream; in response, Hussein's brother Abdallah brought an Arab army from western Arabia to Amman. From there, he hoped to restore Arab rule over a "Greater Syria" which would include Palestine, Lebanon and Syria. Although he never achieved this end, his occupation of Amman forced Britain to agree to the temporary establishment of Trans-Jordan in 1920. This eventually became the Hashemite Kingdom of Jordan, which was recognized by the UN in 1955.

Unreached Peoples

early two million Palestinians form the majority population of Jordan. Originally the native Arab population of the Holy Land, one million Palestinians entered Jordan as refugees after the 1948 Arab-Israeli war. Conflict between the monarchy and the Palestinians grew and came to a head in the civil war of the early 1970's, when King Hussein threw the Palestinian Liberation Organization out of the country.

The Palestinians are now more aware of their national role. Before the creation of Israel most Palestinians favored pan-Arab movements that would remove any distinction between themselves and other Arabs. Since then, having been rejected and mistreated by Western powers, Arab governments, and Israelis alike, the Palestinians have taken on a keen sense of ethnic identity. The rejection they have suffered has been fertile ground for bitterness and violence. As one of the most prominent and articulate groups in the Muslim world, a mass movement to the Christian faith among them would be a major breakthrough in Muslim evangelism. There have been Arab Christians in the Middle East for 2,000 years, and 4-5% of Jordan's population is at least nominally Christian, although Muslim conversion is illegal. Perhaps the limited religious freedom available in Jordan will make such a breakthrough possible through tactful and sensitive means.

Spiritual Competition

$\mathcal{I}$n the best of times Jordan sits on a razor's edge of compromise and last minute maneuvering. The most potent force in the country today is the radical Islamic movement; the Muslim Brotherhood is a particularly well-organized force in Jordan. Fanatical pro-Muslim, pro-Arab and anti-Western solidarity was manifest in the country during the Gulf War, when King Hussein committed a major blunder by siding with Iraq.

Muslim fundamentalists made substantial gains in Jordan's lower house of parliament in 1989 during the first free elections since 1967, despite gerrymandering and a ban on political parties. Since then, the fundamentalists have increased their influence in the government. These gains have prompted King Hussein to take political measures in an attempt to deter even greater successes in new elections, which have been promised. Most telling of his recent actions was a ban on political parties with any non-Jordanian financial or ideological connections, which is clearly aimed at the Muslim Brotherhood. To overcome these restrictions, the brotherhood is reorganizing under new, local charters. Hussein's rule has been equitable, but growing Islamic extremism is a bad omen, both for the king and the church in Jordan.

Noteworthy Trends

$\mathcal{N}$o other non-combatant nation was affected by the Gulf War as much as Jordan. First came the flood of refugees and returning citizens from Kuwait. Then it lost its main trading partner because of sanctions against Iraq. Finally, in retaliation for Jordan's support of Iraq, it was stripped of economic aid by wealthy Desert Storm allies. This triple blow has devastated the Jordanian economy.

Gains in fundamentalist power, the ever present Palestinian issue and the question of the monarchy itself are divisive points that exist all over the Middle East. Jordan was formed precisely because of these tensions and in some measure represents all of them. By signing a peace treaty with Israel in 1994, Hussein rehabilitated himself in Western eyes, but created problems with the radical Islamic elements. The king had carried on secret talks with the Israelis for years, and is generally regarded as one of the fairest and brightest Arab leaders.

Jordan's ability to deal effectively with these transitions and to survive them as a nation is a question being thoroughly scrutinized in Middle Eastern capitals today. If successful, Jordan could be a great stabilizing force in the Middle East. If the country fails, it could be one more catastrophic event in this perpetually troubled area.

National Prayer Concerns

Obstacles to Ministry
Pray about these challenging circumstances:
• Growing Islamic Fundamentalism
Fundamentalists have realized significant political gains
• Evangelical Reluctance to Evangelize Muslims
Many local Christians fear possible reprisals
• Lack of Resources
Economic repercussions from Gulf War are still being felt
• Lack of Quality Christian Teaching
There is significant nominalism in the Jordanian church

Spiritual Power Points
Pray over these influential locations:
• Temple of the Winged Lions (Petra)
Ancient temple dedicated to fertility goddess
• King Hussein Mosque (Amman)
Most well-attended mosque in country
• Village of Adasiya
Stronghold of the Baha'i faith
• The High Place (Petra)
Ancient sacrificial site still widely visited

Festivals and Pilgrimages
Pray during these spiritual events:
• Ramadan & Eid al-Fitr (Varies: '96 = Jan/Feb)
Month of fasting and prayer followed by two day feast
• Eid al-Adha (Varies: '96 = April)
Feast of Sacrifice; coincides with culmination of Hadj
• Yennair Festival (Varies: '96 = May)
Islamic New Year commemorating the hegira
• Mawlid an-Nabi (Varies: '96 = July)
Celebrations honoring Muhammad's birthday

Kazakhstan

Kazakhstan is the fabled land of the steppes, the broad and fertile "great plains" of Russia's wild frontier. A curious blend of east and west, it is a large country, fully one-third the size of the continental United States, and has vast oil, mineral and agricultural resources. With a comparatively small population of only 17 million, Kazakhstan nonetheless surpasses all the other newly formed Central Asian republics in economic potential.

Although the population is nearly half Russian, the future of Kazakhstan is firmly in the hands of the ethnic Kazakhs, who are native to the land. The many Russians and Ukrainians who live in the country have never felt at home there, and since the fall of the Soviet Union they have been leaving in large numbers, taking much of the economic and technical know-how with them. Kazakhstan emerged from the breakup with a full nuclear arsenal, but is committed to dismantling the stockpile and becoming a nuclear free state. There has been widespread concern over the possibility of terrorist theft from their nuclear sites, and the Americans moved a large part of Kazakhstan's nuclear fuel to the US in a secret airlift in 1994.

The high birth rate of the Kazakhs and the flight of Russians and Ukrainians back to their own countries guarantees an increasingly Asian future. President Nazarbayev, although a fixture of the old Soviet order, has been quick to take advantage of this trend. He strongly emphasizes his pure Kazakh ethnic roots and his mastery of the traditional Kazakh folk guitar, even performing on national television. From the grassy steppes once ruled by Genghis Khan to the towering Altai "mountains of gold," Kazakhstan is truly a nation made new.

Basic Facts

Location:
Central Asia

Neighboring Countries
Russia, Mongolia, China, Kyrgyzstan, Uzbekistan, Turkmenistan

Population:
17,206,000

Capital City:
Almaty

Major Cities:
Karaganda, Semipalatinsk, Chimkent, Petropavlovsk

Government:
Republic

Leader:
President Nursultan Abishevick Nazarbayev

Major Religions:
Islam, shamanism

Historical Background

Because of its location halfway between Europe and the Orient, Kazakhstan's history is complex, but from a broad perspective several important threads emerge. Among the earliest inhabitants of the land were the Aryans, a race that originated in the area east of the Caspian Sea and followed a polytheistic religion that eventually evolved into Hinduism when they settled in India.

The Turkish elements that characterize the Kazakh ethnic and linguistic traits of today entered much later in history. Nomadic groups from the northeast slowly migrated to Kazakhstan, forming a part of the early Turkic empire of the late 6th century and then gradually settling the steppes in the 10th and 11th centuries. Many of these early Turks adopted Zoroastrianism, Buddhism and Nestorian Christianity before the arrival of the Arab Muslim forces in the 9th century, although the Turks of the steppe territories of the west did not welcome Islam until as late as the 14th century. Even then it did not penetrate as deeply as it did among the urban Turks of Uzbekistan. In the Soviet era, an influx of Muslim Sufi mystics and the effects of forcibly settling Kazakh nomads has solidified the Islamic identity of the Kazakhs, who have resented more than a century of Russian rule.

Unreached Peoples

Kazakhs account for only about 40% of Kazakhstan's population. A layered mixture of the Turkic and Mongol tribes that washed over the steppes through the ages, the Kazakhs have nonetheless developed a fairly strong national identity. Tribal affiliations related to the Greater, Middle, and Lesser Mongol Hordes still play a major role in the structure of Kazakh society and government.

Due to its location at the crossroads of the old USSR, Kazakhstan has many unreached peoples, mostly of Central Asian origin, such as Uzbeks and Tatars, as well as a number of Tibetan Buddhists such as Buryats and Kalmyks. Other minorities are scattered throughout this vast nation, including Kurds, Koreans and Jews.

Apart from the nine million Kazakhs in Central Asia, there are important Kazakh populations in Mongolia and in the Xinjiang, Gansu and Qinghai regions of China. There is also an influential Kazakh community in Turkey. Nominalism and fear of ethnic tension on the part of the Orthodox and Catholic Christian communities, as well as the historical isolation of the Kazakhs, have conspired to keep the gospel out of their hands.

Spiritual Competition

The Kazakhs are influenced more by ancient shamanistic and Zoroastrian elements than by orthodox Islam. This is not surprising given the proximity of the Altai Mountains, and in particular Mt. Balukha, a principal focus of primitive spiritual worship that has always been prominent. The shamanistic practices and the beliefs of the pre-Turkish Aryans strongly influence the Islam that has managed to penetrate Kazakh culture. More traditional Islam is most prominent in the south, near the historically important Islamic centers in Uzbekistan, although Islam went into serious decline as a result of Soviet repression. The pan-Islamic revival now sweeping the world has begun to raise its head in the country, but the government is committed to remaining a secular state.

Kazakh religion is focused on the ability to influence the spirit world through the practices of a traditional shaman or under the guise of various types of Islamic Sufism. Striking similarities may be observed between the work of the old Siberian shamans and their Muslim counterparts. The most graphic examples include eyewitness accounts of the Muslim shaman Baxsi and the well publicized activities of the Central Asian folk hero Dede Korkut. In both cases the intermediary can allegedly project his spirit into the other world and contact spirits, bringing forth prophecies, hidden wisdom, and healing. Such out-of-the-body travel is a common feature of shamanism worldwide

Noteworthy Trends

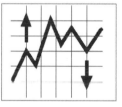

Kazakhstan's economic potential is not lost on president Nazarbayev, who has encouraged privatization and employed a Korean-American economic advisor. He has also shown shrewdness in handling the potentially explosive ethnic questions presented by Kazakhstan's mixed population. He has encouraged Russians to remain in the country while simultaneously establishing the centrality of Kazakh language and culture in the new republic.

This is a difficult period for Kazakhstan. The Soviet system left behind an ecological disaster in the form of large nuclear testing grounds and radioactive pollution. Even more tragic is the depletion of the Aral Sea; once a large saltwater lake providing abundant fishing, the rivers that feed it have been diverted, and it has shrunk by about 50%, killing all life within it and poisoning the people who live around it. Other legacies include the incredibly inefficient Soviet distribution system, which results in the wasting of at least 40% of food production. Moscow's legacy of exploitation and ruin is a specter that is deflating the high hopes of independence. Christians who have moved in to help the Kazakhs deal with these problems have been well received and there is great potential for the Kingdom of God in this newborn nation state.

National Prayer Concerns

Obstacles to Ministry
Pray about these challenging circumstances:
- Ethnic Diversity
Many language groups are spread over vast territory
- Severe Economic Stagnation
Disillusionment is even influencing the Church
- Influx of Cults
Jehovah's Witness and Moonies are winning converts
- Lack of Christian Literature in Kazakh
No full translation of the Bible is yet available

Spiritual Power Points
Pray over these influential locations:
- City of Turkestan
Traditional Islamic stronghold; Sufi pilgrimage site
- Shrine of Ahmad Yasavi (Yasi)
Memorial to great Turkic saint and Islamic mystic
- Mount Balukha
Peak in Altai range long worshipped as a cosmic axis
- Hazret Mosque
Oldest Sufi pilgrimage site in the region

Festivals and Pilgrimages
Pray during these spiritual events:
- Ramadan & Eid al-Fitr (Varies: '96 = Jan/Feb)
Month of fasting and prayer followed by two day feast
- Mawlid an-Nabi (Varies: '96 = July)
Celebrations honoring Muhammad's birthday
- Pilgrimage to Turkestan Mausoleum (All Year)
Tomb of Sheikh Ahmad Yassani, founder of Sufi order
- Pilgrimage to Golovachevka Village (All Year)
Site of the Aisha-bibi & Babadji-Khatun Mausoleums

Korea (North)

$\mathcal{J}$t might be said that North Korea is "a riddle wrapped in a mystery inside an enigma," as Winston Churchill once described Stalin's Soviet Union. One of the harshest Communist regimes in the world, the central government has almost unlimited control over the daily activities of the people. It decides what food will be available, what subjects will be taught in school and what will be seen or heard on the news. North Korea has been walled off from the non-Communist world since the end of World War II when the Soviet Union and the United States could not agree on how to establish a post-war government and the country was split at the 38th parallel. Geographically, the country is 80% mountainous, with long, dry and bitterly cold winters.

While South Korea has become an emerging economic giant, the North is saddled with an extremely unproductive state-controlled economy, which has been spiraling downward since the break-up of the Soviet Union and the withdrawal of its substantial aid. Marshall Kim Il Sung controlled the country since its establishment as a Communist state in 1948 until his death in 1994. His personality cult was evident everywhere: Huge statues of Kim adorn city squares, his picture was painted on buildings, hung in government offices, schools and in homes. His words and deeds have been elevated to mythological, even divine status; citizens were even required to give thanks by saying grace to him before meals. His philosophy of self-reliance, known as Juche, contends that man is the master of his own destiny and must look to no other force but himself. This is the ideological basis of the state, which Kim designed to be self-sufficient and largely cut off from the rest of the world.

Basic Facts

Location:
East Asia

Neighboring Countries
China, Russia, South Korea

Population:
25,548,000

Capital City:
Pyongyang

Major Cities:
Hamhung, Chongjin, Wonsan, Kaesong

Government:
Communist

Leader:
Kim Jong Il

Major Religions:
Officially atheist

Historical Background

Korean legend asserts that Korea was founded in 2333 BC when Tangun, the son of the god-spirit Hwanung, united all the Korean tribes. The earliest beliefs of the people were centered around a world filled with spirits, which were dealt with by a mudang or shaman. Mudangs were generally women and older blind men and are still called on today in times of need.

Confucianism and Buddhism entered the Korean peninsula in the fourth century. By the late 600s a kingdom arose which united Korea and made Buddhism the state religion. Christianity was first known in the 16th century when Korean scholars became interested in the writings of Matteo Ricci, a Jesuit missionary who was resident at the Imperial Court in Beijing. Protestant missionaries began work in the country in the 1880s and saw much success, especially in the north. By 1907 Pyongyang was known as the "Jerusalem of Asia," when one-sixth of its 300,000 people were Christian. Even Kim Il Sung, the ruthless Communist, once played the organ in a church where his mother was a deaconess and his grandfather had been an elder. Most Christians fled to the south or perished under Communist persecution during and after the Korean War.

Unreached Peoples

North Korea, along with South Korea, is the most ethnically homogeneous country in the world, with over 99% of the population being Korean. There are no racial or linguistic minorities. The small non-Korean resident population is nearly all Chinese. The Koreans are ethnically related to the Mongols, with some mixture of Chinese, and the Korean language is a member of the Altaic family of languages which originated in Central Asia.

A fusion of Buddhism and Confucianism, heavily influenced by shamanist and animist beliefs, have historically filled the role of a national religion. A uniquely Korean religion, Chondogyo, emphasizes the divine nature of all men and incorporates aspects of Buddhism, Taoism, and Confucianism. Prior to the Korean War there were approximately 300,000 Christians in the country, but under the Communists the practice of all religion is actively discouraged and has ceased to be a factor in national life. The church in North Korea is one of the most isolated on earth. Nonetheless, the gospel has been carried in by ingenious means such as floating literature ashore from sea and balloon packages by air. The most effective means is probably Christian radio which is broadcast from South Korea and from remote short-wave stations.

Spiritual Competition

*O*fficial opposition to all religion has led to harsh conditions for Christians. The Church in North Korea is one of the most persecuted in the world. In 1945 there were 2,253 churches, but under the Communist regime those Christians who survived went underground. Although there are now three official churches in Pyongyang, one Catholic and two Protestant, they are largely for show. There are no weekly services, and they are only open for arranged, scheduled visits, and on those occasions the people in the pews have apparently been drafted and trained to act like regular churchgoers.

Religious freedom is therefore tightly controlled in North Korea even though the constitution underwent minor revisions in 1992. The constitution promises that "citizens will have freedom of religion," but also adds that "no one can bring religion from the outside, or use it against national security policies." The new wording does little to change reality, which is that Christians are still subject to arrest and imprisonment. The Confucian ideal of filial piety runs deep in Korean society, and despite efforts to place love of country above love of family, the old ways are still strong.

Noteworthy Trends

*E*conomic collapse caused by the withdrawal of Soviet support and trade is forcing the current regime to change or face extinction. The pressure of survival has encouraged two diametrically opposed initiatives: one to produce a nuclear bomb, and the other to pursue reunification with the south. No one on the outside seems quite certain how capable they are of producing the bomb, and it is equally unclear how serious they are about negotiating with the south. Reunification would only be possible if more liberal elements win the power struggle that has been going on since Kim's death. The fact that the nuclear crisis was defused by U.S. diplomacy in 1994 is encouraging.

In spite of the harsh conditions already mentioned, it is estimated that there are now 60–100,000 believers in the country. The number of Christians has been increasing and a noticeable acceleration has taken place since 1988, when the "Love North Korea" symposium was held in Seoul. This gathering helped to wake up the church in the south to the needs in the north and focus their prayer and evangelistic efforts. In addition, aging believers in the north have begun to tell their children of the faith they have kept secret for so many years, and their witness is bearing fruit.

National Prayer Concerns

Obstacles to Ministry
Pray about these challenging circumstances:
- Total Prohibition on Evangelism
Communist government wants total control
- Pervasive Secret Police Network
Regime has informers everywhere
- Relentless State Propaganda
From educational system to public cult of Kim Il Sung
- Small Isolated Church
Cut off from global fellowship and teaching for decades

Spiritual Power Points
Pray over these influential locations:
- Grand Monument on Mansu Hill (Pyongyang)
Focus of Kim Il Sung Worship
- Pohyonsa Temple
Buddhist center at Mount Myohyang
- Tower of the Juche Idea (Pyongyang)
Monument extolling the virtues of Kim Il Sung philosophy
- Mount Paektu (Chinese border)
Sacred peak where Korean race supposedly began

Festivals and Pilgrimages
Pray during these spiritual events:
- Dal-ma-Ji (January/February)
Festival where hills are climbed to meet moon god
- Kim Il-Sung's Birthday (April)
Huge cult extravaganza with parades and celebrations
- Han Sik-il Festival (April)
Family graves are visited and the dead honored
- Chu-Sok Celebration (August)
Buddhist festival with prayers to the dragon god

Kuwait

Before 1990, Kuwait was a small and insignificant Middle Eastern country that was known, if at all, for its oil fields and "Q8" petrol stations, which are a frequent roadstop for European motorists. Kuwait's obscurity ended abruptly in August of that year when Saddam Hussein's Iraqi armored units rolled into the capital and began a brutal occupation. The West, sensing economic hemorrhage if its oil artery were to be cut, reacted swiftly, resulting in the remarkable blitzkrieg known as the Gulf War.

One of the world's richest countries, it was said that in prewar Kuwait one could not find a poor Kuwaiti. Located at the northwest corner of the Persian Gulf, it is wedged between Saudi Arabia and Iraq, and a mere 40 kilometers from Iran. The country is dull and flat with little or no natural water reserves. A fairly young country, it has really only existed as a nation-state for 30 years. However, the ruling al-Sabah family has been in control of the region for almost 240 years, which in effect has constituted a typical Gulf emirate, or mini-kingdom, giving it a more or less de facto national status. Despite its relatively small land area, Kuwait has a strong influence in the Gulf and throughout the Middle East. Its huge oil reserves and industrious citizens have created an ultramodern country with an excellent infrastructure and educational and social services on a par with many western countries. Though the nation was devastated by Iraq in the Gulf War, its $80 billion currency reserves have allowed the country to be rebuilt rather quickly.

Basic Facts

Location:
Middle East

Neighboring Countries:
Iraq, Saudi Arabia, Iran

Population:
1,300,000

Capital City:
Kuwait City

Major Cities:
Hawalli, al-Jahrah, al-Ahamdi

Government:
Constitutional Monarchy

Leader:
Emir Sheik Jabir al-Ahmad al-Jabir al-Sabah

Major Religions:
Islam

Historical Background

$\mathcal{A}$s with many of the modern countries of today's Middle East, Kuwait's formal status as a nation is a new concept. Until well into this century, lines on a map meant nothing to the Arabs of the Gulf, and tribal loyalties were the main cohesive factor. Around 1870, during the decline of the Ottoman empire, the dominant al-Sabah family, chosen by the merchants of the region to represent them, established a treaty of mutual recognition with the governor of Basra. Sheik Abdullah al-Sabah, with the help of the governor of Basra, became the officially recognized governor of Kuwait, then a sub-province of Basra within the Ottoman empire. His son, Mubarak the Great, is considered by most to be the father of the modern al-Sabah dynasty.

Mubarak then secured a protectorate agreement with Britain that was formalized in 1899. Kuwait remained under the British crown until 1961 when they made formal application to the U.N., a move that was blocked by the Arab nationalists in Iraq for two years. Though finally accepted into the U.N., Iraq continued to protest Kuwait's existence, pledging to "end the era of sheikdom" and "extend Iraq's border to the south of Kuwait," a promise they temporarily fulfilled in the invasion of 1990.

Unreached Peoples

$\mathcal{A}$t first glance it seems that Kuwait would be a relatively homogeneous society, and in a statistical sense that is true. The majority of the population - about 80% - is Arab. Before the war however, that number included quite a substantial number of Palestinians, Iraqis, Egyptians and Syrians. Although the Egyptians and Syrians were allowed to return after the war, the Palestinians (of whom there were over 300,000) were forcibly expelled for siding with Iraq.

The returning population of expatriates from other countries is being closely monitored by the Kuwaiti government. Most Asian servant-class residents have been allowed to return. This group includes Filipinos, Indians, Sri Lankans, and Bangladeshis; the national church has included many of these peoples in the past, and people from other Middle Eastern countries traditionally closed to the gospel also work in Kuwait. Even before the war, the comparative freedom for the church in Kuwait allowed these people to be reached without difficulty. While there are a few Arab Kuwaiti converts, in general there is no tolerance for Christian evangelism of Muslims. Although Kuwait was becoming a major crossroads for the Arab world before the war, exactly what form the postwar population will take is yet to be seen.

Spiritual Competition

As with most Islamic societies, there exists in Kuwait a number of significant spiritual forces diametrically opposed to the Kingdom of God. Most of these are in the form of societal institutions or legal restrictions. In Kuwait, most men belong to a diwaniyya, a unique Kuwaiti institution somewhere between a literary-political salon and a weekly stag party. These men-only meetings are a central part of Kuwaiti life and a man may belong to more than one. In addition, since the Gulf War the secret police force has been enlarged to keep a closer watch on the country. These community institutions represent the ties that bind Islam to the fabric of Kuwaiti society.

The Islamic fundamentalist party is also very strong in Kuwait, winning many seats in the latest election, and are now part of the ruling coalition. As a result, the introduction of Sharia (Islamic law) is being debated, and that would undoubtedly result in stricter controls on Christians and evangelism. With limitations on the size of the expatriate community in Kuwait since the war, Kuwaiti believers will need to take the lead in establishing themselves as a legitimate segment of society.

Noteworthy Trends

Since the end of the Gulf War in February 1991, Kuwait has cautiously begun to rebuild, and martial law followed the Sabah family's return from exile in Saudi Arabia. Elections were finally held in the fall of 1992 resulting in a parliamentary coalition that constitutes a democratic challenge to the ruling conservative monarchy of the Sabah family.

Though controls on non-Islamic types of worship remain, there seems to be an openness among the Kuwaiti people that was not found before the war. There is more contact between foreigners and nationals and there is more interest in topics of faith. The congregations in Kuwait, mainly made up of believers from the developing world, are strong and flourishing. Although in some ways this continues the stereotype of Christianity as a religion of foreigners, it does allow a witness in the midst of Kuwaitis. As mentioned, there have been a number of Kuwaiti Arab believers over the years, two of whom were former government officials. With the introduction of democratic reforms, there may now be a legal means by which believers can establish themselves. Prayer for this small but strategic nation at this time could yield dramatic results for the Church.

Obstacles to Ministry
Pray about these challenging circumstances:
• Restrictions on Muslim Evangelism
Evangelizing Muslims can result in arrest and/or deportation
• Active Secret Police
Security forces have been beefed up since Gulf War
• Rampant Materialism
Ostentatious wealth has also effected Christians
• Reduction in Size of Expatriate Community
Lower guest worker quotas mean fewer tentmakers

Spiritual Power Points
Pray over these influential loca tions:
• Shrine of Al Khidr (Failaka Islands)
Ancient shrine and pilgrimage site
• Sief Palace (Kuwait City)
Rebuilt seat of Emir's court
• Benaid al Qarr (Kuwait City)
Shiite suburb with influential mosques and Islamic school
• Shabaan Mosque (Kuwait City)
Center of fundamentalist thought in Shiite neighborhood

Festivals and Pilgrimages
Pray during these spiritual events:
• Ramadan & Eid al-Fitr (Varies: '96 = Jan/Feb)
Month of fasting and prayer followed by two day feast
• Eid al-Adha (Varies: '96 = April)
Feast of Sacrifice; coincides with culmination of Hadj
• Ashura (Varies: '96 = May)
Shiite passion play celebrating Hussein's martyrdom
• Mawlid an-Nabi (Varies: '96 = July)
Celebrations honoring Muhammad's birthday

Kyrgyzstan

The newly created Central Asian republics are not well known in the Western world, and Kyrgyzstan is perhaps the least known of all. A diverse country with over 80 ethnic groups from all over the former Soviet Union, it is an extremely mountainous land, with as much as 75% of its land area lying at elevations over 1,500 meters. Remote and isolated, and "thrust to the very edge of the Islamic galaxy," in the words of its physicist-president, it seemed a likely candidate to emerge from the Soviet Union as the most regressive of the new states. Much to everyone's surprise, quite the opposite has happened.

Kyrgyzstan has been called the real center of democracy in Central Asia. With a freely elected president and a number of legal opposition parties it is not hard to see how it earned this title. The Kyrgyz are also moving very rapidly to reconstruct their crippled economy: Kyrgyzstan is widely considered the most advanced of all the ex-Soviet states in the development of a free market. And this is in spite of the fact that there is very little economy to develop. Kyrgyzstan is a nation heavily reliant on agriculture and farming, an occupation that supports 3.5 million of the country's 4.7 million inhabitants, 75% of whom live in the countryside. The Kyrgyz are pressing on with great courage, optimistic in their ability to turn things around and surprise the watching world yet again.

Basic Facts

Location:
Central Asia

Neighboring Countries:
Kazakhstan, China, Uzbekistan, Tajikistan

Population:
4,696,000

Capital City:
Bishkek

Major Cities:
Osh, Przkevalsk

Government:
Republic

Leader:
President Askar Akayev

Major Religions:
Islam, shamanism

Historical Background

Kyrgyzstan belongs to the area of Central Asia first inhabited by the Indo-Iranians, a nation whose religious philosophy is best represented today in the Brahmins of India, and by the oldest of the Hindu scriptures, the Rig Veda.

The history of this region is that of a series of conquests, including the expansion of the Persian Empire under Cyrus, and later the campaigns of Alexander the Great. The modern Kyrgyz population is descended from the great Turkish race that migrated into this region from the northeast, eventually forming an empire across the Central Asian steppes around 600 AD. The Turks of this period adopted various forms of Zoroastrianism and Buddhism, which were both offshoots of the original Indo-Iranian cult, while maintaining shamanistic practices. Nestorian Christianity also made some headway among the Turks during this period, but eventually faded away.

The Kyrgyz branch of the Turks moved into the civilized heart of Central Asia in the mid 800s. By then the Arabs had brought Islam to the cities of the region, but their religion did not infiltrate the nomadic Kyrgyz fully until the 18th century.

Unreached Peoples

The Kyrgyz are traditionally a nomadic people whose national structure is built around a system of extended families and clans. They are closely related to other Central Asian Turks, especially to the Kazakhs - the Kazakh and Kyrgyz languages are 98% compatible. Many Kyrgyz are still nomadic shepherds who move their flocks to the warmer southern regions in the fall and return them to their mountain feeding grounds in the late spring. The quality and extent of Kyrgyz folk epics and songs are unparalleled among other Central Asians, and form an integral part of the Kyrgyz national identity. These traditional folk art forms have given birth in recent years to several highly gifted and internationally acclaimed writers from Kyrgyzstan.

Thirteen percent of Kyrgyzstan's population are Uzbeks. The Uzbeks, a blend of Persian and Turkic elements, are historically regarded as the elite of Central Asia. Old animosities between the Uzbeks and Kyrgyz have led to some violent clashes between the two groups in towns that border neighboring Uzbekistan. Barriers of religion and terrain have effectively sealed both groups off from the gospel for hundreds of years.

Spiritual Competition

The religious life of Kyrgyzstan is best conceived as divided into two districts, one the more traditionally Islamic southwest and the other the heavily shamanistic northeast. The former region is located near the Islamic heartland of the Fergana Valley, the latter in the remote "Celestial Mountains" of Tian Shan. The differences between the two are perhaps more in form and expression than in essence.

The true religious heart of Kyrgyzstan is a mixture of pre-Islamic Iranian loyalties and shamanism. This is true even in the most Islamic areas, where mystic Sufism is the dominant power. The hidden reality behind even the most pious form of Kyrgyz Islam is revealed in the shrines and pilgrimage sites which dot the landscape. Many of the most important shrines are located around the southern city of Osh. The adjacent Fergana basin is a very influential stronghold. Many sites there are actually of pre-Islamic origin, founded as devotional holy places to ancient Indo-Iranian gods. The most prominent of these, Solomon's Throne, is located on the summit of a mountain near Osh, and is widely renowned across Central Asia as the "second Mecca."

Noteworthy Trends

The attitude of the Kyrgyz government to radical Islam is plain: they have banned religiously motivated political parties and have lent border guards to the neighboring Tajiks in a bid to stem the flow of Afghan Mujahidin into Central Asia. President Akayev's own universal and non-fundamentalist approach was displayed not long ago by his visit to Jerusalem, which was the first visit by a Muslim head of state since Anwar Sadat. However, Kyrgyzstan still has a long spiritual journey ahead of it. Little of the country has been reached with the gospel and many Russian and German Christians who lived there left the country after independence was declared. However, Kyrgyzstan has a very open religious policy for a Muslim country, with almost complete freedom of religion. As a result, hundreds of Kyrgyz have become Christians. Some missions analysts foresee a large movement to the Christian faith by this nominally Muslim people.

The Kyrgyz are encouraging foreign partnerships at this time, and are willing to guarantee direct foreign investments. Muslim brother states, especially Turkey, are jumping at the opportunity to invest their resources and ideology into this very impressionable young state. The same opportunity exists for emissaries of the gospel, provided that they have a measure of optimism equal to the Kyrgyz.

National Prayer Concerns

Obstacles to Ministry
Pray about these challenging circumstances:
- Strong Sufi Muslim Community

Centuries-long tradition of Sufi mysticism in region
- Mountainous Terrain

Over 80 percent of nation comprised of high mountains
- Few Indigenous Churches

Only a handful of Kyrgyz fellowships exist
- Christian Emigration

Many Slavic and German Christians have left the country

Spiritual Power Points
Pray over these influential locations:
- Takht-i-Suleyman (Osh)

Renowned across Central Asia as "second Mecca"
- City of Ak-Beshim

Temple ruins and ancient burial grounds
- Osh Mosque

Largest mosque in the area
- Valleys of the Tian Shan

Strong shamanistic influences remain in local villages

Festivals and Pilgrimages
Pray during these spiritual events:
- Ramadan & Eid al-Fitr (Varies: '96 = Jan/Feb)

Month of fasting and prayer followed by two day feast
- Eid al-Adha (Varies: '96 = April)

Feast of Sacrifice; coincides with culmination of Hadj
- Mawlid an-Nabi (Varies: '96 = July)

Celebrations honoring Muhammad's birthday
- Pilgrimage to Shah Fadl Mausoleums (All Year)

Sacred burial grounds bordering Uzbekistan

Laos

Laos, the "Land of a Million Elephants" is a rustic Southeast Asian republic of mountainous tropical jungle which is totally land-locked and often forgotten in the shadow of its larger neighbors. Laos has been ruled since 1975 by the Communist Pathet Lao, who gained power when the U.S. was defeated in Vietnam. It is sparsely populated and the least aggressive of all Southeast Asian countries, although it has recently been caught up in the senseless and repetitive violence that has plagued the region in this century. Laos is recovering from the aftermath of the war in Vietnam and the ineffective economic policies of the Pathet Lao.

The major people groups of Laos are similar to those in neighboring Thailand, being of the same ethnic stock, speaking essentially the same language, and sharing a common culture and religion. However, they were divided up on the political map when the French imposed artificial distinctions on the region during their colonial rule.

When the Communists took over, Christians in Laos did not experience the same degree of suffering as those in Vietnam and Cambodia. However, the hill tribes, who allied themselves with the U.S. in the Vietnam War, have suffered more than 70,000 casualties in fighting with the Pathet Lao since 1975. The Hmong, who had a strong Christian church in their midst, have suffered the most. As a result of the fighting, most of the trained Hmong church leaders left the nation, and today there are more Hmong churches outside the country than there are in Laos. However, the Hmong church still exists in Laos with people being converted and baptized, and new churches being built and dedicated.

Basic Facts

Location:
Southeast Asia

Neighboring Countries:
Myanmar (Burma), China, Vietnam, Cambodia, Thailand

Population:
4,583,000

Capital City:
Vientiane

Major Cities:
Luang Prabang, Pakse, Savannakhet

Government:
Communist

Leader:
President Kaysone Phomvihan

Major Religions:
Buddhism, spiritism

Historical Background

Traditionally a battleground for neighboring peoples, the present boundaries of Laos did not exist until 1907, when the French divided up the area, then known as Indochina. The first ruler to unite a dominant Lao kingdom was King Fa Ngum, who introduced Buddhism in the 14th century to counteract the popular spirit worship, which was known as the Phi cult. A 10,000 member delegation came from the Cambodian kingdom of Angkor, bringing Buddhist teaching and bearing the Buddhist Phrabang statue, which today is regarded as the most sacred image in Laos.

The Phrabang statue not only had religious significance but also became a symbol of royal authority, with the custodian possessing the divine right to rule. Although the Phrabang statue originally was brought to Laos to replace the primitive Phi worship, it eventually took on additional significance as a Phi relic. In an annual ceremony the king would confirm his acceptance of the authority of the statue, acknowledging its sovereignty over the nation, which was followed by the oath of loyalty to the king, taken by the nobles. As in other parts of Southeast Asia, spirit worship was thus interwoven with Buddhism, creating a more intricate form of spiritual bondage.

Unreached Peoples

The Khmu People are part of a slave class specifically mentioned in the Lao creation myth. They were famous as spirit mediums, supposedly having intimate contact with the guardian spirits of the land. A Khmu shaman was therefore usually employed by the king of Laos, but in spite of this distinction they were despised as an inferior people. Although the first converts of Protestant missionaries were from among the Khmu, the Khmu church remains small. One factor is a high degree of illiteracy, and spirit worship is still the dominant religion of the Khmu.

The Lao Lum (lowland Lao) are the major ethnic group of Laos and are commonly referred to as the Lao. Historically they have imposed their social values, religion, language and political system on the non-Lao peoples. Although they embrace Buddhism, it is a veneer over their ancient allegiance to spirit worship. The church was originally planted among certain Lao Lum who were accused of being "Phi Pop" (demonized), and was therefore slow to gain acceptance among the general population. Surprisingly, this lightly populated country has over 100 different ethno-linguistic groups, most of whom are unevangelized rural tribes numbering less than 100,000.

Spiritual Competition

Buddhism, which is the state religion, poses a strong challenge for the church. Because of its long tradition in the country, it is regarded as a national institution. Christianity, on the other hand, has been suspect because it is considered foreign, and therefore a possible threat to national security.

Despite attempts throughout history to suppress it, the spiritistic Phi cult still permeates all other forms of religion. On Lingaparvata Mountain in southern Laos, the ancient Khmer kings, guarded by a thousand soldiers, offered an annual human sacrifice. This place is called Wat Phu, and is built on the site of an ancient temple which traces its roots back to the Phi cult. The human sacrifice has changed to a buffalo sacrifice and continues to be practiced; the sacrifice of buffalo is also known in Vientiane and Luang Prabang. On a more modest scale, offerings are made at village altars and in homes all over the country. A uniquely Lao custom called the Baci ceremony is often used at weddings, the birth of a child, upon recovery from illness, or on the New Year, and is rooted in the Phi cult.

Noteworthy Trends

In an effort to survive economically, Laos has been strengthening its relationship with Thailand. The two countries are natural trading partners with their common language and culture smoothing the way. Increased trade also means an increase of negative influences crossing the border. Prostitution could experience a resurgence in the current opening of the country, and Buddhism might also be strengthened through renewed relations with Thailand.

Laos is also part of the famous drug-producing region known as the Golden Triangle, and is one of the world's largest producers of opium and heroin; Laotian officials are rumored to be heavily involved in smuggling narcotics. Regarding the church, the Communist government believes that the fall of Eastern Europe was directly tied to political activism in the churches and is wary of a similar occurrence in Laos. There was considerable persecution of Christians after the Communist takeover in 1975.

However, church-government relations have been steadily improving in recent years, and the Christian population has been persistently growing with about 20,000 believers meeting in over 160 churches. Along with the encouraging growth, there is an urgent need for more trained leaders, as most educated Christians have been purged, and it is very difficult for foreign missionaries to establish adequate relationships with believers due to government restrictions.

National Prayer Concerns

Obstacles to Ministry
Pray about these challenging circumstances:
• Government Propaganda
Buddhism and socialism officially linked to nationalism
• Prohibitions on Christian Education
No Sunday school or other formal training is allowed
• Ban on Christian Missionaries
No foreign missionaries are granted access to country
• Discrimination Against Hmong People
Hmong persecuted for cooperation with U.S. during Vietnam war

Spiritual Power Points
Pray over these influential locations:
• Phra That Luang (Vientiane)
Most important Buddhist monument in Laos
• Buddhist Institute (Vientiane)
Main regional organization propagating Buddhism
• Pak Ou Caves (Luang Prabang)
Ancient pilgrimage site studded with Buddhist statues
• Wat Phu (Champasak)
Ancient royal site of human sacrifice and continuing animal sacrifice

Festivals and Pilgrimages
Pray during these spiritual events:
• Pi Mai (Mid-April)
Lao New Year with intensive activity at temples, washing of idols
• Visakha Festival (May/June)
Celebrates birth, enlightenment and death of Buddha
• Awk Phansa (October/November)
End of Buddhist monastic retreat season
• That Luang Festival (November)
Major Buddhist festival conducted at national shrine

Lebanon

$\mathcal{E}$arlier in this century Lebanon was the flower of evangelical Christianity in the Middle East and headquarters for the Christian effort to reach the Arab world. During this period Lebanon was admired by the great powers of the West as the most forward-looking and modern of the Arab States, a land of peace and prosperity. This was an era reminiscent of the biblical land of cedars where the name "Lebanon" was a synonym for beauty and prosperity. In reality this Lebanon was nothing more than a temporary facade, and her true nature has often been a living hell of physical and spiritual conflict. Gone now are the Christian mission agencies. Gone are the tourists and traders. More than three million of the best educated, most progressive people in the Middle East were reduced to primitive tribal barbarity during the ruthless civil war that began in 1975 and ended in 1992.

The famous cedars of Lebanon were long ago stripped from the land, and Isaiah's prophecy that "Lebanon with its majestic trees will fall" has been confirmed in this recent human tragedy. Following judgment, however, is restoration. These same prophecies, together with the current respite from bloodshed, hold out a hope that "the glory of Lebanon" will return:

> Shall not Lebanon in a very little while become a fruitful field,
> and the fruitful field be regarded as a forest? On that day the deaf shall hear
> the words of a scroll, and out of their gloom and darkness the eyes of the blind shall see.
> The meek shall obtain fresh joy in the Lord, and the neediest people
> shall exult in the Holy One of Israel. (Is. 29:17)

Basic Facts

Location:
Middle East

Neighboring Countries:
Syria, Israel, Cyprus

Population:
3,286,000

Capital City:
Beirut

Major Cities:
*Tripoli, Zahle,
Saida (Sidon), Tyre*

Government:
Republic

Leader:
President Elias Hrawi

Major Religions:
Islam, Christianity

Historical Background

Hundreds of Biblical references to Israel's northern neighbor Lebanon and its port cities of Tyre and Sidon establish it as an ancient nation. Home of the seafaring Phoenicians, one of the most influential civilizations of the ancient Mediterranean, this country has been a place of intense spiritual activity from antiquity. Always known as a center of international trade, in the end it was Lebanon's very cosmopolitan nature gone wrong that made it a byword among the nations.

Lebanon was part of the Ottoman Empire for hundreds of years until the empire slumped to defeat at the end of World War I. France then controlled the land until 1941, when it became independent. The fragile governing coalition in which Muslims and Christians ruled together finally collapsed in 1975. The furious civil war which followed all but ruined the once beautiful and prosperous country, especially the international financial capital of Beirut, which had been known as "the Paris of the Middle East."

Over the course of this turbulent history, Lebanon became a magnet for religious outcasts and heretics from both Islam and Christianity, resulting in a complex mix of peoples and ideologies. About 40% of Lebanon's population is Christian, which is one of the largest groups of Arab Christians in the Middle East.

Unreached Peoples

In the Chouf mountains east of Beirut dwell one of the most enigmatic groups in the Middle East, Lebanon's Druze community. The Druze religion is a mystical offshoot of Ismaili Shiite Islam, and is built around the veneration of sheiks and holy ancestors. They are hardy mountain landowners with a penchant for politics and military service, and they are also fiercely loyal to their ethnic heritage. Despite frequent contact with traditional and evangelical Christians, the gospel has made no real headway among the Druze, who believe in a unique form of reincarnation.

The Shiites of Lebanon constitute approximately 32% of Lebanon's population. The Shiites are predominant in the south and east of the country, as well as being a majority in Beirut. They were the most neglected and impoverished segment of Lebanon's society when an Iranian cleric first created the Movement of the Disinherited in the 1970s. His teaching attracted a large following, including many who volunteered to serve in the movement's militia, which became known as Amal, meaning hope. Amal and another Iranian-inspired Shiite movement, Hizbollah, were major players in the civil war.

Spiritual Competition

Lebanon's various Christian, Muslim and Druze factions are deeply entrenched, each finding it nearly impossible to see the other's point of view, even on basic issues. The idea of considering the merits of another's faith is even more remote. A strong sense of rejection dating back to the refugee origins of these communities has been compounded by bitterness over the many lost lives in recent years. All parties now seem gripped in a death lock of extreme intolerance, hatred and paranoia. The non-Christian factions are for the most part unable to separate the real Jesus from the military and political rhetoric of their nominally Christian foes.

The kingdom of darkness has thrived in this environment. While the number of Christian evangelicals decreased in the past twenty years, the most radical of the Islamic factions have grown and have continued to gain in influence. The Iranian-backed Shiites have made the most gains, having grown in popular support, and now have the important Speaker of Parliament position reserved for them by law. Over the past year Iran has targeted the majority Sunni Muslim population for the first time, attempting to spread its brand of radicalism beyond their traditional Shiite strongholds to the larger community.

Noteworthy Trends

The Taif agreement of 1992 has brought comparative peace to the Lebanese. The warring militias are being disarmed under Syrian auspices, and the new government is functioning. The spiritual price for this stability has yet to be counted. The Christian community, tired of the bloodshed, has made some substantial concessions in the accord. Unquestionably, the people that gained the most out of the agreement were the Shiites. Syria's position was also strengthened; their control over Lebanon's destiny is now confirmed. But in the short term, return to normalcy provides at least an atmosphere conducive to spreading the gospel.

Syria's surprising attempts to rein in the Hizbollah following Shiite rocket attacks on Israel in late 1992 shed new light on the positive impact of the Taif agreement. This is confirmed by firsthand reports from the Iranian stronghold of Baalbek that show a remarkable change: due to Syrian influence, very little of Baalbek's once pervasive hostile Shiite religious atmosphere remains in the city. If they can hold the fundamentalists in check, the prospects for a real peace may be quite good. Beirut is slowly being rebuilt, but it will surely be decades before the shattered city is once again spoken of in the same breath with Paris.

National Prayer Concerns

Obstacles to Ministry
Pray about these challenging circumstances:
• Large Muslim Fundamentalist Movement
Pro-Iranian Shiites control much of the country
• Muslim Perceptions of Christianity
Muslims associate Christianity with political parties
• Evangelical Emigration
War time emigration decimated church leadership
• Christian Disunity
Doctrinal and personality disputes weaken fellowship

Spiritual Power Points
Pray over these influential locations:
• Bekaa Valley
Major cannabis and opium growing area
• South Beirut
Stronghold of Muslim radicals including Hizbollah
• Baalbek
Islamic fundamentalist city; former Roman cult site
• Cities of Tyre and Byblos
Ancient centers of Phoenician idolatry

Festivals and Pilgrimages
Pray during these spiritual events:
• Ramadan & Eid al-Fitr (Varies: '96 = Jan/Feb)
Month of fasting and prayer followed by two day feast
• Ashura (Varies: '96 = May)
Shiite passion play celebrating Hussein's martyrdom
• Mawlid an-Nabi (Varies: '96 = July)
Celebrations honoring Muhammad's birthday
• Khilawat Pilgrimages (All Year)
Druze pilgrimages to various holy grave sites

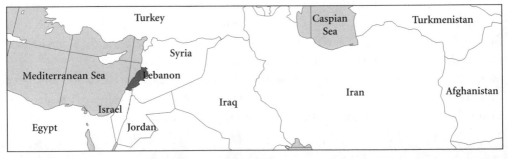

Libya

Libya and its notorious leader Muammar Qaddhafi are synonymous with political instability, Arab nationalism, Muslim zealotry, and state sponsored terrorism. A large country with a small population, Libya is literally split by the desert, which extends all the way from Chad in the south to the Gulf of Sidra on the Mediterranean coast. Cyrenaica, Libya's eastern province, was known in Biblical times as Cyrene, and was the home of a large Jewish community until 1948 when many emigrated to the new nation of Israel. The Cyreneans are also mentioned in the Book of Acts where they were visiting the temple at Pentecost, and Simon of Cyrene was the famous bystander who was pressed into service to carry Jesus' cross to Golgotha.

Like most of North Africa, Libya has an unstable and harsh climate. Sudden sandstorms caused by the hot air of the desert meeting the Mediterranean sea are normal. The interior of Libya is hot and dry, but climactic extremes can result in snow falling on the plateaus adjacent to the coast.

One of Qaddhafi's driving ambitions is the development of a purified Libya, which will be the leader of a pan-Arab alliance that will bring freedom to the Muslim world. This philosophy has defined his foreign policy, and can be seen in Libya's military involvement with Chad, Western Sahara, and Uganda. Libya has attempted to unite with its neighbor Chad, possibly for mineral resources, and more recently with Morocco and Tunisia. None of these attempted unions have been successful, and Qaddhafi's pan-Arab dream appears to be at rest for the moment.

Basic Facts

Location:
North Africa

Neighboring Countries:
*Tunisia, Algeria, Niger,
Chad, Sudan, Egypt*

Population:
5,445,000

Capital City:
Tripoli

Major Cities:
Benghazi, Misurata

Government:
*Islamic Arabic Socialist
Republic*

Leader:
*Colonel Muammar
Qaddhafi*

Major Religions:
Islam

Historical Background

Libya is a country whose history has been shaped by outside forces through invasion and domination by foreign powers. Among the earliest intruders were the Phoenicians, who were followed by a succession of Egyptian dynasties. Even the Berbers, the native inhabitants of Libya, were foreigners, arriving from Southwest Asia.

In the seventh century the Berbers were invaded by Sunni Muslims from Arabia, and the centuries-long process of conversion and assimilation began. It was the invasion of the Shiite Fatamid dynasty however, that was to change the cultural face of North Africa forever. Unable to fully subdue the rebellious Berbers, the Fatamid Caliphate invited warriors from the Arabian peninsula to help them in their jihad (holy war). The 200,000 soldiers brought their families with them, which insured the future of the Arabs in North Africa.

Libya was also ruled by the Ottoman Turks, but they were never able to fully control the land, as there were regular revolts against the Sultan. In the early 1900s, Italy occupied Libya and was finally driven out during World War II, when a number of important battles were fought in the region of Tobruk. Libya finally gained full independence in 1951.

Unreached Peoples

Libyans are predominantly Arabic-speaking Sunni Muslims of mixed Arab and Berber stock. Although there are few pure Arabs or Berbers left in Libya, the people identify strongly with their Arab heritage. Ethnic Berbers comprise about three per cent of the population and are found throughout Libya, but are concentrated in the highlands of Cyrenaica around the town of Aujila. The Berbers are changing from a semi-nomadic to a sedentary culture as the government intensifies its resettlement program.

Apart from the Berbers and Arabs, there is a small minority of Black Africans in Libya, who are descendants of former slaves. Most of these lower class people are farmers and sharecroppers, but some have migrated to urban areas. There are a few nomadic groups, but they are rapidly disappearing. The Taureg, the Tebu, and the Duwud are among several tribes dwelling in the oases of the southern desert. While all these peoples are converts to Islam, they practice magic and other secret arts, which is typical of Africanized Islam.

Finally, Libya has a substantial number of foreign guest workers, who work in the oil fields and other industries. Most are from other Muslim countries such as Egypt and Pakistan, but a significant number (around 10,000) come from South Korea.

Spiritual Competition

*U*nder the revolutionary government the role of orthodox Islam in Libya has become increasingly more important. To fully understand the spiritual situation in Libya, one needs to examine the philosophy of its leader Muammar Qaddhafi. He has repeatedly expressed a desire to exalt Islam and restore it to its proper, i.e., central place in the life of the people. His Islamic ideals have shaped both the domestic and foreign policies of the country since the revolution of 1969. The government is actively propagating Islam in Africa and throughout the world. He is particularly interested in freeing Africa from the influence of Christianity and colonialism.

Like Chairman Mao, Qaddhafi unleashed a "cultural revolution" on his people. In the case of Libya, the intent was to sweep away the vestiges of colonial domination. Like Mao, Qaddhafi also produced a book which contains his ideas, known as "The Green Book," which outlines a world free of economic oppression, social injustice and foreign imperialism. The book also advocates the unity of all Muslims and the Third World people against those who oppress them. As a result of this hyper-Islamic policy, the country is completely closed to evangelism and any other traditional forms of Christian witness.

Noteworthy Trends

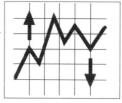

*S*ince 1992 Libya has been suffering under the imposition of UN sanctions resulting from the infamous bombing of the Pan Am flight over Lockerbie, Scotland in 1988. The sanctions have stemmed from the government's refusal to extradite two Libyan citizens who are believed to be responsible for the bombing. The sanctions are apparently having some effect, as Qaddhafi appears to be softening his rhetoric toward the West, as well as distancing himself from state sponsored terrorism.

It is difficult to say whether these conciliatory attitudes are genuine or only an effort to reestablish himself within the Arab fold. If the shift is genuine it would be contrary to his stated views on pan-Arab unity and would appear to herald a significant change in sentiment. Qaddhafi has even hinted at normalizing relations with Israel, having requested permission for a group of Libyan pilgrims to be allowed to visit holy sites in Israel.

Given Qaddhafi's past actions and long-standing hostile attitude toward Israel, caution is required in interpreting his movements. However, if the softening of his position is genuine, the tight restrictions preventing all Christian activity among Muslims in Libya may finally be loosening.

National Prayer Concerns

Obstacles to Ministry
Pray about these challenging circumstances:
• Zealous Islamic Government
Qaddafi has poured money into Islamic missions
• Prohibitions on Muslim Evangelism
Violation of law can result in harsh penalties
• Lack of Indigenous Believers
Only a handful of Libyan believers are known to exist
• Ban on Christian Missionaries
No foreign missionaries are granted access to country

Spiritual Power Points
Pray over these influential locations:
• Conference for the Islamic Call (Tripoli)
Headquarters of major Islamic mission organization
• Gamal Abdel Nasser Mosque
Former Catholic cathedral; now a key Islamic center
• Al Fateh University (Tripoli)
Training center for Muslim intellectual leaders
• Sanusi Monastery (Jaghbub)
Renowned Islamic center of scholarly pursuits

Festivals and Pilgrimages
Pray during these spiritual events:
• Ramadan & Eid al-Fitr (Varies: '96 = Jan/Feb)
Month of fasting and prayer followed by two day feast
• Eid al-Adha (Varies: '96 = April)
Feast of Sacrifice; coincides with culmination of Hadj
• Yennair Festival (Varies: '96 = May)
Islamic New Year commemorating the hegira
• Mawlid an-Nabi (Varies: '96 = July)
Celebrations honoring Muhammad's birthday

Malaysia

Malaysia is a warm tropical nation of wide beaches, sparkling islands and beautiful rain forests, nurtured by British colonial charm and a robust economy, which yields a good standard of living. Simple and sophisticated, the country is a mix of ancient cultures which have kept in step with the 20th century. While gaily painted ox carts amble along country roads, the latest automobiles speed along modern highways. Malaysia has been described as a glimpse of the past and present in perfect harmony.

Situated in the very heart of Southeast Asia, Malaysia is the only Asian country that is part of both the mainland and the vast Indonesian archipelago that stretches east into the Pacific. It consists of two geographical and political segments, which are separated by 400 miles of the South China Sea. West Malaysia occupies the southern third of the Malay Peninsula, and East Malaysia consists of two states, Sabah and Sarawak, located in the northern quarter of the jungle island of Borneo.

A multiracial nation, it is a human kaleidoscope of brilliant colors and cultures. The population falls into four broad categories: native Malays comprise 52% of the total, most of them living in rural areas as peasants or in coastal regions as fishermen. The second largest ethnic group are the Chinese, who make up about 30%, and who also control much of the economy, monopolizing commerce and trade, and providing a large part of the professional and general labor force. Indians form 10% of the population, and the remainder are native tribal groups, descendants of the earliest inhabitants of the area. Malaysia is a young country, and according to the last census, approximately 70% of its people are less than 30 years old.

Basic Facts

Location:
Southeast Asia

Neighboring Countries:
Thailand, Indonesia, Singapore, Brunei, Philippines

Population:
19,186,000

Capital City:
Kuala Lumpur

Major Cities:
Ipoh, Penang, Johor Baharu

Government:
Federal Parliamentary Democracy with a Constitutional Monarch

Leader:
Prime Minister Datuk Seri Mahathir bin Mohamad

Major Religions:
Islam, Buddhism, Chinese religions, Christianity, Hinduism

Historical Background

As early as 2000 BC, ancestors of today's Malaysians migrated from the Asian mainland to the Malay Peninsula, and Chinese and Indian influence date from around the first century AD. The Malay Peninsula and even remote Borneo were integrated into a larger economic and cultural system from about 300-400 AD, linking the trade routes between China and India. The early Buddhist Malay kingdom of Sri Vijaya dominated much of the peninsula from the 9th to the 13th centuries, followed by the powerful Hindu kingdom of Majapahit, which gained control in the 14th century.

About 1400, Prince Parameswara fled from the forces of Majapahit and established a new kingdom on the coast at Malacca. Soon afterwards he converted to Islam, and this promoted stronger ties with Malacca's Indian and Arab trading partners. After his death in 1444, a zealous Muslim came to power and proclaimed Malacca a Muslim state. The conversion of Malays to Islam accelerated, and by 1500 the new faith was well established throughout the peninsula. Since Malacca had developed into a major trading center, its prosperity and expansion were linked with the propagation of Islam. The British colonized Malaysia in the 19th century and granted it independence in 1957.

Unreached Peoples

The 52,000 Orang Asli people are particularly interesting, and are representative of the original indigenous people. They live as nomads engaged in hunting and subsistence agriculture in the interior jungle of the peninsula. Although the Orang Asli are considered by the Malays to be Muslim, in reality they dislike Islam and its restrictions. They remain committed to their traditional ways and are bound by animism. However, about 10% have become Christian, and churches have been planted, but there is a great need for the scriptures in their languages.

Large numbers of mainland Chinese migrated to Malaysia in the late 19th century. Speaking at least nine major dialects, the Chinese generally remain isolated from Muslim Malay society. They maintain a closely knit structure of clans, as well as voluntary associations such as benevolent societies and trade guilds. Over 75% of the Chinese are urban dwellers, and nearly every Malaysian town has a Chinese majority. They are chiefly Confucianists, but many combine several systems of belief - Confucianism, Buddhism, Taoism, animism, ancestor worship, and deification of local heroes. Only about 4% of the Chinese profess Christianity. The Indian population is mostly Hindu, and there are many shrines and holy places in the country that are reminiscent of India.

Spiritual Competition

The one universal element of native Malay culture is the Muslim faith, and the propagation of any other religion to Malays is strictly prohibited by state laws. Malays who have become Christians have not only suffered social ostracism, but have also experienced the loss of legal rights, privileges, jobs and even imprisonment; some have had to leave the country. Although Malay Christians meet together secretly in house groups, there is no viable Malay church.

The interlocking relationship of mosque and state is a powerful one, and government leaders are designated as the religious heads of their areas of jurisdiction. Instruction in Islam is mandatory in all government-assisted schools.

However, the orthodox teachings of Islam do not fully reflect the true Malay belief structure. In practice, ancient customs, beliefs in spirits and other primal elements combine with Islam to create a complex religious system. Festivals are also deeply entrenched in the lives of the people. One example observed by the Chinese is the well-known "Hungry Ghosts" festival, when offerings are set out to placate wandering evil spirits, a practice which has dark overtones of demonic worship.

Noteworthy Trends

Reference is often made to the four economic "little dragons"—Singapore, Hong Kong, Taiwan, and South Korea. Recently there has been talk of "the fifth dragon," which is Malaysia. In 1993, Malaysia's GNP overtook that of South Korea. The country's economic boom can open doors for businessmen, although the Malaysian church, which is mostly Chinese, is fairly strong. All things considered, Malaysia is a very open and westernized society, especially considering the fact that it is a Muslim country. However, the slim Muslim majority, who consider themselves "the sons of the soil," constantly try to impose their will on the other citizens, and Buddhists, Hindus and Christians have banded together in an unlikely alliance to limit Islamic pressure and influence.

There are as many Malaysian students studying overseas as there are enrolled in domestic universities. Malaysia sends far more students overseas for education than any of its regional neighbors. For example, 13,000 students are studying in Britain, which is even more than Hong Kong sends. In the U.S., Malaysia's 13,500 students account for 3% of the total foreign student body - making it the eighth largest group. Another 10,000 Malaysians are studying in Australia. This trend foreshadows an even more cosmopolitan future for this interesting country.

National Prayer Concerns

Obstacles to Ministry

Pray about these challenging circumstances:

• Muslim Evangelism Strictly Prohibited

Many Christians have been imprisoned for witnessing

• Lack of Malay Believers

Most Christians found among minority Chinese, tribals

• Growing Islamic Extremism

Muslim activists have engineered discriminatory laws

• Widespread Animism in Sarawak & Sabah

Spiritism and ancestor worship still flourish

Spiritual Power Points

Pray over these influential locations:

• Shah Alam Mosque (Selangor)

Largest mosque in the world

• Serpent Temple (Penang)

Sacred temple where snakes are worshipped

• Islamic Center (Kuala Lumpur)

Main government institution propagating Islam

• Kek Lok Si Temple (Penang)

Huge Buddhist temple; site of religious celebrations

Festivals and Pilgrimages

Pray during these spiritual events:

• Thaipusam (January or February)

Passionate Hindu procession honoring Subramaniam

• Ramadan & Eid al-Fitr (Varies: '96 = Jan/Feb)

Month of fasting and prayer followed by two day feast

• Kaamatan Festival (May)

Rice harvest fete observed by tribal Kadazans

• Gawai Dayak Festival (June)

Sarawak harvest festival involving ritual sacrifice

Maldives

Strewn like a lost treasure of 1,200 pieces of jade, the exotic Maldive Islands lie in a thousand mile-long string, running southwest from the tip of India into the warm Indian Ocean. These coral islands are perched on the peaks of an ancient submerged volcanic mountain range, and are protected from the ocean and the effects of the monsoons by barrier reefs. With sandy beaches, luxuriant palm groves and crystal waters, the islands are considered one of the world's last unspoiled getaways. More than 100,000 people come to the Maldives each year, and most tourists consider diving a must, as the coral reefs harbor an abundance of beautiful tropical fish and marine life.

The government reports that only 200 of the islands are actually inhabited, and none of these small, low-lying islands reaches more than two meters above sea level. Grouped in clusters called atolls, they are connected by a flotilla of water taxis. But this is not quite the paradise it appears to be, as the inhabitants face many harsh realities, including the highest divorce rate in the world (which is attributable to a curious lifestyle of promiscuity and adultery—many women marry four or five times); an average life expectancy of only 52 years, and a subsistence economy. But perhaps the greatest threat to the Maldivian nation is global warming. If the worst-case scientific theories concerning the melting of the polar ice caps come true, the islands could be all but submerged in a few decades. The government is well aware of this and has expressed its concern to the UN.

Basic Facts

Location:
South Asia

Neighboring Countries:
India, Sri Lanka

Population:
248,000

Capital City:
Male

Major Cities:
Gan

Government:
Islamic republic

Leader:
President Maumoon Abdul Gayoom

Major Religions:
Islam

Historical Background

The history of the Maldives can be divided into two stages - before and after their conversion to Islam in 1153 AD. At some point in ancient history, people from an unknown land arrived on the islands and settled; they became known as the Redin, a sun-worshipping tribe who were probably the first inhabitants. It is the Redin who are credited with leaving a pagan heritage of beliefs and customs involving evil spirits, or jinn, which are still a major force in Maldivian spirituality. Around 500 BC the Redin appear to have left or were absorbed by Buddhists or Hindus from Sri Lanka and India.

Abu Al Barakat, a North African Arab, is given credit for converting the Maldivians to Islam when he killed Rannamaari, a sea jinn, who had been preying on young women in Male. As the story goes, Barakat took the place of a potential sacrificial virgin and drove this evil spirit away by reading from the Koran. This may seem far-fetched, but it has been determined that certain Hindu sects did practice human sacrifice; skulls of young women have been uncovered where the temple once stood. The Maldives have been independent except for a short period as a nominally British protectorate, which ended in 1965.

Unreached Peoples

The Maldivian population is 98-99% indigenous, and it is believed that many of the original settlers were Indian and Sri Lankan. There has also been a great deal of intermarriage and mixing with Arabian and African people. Presently, Maldivian ethnic consciousness is a blend of these cultures, reinforced by religion and language. The official language is Dhivehi, which is related to Sinhala, the tongue of Sri Lanka. The Maldivian people are ethnically homogeneous, so there are no unreached people groups apart from the nation itself, which is one of the most unevangelized on earth.

The Maldive Islands have a developing economy based on fishing, tourism and shipping, with fishing employing almost 40% of the labor force. Poor soil and limited availability of arable land limit agriculture, and despite efforts to enhance output, nearly all food must be imported. In addition, great needs exist in the area of preventative medicine and health care, with one community health worker per 4,000 people outside of Male. Obtaining sufficient fresh water is also a significant problem in a country that is an archipelago of small dry islands.

Spiritual Competition

All Maldivians are Muslims of the Sunni sect, and no other religions or Islamic sects are permitted in the country. It is one of the few countries in the world that has never had any sort of Christian church existing in it at any time in its history. There are no Christian radio programs, there have never been any resident missionaries, and all incoming mail is scrutinized for anything other than Islamic teaching. The Scriptures have not yet been translated into Dhivehi, although there is a draft of the Gospel of Luke. There are Western and Sri Lankan expatriates residing in the country, but no Christian meetings are allowed, nor may Christian literature be imported.

These islanders still have a great fear of jinn, the evil spirits which are blamed for everything which cannot be explained by education or religion. To counteract the jinn there is fandita, which are the spells and potions provided by what is called the hakeem, or medicine man. The hakeem might cast a curing spell by writing phrases from the Koran on pieces of paper which are tied to the patient, or having the patient drink a magical potion.

Noteworthy Trends

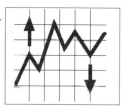

As mentioned, the felt needs and problems of the Maldivians focus on four areas: food, water, fuel, and health. Considering the problems faced by the nation, there are open doors for Christians to reside in the Maldives and help meet these needs. The government has been very receptive to foreign aid programs which have specific plans with reasonable expectations and results.

In 1972 an Italian tour operator visited the Maldives and saw the immense tourist potential. Word spread, and by 1977 there were eleven tourist resorts; a steady stream of development continued and by 1989 there were 59. These not only provide opportunities for Christians to come as tourists, but also to come and fill strategic management positions in the developing tourist industry.

However, the government is becoming more and more hyper-Islamic, and keeps these resorts strictly quarantined from the general populace, lest they be polluted by the non-Muslim paganism and materialism of the Europeans who frequent the islands. The tourist spas are located on uninhabited islands to minimize contact; the only exposure foreigners might have with the natives is in a stroll through the unimpressive capital of Male, where souvenirs and handicrafts may be purchased.

National Prayer Concerns

Obstacles to Ministry
Pray about these challenging circumstances:
• Lack of Christian Witness
No Scriptures, Christian radio, or national missionaries
• Anti-Conversion Laws
Repercussions can include banishment to outer islands
• Meager Tentmaker Opportunities
Few Christian workers have managed to get residency visas
• Geographic Challenges
Maldivians inhabit over 200 coral atolls in Indian Ocean

Spiritual Power Points
Pray over these influential locations:
• Grand Friday Mosque (Male)
Main Islamic center in the country; accommodates 5,000
• Islamic Center (Male)
Near Grand Mosque; includes library and conference area
• Hukuru Miskii (Meduziyariy Magu)
Mosque includes tomb of Sultan Ibrahim Iskandhar
• Mulee-Aage (Male)
Official residence of Islamic president of Maldives

Festivals and Pilgrimages
Pray during these spiritual events:
• Ramadan & Eid al-Fitr (Varies: '96 = Jan/Feb)
Month of fasting and prayer followed by two day feast
• Hijri Festival (Varies: '96 = May)
Islamic New Year commemorating the hegira
• Eid al-Adha (Varies: '96 = April)
Feast of Sacrifice; coincides with culmination of Hadj
• Mawlid an-Nabi (Varies: '96 = July)
Celebrations honoring Muhammad's birthday

Mali

Mali is a land on the edge - on the edge of the Sahara Desert, which is steadily drifting south, devouring precious grazing and farm land, and on the edge of ethnic and cultural mixing, a country where North African Arabs and Berbers co-exist with black Africans. It is also a nation on the edge of disaster, as drought and famine constantly threaten to extinguish all life.

Mali has been at the crossroads of Africa for centuries. Trading routes crisscrossed the land when it was the seat of the ancient kingdoms of Ghana, Mali, and Songhai. Slaves and precious commodities brought from the south were traded in the Middle East and Europe for salt, weapons, jewelry and copper. Legendary Timbuktu once boasted an Islamic university with 25,000 students at the pinnacle of the Malian empire.

History has since bypassed this glorious era, and the cumulative effect of drought, desertification and a burgeoning population has transformed a once fertile land into shifting sand dunes. Tuareg nomads in the north have lost their huge herds of cattle to drought and have been forced to settle as paupers in shanty towns around the cities.

Landlocked Mali is the largest country in West Africa, and is dominated by the Niger River in the south, referred to locally as the King of Rivers. The river is a major transportation route, providing the main access to the interior during the high water season. The river delta country of the south is very productive in the wet season and produces the majority of Mali's food. Mali's plight can be illustrated by the fact that 80 percent of its land is desert or semi-desert, and only two percent is arable.

Basic Facts

Location:
West Africa
Neighboring Countries:
Mauritania, Senegal, Guinea, Côte d'Ivoire, Burkina Faso, Niger, Algeria
Population:
10,878,000

Capital City:
Bamako

Major Cities:
Kayes, Mopti, Segou, Sikasso, Timbuktu

Government:
In transition

Leader:
President Alpha Oumar Konare

Major Religions:
Islam, African traditional religions

Historical Background

For almost a thousand years the slave trade, gold, salt and ivory were ferried by camel caravans across the Sahara desert through Mali. In the 11th century the trade routes were controlled by the fabulously wealthy Mali empire, from which present day Mali derives its name. The wealth of the trading empires was enormous and salt traded at the same price as gold. However, the development of maritime trade eclipsed the old land routes and thereafter Mali never kept pace with the rest of the world.

Significantly, the original ancestors who first settled the area which is now Mali were said to have entered into allegiances with the deities and spirits in order to develop and control the land for agriculture. Thus, when Islam was introduced in the 11th century (primarily through trade relationships) kings often made superficial conversions for economic gain. Because the king's right to rule was derived from his descent from the original ancestors, he needed to carefully observe the ancestral and land cult rites in order to maintain the loyalty of his subjects. In such an environment, wholesale conversion to Islam came slowly and with much syncretism.

Unreached Peoples

The centuries-old world of the Dogon people remains unchanged. Foxes speak as spirit oracles, foretelling the future, and diviners regularly seek information from the spirit world through sand grids, which represent an elaborate cosmology. The hogon (shaman) oversees the spiritual life of the village, where most people still cling to a bizarre belief system of talking animals, and spirits that stalk the countryside. Although about 40 percent of the Dogon profess to have become Muslim, they still follow traditional beliefs. Christian missionaries have labored among the Dogon for a number of years with some fruit.

The Fulani, a pastoral people with some non-Negroid traits, have had a strong Muslim element for centuries and have produced some of the leaders of Islam in West Africa. Pioneer Christian missionary work has begun among some groups, but many still have no opportunity to hear the gospel.

Spiritual Competition

$\mathcal{I}$slam is predominant in Mali as proclaimed by the country's motto "One People, One Aim, One Faith." Vigorous Islamic missionary activity fueled by Saudi Arabian and Libyan petrodollars has eroded the number of animists and strengthened the position of Islam. Most Muslims belong to either the Tijaniya or Qadiriya, which are West African Islamic brotherhoods. Recently, Wahhabi fundamentalists from Saudi Arabia have also gained many adherents. However, pacts made with ancestral spirits, combined with the effect of the supernatural, has resulted in a substantially animistic religion overlaid by a veneer of Islam.

Although Christians account for only four percent of the population, both Protestants and Catholics have grown steadily, with a significant number of converts from Muslim backgrounds. Unfortunately, the church in Mali faces the same problems with syncretism as does Islam, and this is especially evident in areas where there has been explosive growth and limited follow-up. Although animists officially compose only about ten percent of the population, most people practice some form of animism, with those people worshipping spirits and ancestors found at all levels of society.

Noteworthy Trends

$\mathcal{T}$he disastrous 1980 Sahel famine which affected most of Mali brought considerable help from Christian missions and aid organizations, resulting in greater openness to the gospel. At the same time, the selfishness and misrule of Muslim leaders became apparent, leading to considerable disillusionment with Islam. The current regime maintains a secular state with freedom of religion despite the large Muslim majority, leaving a unique window of opportunity for Christian missions to reach into the Muslim world without legal restrictions.

In 1990, the Tuareg people in the northeast rebelled against the central government. The situation has stabilized since the conflict but the incident has strained the country's unity. The promised transition from a military regime to civilian democratic rule has been slow and difficult, and relations with neighboring countries have been strained. More importantly, the insurrection has severely impaired Christian missionary work among the Tuareg, where one or two congregations had resulted from difficult pioneering work among these desert people.

Despite this, Mali is an important and strategic center for the church's missionary effort in Africa. The country's central location and lack of government restriction make it a prime target in this heavily Muslim area. Dedicated workers with vision and strength are needed to meet Mali's challenge.

National Prayer Concerns

Obstacles to Ministry
Pray about these challenging circumstances:
• Large Muslim Population
Eight out of ten citizens profess some faith in Islam
• Low Literacy Rate
3rd lowest in world; limits impact of Christian literature
• Strong Animist Influences
Especially among the Dogon people
• Severe Poverty and Health Problems
Highest infant mortality rate in world; desertification

Spiritual Power Points
Pray over these influential locations:
• Bandiagara Cliffs
Burial caves of the ancient Tellem people
• Dogon Togu-na
Male meeting hut adorned with carved ancestral spirits
• City of Timbuktu
Headquarters of the Dou, an African secret society and historic center of Islamic teaching
• Djenne Mosque
Main mosque in traditional center of Islamic learning

Festivals and Pilgrimages
Pray during these spiritual events:
• Ramadan & Eid al-Fitr (Varies: '96 = Jan/Feb)
Month of fasting and prayer followed by two day feast
• Fete des Masques (April/May)
Five-day animist festival celebrated in Dogon villages
• Tabaski/Eid al-Kabir (Varies: '96 = April)
Islamic sacrificial feast; most important in West Africa
• Sigui Ceremony (Every 60 Years)
Dogon debut of new serpent-styled Grand Mask

Mauritania

Mauritania is one of the most isolated countries in the world, covered in a pall of dust from Saharan sandstorms for as much as 200 days a year. This ancient nation forms the divide between Muslim North Africa and black West Africa. A harsh, dry land of desert and rocky escarpments, Mauritania is located on Africa's west coast, where the Sahara Desert meets the Atlantic. In the parched interior, oases with date palm groves provide shelter and relief, but cultivation is only possible along the banks of the Senegal river in the extreme south. Nomadic herding provides a meager livelihood for most of the country, while the coast has some of the world's best fishing grounds, and the interior has rich deposits of iron ore.

Mauritania has one of the world's largest wandering populations, with 80 percent of the people being either nomadic or semi-nomadic. The social structure of Mauritania has been drastically affected by a vicious spiral of drought, human migration, food shortages and desert onslaught.

As the sand dunes shift, so life is shifting dramatically for those in Mauritania, where infant mortality is high and life expectancy is low. In 1990 the infant mortality rate was 96 per 1,000, and life expectancy was 44 years for men and 49 years for women. Accordingly, the population is young; in 1985, over 46% were under 15 years of age. The Sahel drought of the 1970s and wars in neighboring Western Sahara have forced many of the proud and independent nomads to leave the desert and settle in shanty towns around the capital of Nouakchott.

Basic Facts

Location:
North Africa

Neighboring Countries:
Morocco, Algeria, Mali, Senegal

Population:
2,329,000

Capital City:
Nouakchott

Major Cities:
Nouadhibou, Kaedi

Government:
In transition

Leader:
President and Premier Maaouya Ould Sidi Ahmed Taya

Major Religions:
Islam

165

Historical Background

Berber farmers and herdsmen from North Africa began migrating southwards into the region as early as 200 BC, pushing the native black population out before them. The Berbers thus gained control of one of the most lucrative of the trans-Saharan trade routes between northwest Africa and the Sudan, while the southeast region of Mauritania was dominated by the kingdoms of Ghana, Mali, and Songhai. The power of the Berbers was eclipsed by invading Arabs in the 12th century, and intermarriage between the two groups resulted in the formation of the Moors, who later invaded Spain.

Trade in slaves and gum arabic eventually drew the Dutch, English and French to Mauritania; the country became a French colony in 1920 and an overseas territory in 1946. Full independence was gained in 1960. Soon after independence the government became embroiled in the Western Sahara war, which led to a break in diplomatic relations with Morocco. The government eventually renounced all land claims in Western Sahara. Further political turmoil resulted from the government's policy of "Arabization" of the black population in the south, which caused the expulsion of the Senegalese living in Mauritania; the ensuing refugee crisis also forced Mauritanians to leave Senegal, the country which is located on its southern border.

Unreached Peoples

The Moors make up 82% of the population, while the remaining 18% are black Africans. The Moors are divided along a rigid hierarchical two-caste system. The Bidan or "white" Moors hold a slight majority (55%) over the Haratin, or "black" Moors. The white Moors are both the warrior class and the religious elite, while the Haratin are considered to be essentially a slave class. Incredibly, slavery was only officially abolished in July 1980. By the mid-80's there were still an estimated 100,000 slaves in the country.

Mauritania is ethnically divided between the Moors and the southern black population, and it is politically divided along similar lines. The Moors tend to look toward Morocco and the Arab world for their identity, while the black population of the south aligns itself with the West African states. Of these Negroid peoples, the largest is the Toucouleur, who incorporated the Wolof and Soninke peoples into their society. The Toucouleur are Muslim, but like many of their neighbors, they believe in divination and supernatural powers associated with Islamic holy men.

Spiritual Competition

Mauritania has been under the pervasive control of Islam for over 1,000 years, and is one of the most closed countries of the Muslim world. Islam's hold is so entrenched in this area that Chinguetti in the central Adrar region is considered the seventh holy city of Islam. Virtually all Mauritanians are Sunni Muslims, and laws forbid Mauritanians from even hearing the gospel, much less converting to Christianity. As in other nations of West Africa, the centers of religious power are located in the two Muslim brotherhoods, the Qadiriya and the Tijaniya. The Tijaniya is essentially a zealous missionary order, which has spread into many areas of West Africa.

The spiritual growth of Christian believers in Mauritania is complicated by the lack of biblical texts in Hassaniya Arabic, the national language, as well as the fact that there are no radio broadcasts into the nation. According to their law, Mauritanians who confess Christ face the death sentence if discovered. Some of those who have shown interest in the gospel have suffered imprisonment and torture. Despite the laws and penalties against conversion, there are a growing number of national believers, who are desperately in need of supportive prayer.

Noteworthy Trends

Although the country's economy was based almost entirely on the export of high-grade iron ore, the fishing industry has become the largest generator of income. The government has placed considerable emphasis on the development of the fishing industry, and a deep water port was opened in 1986. The government's emphasis on new development and the continued need for humanitarian aid provide opportunities for foreign Christians to work as tentmakers in Mauritania. As a result of the severe drought in 1980, church aid organizations were able to enter Mauritania. Contrary to expectations, the workers found much openness to the gospel.

Over one-half million Mauritanians seek work outside their homeland, mainly in West Africa, the Middle East, and Western Europe. Mauritanians who live overseas are more open to the gospel than before. A young Moorish woman studying in France said that she experienced freedom there, but added, "Once back home, it's finished. I am again a member of my family, a member of the caste I belong to." Pray that those Mauritanians outside the country will have a chance to hear the gospel and that the fledgling church in Mauritania will grow and flourish in that secluded and barren land.

National Prayer Concerns

Obstacles to Ministry

Pray about these challenging circumstances:

• Law Forbidding the "Renunciation of Islam"
Converts to Christianity can be dealt with harshly
• Interracial Tensions
Stratified caste system places Bidan Moors over Blacks
• Harsh Physical Conditions
Traditional nomads have been forced into urban shanties
• Small Indigenous Church
Few Mauritanian fellowships exist, with little leadership

Spiritual Power Points

Pray over these influential locations:

• Adrar Region
Reported location of ongoing slave trading
• Koumbi Saleh
Ruins of West Africa's first medieval empire
• City of Chinguetti
The seventh holy city of Islam; significant spiritual center
• Tomb of Ibn 'Abdallah Yacin (Oued Korifla)
Venerated burial site of orthodox Islamic leader

Festivals and Pilgrimages

Pray during these spiritual events:

• Ramadan & Eid al-Fitr (Varies: '96 = Jan/Feb)
Month of fasting and prayer followed by two day feast
• Tabaski/Eid al-Kabir (Varies: '96 = April)
Islamic sacrificial feast; most important in West Africa
• Yennair Festival (Varies: '96 = May)
Islamic New Year commemorating the hegira
• Mawlid an-Nabi (Varies: '96 = July)
Celebrations honoring Muhammad's birthday

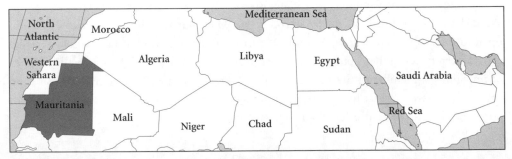

Mongolia

Modern Mongolia is the remnant of an empire once so vast it was said to have encompassed "all the lands from the rising of the sun to its setting." With borders stretching from the Pacific Ocean to the Adriatic Sea, the dominion of the ancient Khans dwarfed even the legendary conquests of Alexander the Great and the Roman Caesars. Throughout history Mongolia has managed to arouse greater curiosity and deeper fears than almost any other country. From the scorched-earth campaigns of Genghis Khan to the narratives of the intrepid Marco Polo, the outside world has found itself alternately terrified and fascinated by this mysterious kingdom.

Those who insist that Mongolia is the proverbial "uttermost ends of the earth" are not without their reasons. With less than 2.6 million people spread across nearly 600,000 square miles (1.5 million sq km), Mongolia is the least densely populated nation on earth. In fact, the country holds the unique distinction of being the only place in the world to host more horses than people. As one visitor wryly observed, "Strictly speaking there are no proper roads in Mongolia—just a series of widely divergent tracks from which you hopefully select the most promising."

From early November to late June, the temperatures plummet until a man's breath hangs lifeless in the air. On other days, according to the Mongols, persistent north winds "dry the ponds and blow the fish into the pastures." Cold and isolated, Mongolia's geography reflects in many ways her spiritual condition. Until the early 1980s, despite the efforts of British, Swedish and Danish missionaries, Mongolia had never yielded a successful church plant—or even a single convert in modern times!

Basic Facts

Location:
Central Asia

Neighboring Countries:
Russia, China, Kazakhstan

Population:
2,596,000

Capital City:
Ulan Bator

Major Cities:
Darhan, Choybalsan, Moron, Tsetserleg

Government:
Republic

Leader:
President Punsalmaagiyn Ochirbat

Major Religions:
atheism, Tibetan (lamaistic) Buddhism, shamanism

Historical Background

$\mathcal{I}$n 1206, Genghis Khan established the first united Mongol nation. To fuel his greater ambitions, however, the famous warlord subsequently led his mounted warriors on a series of ruthless campaigns across Asia and Eastern Europe. "The greatest joy," he once boasted, "is to vanquish your enemies and chase them before you, to rob them of their wealth and see those dear to them bathed in tears..."

When Kublai, his grandson, came to power in 1261, the Mongol capital removed to Peking. From there Kublai welcomed distinguished foreign travelers such as Marco Polo. While Kublai's mother, the princess Sorkatani, was said to be a devout Christian, the Khan himself relied heavily on the advice of some 5,000 astrologers and soothsayers.

The 16th century not only saw the Mongol empire fall to the Manchus, it also marked the arrival of Lamaistic (Tibetan) Buddhism. Blending easily with the native shamanism, the faith spread rapidly until it was derailed by Asia's first Communist regime in the 1920s. Within the space of two decades, the ranks of the Buddhist clergy were reduced (through imprisonment and execution) from about 150,000 to less than 200. In 1990, the Communist Party finally relinquished power.

Unreached Peoples

$\mathcal{A}$lmost 90% of Mongolia's 2.6 million inhabitants are descendants of the Hsiung-Nu, or Huns, who wandered across Central Asia thousands of years ago. The Khalka Mongols are by far the dominant group in the country, constituting over 75% of the population. Largely Buddhist before the Communists took power, today most Khalka claim to be non-religious. In happy contradiction of this fact, however, many Khalka have lately been quite responsive to the gospel.

The Oirat Mongols (including the Durbets, Bait, Olot and Darkhat) live in the western regions of the country. They are reputed to be even less spiritually minded than the Khalka. Of the nation's other small Mongol minorities, the most notable are the Dariganga in the southeast corner, and the northern Buryats. While scholars debate their precise origins, the Buryats themselves claim to be the descendants of either a gray bull or a white swan. In the forests of the northwest, about 300 nomadic Tsaatang animists live in bark-covered tents.

The final 10% of Mongolia's population is made up of Turkic-speaking minorities—Kazakhs, Uzbeks, Uighurs, Khotons and Tuvinians. Mainly Muslim and animist, Christians have only recently been able to take the gospel to their remote region.

Spiritual Competition

Almost 70 years of Communist domination has left a spiritual vacuum in Mongolia. Once the state religion, Buddhism was all but obliterated. Although it is making a comeback, it is unlikely that it will reach its former high-water mark which saw nearly half of the adult male population serving as monks. When the Dalai Lama (the leader of Tibetan Buddhism) visited Ulan Bator in 1991, only a few thousand people went to the national stadium to hear him. While in the rural areas there are those who would once again follow Buddhism, they have forgotten how to practice it and have no one to teach them. There is also an influential element in the government which would like to see Buddhism reinstated as the national religion – or at least given special status.

The Mongols have always been sensitive to supernatural forces. Shamanism and lamaism merely give names to their fears. For a substantial number of Mongols, ritual spirit appeasement is still necessary to avert disaster – a killing freeze, a deformed child, an epidemic in the herd. Because of this, in isolated country gers as well in urban apartments, cases of demonic influence and possession are not uncommon. Accordingly, those who would minister successfully in this land must have confidence in the delivering power of God.

Noteworthy Trends

Now that Mongolia has embarked on the tenuous journey toward democracy, there is a renewed hope that the country's darkest days are behind her. In 1990, when Mongolia opened to the Western world, there were four known Mongol believers. Within less than three years, there were between 1,000 and 1,500 Mongols meeting for worship and Christian teaching in fellowships throughout the country. Most of these are young people between the ages of 14 and 25 and many have yet to make a sincere commitment to Christ. However the evidence speaks for itself: Mongols are interested in the gospel and this may be the beginning of an awakening. (An exciting Book of Acts-style move has already taken place in Mongolia's Bayan Olgiy Province).

Mongolians place a high priority on education and value an intellectual approach to learning. Given these factors and a national literacy rate of 90%, it is significant that the Mongolian New Testament rolled off the press just as the country opened to the Western world! A ministry partnership is in place helping to organize the flow of God's Word and work within the country—a work that has attracted Germans, Koreans, Japanese, Americans, British and Navajos. Pray that power struggles within the Church will not further disrupt the work.

National Prayer Concerns

Obstacles to Ministry

Pray about these challenging circumstances:
• Lack of Christian Heritage
Nearly all Mongol Christians have converted since 1990
• Revival of Old Spiritual Practices
Interest in Buddhism and shamanism picked up after the Communist decline
• Weak National Infrastructure
Poor travel and communication links make ministry planning a challenge
• Lack of Trained Indigenous Leaders
New converts are rapidly outpacing available disciplers

Spiritual Power Points

Pray over these influential locations:
• Karakoram (Central Mongolia)
Ruins of Genghis Khan's ancient capital
• Gandan Monastery (Ulan Bator)
Main Tibetan Buddhist monastery in country
• Union of Mongolian Astrologers (Ulan Bator)
Center for revival of Zurhai astrological monasteries
• Erdenezuu Monastery (Karakoram)
First Buddhist center in Outer Mongolia

Festivals and Pilgrimages

Pray during these spiritual events:
• Tsagaan Sar & Monlam Chenmo (February/March)
New Year and Great Prayer Festival
• Sakadawa (May)
Celebrates birth, enlightenment and death of Buddha
• Dzamling Chisang (June)
Purification festival with offerings to guardian spirits
• Naadam (July)
Major festival with origins in ancient Obo worship

Morocco

Morocco is the western outpost of the Middle East, and is considered by many to be the most interesting and exotic of the Arab countries. Lying on the northwest corner of Africa, Morocco is separated from Europe by the narrow Strait of Gibraltar, a 45 minute hydrofoil ride from Spain. This ancient nation has long been the crossroads between Arab North Africa and Europe. Once the home of a large and cultured Christian population that produced notable church fathers like Tertullian, Morocco fell to the Arab invaders in the 8th century and has been Muslim ever since.

This land of high mountains, sunny beaches and remarkable desert cities of winding alleys and scented bazaars has attracted travelers, invaders and pilgrims for centuries. This is still the case, as tourism is a mainstay of the Moroccan economy. While closely tied to Europe, Morocco remains an oriental land held in the grip of magical-mystical Islam. So pervasive is the occult realm that at night in the old city of Marrakech the Jamaa el Fna square— also known as the "assembly of the dead"—becomes a showcase of the secret arts. As twilight falls, a strange mix of many types of dark spiritual practices can be found. An observer wrote that "My impression, as I walked through circles of witch doctors, was that Hell was better organized." It is this fascination with the occult, as well as the strong spirit of intolerant, militant Islam that has hindered the advance of the gospel for many centuries in this ancient land.

Basic Facts

Location:
North Africa

Neighboring Countries:
Western Sahara, Algeria, Spain

Population:
29,116,000

Capital City:
Rabat

Major Cities:
Casablanca, Marrakech, Fez, Tangier

Government:
Monarchy

Leader:
King Hassan II

Major Religions:
Islam

Historical Background

The country has an enviable strategic position. Its location along the Strait of Gibraltar at the mouth of the Mediterranean has formed much of its history. Every major European power, including the Romans, felt the necessity to control the area, and in the process left their marks. In the centuries before Christ, Carthaginian traders were among the first settlers on the coast, establishing trading posts for forays into the Mediterranean. The Carthaginians were followed by the Phoenicians and the Romans, but the most lasting impact on Morocco's history was to be the arrival of Islam in 788.

At that time, most of the population, including the Christian Berber tribes of the Atlas Mountains, were forced into the fold of Islam. Various political dynasties subsequently ruled, and under the Muslim mantle Morocco became a center of learning and Islamic culture. Following centuries of dynastic rule it was a protectorate of France, from the early 1900s until 1956. Spain administered the Saharan zone (now the Western Sahara) until it withdrew from the territory in 1975, and since then the Western Saharan Polisario Front has been waging a protracted guerrilla war against Moroccan forces for the control of the area.

Unreached Peoples

Almost all Moroccans belong to either Berber, Arab, or Arab-Berber stock. The Arab invaders left their indelible stamp upon the culture, introducing their religion and language. A majority of Morocco's population of 29 million live west of the mountains, which insulate the country from the Sahara desert. Fez, an Arab city, is Morocco's cultural and religious center, while the more Berber Marrakech is a major tourist area.

The Berbers of the high Atlas who comprise 35% of the country's population are the original Moroccans and descendants of the people who migrated from the eastern Mediterranean area to North Africa about 2000 BC. Extended families of cousins, siblings and parents live in fortress-like Berber hamlets built around fortified communal granaries. Rather than being absorbed by Islam, the Berbers have adapted the religion to suit their needs. Although Sunni Muslims, the Berbers have maintained a strong attachment to pre-Islamic religions, particularly the veneration of saints and the use of amulets to ward off harm and "the evil eye." There are three main Berber language groups and many dialects. There has been an encouraging spiritual response among the Berbers, who appear to be more open to the gospel than those of Arab stock, in part because they are aware of their Christian past.

Spiritual Competition

Morocco is a Muslim kingdom, and the government is determined to preserve Islam as the religion of all Moroccans. Pride in her glorious past as a center of Islamic civilization and learning as well as prejudice against Christianity are formidable barriers, and it has been estimated that 80% of the population has never heard the gospel. While Sunni Islam is the official religion, a pervasive attraction for the mystical exists. This can be seen in the igurramen, or Berber saints, who are said to possess magical powers to heal and settle disputes. Folk Islam is practiced by Berbers and many of the Arab peoples of Morocco.

The official government attitude toward the Church has become more problematic and oppressive in recent years. Moroccan intelligence and security is very concerned about the spread of Christianity among Muslims, and has cracked down with severity, opening mail, conducting surveillance, and even jailing and torturing converts. Christian radio and Bible correspondence courses have had a good impact in the past, but the security forces are now closely monitoring these channels. The small house churches are very isolated and fearful, and are in dire need of prayer and material support.

Noteworthy Trends

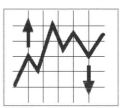

The reign of King Hassan has hardly been trouble free. A third constitution has been finalized which appears to give increased liberties to citizens, including greater freedom of religion. Islamic fundamentalists are a minority movement in Morocco compared to neighboring Algeria, where the country is on the brink of a civil war between government forces and fundamentalists. There is great concern that should the hard-line militants prevail in Algeria the movement could easily spread across the border to relatively peaceful Morocco. This factor, combined with the pesky problem of Christianity and the ongoing war in Western Sahara has only made the government more paranoid and repressive. Morocco's human rights record is bad and likely to get worse in view of the impending conflicts.

The Western Sahara conflict is also proving to be a severe drain on Morocco's economy. It does not appear however, that King Hassan will willingly give up the Western Sahara to the Polisario Front, due to his heavy ideological investment in the war and the many lives already lost. Like other totalitarian Arab governments, Hassan is stubbornly marching down the path of self-vindication and non-compromise, failing to understand that it is precisely this attitude that galvanizes his foes. Needless to say, none of this bodes well for the young church.

National Prayer Concerns

Obstacles to Ministry
Pray about these challenging circumstances:
• Persecution of National Believers
Christians have been beaten, tortured and imprisoned
• Prevalence of Folk Islam
Ritual superstition is widely observable
• Muslim Perceptions of Christianity
Often associated with French and Spanish colonialism
• Distrust Among Believers
Deep suspicions have arisen, making unity difficult

Spiritual Power Points
Pray over these influential locations:
• Jamaa el Fna (Marrakech)
Spiritual gathering place for fortune tellers, sufis etc.
• City of Fez
City includes numerous medresas (seminaries), mosques and holy sites
• City of Ouezzane
Center of the Wazzaniyyah, an Islamic mystic brotherhood
• Kairouyyin Mosque (Fez)
Largest mosque in North Africa; important Islamic center

Festivals and Pilgrimages
Pray during these spiritual events:
• Ramadan & Eid al-Fitr (Varies: '96 = Jan/Feb)
Month of fasting and prayer followed by two day feast
• Sidi ben Yasmin Moussem (June)
Week of religious chants & music to honor Islamic saint
• Bousselham Pilgrimage (June/July)
Annual pilgrimage with animal sacrifices
• Moussem of Sidi Alla el Hadj (August)
Religious celebrations held near numerous saints' tombs

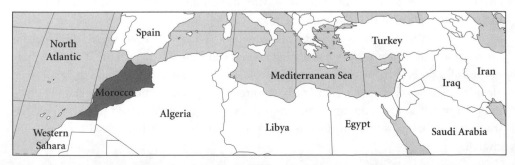

Myanmar (Burma)

$\mathcal{A}$ sleepy and tropical Buddhist land that reminds visitors of a Rudyard Kipling novel, Myanmar is surrounded on three sides by mountains and on the fourth by the sea, and is a country where time seems to have stopped decades ago. Its geography makes it rather inaccessible, and since independence from Britain in 1947, it has become politically isolated as well. Myanmar, or Burma, as it was known until 1989, is the world's largest heroin producer. The opium poppies are grown in the legendary "Golden Triangle," which is controlled by warlords and lies in the northern part of the country, encompassing northern Thailand and the high plateau of neighboring Laos.

Mountains and plateaus surround the central lowland area where most of the population lives. There are 67 tribal groups living in the mountainous frontier areas who are generally scorned and dominated by the majority Burmans. The unsettled domestic situation has contributed to the gradual sealing off of the country, making foreigners, including missionaries, unwelcome.

The current government of military thugs seized power in 1962 and set themselves up as an independent socialist state. Unfortunately, they seemed to know little about either socialist economics or the rudiments of governing, and the regime soon became xenophobic, erratic, repressive and broke. Today the nation is a seedy and decaying backwater. The once stately British capital of Rangoon is a maze of crumbling, mossy buildings and deteriorating roads, where consumer goods are mostly smuggled in from across the Thai border and sold in ramshackle storefronts and open-air bazaars. The major marketplace in the capital was built by the government to function as a central clearing house for smuggled contraband—even though all transactions carried out there are technically illegal.

Basic Facts

Location:
Southeast Asia

Neighboring Countries:
Bangladesh, India, China, Laos, Thailand

Population:
46,275,000

Capital City:
Yangon (Rangoon)

Major Cities:
Mandalay, Karbe, Moulmein, Insein, Thingangyun

Government:
Military

Leader:
General Than Shwe

Major Religions:
Buddhism, animism, Christianity

Historical Background

The first known religion of the earliest inhabitants of Myanmar was spirit worship. Although Buddhism was the prevailing organized religion of the Pyu and Mon peoples who preceded the Burmans, it was never able to replace or eradicate the allegiance to spirits. In the 11th century, King Anawrahta was the first leader to unite the Burmese empire, which included much of present day Myanmar. He became a Buddhist early in his reign and made Buddhism the state religion; his capital, Pagan, became a major Buddhist center.

In 1287 the Mongol armies of Kublai Khan seized Pagan, finally withdrawing in 1303. Myanmar was not dominated by another foreign power until 1886 when the British annexed it as the colony of Burma. The colonial period lasted until 1947, although the Japanese also invaded and prevailed from 1942-45. After independence, Buddhism was again made the state religion, although this is no longer the case. Hinduism, which was an early influence in much of Southeast Asia, never gained much of a following in Myanmar despite its proximity to India. The present government closed the country to foreign residents in 1964. Since then the economy has gone from bad to worse despite the presence of a friendly, educated, and largely English-speaking population.

Unreached Peoples

The majority Burmans have had vigorous missions activity directed toward them in the past. Perhaps the most famous missionary to work among them was the American Baptist Adoniram Judson, who arrived in 1813. Despite his efforts and those of many other dedicated servants, the gospel has never had a significant impact on these people. Only about two per cent of all the Christians in Myanmar come from among the Burmans, who continue to follow Buddhism with a strong undercurrent of spirit worship. Most Christians are found among the hill tribes. Buddhism has been particularly resistant, especially the monastic orders, who dominate Burmese spiritual life.

The Rohingya are a Muslim people who have lived in Myanmar for centuries. Their ancestors were Arab, Moorish, Mughal, and Bengali traders who opened ports in the Arakan region (a mountainous coastal area close to Bangladesh). Despite their long history in the country, the ruling military junta sees the Rohingyas as aliens in a Buddhist land and has launched various campaigns against them which have resulted in torture, rape, and murder. In 1978 approximately 300,000 Rohingya fled to Bangladesh, many of whom eventually returned; in February 1992, thousands more again fled across the border. There are no known believers among the Rohingya.

Spiritual Competition

Buddhism has a strong hold in Myanmar and is considered the national religion. Yet, as mentioned earlier, it has never eradicated the older animism embraced by the ancient and primitive peoples. Many Buddhist pagodas are either built on the site of older nat (spirit) shrines, or else the nat shrines are incorporated into the Buddhist structure. One such example is Shwe Zigon, the holiest of Pagan's Buddhist stupas, where the most historic nat shrine is included in the complex.

Until 1551, when a strict Buddhist king forbade the sacrifice of live animals, many kings sacrificed horses and cattle on Mt. Popa (an extinct volcano in the central part of the country), site of the Mahagiri nat, the most famous of all nats. There are a total of 37 nats enshrined on the summit of Mt. Popa, which is part of the vast array of shrines and temples at Pagan. Many homes still have a dried coconut hanging on the wall which is meant to be a little dwelling for the Mahagiri spirit should it choose to make a welcome visit to the house. Fortunately, Burmese-style Buddhism is a relatively tolerant religion, and the Burmese church has been allowed to grow without serious opposition, even from the repressive government.

Noteworthy Trends

For more than 40 years, there has been continual armed conflict between the central government, dominated by Burmans, and the ethnic minority hill tribes, who want independence. At times the conflict has escalated to all-out warfare, even to the extent of the various tribes unifying their armies in opposition to the government. Christians, the majority of whom are from the hill tribes, are caught up in this tragic conflict. Although the vastly superior government army has inflicted horrible destruction, it has not been able to stop the guerrilla activities of the tribes. Peace initiatives backed by Thailand and China have thus far not been very successful.

After a series of popular uprisings in 1988, including one massacre in the capital in which 3,000 marchers were gunned down by the army, the regime allowed free elections in 1990. When the opposition party, headed by a woman named Aung San Suu Kyi won 85% of the vote, the government nullified the results and put Suu Kyi under house arrest where she remains today; she was awarded the 1991 Nobel Peace Prize for her courageous efforts. If the military regime falls, Myanmar could again become a thriving country, as it has good agricultural potential, and could earn tourist dollars because of its unique and friendly culture.

National Prayer Concerns

Obstacles to Ministry
Pray about these challenging circumstances:
• Xenophobic Government
Dictatorial military regime has isolated country
• Prevalence of Buddhist Animism
Idolatry and superstition deeply ingrained in culture
• Opium Production in North
Golden Triangle region can be extremely hazardous
• Shortage of Christian Literature
Strict import restrictions have exacerbated problem

Spiritual Power Points
Pray over these influential locations:
• Shwedagon Pagoda (Rangoon)
Renowned Buddhist reliquary and worship complex
• Mt. Popa
Spiritual axis of pre-Buddhist Burma
• Shwe Zigon (Pagan)
Most popular pilgrimage shrine of Pagan, the spiritual capital of Myanmar
• Kuthodaw Pagoda (Mandalay)
Houses slabs containing the entire Buddhist canon

Festivals and Pilgrimages
Pray during these spiritual events:
• Wesak Festival (May/June)
Celebrates birth, enlightenment and death of Buddha
• Rains Retreat (July-October)
Celebrations honoring Buddha's conception
• Thitingyut Festival (October)
Huge celebration of Buddha's descent from heaven
• Pagoda of the Eight Weekdays (All Year)
Offering pilgrimage to Shwedagon "planetary posts"

Nepal

Nepal was closed to the world until it opened its borders in 1951; since then the country has come to represent all the enchanting allure of the inscrutable Orient. Because the culture and architecture has been well preserved, the country has often been called a "living museum" of Asian culture. To cross a street is to travel across centuries. Amazing physical variety also fashions this incredible land: the world's highest peaks, lowland plains where tigers and rhinoceros roam, and radical variations in climate. Even the name of the capital, Kathmandu, has a ring of the exotic. The people of Nepal are as kaleidoscopic as the terrain. In the mountains along the northern border, the ethnic groups are closely related to Tibetans and follow Tibetan Buddhism. Indian and Hindu influence are more clearly evident in Kathmandu, and further south a Muslim minority is also found.

Nepal is a favorite destination of trekkers and adventure seekers who arrive from all over the world. The Himalayan mountains and foothills offer a veritable hiker's paradise, with magnificent views of snow capped summits, forests of rhododendrons, isolated hamlets, intricate temples, and great ridges carpeted with alpine flowers.

Although Nepal is the birthplace of Buddha (ca. 560 BC), the country is now largely Hindu, and is the world's only Hindu kingdom; the king is widely regarded as a deity. Buddhist and Hindu temples and shrines compose a dizzying array of sacred spots in the Kathmandu Valley. Many Westerners are drawn to Nepal for spiritual reasons, and large numbers of Europeans and Americans can be found around the capital, dabbling in Hindu and Buddhist meditation or studying under gurus and holy men.

Basic Facts

Location:
South Asia

Neighboring Countries:
China (Tibet), India

Population:
20,188,000

Capital City:
Kathmandu

Major Cities:
Pokhara, Biratnagar;
Birganj

Government:
Democracy

Leader:
Prime Minister Man
Mohan Adhikary;
King Birendra

Major Religions:
Hinduism, Buddhism

Historical Background

Traditionally, legends conveyed history to the Nepalese people, attributing unknown beginnings to great heroes and gods. The modern history of the country began in 1769, when the king of the Gurkhas was able to unite the petty principalities of the Kathmandu Valley. This kingdom was in turn taken over by the Rana family in 1846, who held power until 1951, while reducing the king to a figurehead.

Shamanism (a belief in the ability of certain persons to communicate with the spirit world) appears to have been one of the earliest religions in Nepal. Buddhism then entered the region, and was the dominant religion until the fourth century, when the ruling class began to accept Hinduism. Hinduism did not displace Buddhism but rather fused with it, allowing shamanism to survive as well. Since both Hinduism and Buddhism tend to be all-encompassing in their beliefs, they mix together easily in Nepal. Shamans can be found in all ethnic groups today. As a result there is a high degree of demonic activity in the country, and Nepalese Hinduism and Buddhism are saturated with spirit contact and occult practices such as tantra, a symbolic fusion of good and evil through bizarre rites.

Unreached Peoples

Hindus comprise the majority of the population and are composed of a number of ethnic groups of Indian origin. Most are engaged in agriculture and are found in the lowland areas of the south as well as the valleys. They have been responsive to the gospel, as missionaries and evangelists in Nepal have seen considerable success over the last several decades. In 1960 there were 25 national Christians; today there are upwards of 100,000. The church in Nepal is much more inclusive than in India, cutting across caste and tribal lines.

The Sherpas are perhaps the best known of all Nepalese people groups, having become famous worldwide for their mountaineering skills and cheerfulness. They are closely related to the Tibetans, being of the same ethnic stock and following the same form of Buddhism. As with other Tibetan Buddhists, it often takes twelve years or more from the time they first hear the gospel until they make a decision to become Christians. There are perhaps only 20 believers among the 29,000 Sherpas, a number which has been growing slowly in recent years. The Muslim minority in the south is virtually unevangelized, and isolated Buddhist groups in the mountainous north are also unreached.

Spiritual Competition

Hinduism is the state religion, and although religious tolerance is traditional in Nepal, the tolerance has not always applied to Christianity. The constitution prior to 1990 (when a change of government took place) provided that "every person may profess and practice his own religion," but did not permit proselytism. The law was strictly enforced, and in the late 1980s Nepal had hundreds of Christians languishing in substandard prisons. However, an amnesty has been granted to all Christians formerly held in prison—there were over 200 believers in jail in 1989. Aggressive evangelism is still illegal, but the church has enjoyed greater freedom since then.

Nepal is known for its continuous festivals, and hardly a day passes without festivities, ceremonial observances, or pilgrimages taking place in some part of the country. Almost all of these events have religious significance and serve to strengthen the Hindu and Buddhist faith of the people. There is still considerable opposition on a local or family level if a Hindu or Buddhist converts to Christianity. Foreign and native evangelists are quite active, but there is a real need for tact and sensitivity to avoid a backlash reaction.

Noteworthy Trends

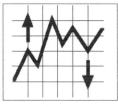

The popular democratic revolt of 1990 ushered in a new constitution and elected government. Although the constitution is not substantially different in terms of religious freedom, the interpretation of it seems to be more relaxed, and Christians are taking greater liberties without repercussions. The Nepalese church was already very active in evangelism, and they are now able to make more public professions of their faith. One way they have done this is through Christmas and Easter marches—the first time in their history they have been able to freely make such public statements.

A significant movement has been taking place among the Tamangs, who traditionally followed Tibetan Buddhism as well as Hinduism and animism. Entire villages and high percentages of people in some areas have been turning to Christianity. It is safe to say that over 15,000 Tamangs have embraced the Christian faith in the last ten years. This kind of overwhelming response is unknown among any other Tibetan Buddhist peoples. Nepal has been one of the great mission success stories of recent years, but prayer is still needed for the unity of the church, which is showing signs of internal tension.

National Prayer Concerns

Obstacles to Ministry
Pray about these challenging circumstances:
• Large Hindu Majority
Government and national populace strongly Hindu
• Demonic Influences
Demonic bondages are powerful and widespread
• Social Ostracism
Repercussions for converts especially severe in rural areas
• Christian Disunity
Divisions have emerged around racial and doctrinal issues

Spiritual Power Points
Pray over these influential locations:
• Pashupatinath Temple & Bagmati River
Main Hindu temple and worship site in Nepal
• Town of Bhaktapur
Major Buddhist, Hindu and animist ritual center
• Mts. Machapuchare, Annapurna & Khumbila
Abode of Hindu, Buddhist and Sherpa animistic deities
• Boudhanath & Swayambhunath Stupas
Central Tibetan Buddhist worship and training sites

Festivals and Pilgrimages
Pray during these spiritual events:
• Shivarati (February)
Major Shiva festival at Pashupatinath Temple
• Macchendranath Festivals (April)
Major Buddhist and Hindu chariot pageants
• Indra Jatra Festival (September)
Sacrifices, dances and parading of the Kumari goddess
• Annapurna Sanctuary Pilgrimage
Includes 2,000-year old sacred grove and Hinko cave

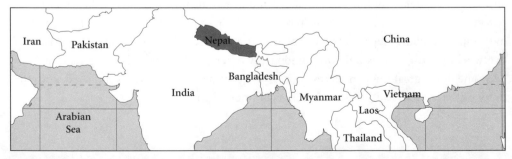

Niger

The dry, hot and dust-laden wind known as the harmattan blows off the Sahara with such blistering intensity that rain often evaporates before falling to the ground, leaving little doubt that Niger is located in one of the hottest regions of the world. Niger is also noteworthy in that it is one of the least urbanized nations on earth. 82% of the population is either nomadic or lives in tiny villages. Even the capital, Niamey, which is the largest population center, has a sizable number of nomads continually drifting in and out of the city.

The Sahara Desert dominates much of the country, covering the land like a great sandy blanket. As a result, 90% of the population clusters along the Niger River in the southwest corner of the country, one of the few regions where crops are able to grow. The rest of the land is barren waste, where desert oases and nomadic bands are among the few signs of life.

Agriculture is at best a hit-and-miss undertaking. All too often fields of dead and dried millet bear mute testimony to the scant rainfall, and at least 60% of the livestock was lost during the droughts of 1969-74. Only the export of uranium kept the economy functioning during that difficult time, but uranium prices have since dropped.

The country came into being when the French combined several areas which had been zones of refuge for people victimized by military and religious struggles. The resulting population mix consists of approximately 75% black African peoples and 25% Berbers. Almost all segments of the populace adhere to Islam.

Basic Facts

Location:
West Africa

Neighboring Countries:
Libya, Algeria, Mali, Burkina Faso, Benin, Nigeria, Chad

Population:
8,313,000

Capital City:
Niamey

Major Cities:
Zinder, Maradi, Tahoua, Agadez

Government:
Republic (military currently in power)

Leader:
President Mahamane Ousmane

Major Religions:
Islam, African traditional religions

Historical Background

Niger was once controlled by wealthy empires which ruled much of the Sahel (the fringe of the Sahara). Their wealth was derived from control of the trans-Saharan trade in slaves, gold, and salt. With the advent of European involvement in Africa and the increase in maritime trade, trans-Saharan routes diminished in importance. Ruins of cities in the Sahara attest to the fact that a highly civilized people inhabited what is now Niger thousands of years ago. Islam entered the area in the 10th century but was limited to the aristocracy and urban elite until the 19th century when it finally took root among the outlying people. The earliest leaders who converted did so to gain trading advantages, while holding only loosely to Islamic customs and rituals. Even when Islam began to make headway in the rural population, it did not undermine traditional beliefs. Animistic rituals not only continue alongside Islam, but are accepted without question.

Christianity arrived in Niger in the 7th century when Berber Christians were driven south by Islamic jihads (holy wars). Gradually, however, due to isolation from other Christians, the faith died out and was not known again until the twentieth century.

Unreached Peoples

The Tauregs are a nomadic Muslim people, ethnically related to the Berbers of North Africa, giving them an almost Arab appearance. They were driven south into the desert about same the time as the aforementioned Islamic invasion of North Africa. During the 6th century, Tauregs in the desert oases had significant contact with Byzantine Greek Christianity. Their present fixation with crosses (21 different types), perhaps dates back to this period. They have however, shown only a marginal interest in the gospel. While a vital and consistent witness has been extended to them for over 40 years, a major breakthrough has yet to come.

The Wodaabe are an animistic people who are part of the Fulani ethnic group. Their name literally means "people of the taboo," and they have traditionally resorted to secret potions in their attempt to wrest a bare subsistence from the harsh environment. Loyalty is their highest value, making a change of religion nearly impossible. As one said, "We would rather die than change." After more than 20 years of patient Christian witness, there are now over 60 Wodaabe believers and even a Bible school graduate.

Spiritual Competition

Although over 90% of the population is consid-ered Muslim, the new constitution has established Niger as a secular state. The current administration maintains an attitude of religious toleration, helping to make it one of the most accessible countries in West Africa for missionaries. But despite the ease of access, it is still one of the countries least touched by the gospel.

As in other countries of North and West Africa, the most powerful religious orga-nizations are the Muslim brotherhoods. (For more detail on the brotherhoods, see Senegal.) Islam in this area has absorbed many of the traditional religious practices. These traditional religions are very territorial in nature - restricted to a particular piece of land and the sky above it. A man is attached almost irretrievably to his society, his ancestors, the gods and forces of the land. Change comes slowly, since a change of religion removes one from the social order and the land of the tribe.

One particularly powerful traditional religion is the Bori cult, which involves con-tact with spirits, sacrifices, seances, and possession dances. The leader is said to be a woman who has control of many prostitutes. While institutional Islam frowns on such a cult, many Muslims participate nonetheless.

Noteworthy Trends

The church in Niger is the only one south of the Sahara where numbers have declined since colonial times. One of the reasons for the decline is that the Catholic Church is predominantly expatriate, with little impact on the indigenous peoples. Despite declining numbers, there is a surprising openness to the gospel. Many Muslims are willing to listen to the Christian message due to the credibility and consistent witness of many Christian ministries, especially in providing famine relief.

In April, 1993, President Ousmane came to office following the first fair, demo-cratic elections in 33 years of independence. However, he inherited a country on the brink of chaos and disaster, as most of the 38,000 civil servants had not received their salaries for at least three months. A Taureg insurrection had paralyzed the transition government prior to the elections, and even now cease-fires between the Tauregs, the government, and other rebel groups are tenuous. The country remains virtually bankrupt, and prospects for increased earnings are slim due to the lifeless uranium market and no other significant export com-modities. Only the largess of the French government has kept the country afloat during the transition to democracy.

National Prayer Concerns

Obstacles to Ministry

Pray about these challenging circumstances:
- Strong Islamic Presence

Over 80 percent Muslim; Islamic university in capital
- Difficult Physical Terrain

Much of the country is inhospitable desert with poor roads
- Cultural Barriers

Tuareg and Wodaabe especially resistant to change
- Tensions Between Christians

Strained relations between different national church groups

Spiritual Power Points

Pray over these influential locations:
- Kaouar Oases

Center of strong Senousi proselytizing
- Village of Lugu

Important center for animist rituals
- Sarari-n-Mesall Aje (Agadez)

Significant mosque and pilgrimage site
- City of Say

Center of Islamic learning and piety

Festivals and Pilgrimages

Pray during these spiritual events:
- Bori Festivals (Monthly)

Ceremonies in which the gods possess initiated women
- Ramadan & Eid al-Fitr (Varies: '96 = Jan/Feb)

Month of fasting and prayer followed by two day feast
- Gerewol Festival (September)

Magic ritual courtship celebrations of the Wodaabe
- Bude N'Daji Celebration

Ritual sacrifices to the Dogoua spirit

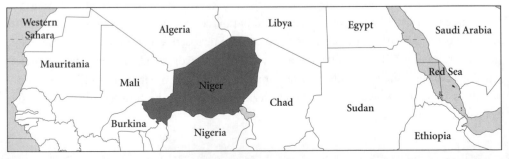

Nigeria

Nigeria is a nation divided. Africa's most populous and potentially wealthy nation is the largest country in West Africa, and is actually a federation of 30 states, divided largely along ethnic and religious lines. The north is predominantly Muslim, while the south is mainly Christian, and tensions always run high between the two religions.

This is a country of significant natural wealth (mainly oil), but it has suffered three decades of mismanagement, political turmoil and civil war. A Nigerian leader recently noted that "...the challenge is to alleviate the economic malaise of our people, who have continued to suffer in times of plenty."

Nigeria's huge and ethnically diverse population of 100 million speaks over 200 languages and accounts for one-fourth of the total population of sub-Saharan Africa. Cultural differences in Nigeria have often resulted in bloodshed and turmoil. From 1967 to 1970 differences between east and west resulted in the tragic Biafran war. More recently, in the early 1980s, sporadic Muslim vs. Christian sparring and violence has created turmoil in the northern states where Muslims form the majority.

While Nigeria is a secular country with freedom of religion specified in her constitution, most post-independence governments and military juntas have given preferential treatment to Muslims, and often ignore incidents of Muslim persecution of Christians. Tensions between Muslims and Christians run high over the desire of some Muslims to introduce Sharia (Islamic law) to the country. Nigeria has closer links with the more distant English-speaking countries such as Ghana and Sierra Leone than with its adjacent French-speaking neighbors of Benin, Niger and Cameroon.

Basic Facts

Location:
West Africa

Capital City:
Abuja

Leader:
General Sani Abacha

Neighboring Countries:
Benin, Niger, Chad, Cameroon

Major Cities:
Lagos, Ibadan, Ogbomosho, Kano

Major Religions:
Christianity, Islam, African traditional religions

Population:
100,580,000

Government:
In transition

189

Historical Background

What is now called Nigeria was originally several separate kingdoms, and some of the older cultures can be traced back 2,000 years. The earliest recognizable Nigerian society was that of the Nok people, who existed between 500 BC and 200 AD in the area south of the Jos plateau. In the 7th and 8th centuries the kingdom of Kanem-Bornu, which originated in the region of Lake Chad in northeastern Nigeria, dominated from West Africa to the Sudan. There is some evidence of contact between the kingdom of Kanem-Bornu and the Christian kingdoms of Nubia along the middle Nile before the latter were overrun by Islam.

Nigeria was also influenced by the Atlantic slave trade, which was initially dominated by the Portuguese and later by the Dutch and English. A majority of the trade concentrated in the Niger delta where coastal tribes organized to take advantage of the slave trade, acting as middlemen to protect themselves from becoming victims.

Nigeria's modern history has been dominated by bloodshed, strife, political turmoil and civil war. Nigeria underwent six coups in twenty years, and movement towards free and democratic elections are constantly undermined by the Muslim-dominated military junta.

Unreached Peoples

The urbanized Yoruba of the west are one of the three dominant peoples of Nigeria. They are largely Christian, with a 25% Muslim minority, and are very influential in business. Muslim missionary efforts coupled with monetary enticements and favors have brought some into the fold of Islam, and traditional beliefs are still strong among many of the Yoruba.

The Ibo of the east are the second largest people group in Nigeria. They used to keep slaves for religious rituals, and these slaves were sacrificed upon the death of a king. These practices may have come from the bloodthirsty kingdom of Benin to their west, where human sacrifice played an important part in insuring spiritual and political power. A high percentage of the Ibo are now Christian.

The Hausa and the Fulani of the north are both largely Islamic tribes. Although outwardly Muslim, some 30% of the Hausa actually follow traditional religions, and there have been some advances for the gospel among these people. There are nearly ten million Fulani in Nigeria, where they constitute much of the ruling class. Some Fulani have responded to the gospel, and there may now be 2,000 Christians among them.

Spiritual Competition

$\mathcal{T}$he spiritual makeup of Nigeria closely mirrors the nation's ethnic and cultural divisions. There are no definite statistics, but the country is approximately 50% Christian and 40% Muslim, with the remainder still following traditional African religions. The South's Christian majority was influenced by European missionaries at the turn of the century, while the Muslim north was converted by neighboring Islamic states. The middle zone is nominally Christian but hotly contested by Muslim missionaries who are aggressively seeking converts there.

Expatriate missionaries are welcomed by the Nigerian church, but visas are difficult to obtain due to Muslim influence in the political system. The same does not hold for Muslim evangelists and missionaries who have few restrictions placed on their travel. Although there are no anti-conversion laws, converts from Islam, especially in the north, face considerable pressure and hostility from relatives and the authorities. The religious unrest that has sporadically rocked northern Nigeria for the last decade has cost over 6,000 lives in clashes between Muslims and Christians. Countless churches and mosques have been destroyed in the conflicts.

Noteworthy Trends

$\mathcal{A}$ rapidly growing population of 100 million, low per capita income, and constant political uncertainty are serious challenges facing the country as it approaches the turn of the century. The "giant of Africa" is in serious trouble.

The transition from military to civilian government in Nigeria has been a fickle affair. A Nigerian wryly remarked that the transition is like Jesus Christ's second coming, saying that "It has been promised, but nobody knows when it will be." The last presidential elections were canceled and the military appears to be more firmly entrenched in Nigerian politics than ever before.

The Nigerian church has experienced rapid growth which has greatly accelerated over the last 15 years. There are over 160 accredited Bible schools and seminaries, supported by numerous theological education and church leadership programs. Nigeria has become one of the major missionary-sending countries of the developing world, but faces significant challenges in the future. One of the most important is providing sufficient follow-up and balanced teaching to accompany evangelistic results and to counteract doctrinal distortions. Pray that God would encourage, empower and purify the national church and give them a vision for the unreached people of Nigeria.

National Prayer Concerns

Obstacles to Ministry

Pray about these challenging circumstances:

• Muslim Attacks on Christians
Extremists in north have burned churches, beaten many
• Christian Syncretism
Animist secret societies have roots in church as well
• Serious Urban Crime and Congestion
Lagos is one of the most dangerous cities in Africa
• Lack of Christian Maturity
Power seeking and selfish attitudes are too common

Spiritual Power Points

Pray over these influential locations:

• City of Kano
Oldest city in West Africa; Islamic spiritual center
• Oshun Shrine (Oshogbo)
Sacred site of the Yoruba peoples
• Egbo House (Lagos)
Headquarters of one of the more significant animist tribes
• Sultan's Palace (Sokoto)
Seat of the spiritual leader of Nigeria's Muslims

Festivals and Pilgrimages

Pray during these spiritual events:

• Ramadan & Eid al-Fitr (Varies: '96 = Jan/Feb)
Month of fasting and prayer followed by two day feast
• Okere Juju (May/June)
Five week festival of purification and flagellation
• Egungun Festival (June)
Egungun secret society dancers are possessed by spirits
• Oshun Festival (August)
Yoruba festival involving dance and ritual sacrifice

Oman

Situated on one of the world's busiest maritime trade routes, the Sultanate of Oman has long been one part myth and two parts living legend. For centuries Omani shipwrights constructed merchant vessels that roamed from Zanzibar in the south to China in the east – all in quest of timber, spices, pearls and ivory. Some scholars believe that the legendary voyages of Sinbad were actually based on a composite of Arab captains and merchants that had ventured to the limits of the known world during the golden age of Arab exploration between the 8th and 11th centuries. Whereas in days gone by Oman's primary export was frankincense, today it is oil.

Even jaded Middle Eastern travelers are routinely captured by the nation's stark physical beauty. For overland visitors the attraction is a dramatic lunar landscape dotted by ancient forts, deep gorges and vivid green oases. Those approaching by sea are equally bedazzled by the razor sharp lava ridges that descend to create a fjord-like coastline. Most unexpected of all, is the nation's lush southwest – an Arabian anomaly produced by summer clouds that are tripped up and wrung out by the Qara Mountains.

Besides claiming the further dubious distinction of being the hottest place on earth where human beings routinely live and work – over 135° in its sun-baked interior —Oman is also a sensual bouquet of cultural diversity. At no time is this fact more in evidence than on summer evenings when weary workers shake off the lingering daytime heat with food, fellowship and song. The music, like Omani society, is an exotic hybrid of Indian lilt, African rhythm and Arab expressiveness.

Basic Facts

Location:
Middle East

Neighboring Countries:
United Arab Emirates,
Saudi Arabia, Yemen

Population:
1,735,000

Capital City:
Muscat

Major Cities:
Matrah; Salalah; Nizwa;
Al-Buraymi; Sur

Government:
Sultanate (Monarchy)

Leader:
Sultan Qaboos bin Said

Major Religions:
Islam

Historical Background

While some Omani traders were hauling copper to Sumer as early as 2200 BC, Arabs from other parts of the Arabian Peninsula did not begin settling the region until the first six centuries AD. Many were drawn by Oman's sacred frankincense groves. While the Omanis were among the earliest of Muhammad's converts—embracing Islam by the middle of the 7th century—their fierce independence prevented them from paying taxes to the reigning caliphs in Damascus and Baghdad.

A darker chapter in Omani history reveals an involvement with piracy and slavery. While much of this activity was confined to the waters of the Persian Gulf, other raids ventured as far as East Africa. In the 17th century, Oman replaced the Portuguese as the controlling power in the East African city of Mombassa. And while the Omanis have long since gone, their Islamic religion has remained behind as an active force.

On a more encouraging note, Oman was the country in which Samuel Zwemer, the great missionary to the Muslim world, began his ministry in the late 19th century. About eight decades later, in 1970, the country's doors opened further when the austere and isolationist Sultan Said bin Taimur was deposed by his Sandhurst-trained son in a bloodless coup.

Unreached Peoples

First time visitors to Oman can easily feel as though they have been caught in a time warp. In many areas of the country women still wear full face masks—some almost bird-like in appearance—to shield their features from male eyes. Omani men, meanwhile, parade in battle fashion. In the interior, this generally means lacing themselves with decorative cartridge belts and WW I vintage carbines. Even more ubiquitous is the khanjar—a traditional curved dagger worn in elaborate silver scabbards tucked into brocade waist sashes.

Oman's patchwork population is largely a reflection of its turbulent history. Many of the dark-skinned Zanzibaris, for instance, are the descendants of East African slaves. Also evident, however, are remnant populations of ancient tribes that lived here before the advent of Islam—the Mahra hill peoples from the Dhofar Region, the traditionally nomadic Harais and Jeballi, and the Shihuh who live on the bleak mountains of the Musandam Peninsula (although younger Shihuhs now work in the nearby Emirates). Desert Bedouin work as roughnecks and drivers in the country's oil fields. Unfortunately, there are almost no Omani believers. Most coastal people are Ibadi Muslims. The rest (mainly from India, East Africa and Baluchistan), are Sunnis and Shiites.

Spiritual Competition

While the dominant role of Islam comes as no surprise, what is unexpected is the continuing influence of the occult in modern Oman. While much of this influence is confined to the nation's interior, the region's unusual specialty is well known throughout the Gulf. Speaking of the Omani interior, one Middle Easterner recently remarked to a Christian expatriate: "There are real magicians there." As if this were not enough, there is also a voodoo-like religion presently operating in Oman that comes as a byproduct of the nation's African influence.

By far and away the biggest problems facing Christian workers in Oman, however, are the cultural attachments to Islam and governmental prohibitions on Muslim evangelism. Shiite fundamentalists can be found in Mutrah's old town, and women are still shrouded in the loose-fitting long black aba. In addition, many parts of the country rely on Sharia law, and Quranic education is compulsory.

Despite the strict anti-proselytizing measures, non-Muslim foreigners (Christians and Hindus) are allowed to worship at designated locations. The government has even donated land for building Christian churches and a new Hindu temple.

Noteworthy Trends

Situated on the strategic Straits of Hormuz, Oman will always be a key player in any conflict involving the flow of oil out of the Persian Gulf. What is more, Sultan Qaboos, the fourteenth of the Al Bu Said monarchs, is a just, friendly-to-the-West ruler who can be counted on to maintain a policy of political moderation and economic modernization. The immediate threat facing the Sultan and his country is the fact that Oman's oil reserves are due to run out within the next 10-20 years. If diversification tactics are not sufficient to stave off a significant economic downturn, resulting social unrest could be exploited by Islamic extremists.

Another unfortunate trend in the last ten years has been the shrinking of an already puny indigenous church. Two small groups that had existed earlier have since dissipated as a consequence of inter-faith marriages and other factors. And while there are no known indigenous fellowships at present, the good news is that there were several new professions of Christ during the spring and summer of 1993.

Another encouraging trend has to do with improving access to Oman's unreached peoples. After years of isolation, the country is now planning to host upwards of 50,000 tourists by 1995!

National Prayer Concerns

Obstacles to Ministry

Pray about these challenging circumstances:

• Muslim Evangelism Strictly Forbidden

Foreigners are closely watched – especially at Sultan Qaboos University

• Occult Activity in Interior Villages

Practices go beyond traditional folk Islam; demonic magic and witchcraft are active

• No Indigenous Christians

Only a handful of national believers are known to exist; churches are for expatriates only

• Isolation of Certain People Groups

Areas such as the Ar Rub' al Khali and Musandam Peninsula are difficult to access

Spiritual Power Points

Pray over these influential locations:

• Ru'us Al Jibal

Sacred mountain home to the animist Shihuh tribe

• City of Nizwa

Former capital of Oman; regarded as holy city of Ibadism

• Khor and Ali Musa Mosques (Muscat)

Significant mosques sometimes visited by Sultan Qaboos

• Dhofar Region

Home of superstitious Mahri people; the area traditionally manifests a strong spirit of rebellion

Festivals and Pilgrimages

Pray during these spiritual events:

• Ramadan & Eid al-Fitr (Varies: '96 = Jan/Feb)

Month of fasting and prayer followed by two day feast

• Eid al-Adha (Varies: '96 = April)

Feast of Sacrifice; coincides with culmination of Hadj

• Ashura (Varies: '96 = May)

Shiite passion play celebrating Hussein's martyrdom

• Mawlid an-Nabi (Varies: '96 = July)

Celebrations honoring Muhammad's birthday

Pakistan

Pakistan is defined by the natural borders provided by the great Himalayan mountains to the north and the Arabian Sea on the south. The Indus River which runs down the center of the country provides the agricultural fertility that has attracted most of Pakistan's large population. This remarkable study in contrasts is not limited to physical geography. Although inhabited for at least 7,000 years, the modern nation of Pakistan is less than 50 years old. Culturally and ethnically it is a melting pot, but one that might better be described as boiling: this is a place where the similarities and distinctions of its peoples both tie the nation together and also threaten to tear it apart due to its complexities. There is no single Pakistani race, culture or history—the name Pakistan itself is said to be an acronym derived from the names of its various peoples. Such an acronym suggests that this country is the embodiment of a compromise, a nation resting more on theory than fact.

The political borders of Pakistan place it at the fracture zone of south and central Asia. Disputes with India and China, and a long porous border with disintegrating Afghanistan represent only a foretaste of the regional tensions that threaten to make Pakistan's future even more uncertain. Born in blood, Pakistan emerged as a new country in 1947 when the British gave India its independence and partitioned off Pakistan as a home for the Muslims. The civil carnage that followed took an estimated six million lives in brutal and ruthless slaughter between Hindus and Muslims. A half century later there is still great tension and animosity between the two countries and religions.

Basic Facts

Location:
South Asia

Neighboring Countries:
Iran, Afghanistan,
Tajikistan China, India

Population:
141,599,000

Capital City:
Islamabad

Major Cities:
Karachi, Lahore,
Faisalabad, Hyderabad,
Rawalpindi

Government:
Islamic republic with a
parliamentary democracy

Leader:
Prime Minister Benazir
Bhutto

Major Religions:
Islam

Historical Background

The Indus valley civilization of the 2nd and 3rd millennia BC is among the world's oldest. The Harrapan people built cities there and used a writing system derived from the Sumerians, with whom they traded. Evidence suggests that there was more than merchandise traded between them. A striking example was found in the northwestern Mesopotamian city of Mari: one of the earliest examples of the sacred tree cult, complete with a serpent, was discovered near the temple of Inana, or Ashtoreth. The source of both the greenish stone vessel and the workshop that carved its image was far away in the Indus valley of modern Pakistan. The seafaring middlemen of Bahrain were the link between the two cultures.

The Indo-Iranian peoples of Central Asia wiped out the Harrapan culture, bringing into India the language and culture that came to dominate the region. Their Iranian-based polytheistic religion is similar to that described in the earliest Hindu scripture, the Rig Veda. This Iranian proto-religion and its offshoot, Zoroastrianism, remained strong until the middle ages. The Islamization of north India began with the Arab conquests of the 8th century. The Ghaznavid Turks completed the process in the 1200s.

Unreached Peoples

A slight majority of Pakistan's people, about 60%, are Punjabi. The name of their homeland, Panj-ab, means five waters, and is derived from the five rivers that have given life to this region for thousands of years. The Punjabi culture is centered on the extended family. This identity of kinship is the only source of prestige in the Punjabi culture; individuality is secondary to one's status as a member of the group. Beyond this, the extended families are themselves grouped into biraderi. Relationships between families in this larger group are established and maintained through a strict system of gift giving. Accordingly, each family is responsible for giving reciprocal gifts to related families. Each successive gift has to be of greater value than the previous gift, thus maintaining a kind of binding indebtedness to each family.

The Sindhi people of the southern Indus valley account for 12% of the national population. They exhibit traces of Arab culture more than any other group in Pakistan, for Sind was occupied by the Arabs for 275 years. This is especially evident in the Sindhi language, family customs and art. The other major ethnic groups are the various Iranian peoples such as the Pathans and Balochs, and the Urdus, who are Muslims who immigrated from India.

Spiritual Competition

The one thing that is common to most Pakistanis is their Islamic religion; about 96-97% of the country is Muslim. As a nation founded upon religious tensions between the Hindu and Muslim populations of British India, it is this single identity alone that binds the nation together. However, over three percent of the population are Christian or Hindu, and both groups suffer from considerable discrimination. The adoption of the orthodox Islamic Sharia law by the same government that "rescued" the country from civil unrest in 1977 seems to prove the point that conservative Islamic ideals were adopted mostly to shore up the failing national identity and avert civil war.

Pakistani religion exhibits many facets of Islam. Both the extremely influential puritanical groups, some of which have a global influence, and the more grass-roots and mystical Sufi networks are deeply entrenched here. The Punjabis, for example, are known for their unusually deep devotion to mystical holy men. This custom is rooted firmly in Hinduism and other pre-Islamic religions, and probably illustrates the spiritual bent of most Pakistani Muslims. The tight control of family institutions in the native Pakistani cultures also contribute considerable resistance to the spread of the gospel. Bitterness and rejection of other peoples and views are also strong binding forces in this country.

Noteworthy Trends

Now that Pakistan is an officially Muslim state, the rights of Christians in the country have been sharply curtailed. Christians are not allowed to defend themselves or give testimony in Muslim courts that decide on issues of murder, rape, theft and blasphemy. Christians are not only kept from defending themselves, but in the case of assault by a Muslim, the Christian has no legal means to press charges. This can result in lengthy prison terms even when the defendant is found innocent. It also makes the blasphemy law a powerful weapon in the hands of fundamentalists.

The civil war in bordering Afghanistan is divided along ethnic lines between the Pashtun and other tribes, and many in the country are pressing for some form of ethnic autonomy. Since 10% of Pakistan is also Pashtun, the prospect of a strong separatist movement is not at all far fetched.

Since 1947 there have been three wars with India, and the last one almost resulted in a nuclear exchange, as both countries are believed to possess nuclear weapons, despite their denials. The combination of internal instability and hair-trigger military posturing means that Pakistan could easily become one of the most explosive and dangerous nations in the world.

National Prayer Concerns

Obstacles to Ministry

Pray about these challenging circumstances:

• Growing Islamic Fundamentalism
Enforcement of Sharia law is being pushed hard
• Prevalence of Folk Islam in Rural Areas
Strong superstitions exist in northern regions
• Christian Disunity
Caste consciousness and lack of mature leadership
• Lack of Resources
Christians are poor; church buildings in short supply

Spiritual Power Points

Pray over these influential locations:

• Lal Qalandar Shah Baz Shrine (Sehwan Sharif)
Pilgrimage site associated with revered Muslim saint
• City of Multan
Called the city of Mosques, shrines and sacred tombs
• Badshahi Mosque (Lahore)
Prominent Islamic center
• University of Quaid-i-Azam (Islamabad)
Center of Islamic learning and outreach

Festivals and Pilgrimages

Pray during these spiritual events:

• Ramadan & Eid al-Fitr (Varies: '96 = Jan/Feb)
Month of fasting and prayer followed by two day feast
• Shab-e-Mairaj (Varies: '96 = April)
All-night celebration of Muhammad's ascension
• Shab-i-Barat (April)
Remembrance of the dead; illumination of mosques
• Ashura (Varies: '96 = May)
Shiite passion play celebrating Hussein's martyrdom

Qatar

One hundred years ago when Qatar's island neighbor Bahrain was still considered a tiny backwater, Qatar itself was known only for its proximity to Bahrain. It was one insignificant place living in the shadow of another. At that time no one foresaw that this small peninsula of sand and stone held locked within it enough petroleum treasure to satisfy the needs of millions. That same treasure has done even more for the small population living there.

Qatar is now a typical Gulf Arab nouveau riche success story: a conservative Muslim nation surprisingly but happily thrust into the economic front lines of the twentieth century. For the average Qatari, this new-found oil wealth is not unlike winning the lottery—the native residents control a swelling influx of easy petrodollars, while employing a cosmopolitan mix of expatriates to manage the technology and do the hard work.

In spite of their recent windfall of wealth and prominence, the Qataris remain a rather simple and humble people, seemingly unaffected by their global status. Ruled by a traditional monarchy, the biweekly tradition of mejlis still exists, where open court is held and the emir is available to listen to the pleas of any of his subjects. The emir himself still personally signs the government checks and oversees the day-to-day matters of running his beloved country. Despite its enviable image, Qatar remains beautiful in its simplicity and traditional refinement.

Basic Facts

Location:
Middle East

Neighboring Countries:
Saudi Arabia, United Arab Emirates, Bahrain

Population:
516,000

Capital City:
Doha

Major Cities:
Dukhan, Umm Said, Ruwais

Government:
Traditional emirate

Leader:
Emir Khalifah ibn Hamad ath-Thani

Major Religions:
Islam

Historical Background

*Q*atar does not have the deep historical roots of neighboring Oman and Bahrain. It is ruled by the ath-Thani clan, whose origins are similar to the extended royal family that rules Saudi Arabia. The ath-Thanis first arrived in Qatar during the 1700s as part of a migration of tribes from central Arabia. These tribes were connected by their common commitment to a Muslim reform movement known as the Wahhabis, who sought to cleanse Islam from pagan practices which had crept in from pre-Islamic societies.

By the early 1900s this reform-minded movement had coalesced into a powerful political and military force which came to dominate all of Arabia, and in the end it emerged as the Kingdom of Saudi Arabia. Qatar and the other Gulf sheikdoms escaped assimilation because of British and European control of the Arabian coastline. At that time, Qatar's only real economy was based on pearl diving, but oil was soon discovered and the rulers signed an oil concession treaty in 1935 and remained under British protection until it was granted independence in 1971. Qatar's tenure as a British protectorate served it well, opening an economic doorway to the West and introducing the now indispensable English language.

Unreached Peoples

*A*s little as 20% of Qatar's total population consists of native Qataris. The remainder of the population is made up of immigrant Arab workers, south Asians, Iranians and Western businessmen. About 15% of Qatar may be Shiite Muslim. This sect is an anti-establishment branch of Islam made famous by the Shiites in Iran and Lebanon who are behind much of the instability in the Middle East today. Iran has encouraged and supported uprisings in all the Gulf states where Shiite minorities form a strategic block of workers in the critical oil industries.

One in 15 native Qataris is a member of the ruling ath-Thani clan. The ath-Thanis set the tone for Qatar and define its customs and laws. The character of their rule is a softer version of Saudi puritanism, with some grace given for "discreet" personal behavior. Their patronage of culture and the arts, their restrained economic policies and manifest generosity suggest a certain humility and softness that would not necessarily be expected from a puritanical Islamic regime. Any spiritual breakthrough among this clan would have widespread results. Expatriates are allowed some freedom of religion, but are strictly forbidden to evangelize Muslims. The Anglican Church is the only Christian denomination given official status.

Spiritual Competition

*L*he Wahhabi interpretation of Islam is stringent, relying heavily on the letter of the law. In the Sharia Islamic law (based on the Koran) this can mean stoning, amputation, beheading and other severe punishments for the slightest infringements of Muslim protocol. At the heart of Wahhabism is a strong emphasis on the unity of God (Allah). In that unity, true Muslims are expected to keep themselves free from anything that might detract from Allah's central and supreme place in the universe. Nothing is to be compared to him and no earthly authority is to stand in his place. One proverb holds that "anything you may think Allah to be, that you can be sure he is not."

During Wahhabi military campaigns, the holy warriors undertook to destroy any mosques or shrines dedicated to sheiks and holy men. Their purges included destroying the most sacred sites of Shiite Islam, such as Karbala and Nejaf (located in southern Iraq.) Wahhabis still consider the Shiites a barely tolerable aberration. Wahhabi control over Mecca, Medina and other sacred pilgrimage sites is an increasingly explosive issue among Shiite Muslims, who regard the conservative Arab Sunnis with disdain. This tension is similar to the Christian division between Roman Catholicism and conservative Protestants.

Noteworthy Trends

*Q*atar has experienced remarkable stability since its independence in the early 1970s. The ruling family has followed prudent and restrained financial policies and distributed the national wealth equitably. Their cultivation of a moderately free press and a rich cultural heritage has lent dignity and meaning to the citizens. Qatar has evolved since independence into the premier cultural center of the Gulf. It preserves local history and culture not only in its widely acclaimed museum but also in the respected Gulf Folklore Center.

Qatar's conservatism however, has manifested itself spiritually in the form of a severe attitude toward Christianity. There is no native church in Qatar and evangelism is strictly prohibited. Although Qatar's conservative policies have for the most part kept it free from entanglement in great international issues, it is not entirely immune. As a member of the Gulf Cooperation Council, it has shown a tendency toward understanding, if not supporting, the Iranian point of view. It remains susceptible to Iranian influence as the latter attempts to exploit regional fears by playing Qatar and other sympathetic Gulf states against each other.

National Prayer Concerns

Obstacles to Ministry

Pray about these challenging circumstances:

• Muslim Evangelism Strictly Forbidden
Imprisonment or deportation are minimum penalties
• No Official Indigenous Church
Handful of national believers forced underground
• Anti-Christian Propaganda
Recent influx from Saudi Arabia
• Prevalence of Materialism
Many citizens are concerned only with the good life

Spiritual Power Points

Pray over these influential locations:

• Grand Mosque (Doha)
Major worship center in Al-Jassrah district
• Headquarters of Qatar General Petroleum Corp. (Doha)
Economic power center situated in West Bay district
• Emiri Palace (Doha)
Seat of Emir Khalifa ath-Thani
• Qatar University
100,000-square-meter campus houses Islamic studies

Festivals and Pilgrimages

Pray during these spiritual events:

• Ramadan & Eid al-Fitr (Varies: '96 = Jan/Feb)
Month of fasting and prayer followed by two day feast
• Leilat al-Meiraj Festival (Varies: '96 = April)
Special events celebrating the ascension of Muhammad
• Eid al-Adha (Varies: '96 = April)
Feast of Sacrifice; coincides with culmination of Hadj
• Yennair Festival (Varies: '96 = May)
Islamic New Year commemorating the hegira

Saudi Arabia

This dune-swept land of Arabian nights and desert oases is one of the largest and wealthiest states in the Middle East. While foreign geologists and politicians may view the large subterranean oil reserves as a random quirk of nature, Saudis see it as nothing less than "the treasure chest of Allah"—delivered to their custody because they have been good Muslims.

From the Saudi point of view oil is not the only divine gift that they have been "chosen" to steward. As birthplace of the Islamic faith, the country is host to the two holiest shrines in the Islamic world - Mecca (the site of the Grand Mosque and holy Kabah) and Medina (the location of Muhammad's tomb). It was also well known to the Biblical writers. Places like Dedan, Tema and Sheba, were all located on the Arabian Peninsula. The land of Uz, the setting of the ancient Book of Job, may also have been in Arabia.

The Saudis have taken seriously the responsibility to use their oil money for the greater glory of Islam. The Muslim World League operates out of Mecca and strenuously lobbies for Muslim religious rights around the world, while at the same time denying all religious freedom in their country. They have also built the world's largest presses to print Korans and Islamic literature for world distribution, and have used petrodollars to build ostentatious mosques around the globe, while denying expatriate Christians in Arabia the right to gather for an informal Bible study. Despite their flagrant violations of human rights accords, the Saudi regime is coddled by the West because of their large oil reserves and strategic location in the Gulf, which serves to neutralize Iraq and Iran.

Basic Facts

Location:
Middle East

Neighboring Countries:
Kuwait, Iraq, Jordan, Egypt, Yemen, Oman, United Arab Emirates, Qatar, Bahrain

Population:
17,118,000

Capital City:
Riyadh (royal), Jiddah (administrative), Mecca (religious)

Major Cities:
Medina, Taif

Government:
Monarchy, with a Council of Ministers

Leader:
King Fahd Bin Abdul Aziz

Major Religions:
Islam

Historical Background

*O*riginally the Arabian peninsula was inhabited by nomadic tribes, with settlements found in the coastal areas. The three principle deities of this region were the Sun, Moon, and Venus, represented by a disk, a crescent, and a star respectively. These same symbols can still be found in various forms in modern Islam. Just as the crescent is the predominant symbol of Islam, so the moon was the dominant deity of its day.

Other features of the ancient religions also seem to have been preserved in Islam. The black stone embedded in the wall of the Kabah (a small stone building within the Grand Mosque) is similar to the sacred stones formerly worshipped by the nomadic peoples of this area. Arab scholars affirm that the pagan ceremonies of the great feast at Mecca have been preserved virtually unchanged in the rituals of the Hadj (pilgrimage to Mecca). Likewise the minarets of Islam, although much larger, are strikingly similar to the ashura posts found next to ancient altars. These posts were topped by the symbol of the deity they represented., just as mosques often have a crescent moon symbol over them

Unreached Peoples

*T*he Arab Muslims who compose the majority of the indigenous population are almost entirely unreached. They are kept isolated from the gospel by very strict laws forbidding the propagation of any religion except Islam. These laws are rigidly enforced by the religious police, the Mutawa. Violations can be punished by death for Saudi converts; one such believer was beheaded in 1992. Most are discreetly poisoned, which is the prescribed means of death for an apostate Muslim. Because of this situation, it is essential to capitalize on opportunities to reach Saudis while they are working or studying abroad.

The Bedouin tribes which still roam the vast desert areas just as their ancestors have for thousands of years, are equally unreached. While Islamic law and the Mutawa make Christian evangelism extremely difficult throughout the kingdom, it is the nomadic lifestyle of the Bedouins which keeps them particularly isolated. However, the police do not have sufficient manpower to bother with them, making evangelism a possibility for those who can contact these hospitable people. There are quite a few secret Saudi believers, who are usually converted through dreams or Christian radio, but they are unable to form a viable church because of the police. There are also large numbers of Asian workers in the kingdom who may be discreetly evangelized.

Spiritual Competition

Islam holds a vise-like grip on the entire kingdom, even tightly monitoring the activities of the millions of foreign workers. The responsibility for maintaining the purity of the faith and enforcing Islamic law falls to the Mutawa. These religious police function as an autonomous body, and do not report to the king or the government. Although the current monarchy represents a moderate, conservative force within the Islamic world, they have not dared to take a strong stand against the Mutawa for fear of a Muslim extremist backlash.

The ancient spiritual forces already alluded to are still potent. Five times a day millions of Muslims around the world bow down to Mecca, to pray, unwittingly renewing their allegiance to the old spiritual powers behind Islam. The roots of the militant face of Islam may still be visible in the star god (Venus), who was revered as the god of war. In this light the aggressive power and spread of Islam is not surprising, and it is interesting to note that the faith of Muhammad took over the Middle East by the power of the sword. Islamic nations continue to rattle their sabers throughout the world, and most have bad, if not brutal civil rights records.

Noteworthy Trends

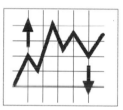

When Saudis speak of traveling abroad, they talk of "going outside"—the idea being that they are imprisoned in their own country and will be going to a freer environment. Among the well educated there is a desire for more freedom and social liberalization, and there has also been a marked increase of interest in the gospel among Saudis. Despite the very real threat of imprisonment and execution, there have been an unprecedented number of Christian converts.

When the Gulf War began, Western women were told to wear veils, and such things as painted toenails were no longer tolerated. Husbands whose wives were not veiled were sometimes beaten. Previously these and other "grievous" offenses had gone unchallenged among foreigners. The harassment has not only continued but has intensified.

Saudi Arabia's large extended royal family is corrupt and extremely materialistic, often passing the time by flying around the world investing in real estate and buying luxury items. However, this lifestyle could soon backfire on them, as other Muslims, both in Arabia and abroad see them as unholy and unworthy guardians of the sacred shrines. It may only be a matter of time before there is a serious attempt to overthrow them.

Obstacles to Ministry

Pray about these challenging circumstances:

• Muslim Evangelism Strictly Forbidden
Imprisonment or deportation are minimum penalties
• Harsh Penalties for Conversion
Saudi converts face certain prison and possible death
• Pervasive Religious Police Network
The Mutawa are militant guardians of orthodoxy
• Prevalence of Materialism
Many citizens are concerned only with the good life

Spiritual Power Points

Pray over these influential locations:

• Grand Mosque (Mecca)
Holy site contains Kabah shrine and well of Zamzam
• Islamic University (Riyadh)
1000-acre international Islamic training complex
• Medina Mosque (Medina)
Muhammad's burial site—major pilgrimage site
• Devil's Pillars at Mina
Sacrificial pilgrimage site where devil once appeared

Festivals and Pilgrimages

Pray during these spiritual events:

• Ramadan & Eid al-Fitr (Varies: '96 = Jan/Feb)
Month of fasting and prayer followed by two day feast
• The Hadj Pilgrimage (Varies: '96 = April)
Main Islamic pilgrimage—two million visitors annually to Mecca
• Mawlid an-Nabi (Varies: '96 = July)
Celebrations honoring Muhammad's birthday
• Pilgrimage to Muhammad's Grave (All Year)
Medina—second holiest site in Islamic world

Senegal

Senegal is a country saved by its rivers. If it were not for the Senegal and Gambia rivers, the land would suffer the same fate as neighboring Mauritania, a barren land which one writer has described as "a howling emptiness of sun-smitten desert." Existence in drought-plagued northwest Africa has never been easy. Dakar, the Senegalese capital fondly known as the "Paris of Africa," was an uninhabited wasteland until the French constructed a pipeline to bring in drinking water.

Senegal was first colonized by the Portuguese, and later was taken over by the Dutch, the English, and finally by France in 1880. Prior to the French colonization, the interior of Senegal was never exploited; instead, the colonial powers were attracted to the small island of Goree, off the coast of Dakar. Also known as the "island of sorrows," Goree served as a major shipment point for the transatlantic slave trade. The entire west coast of Africa suffered under the terrible legacy of slavery, a story that Alex Haley immortalized in his book Roots, which is set in the area of the Gambia river which flows through Senegal. The banks of the Gambia River actually form the nation of Gambia, a small finger-shaped state which divides Senegal in half.

After independence from France in 1960, the secular state of Senegal elected a Catholic president, who ruled for 20 years. While the nation is approximately 90% Muslim, religious tolerance prevails to a greater degree than in most Muslim-dominated nations.

Basic Facts

Location:
West Africa

Capital City:
Dakar

Leader:
President Abdou Diouf

Neighboring Countries:
Mauritania, Mali, Guinea, Guinea-Bissau, Gambia

Major Cities:
Thies, Kaolack, Saint-Louis

Major Religions:
Islam, African traditional religions

Population:
8,448,000

Government:
Republic

Historical Background

Huge stones set in a circle, reminiscent of an African Stonehenge, as well as pottery and other artifacts are all that remain of the ancient civilizations that have long vanished in the dusty history of Senegal. Early references indicate that religious life was dominated by priests or wizards who were believed to have great spiritual power. The role of the wizards or soothsayers later became integrated with that of the Muslim spiritual leaders known as marabouts, who are revered as magicians. Keeping a balance of spiritual forces is of paramount concern to the Senegalese, and the death of a king signaled a disturbance in the spirit realm, which required powerful occult rites to restore equilibrium.

The Almoravids, a radical Muslim people from the lower Senegal River valley, converted the Tukulor people of Mauritania to Islam in the 11th century. They were also instrumental in bringing about the demise of the empire of Ghana before conquering Morocco and invading Spain. In the 14th century, the vast empire of Mali controlled present day Senegal, but was unable to convert the entire population to Islam. Widespread Islamization took place only in the 19th century, partly as a form of passive resistance to French colonization.

Unreached Peoples

As the largest ethnic group in Senegal, the Wolof tend to dominate political and economic life, and their language is the trade language of the country. The Wolof hold most of the government positions and are the prominent businessmen and religious leaders of the community. They have an uncanny ability to assimilate the cultural traits of their neighbors, while at the same time maintaining a distinct culture of their own. Although almost totally Muslim, they are obsessed by a fear of the spirit realm, often covering their bodies with amulets, charms and talismans to ward off spells such as the evil eye. Despite a concerted effort by Christian missionaries, the Wolof remain strong Muslims. However, there are possibly 150 Christian believers among the Wolof.

The Tukulor were the first Senegalese to become Muslims and consider themselves to be the defenders of the faith, with many of them literate in Arabic. The Tukulor are mainly farmers, but worsening conditions caused by severe droughts are increasing their migration to towns. Recently there has been a promising Christian movement among these resistant people, and there are now approximately 15 believers among them.

Spiritual Competition

Muslim brotherhoods, which are influential throughout West Africa, dominate the fabric of Senegalese life, with 85% of the men belonging to one of these religious societies. They are organized around a hierarchy of charismatic leaders who are reputed to possess great spiritual power. Contrary to orthodox Islam, the brotherhoods teach that a person must become the disciple of a marabout to gain salvation. There may be over 100,000 marabouts in Senegal, and the ones with larger followings have considerable economic, spiritual, and political power, since the followers must support them either with their own labor or cash donations. Loyalty to one's marabout is therefore a cornerstone belief of the orders. Membership in brotherhoods embodies several important traditional Senegalese life forces: fear, magic and cooperative efforts.

There are no doctrinal differences between the brotherhoods in Senegal; the only distinguishing feature of each group is the personal devotion given to different spiritual leaders. Magic and fear of spirits continue to saturate the social fabric of the country. Animistic rites and initiations marked by trance and possession are still actively practiced in many areas.

Noteworthy Trends

Although the population is predominantly Muslim, the nation is marked by a tolerance for other religions. This tolerance can be credited in part to the Catholic schools, where many of Senegal's leaders were educated. While there are few Christians, their influence has been disproportionate, due in part to the prominence of their educational institutions. Unfortunately, most Christians are nominal, and their lives give a diminished witness to the true gospel.

The Casamance, which lies in the southern part of the country, has been destabilized since 1983 by the Jola secessionist guerrilla movement. Various peace initiatives have faltered, and the confrontation has become a stalemate. The fighting has caused dangerous conditions for missionaries working in the area.

Missionaries have labored for many years in Senegal, but without significant fruit or a major breakthrough. A veteran missionary observed that "There is a spiritual force which is binding Senegal. We, as missionaries, are not spending enough time in real concentrated prayer." However, significant opportunities exist for Christian witness in this Muslim country. Pray that God would send workers, as well as raise up a national church.

National Prayer Concerns

Obstacles to Ministry
Pray about these challenging circumstances:
• Rapid Growth of Islam
The religion has spread to over 90 percent of population
• Major Cultural Belief
To be Senegalese is to be Muslim
• Disheveled Economic System
Real per capita income has not risen since 1960
• Small Evangelical Population
Full-time Christian workers are even rarer

Spiritual Power Points
Pray over these influential locations:
• Tomb of Amadou Bamba (Touba)
Holy pilgrimage site and seat of Mouride Grand Caliph
• Tivaouane
Pilgrimage site and seat of the Tijani Islamic brotherhood
• Goree Island
Major slave transshipment center for 300 years
• Sacred Grove (Casamance Region)
Spiritual initiation grounds for the Diola people

Festivals and Pilgrimages
Pray during these spiritual events:
• Ramadan & Eid al-Fitr (Varies: '96 = Jan/Feb)
Month of fasting and prayer followed by two day feast
• Tabaski/Eid al-Kabir (Varies: '96 = April)
Islamic sacrificial feast; most important in West Africa
• Great Magal Pilgrimage (July/August)
Mouride Muslims journey to the Tomb of Amadou Bamba
• Bakut Ceremony (Every 15 to 30 Years)
2-month initiation rites for Diola males in SW Senegal

Somalia

Somalia has been described as a "living hell on earth." This country, now well-known to Westerners, is located on the Horn of Africa, and has been brought to its knees by the modern plagues of civil war, clan rivalries and famine. At independence, Somalia was hailed as a model for African stability. It was a country without ethnically differentiated tribes; people shared a common language and a common religion, Islam, as well as the same culture and history. However, instead of fulfilling its promise for unity and stability, Somalia has become synonymous with chaos, anarchy, starvation and despair. A young Somali observed that "You can find Somalia on a map, but the country is dead."

Somalia is a land with a long history. In ancient times the Egyptians knew Somalia as the Land of Punt, which was famous for its trade in frankincense and myrrh. The long and fairly narrow country is bordered by Kenya, Ethiopia and Djibouti, as well as the Gulf of Aden in the north and the Indian Ocean in the east. Because of its location, Somalia's real value lies in its position on the entrance to the Suez Canal, offering a convenient window on the troublesome Middle East.

The Somali people are fiercely independent and predominantly Muslim. Prior to the clan wars and the United Nations intervention, a majority of Somalis (60%) were nomadic or semi-nomadic. Most of the land is scrub desert, but the south central region of the country is the traditional agricultural area where the Giuba river provides sufficient water for cultivation. However, production is plagued by outmoded farming methods and civil strife.

Basic Facts

Location:
East Africa

Neighboring Countries:
Djibouti, Ethiopia, Kenya

Population:
8,505,000

Capital City:
Mogadishu

Major Cities:
Hargeysa, Kismayo, Marka, Berbera

Government:
In transition

Leader:
In transition

Major Religions:
Islam

Historical Background

Arab traders established outposts in Somalia about 900 AD and their descendants brought the religion of Islam with them. Islam became so entrenched that Somali tribes participated in a jihad or holy war against the Christian Kingdom of Ethiopia in the 16th century at the request of a Muslim coalition that was attempting to subdue the peoples of Sudan and Ethiopia. The Portuguese intervened and saved Ethiopia from being overrun by the Islamic onslaught, which forced Somalia into a southward expansion. Later the country's strategic trade and political location drew the attention of the colonial powers of Great Britain, France, and Italy. All three of the European powers emerged with protectorates in the region.

With independence from Britain and Italy, Somalia entered a period of relative peace. This peace was shattered when General Muhammad Siad Barre took over the country in 1969 and ruled it with an iron hand. By 1988 the country was experiencing a great deal of internal unrest. In 1991 Barre fled the nation, and the capital, Mogadishu, was rapidly being reduced to a heap of rubble by two opposing clan warlords. It was at this point that the world's attention was focused on Somalia, and the United Nations mounted its ill-fated peace-keeping initiative, aptly named "Operation Hope."

Unreached Peoples

Somalia is perhaps the most ethnically homogeneous country in Africa. The Somalis, who comprise 95% of the population, are thought by some scholars to be descendants of Noah's grandson Cush, and have only recently developed a written script. Illiteracy was substantially eradicated by the adoption of the standardized alphabet. As a result of their prior lack of a written language, the Somalis are a people with an oral tradition who utilize poetry and songs.

Somalis divide themselves into several tribes, each of which can trace its lineage back to a single patriarchal figure. The main tribes, are the Ishaak, the Hawiya, the West Somali (Dir), the Geri, the Ogadeni, the Sab, and the Mijurtein. The remaining 5% are African peoples who were not forced into Kenya or Ethiopia by Somalia's southward migration. Somalis owe strict allegiance to their clan and its leaders, causing tribal and clan divisions. These deep seated rivalries between the clans have been the downfall of the nation, causing splits in a homogeneous population who share the same language, culture and religion.

Spiritual Competition

Since their acceptance of Islam, the religion has become an integral part of the national culture, and is entrenched in Somali life to the extent that "to be Somali is to be Muslim." The Somalis have been characterized as liberal or "mellow" Muslims in terms of lifestyle, but fanatical when it comes to the issue of abandoning their religion and following another faith.

As mentioned, clan loyalty is a potent force in the Somali culture. The ongoing civil war is evidence that clan rivalry is one of the strongest spiritual forces in the country. It would seem that clan loyalty is even stronger than traditional Islamic ties.

Violent civil war and extreme poverty over the last few years have made evangelism difficult. Most mission organizations were forced to leave the country in 1974, and no missionary visas have been reissued. There are approximately ten thousand Somalis living in Toronto, Canada, as well as in other countries, and there are reports that the expatriate Somali church is growing in these countries. The gospel is also beamed into Somalia by radio, but follow-up work is impossible due to the present conditions.

Noteworthy Trends

Somalia was the first nation where military intervention by Western allies has been used to insure the safe delivery of relief supplies. Somalia had finally fallen apart. The result of years of arms sales and international manipulation by the Soviet Union and the U.S. was noted by a journalist who remarked, "Somalia is a place where guns are easier to find than a toothbrush."

The possible scenario of continuing civil war and famine in Somalia is frighteningly real. The UN peace-keeping effort has not managed to remedy the underlying causes of inter-clan warfare, and the country still has problems feeding itself. The paramount question remains - what does the future hold for Somalia? The answer to this question is not difficult: so long as the spirits of violence and clan hatred control the minds of the people, the future is not promising.

The witness of the gospel in Somalia is maintained by Christian development organizations who serve the refugees of this shattered land with hearts of compassion. It is also a unique opening, which could soon close. Let us pray that God continues to open doors to the people of Somalia, and that they might reflect on the root of their suffering and turn to be truly healed.

National Prayer Concerns

Obstacles to Ministry
Pray about these challenging circumstances:
- Violent Civil War

Cause of well-publicized terror and starvation
- Social Disorder

Many have turned to khat (a narcotic) chewing and crime
- Dominance of Islamic Faith

98 percent of population professes allegiance to Islam
- Small and Ill-Equipped Church

There are few believers and even fewer trained leaders

Spiritual Power Points
Pray over these influential locations:
- Tomb of Sheik Isxaaq Ibn Ahmed (Maydh)

Ancestor of the Isxaaq clan; prime pilgrimage site
- Mnara Tower (Brava)

Ancient minaret and pilgrimage site
- City of Baardheere

Historically famous center of Islamic teaching
- Tomb of Sheik Jabarti Ibn Ismail (Ceerigaabo)

Pilgrimage site associated with founder of Daarood clan

Festivals and Pilgrimages
Pray during these spiritual events:
- Ramadan & Eid al-Fitr (Varies: '96 = Jan/Feb)

Month of fasting and prayer followed by two day feast
- Pilgrimage to Tomb of Sheik Aweys (Varies according to lunar calendar)

At Biyooley in Bakool Region commemorating his death
- Pilgrimage to Tomb of Sheik Nuur (Varies according to lunar calendar)

Commemoration of his death near Jilib in Beledul Kariim
- Pilgrimage to Sheik Mumin Abdullahi's Tomb (Varies according to lunar calendar)

Grave of respected Muslim teacher

Sri Lanka

Sri Lanka, known as Ceylon under British colonial rule, is a teardrop shaped island located off the southern tip of India. Its palm-fringed beaches are washed by the clear warm waters of the Indian Ocean, giving it the deceptive air of a tropical paradise. In the interior, there are fertile farmlands, lush forests, and cool green mountains, where the world's best tea is grown. While Buddhism is the state religion, Hindus, Muslims and Christians have lived here for centuries.

Sri Lanka's lengthy and interesting history has recently turned rather tragic with the brutal and bloody conflict between the Tamil Hindu minority and the Sinhala Buddhists, who dominate the country. A large Tamil presence has been on the island for over 1,000 years, but during the British colonial period (1796-1948), large numbers of Tamil people were brought in from India to work on the plantations. Friction between the two groups was common, with violent outbursts erupting from time to time. In 1983 the tensions spilled over and the country was plunged into total anarchy, with terrorist bombings and indiscriminate massacres making world headlines for the last decade. Today the terrorist activity continues, such as the 1993 assassination of President Premadasa.

Sri Lanka is one of the few Buddhist nations left in the world. Colonial Christianity still has a strong cultural influence in the cities, but the outlying areas are heavily Buddhist. The government strives to be democratic, but the strong Buddhist lobby emanating from the ancient orders of monks is pushing the nation closer to Buddhist ideals and principles.

Basic Facts

Location:
South Asia

Neighboring Countries:
India, Maldive Islands

Population:
18,320,000

Capital City:
Colombo

Major Cities:
Jaffna, Galle, Kandy

Government:
Republic

Leader:
President Dingiri Banda Wijetunga

Major Religions:
Buddhism, Hinduism, Christianity, Islam

Historical Background

In the sixth century BC, Aryan invaders from India overcame the indigenous primitive peoples to establish the Sinhala culture. Buddhism was introduced in 247 BC and the Sinhala civilization flourished, as Buddhism spread rapidly. Four hundred years of colonial rule began in 1505. First to come were the Portuguese, who introduced Christianity, followed by the Dutch in 1658, and finally the British, who granted independence in 1948.

The tension between the Tamil and Sinhala peoples is deeply rooted in Buddhist mythology which asserts that the island not only belongs to the Buddha, but should only be inhabited and ruled by Buddhists, ostensibly by a decree of the Buddha himself. The story goes that on his first visit to Sri Lanka, the Buddha was given the island by ruling spirits called yakkhas, a band of elemental rogues whom he later drove out of the country.

One of the Buddha's teeth was preserved as a symbol of royal authority and is now enshrined in the ancient royal capital of Kandy. During the reign of Sirimeghavanna (301-328), the king was said to have ceremonially offered the entire kingdom to the tooth relic. The annual tooth relic festival is a reaffirmation of the sovereignty of the Buddha over the island.

Unreached Peoples

While Hindus, Muslims, and Buddhists are found almost entirely within separate people groups, Christianity cuts across ethnic lines. Most Christians are among the more prosperous, leaving the poor, particularly in the urban slums, with little witness.

The Muslims, who are sometimes called Moors, are partly descended from Arab seafarers. They live mainly in the northern coastal areas where they are generally traders, bureaucrats, and farmers. Until recently there were few Christian converts out of Islam, but the situation has improved recently, as specific outreach toward them is bearing fruit. There is a need for a specific ministry to the Muslim Malays, who although small in number, may be more responsive to the gospel than the Moors, as they practice a diluted form of Islam.

Sri Lanka is the world stronghold of Theravada Buddhism (the older variety which puts more emphasis on the historical Buddha and his teachings). The government is influenced by the Mahasangha, a powerful Buddhist lobby, whose policy is to keep Sri Lanka Buddhist. This situation results in a subtle erosion of Christian religious freedoms, particularly in the rural areas.

Spiritual Competition

For centuries Sri Lanka has been a powerful Buddhist missionary sending base, spreading its influence throughout Southeast Asia. With its many temples and shrines, some of which rival the great pyramids of Egypt in height, Buddhism still holds a powerful influence over most of the Sinhala people, who compose 70% of the population. Even today Buddhist missionaries are still carrying their message beyond the shores of this nation. The United States in particular has been targeted by Buddhists, and substantial gains have been recorded by them in the last decade. According to the Gallup Poll, approximately 30% of Americans now believe in reincarnation.

Somewhat tragically, the Church itself has often been its own stiffest competition. Sri Lanka is the only non-Muslim Asian country where the Christian church has steadily declined in numbers and influence during this century. This is attributed to several factors: nominalism, lack of desire to evangelize non-Christian religions, and emigration of many Christians to Australia, Canada, and England. The church in Sri Lanka became fat and spoiled under colonial rule, living a privileged life reflective of its support by the ruling classes. Financed by the colonial government from the outset, the church commenced and was maintained as a Western institution, while national culture and language were ignored. No new missionary visas are being issued; like many Asian nations, Sri Lanka is engaged in a general phase-out of foreign missions.

Noteworthy Trends

Although the older churches are largely stagnant and declining in numbers, the newer Pentecostal and evangelical churches are experiencing rapid growth. They have a strong emphasis on evangelism and now have many more members than the traditional churches. In addition, a number of missions and parachurch organizations are effectively engaged in ministry.

The massive civil unrest that began in 1983 and continues with acts of terrorism has caused many Sri Lankans to reassess their spiritual values. A greater degree of openness to the gospel has come in the midst of the uncertainty and great suffering, even among the usually resistant Muslims.

In 500 AD King Kasayapa built a fortress called Sigiriya atop the 300 foot vertical cliffs of a lofty mesa. The citadel was constructed as a hideaway from his vengeful half-brother, because King Kasayapa had buried their father alive. The ruins of the fortress are a mute reminder that the blood of the father cries out from the ground for justice, just like the blood of many innocent victims of the current brutal civil war. Pray that the spirits of violence, hatred, and revenge may be countered by the clear and penetrating gospel of the only Prince of Peace.

National Prayer Concerns

Obstacles to Ministry
Pray about these challenging circumstances:
• Buddhist State Religion
Supporting a 70 percent Buddhist population base
• Tamil Conflict
War with Hindu Tamil separatists has destabilized nation
• Weak National Church
Nominalism, lack of evangelism and declining numbers
• Leadership Vacuum in Church
There is an acute need for full-time pastors and lay leaders

Spiritual Power Points
Pray over these influential locations:
• Adam's Peak
Major Hindu, Buddhist and Islamic pilgrimage site
• Kelaniya (Colombo)
Important Buddhist temple near the capital
• Anuradhapura
Ancient center of Buddhism; includes sacred Bo tree
• Temple of the Tooth (Kandy)
Sacred tooth relic of the Buddha is preserved here

Festivals and Pilgrimages
Pray during these spiritual events:
• Sinhala & Tamil New Year (April)
Includes anointing with oil at key astrological times
• Wesak (May)
Celebrates birth, enlightenment & death of Buddha
• Esala Perahera (July or August)
Big event in Kandy honors sacred relic of the Buddha
• Pilgrimage to Saman's/Adam's Peak (December to April)
Annual pilgrimage for Hindus, Buddhists and Muslims

Sudan

The Sudan is a schizophrenic nation with two peoples and two identities. It is also a land of famine that is caught up in a brutal civil war. Ignored by the West and forgotten by the Church, the Christians in the south feel "Like a voice crying in the wilderness." The courage and strength of the Sudanese Christians has been forged with great suffering: "Though we are hungry, thirsty and dying of disease, we will take up our cross to show the world that we are Christians," declared a Sudanese pastor.

Sudan stretches more than 1200 miles from north to south and is the largest nation in Africa. The Nile river provides a band of life in the hostile northern deserts while a vast swamp called the Sudd dominates the center of the country. The land of the tropical south has great potential to produce sufficient food, but the war makes normal farming very difficult, perpetuating the famine conditions.

In biblical times Sudan was known as the land of Cush. At this ancient crossroads Egyptians, Nubians and Arabs, animists, Christians and Muslims have all been fused into a divergent nation. In some rare cases these disparate elements have blended together in peaceful coexistence, but this has been the exception. Northern Sudan is mostly populated by Muslim Arabs, who dominate the political and military structures of the nation. The south is inhabited by black Africans, who are a mixture of tribal animists and Christians. The natural divides between religion and climate are magnified by the ten year-old civil war, which has cost one million lives in the south alone.

Basic Facts

Location:
East Africa

Neighboring Countries:
Egypt, Libya, Chad, Zaire, Uganda, Kenya, Ethiopia

Population:
29,116,000

Capital City:
Khartoum

Major Cities:
Omdurman, North Khartoum, Port Sudan

Government:
Military

Leader:
Prime Minister General Umar Hazzan Ahmad al-Bashir

Major Religions:
Islam, animism, Christianity

Historical Background

The banks of the Nile river in Sudan supported a thriving ancient civilization from the 11th to 4th centuries BC. This culture was largely Egyptian in character, with the central religious deities imported from Egypt. Christian missionaries first reached Sudan in the sixth century AD, and were successful in converting native kingdoms they found there. The Christian influence did not last however, and Sudan was slowly converted to Islam by teachers and traders who followed the Nile River south.

Egypt conquered Sudan in 1821, followed by the British, and their joint rule was a consolidating factor for the land. The British occupation of the Sudan inspired a massive revolt led by a Muslim cleric, whose forces beheaded General Gordon and routed the British forces in Khartoum, but were later crushed by Lord Kitchener's combined Anglo-Egyptian army. Since independence in 1956 the country has been rocked by two civil wars, coups, and countercoups, as well as a succession of leaders who have taken increasingly stronger Islamic positions. In 1989, the government effectively adopted Sharia (Quranic) law as the system of government for the nation, further accelerating the war between the Muslim north and the Christian/animist south.

Unreached Peoples

According to the government, Sudanese Arabs form a 51% majority in the country, living mainly in the north and central areas. Mysticism has played a large role in the spiritual life of the Sudanese Muslims, with Sufi brotherhoods well established among the predominantly Sunni Muslim community. There are very few Christian converts among the Sudanese Arabs, and the extremely militant National Islamic Front (NIS) makes evangelism very difficult among them.

Quite a different picture emerges in the south. As mentioned, the southern Sudanese are black Africans, composed of a blend of Christians and animists. The Dinka and the Nuer are among the largest southern tribes, while the Nuba also comprise a substantial tribe further to the north. Opportunities to reach the animists of the south are made difficult by the war and the government's forceful Islamization policy. Animists are already under great economic and social pressures to convert to Islam. There are documented cases where the government has refused relief and food aid to Christians or animists, then provide the aid if they become Muslim. The people of the south are at severe physical risk from the war and famine, but despite tremendous hostility and hardship, the church there has been experiencing great growth.

Spiritual Competition

Sudan's brand of Islam is styled after the leader of the National Islamic Front, Hassan Turabi. The NIS virtually controls the country, enforcing Sharia law and controlling the state through a network of fundamentalist supporters. Turabi was the author of Sudan's Islamic law code and is a powerful ideologue who has painstakingly built his support base over a period of many years. His supporters include sympathetic Sudanese businessmen who provide the NIS with needed financial backing.

Turabi is western-educated and seeks to place a moderate face on the aims of his movement. However, in statements to his supporters he is more forthcoming, saying that "Democracy is a form of factionalism . . . that is antithetical to the Muslim's ultimate responsibility to God." Since coming to power, Turabi has forged strong links with Iran, opening his country to the Iranian revolutionary guards, who have established ideological and military training centers. These centers, which are intent on exporting the Sudanese version of Islamic jihad have targeted Ethiopia, Kenya, Djibouti, and Somalia. There is great persecution of the Sudanese church by the Arab military - Christian villages are sometimes plundered, the men killed, and the women and children taken as slaves.

Noteworthy Trends

Sudan was never a wealthy country, but civil war and the Muslim government's genocidal activities against the south have combined to increase the level of suffering to a degree that may be irreversible. Nearly two million refugees now crowd into cardboard huts surrounding the capital of Khartoum. Combined with the existing refugee burden, infighting among the opposition in the south has caused famine to afflict almost one million people in 1994. The Muslim regime denies that a hunger problem exists, preventing the delivery of Western aid and assistance to the imperiled south.

Turabi is working hard to solidify his grip on power. All university students have to take a two month course prior to university entrance where they are trained in military tactics and in Turabi's radical Islamic ideology. Fear of the secret police and the informant network is widespread and effectively keeps a lid on dissent. The tide appears to be turning against the Christian resistance in the south. If the civil war ends with a Muslim victory, the north will finally have the opportunity to force their brutal policies on the Christians and animists of the south. Pray to God that his sovereign hand would block the forces of Islam from destroying the courageous and battered church of southern Sudan.

National Prayer Concerns

Obstacles to Ministry
Pray about these challenging circumstances:
- Brutal Fundamentalist Muslim Regime

Thousands have been evicted, tortured and starved
- Muslim Evangelism Strictly Forbidden

Outreach can lead to death—especially in the north
- Animist Influence

Especially in south and in Nuba mountain region
- Lack of Resources

Many Christians have lost everything in recent years

Spiritual Power Points
Pray over these influential locations:
- Hamed al Niel Mosque (Omdurman)

Islamic pilgrimage site
- Temple of Amun (Jebel Barkal)

Sacred ancient temple and religious center
- Nuba Mountains

Sacred home of the Nuba; site of Christian persecution
- Village of Kafia Kingi

Center of the Fakirs, diviners who use spells and potions

Festivals and Pilgrimages
Pray during these spiritual events:
- Ramadan & Eid al-Fitr (Varies: '96 = Jan/Feb)

Month of fasting and prayer followed by two day feast
- Eid al-Adha (Varies: '96 = April)

Feast of Sacrifice; coincides with culmination of Hadj
- Mawlid an-Nabi (Varies: '96 = July)

Celebrations honoring Muhammad's birthday
- Pilgrimage to Mahdi's Tomb (All Year)

Obligation of all Sudanese Muslims

Syria

Situated between the Mediterranean and the Euphrates, the land of Syria has been in the thick of Middle Eastern intrigue—and conflicts—for over four thousand years. As a remnant of the great Assyrian Empire, the modern Syrian Arab Republic is still consumed with nostalgia for "Greater Syria"—a living psychological reality that has led to frequent clashes with its neighbors.

Syria's antiquity is plainly visible. Besides the ruins of Crusader castles, Roman aqueducts and ancient Canaanite cities, the Syrian capital of Damascus has been inhabited continuously since 2000 BC.—a fact, as its citizens proudly point out, that makes it the oldest capital city in the world. To this day, it is possible to walk down the Street Called Straight where Saul of Tarsus received his sight and a call to missions.

It is a mistake, however, to assume that Damascus is nothing more than an urban antique. It remains a throbbing Islamic citadel; a sacred place that hosts the Umayyad Mosque and annually serves as a final staging area for Hadj pilgrims heading toward Mecca.

Physically, Syria's landscape turns rugged after one heads inland from the country's northern Mediterranean beaches. In addition to encountering the Anti-Lebanon Mountains which form the de jure boundary with Lebanon, the country's eastern reaches (with the exception of the Euphrates River basin) are dominated by inhospitable desert. The volcanic southern plateau which culminates in the famed Golan Heights (presently under Israeli control) is home to the mysterious Druze community.

Basic Facts

Location:
Middle East

Capital City:
Damascus

Leader:
President Hafez al-Assad

Neighboring Countries:
Lebanon, Israel, Turkey, Jordan, Iraq, Cyprus

Major Cities:
Hamah, Homs, Latakia, Aleppo

Major Religions:
Islam, Christianity

Population:
14,904,000

Government:
Republic

Historical Background

Centuries ago, Syrian culture and language (Aramaic) represented the dominant force in the Near East; and well before the advent of Islam, the nation's spiritual legacy was already dark. Besides worshipping the moon goddess, Sin, Syria's early inhabitants also set up altars to Baal on the same mountains that the Romans used to offer sacrifices to Jupiter.

While the region was heavily Christianized in the early centuries AD, the Syrians' unorthodox view of Christ created grave tensions between the resident community and Church leaders in Constantinople. So serious was this breach that when invading Islamic armies moved into the region in the 7th century, many Christians greeted them as liberators.

In 637 AD, Islamic forces achieved a decisive military breakthrough against the Byzantines at the battle of the Yarmuk River. Following this victory, Syria became the seat of the first Islamic dynasty. During their reign, the Umayyads of Damascus directed an Islamic expansion that stretched from France all the way to China. One especially busy caliph, Abd al-Malik, not only built the famed Dome of the Rock on the site of Solomon's Temple in Jerusalem, but managed to impose Arabic as the official language of the entire Middle East.

Unreached Peoples

Syria's largest unreached ethno-religious people—by far—are the Sunni Muslim Arabs. Representing approximately three quarters of the country's dominant Islamic population, most Sunni have yet to receive a clear presentation of the gospel. The minority Alawites, an unorthodox offshoot of Shiite Islam, comprise another 12% of the total population. Traditionally the Alawites have resided in the northwestern parts of Syria where, until recent times, they remained as part of the national underclass. By patiently and shrewdly building upon their tight-knit tribal network, however, the Alawites (which include among their ranks President Hafez al-Assad) have slowly taken control of important sectors of the armed forces and the government.

The Druze, a secretive and unreached sect living primarily on the southern plateau known as Jabal ad Duruz (Mountain of the Druzes), adhere to a curious doctrinal admixture of monotheism and reincarnation. They are joined in spiritual need by the Cherkess who are related to a Muslim people found in the Transcaucasia region, the Kurds who live in the country's northwest corner, and the Bedouin who have roamed Syria's deserts for thousands of years. The latter, though nearly one million strong, have no known Christians among them.

Spiritual
Competition

$\mathcal{J}$n addition to the challenges one would expect from Islam in a venerable Middle Eastern nation, Syria also harbors many hindering spirits from her pagan past. Besides the Druze belief in cosmic emanations and the transmigration of the soul, many Bedouin cling to strong animistic superstitions. The 25,000 member Yezhidi community honors Satan outright.

Syria's ruling Baath party represents something of a two-edged sword. On the one hand, Baathism is a fiercely nationalistic philosophy which elevates Arab identity to the level of religious devotion – and Baathists in Syria, as in neighboring Iraq, have proven to be ruthless in their suppression of rivals. On the other hand, the ruling Baathists have made Syria the only Middle Eastern nation with a Muslim majority that does not enshrine Islam as the state religion. This fact, combined with the government's general suppression of Islamic activists, has meant comparative freedom for Syrian Christians.

The key word here is comparative however. For the same security forces that keep Islamic fundamentalists in check also keep close tabs on the Church. Over the years this has had a chilling effect on nearly all community evangelism.

Noteworthy
Trends

$\mathcal{T}$wo recent events—the collapse of the Soviet Union and the Gulf War—have had a profound impact on Syria's traditional anti-Western posture. While the former deprived the country of significant foreign aid and political support, the latter restored Syrian stature in the Middle East and highlighted the rewards of participatory politics. The hope is that improved relations with the West will make it easier for Christian personnel to access the country.

Another important development affecting Syria is the recent joint recognition and limited autonomy agreement between Israel and the PLO. Syria still harbors some of the most radical Palestinian elements—like Ahmed Jibril of the PFLP—that have announced intentions to violently disrupt any future peace accords. It remains to be seen how far the Syrian government will allow these factions to go, and whether their actions will return Syria to the list of outlaw nations.

Also bearing closer scrutiny is the reported poor health of political strongman Hafez al-Assad. If the Syrian President should die or become otherwise incapacitated, there is great potential for radical change—including the emergence of an Islamic fundamentalist movement.

Obstacles to Ministry
Pray about these challenging circumstances:
• Growth of Muslim Fundamentalist Movement
Undercurrent may become a force when ailing president Assad is gone
• Large Druze Population
The secretive Druze community is extremely difficult to penetrate
• Christian Emigration
A significant number of Syrian believers have left the country
• Lack of Full-Time Christian Workers
National evangelists and teachers are in short supply

Spiritual Power Points
Pray over these influential locations:
• Umayyad Mosque (Damascus)
Ancient dynastic-era mosque; one of Islam's holiest shrines
• Qanawat (Southern Syria)
Druze stronghold on Jabal ad Duruz (Mountain of the Druzes) near Jordan
• Tomb of Sayyidah Zaynab (Damascus)
Important Islamic pilgrimage site
• Jabal Aqra (Baal Zaphon)
Canaanite and Roman Sacrifice site; the dwelling of Baal

Festivals and Pilgrimages
Pray during these spiritual events:
• Ramadan & Eid al-Fitr (Varies: '96 = Jan/Feb)
Month of fasting and prayer followed by two day feast
• Eid al-Adha (Varies: '96 = April)
Feast of Sacrifice; coincides with culmination of Hadj
• The Hadj (Varies: '96 = April)
Damascus is a major staging area for Islam's all-important pilgrimage to Mecca
• Pilgrimage to Tomb of Sayyidah Zaynab (All Year)
Damascus burial site of revered Islamic saint

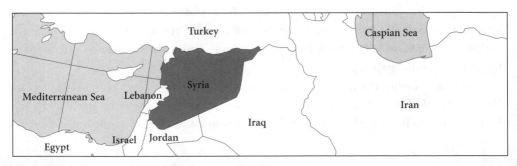

Tajikistan

$\mathcal{O}$f all the republics of the former Soviet Union, Tajikistan is the most destitute and needy. Trapped in a downward spiral by civil war and economic woes, it is also cut off from the world because of its location and topography.

Situated high in the Pamir and Tian Shan mountains along the Afghanistan border, the land of Tajikistan has often been called "the roof of the world." Just as in other Central Asian nations, the idea of an independent Tajik state is a new one, slowly evolving out of the divisive ethnic policies of the Soviet Union. Its borders were arbitrarily and artificially set by Stalin's erratic and irrational resettlement programs in 1929. Sixty-five years later, the Tajiks are still gradually developing an independent identity based on racial and linguistic ties to nearby Persian relatives, found today in Iran and Afghanistan. However, the heart of Tajik culture and history is found in the great historical cities of Samarkand and Bukhara, which are unfortunately now located next door in the republic of Uzbekistan.

Forced into the mountains over many centuries of conflict, the peoples of Tajikistan are known for their skilled use of the sparse terrain they inhabit. They have been practitioners of terraced farming and irrigation for centuries. Even the ruinous Soviet policy of forcing the Tajik population into cotton growing communes has not managed to break their ties to mountain village life. Still, many political forces are moving to exploit this often wounded people, as the Tajiks struggle for a new national identity in the wake of Communism's collapse.

Basic Facts

Location:
  Central Asia

Neighboring Countries:
  Uzbekistan, Kyrgyzstan, China, Afghanistan

Population:
  6,311,000

Capital City:
  Dushanbe

Major Cities:
  Khudzand, Kurgan-Tyube, Kulyab

Government:
  Republic

Leader:
  President Imomali Rakhmonov

Major Religions:
  Islam, shamanism

Historical Background

Like all nations located along the great Silk Route, Tajikistan has been the site of numerous conquests and has witnessed large scale upheavals of culture and religion. The Tajiks are the oldest surviving ethnic group in Central Asia, and their earliest ancestors were Indo-Iranians, the forebears of the modern peoples of Iran and India. The ancient residents of Tajikistan were most likely adherents of the Vedic religion that gave birth to Hinduism.

The Tajiks enter written history upon the arrival of the Persian Empire's armies in the Oxus river region in the 6th century BC. With the occupation of the area by the Persians, Zoroastrianism became the dominant religion and remained so until the Arab conquests of the 7th century.

The identifying characteristics of the modern Tajiks only began to emerge during the rule of the Samanids, an Islamic Persian dynasty that revived many Zoroastrian cultural elements in the 9th century. The empire was short-lived, and was overwhelmed by various Turkish and Mongol forces, but the distinctly Persian flavor of the original Indo-Iranian peoples of Central Asia was preserved in the Tajik people.

Unreached Peoples

Uzbeks form a large minority group, about 25 percent of Tajikistan's population. The Uzbeks are a Turkish-speaking people of mixed ethnic origins, and are one of the largest Muslim nations in the former USSR. Resentment over what many Persian-speaking Tajikistanis saw as the favored status of the Uzbeks under Soviet rule has resulted in persecution of the Uzbeks following Tajikistan's independence.

The majority people of the country are Tajiks, for whom the nation is named, and constitute the oldest ethnic elements in Central Asia. Until the formation of the Soviet Union earlier in this century the distinction between the Uzbeks and Tajiks was not clear. When forced to identify themselves as one or the other by the new Soviet system, it was not uncommon for family members to profess different ethnic affiliations. In the end some people in the same family had become Uzbeks, and others Tajiks. This was due to the bilingual and cosmopolitan culture that had characterized the area for centuries. The extreme isolation of these peoples living in the wild vastness of the rugged mountains, as well as their fiercely clannish loyalties have been an effective deterrent to Christian evangelists.

Spiritual Competition

The Tajiks were early converts to Islam, and although they are mostly orthodox in creed, many pre-Islamic practices are carried on at the popular level. This is visible today in the continued veneration of Indo-Iranian gods. These pre-Islamic deities are direct connections to the earliest forms of spiritual deception in Central Asia. The identities of gods such as Garm and Sebzoush were preserved throughout the Islamic period, concealed as memorials to Muslim saints. Shamanistic practices have also been retained in Tajikistan. Healers and soothsayers are sought to deal with day-to-day supernatural needs. There is unquestionably a very raw form of spiritism still present in the country, especially in the mountain areas.

Tajikistan is a prime target for Islamic fundamentalist elements. Both the influences of their Iranian cousins and the excitement created by the Islamic Mujahidin victory in Afghanistan are having a powerful influence on the Tajiks' religious views. Saudi Arabia has also put considerable resources into fostering an Islamic revival here. The number of mosques in the country has increased from 18 to over 2,000 between 1990 and 1993.

Noteworthy Trends

Of all the newly created Central Asian countries, Tajikistan has had the most difficulty in making a peaceful transition to self rule. Ethnic violence, Muslim fundamentalist activity and clan warfare have been the rule rather than the exception since September 1991. Several changes in government have occurred since then, and the situation continues to be unstable.

As citizens of the poorest of the new republics, Tajiks suffer deeply at every level, with even their traditional livelihood decimated by Soviet central planners. They are desperate to form relationships with potential foreign helpers, and this could be a great opening for the gospel. At the same time, Iranian economic incentives have led the Tajiks to adopt the Iranian alphabet in contrast to the other Central Asian republics, who are moving toward the Roman script of Turkey. This step will affect Tajikistan's relations with other nations in the area, but it is unlikely that Iran can achieve its ultimate goal of reproducing itself in an Tajik Islamic Republic. There is a network of Christian mission agencies that are attempting to reach the nation, and the Bible was printed in Tajik for the first time in 1992.

National Prayer Concerns

Obstacles to Ministry
Pray about these challenging circumstances:
• Major Civil Unrest

Fighting has caused severe social and economic chaos

• Growing Islamic Extremism

Iranian-influenced groups are calling for Sharia law

• Animist Influence

Stronger than many realized – especially in mountains

• Small and Ill-Equipped Church

Few believers and serious shortage of Christian literature

Spiritual Power Points
Pray over these influential locations:
• Tomb of Yaqub Charkhi (Dushanbe)

Disciple of famous Naqshbandi master, Khoja Ahrar

• Adzhina Khan Mosque and Training Center (Ura-Tyube)

Huge center of Islamic learning and outreach

• Khadzha Mashad Mausoleum (Saiat)

Sacred burial place and pilgrimage site

•Kanibadam Madrasah

Renovated Islamic center

Festivals and Pilgrimages
Pray during these spiritual events:
• Ramadan & Eid al-Fitr (Varies: '96 = Jan/Feb)

Month of fasting and prayer followed by two day feast

•Mawlid an-Nabi (Varies: '96 = July)

Celebrations honoring Muhammad's birthday

• Pilgrimage to Shaartuzski (All Year)

Site of Khodja Durbab & Khoda Mashad Mausoleums

• Pilgrimage to Kalia Kakhkakha (All Year)

Ancient site of the "Temple of Idols"

Thailand

Thailand, which literally means "Land of the Free," is one of the most cohesive and integrated societies in Southeast Asia. This is primarily because it has never been ruled by a Western power and was therefore not subject to arbitrary divisions based on colonial expediency rather than ethnic affinity. The country is shaped like the ear of an elephant, which is appropriate for a land where elephants are commonly used as beasts of burden and the white elephant is revered as sacred. "The land of the smile" is predominantly Buddhist, with 95% of the population adhering to this ancient faith.

About 75% of the people are Thai, who are ethnically related to the Lao as well as to the Shan of Myanmar. The Thai are a settled agricultural people with 87% of the population living and dying in the province in which they were born. Thailand is mostly rural, with 80% of the population living in villages, usually located near rivers or canals, which are still an important means of transportation. However, most farms are quite small and only provide a meager living for farmers.

Bangkok is the major metropolitan area, as well as the political, commercial, educational and religious center of the nation. Urban migration to Bangkok and provincial capitals has increased significantly during the past decade. The city is a bustling, crowded, megalopolis of impressive buildings, massive traffic jams and the usual urban social ills. Bangkok is the prostitution center of Asia, if not the world, a sad fact which gives an otherwise noble nation a moral black eye. About two million Thais derive their income from the tawdry "sex industry."

Basic Facts

Location:
Southeast Asia

Neighboring Countries:
Myanmar (Burma), Laos, Cambodia, Malaysia

Population:
59,605,000

Capital City:
Bangkok

Major Cities:
Chiang Mai, Hat Yai, Khon Kaen

Government:
Constitutional monarchy

Leader:
Prime Minister Chuan Leekpai, King Bhumibol Adulyadej

Major Religions:
Buddhism

Historical Background

Hinduism was the first major religion to prevail in early Thailand during the time when the kingdom of Funan dominated much of Indochina. Its influence can still be seen today, as evidenced by the national emblem, the Garuda, which is a winged creature used as a mount by the Hindu god Vishnu. When the first Thai people began arriving from southern China late in the 11th century, the original people of the land were under the control of the Cambodian Khmers. These Thais also came under Khmer rule until 1253 when hundreds of thousands of Thais began to flee China because the Mongols invaded their land. Aided by the massive influx of refugees, the Thais were able to rid themselves of the Khmer and establish the first Thai kingdom in 1257. The Thais began to adopt many Khmer ways, including their religion, Buddhism.

In 1782 the Chakri dynasty was founded with Bangkok as its capital. A military coup ended the absolute monarchy in 1932, which began a continuous series of military coups and new constitutions. The current king is part of the Chakri dynasty, and although he holds no political office, the respect and reverence he commands make him the single most important influence for political and social stability.

Unreached Peoples

The Thai are a Mongoloid people who are almost uniformly Buddhist. Although Christianity was introduced into Thailand as early as 1511 when the first Catholics arrived, it has seen a modest number of converts, and only about 1% of the population claim to be Christian, either Protestant or Catholic. Christian missions have had freedom to proclaim the gospel among the Thais, but in spite of several hundred years of witness, the Thais have remained largely apathetic. Almost every Thai home has its own altar or spirit house where offerings are placed. As in most of Southeast Asia, popular Buddhism here is heavily laced with appeasement and accommodation of spirits.

The Chinese are the largest non-Thai ethnic group and constitute about 15% of the population. They make up more than a third of the population of Bangkok, and dominate the nation's economy, controlling about 85% of finance and industry. The Chinese are subdivided into different groups according to their dialect and their province of origin in China. They have become well integrated into Thai society due to the pressures of Thai nationalism.

Spiritual Competition

$\mathcal{T}$hai Buddhism is a mixture of pre-Buddhist Hindu beliefs and practices, interwoven with spirit worship and orthodox Buddhist philosophy and rituals. These beliefs and practices have changed little over the centuries and overlap into social and economic life. Buddhism is the state religion, and the constitution requires that the king be a practicing Buddhist. The king in turn appoints the patriarch who presides over the supreme council of Buddhist monks.

Religion is probably the most visible force in national life. Temples, known as wats, dot the landscape as frequently as Buddhist festivals do the calendar. The government is the legal owner of all wat lands, administers religious education, and operates a large Buddhist publishing house. The king himself maintains 115 royal wats as well as two Buddhist colleges.

The Emerald Buddha is housed in a special temple on the grounds of the Grand Palace in Bangkok. It is revered as the guardian of the Chakri dynasty as well as the kingdom over which it rules. For centuries it has been the symbol of the divine right to rule in various kingdoms of Indochina and is one of the most sacred of all images in the area.

Noteworthy Trends

$\mathcal{W}$hile the "normal" transition in government has generally taken place in the form of military coups since the 1930s, the present military leadership appears less interested in politics. Whether this is actually true remains to be seen. The image of the military was severely tarnished by the violent and bloody suppression of pro-democracy demonstrations in 1992, and they are working to renew public trust. If the military does distance itself from politics, political influence will probably shift away from the strongholds of the Chakri dynasty (with its official and ceremonial ties with Buddhism) to a more secular electorate. What this shift could mean for the church and national outreach is not clear.

The slow growth of the church in Thailand is a real concern for prayer. Only about half of the believers are ethnic Thai, and the rest are Chinese or tribal minorities. Syncretism, lack of real spiritual concern, lax church discipline, immorality of Christian leadership, and misuse of church funds have plagued churches. However, Biblical foundations have been laid and there is great potential. Many Thai believers spend one day each month fasting and praying for their country.

National Prayer Concerns

Obstacles to Ministry
Pray about these challenging circumstances:
• Buddhist World View
Christianity is perceived to be a foreign import
• Limitations on Missionary Visas
Quota system keeps foreign influence in check
• Widespread Moral Decadence
Sexual immorality is especially rampant in Bangkok and Pattaya
• Lack of Mature, Visionary Leadership
Recent church scandals have hurt cause

Spiritual Power Points
Pray over these influential locations:
• Wat Phra Keo (Bangkok)
House of the revered Emerald Buddha
• Wat Phra Budohabhat (Sarapburi)
Temple complex enshrining Buddha's footprint
• Phra Pathom Chedi (Nakom Pathom)
Complex where Thailand's Buddhism was established
• Village of Ban Kon Yang
Karen animist center

Festivals and Pilgrimages
Pray during these spiritual events:
• Songkran Festival (April)
Water festival with idol worship and purification rites
• Vaisakha Bucha (May)
Celebrates birth, enlightenment & death of Buddha
• Vassa & Kathina (October/November)
Monastic retreat season followed by meritorious giving
• Loy Krathong (November)
Festival of Light; thanksgiving to goddess of rivers

Tibet

Yaks and yetis, wizards and lamas all share in the mystique of Tibet. Part fact, but mostly fiction, this mysterious and enchanting "Shangri La" has been an adventurer's destination for centuries. Situated on the highest mountain plateau in the world, with an average elevation of over 13,000 feet, Tibet is often called "The Rooftop of the World", and "The Land of Snows".

The enigma of Tibet has been amplified by its geographic and political isolation. In 1979, when China first opened Tibet to foreign tourists, only about 1,200 Westerners had ever seen Lhasa, including about 600 members of the Younghusband expedition who had fought their way into the capital in 1903-4. Many thousands of tourists have now shared in this rare opportunity, usually by flying into Lhasa, a relative lowland at "only" 12,000 feet above sea level.

Lhasa is the spiritual center of Tibet, housing the imposing Potala, the highest palace on earth. Formerly the winter home of the Dalai Lama, the god-king of Tibetans, the 1,000 room Potala dominates the entire valley, rising 700 feet above the city. However, the most sacred of all temples for the Tibetans is the Jokhang, a relatively small and unobtrusive building in the center of Lhasa. It has none of the architectural wonder of the Potala, yet it is circled incessantly by pilgrims seeking merit.

Not surprisingly, Christianity has never fared well in this remote Buddhist land. In 1716 an Italian Jesuit, Ippolito Desideri, was able to establish residence in Lhasa. Rome forced Desideri to leave in 1721 and replaced him with the Capuchins, who were expelled in 1745. There had been only seven conversions by 1733, and nothing is known of the fate of these early believers.

Basic Facts

Location:
South Central Asia

Neighboring Countries:
China, Nepal, Bhutan, India, Myanmar (Burma)

Population:
2,200,000

Capital City:
Lhasa

Major Cities:
Xigaze, Qamdo, Gyantze

Government:
Communist (governed by China)

Leader:
In Transition

Major Religions:
Tibetan (lamaistic) Buddhism

Historical Background

Prior to the advent of Buddhism, a religion called Bon, as well as other forms of shamanism existed. Since the Bon gods were exceedingly wicked and cruel, they had to be constantly appeased through various offerings and sacrifices. The casting of spells and other forms of sorcery were common practices of the Bon religion. Buddhism entered Tibet through King Songsten Gampo (627-649) when he married Buddhist wives from Nepal and China. Buddhism absorbed many of the practices and beliefs of Bon, with the monks (lamas) filling the role of the shaman. As a result, Tibetan Buddhism incorporates a high degree of witchcraft and magic and is a very potent and insidious snare to its followers.

In 1578 the Mongol ruler Altan Khan conferred the title of Dalai Lama (Ocean of Wisdom) on Sonam Gyatso, thus beginning the tradition of spiritual leadership in Tibet which later also included temporal leadership. In 1720 the Chinese invaded Tibet and were able to exercise varying degrees of control until the mid-1800s. The Chinese Communists entered Tibet in 1950, and in 1959 the 14th Dalai Lama fled to India, where he remains today with his government-in-exile.

Unreached Peoples

All people groups in Tibet are considered unreached with no more than a handful of believers inside its borders. The Tibetan people are composed of a multitude of tribal groupings scattered throughout the mountainous region in tiny villages and settlements. Many still wander as nomads, tending their herds of yak and sheep.

The New Testament is available in Tibetan but must be smuggled into Tibet. Even when it is read, it is not easily understood, since all Tibetan religious vocabulary is Buddhist, and Christian concepts are not comprehended without thorough explanation.

The Khampas are one of the largest tribes in Tibet. Their homeland is the eastern region near the Sichuan Province of China. They are known as fierce warriors and were among the staunchest fighters in the struggle to resist the advance of the Chinese People's Liberation Army in 1950. Khampa men are easily recognized by their red headgear and often serve as butchers - considered an ignoble profession among Buddhists. Some Khampas have had an opportunity to hear the gospel, especially prior to 1949, when missionaries were working in Tibetan-Chinese border areas. However, it is not known if there are any Khampa believers today.

Spiritual Competition

Tibetan Buddhism has been an impenetrable fortress for the gospel, and relatively few Tibetans have ever converted to Christianity. For hundreds of years prior to Communist control, Tibetans steadfastly resisted any foreign intrusion, forcing missionaries to work along the borders. The prevailing belief is that to be a Tibetan is to be a Buddhist. Almost without exception, whether it be in a Chinese-style apartment in Lhasa or a nomad's black tent on the open plateau, every Tibetan home has an altar where incense is burned and fresh offerings are placed regularly. The temples and shrines are among the busiest in the world with pilgrims streaming through them year round.

The influence of the Chinese in Tibet has been mixed. While a horrendous price was paid by the Tibetans in starvation, torture and death, Tibet is now accessible to the outside world as never before. While the government attitude toward Buddhism has moderated, they continue to vigorously repress Christianity, to keep the Buddhist monks (who are prime agitators for independence) from having another point of contention. Since the open proclamation of the gospel is prohibited, it is difficult to assess the current openness of the people.

Noteworthy Trends

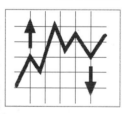

In 1992 Lhasa was designated as a special economic zone where foreign investment and joint ventures are welcome, thus affording greater tent making possibilities for Christians. In addition, the new status may signal an increase in unbridled materialism, as is the case elsewhere in China, taking people's time and drawing them away from spiritual things (which may not be all bad if it draws them away from Tibetan Buddhism).

At the same time, sporadic demonstrations for independence from China keep the political climate tense. Often fueled by unrealistic hopes that U.S. or British warplanes will come streaking over the mountains at any moment to blast away the Chinese as they did to Iraq during the Persian Gulf War, some Tibetans cling to a fantasy of outside intervention in their hope for independence. The demonstrations usually result only in further restrictions.

While most Westerners see the obvious poverty and filth of Tibetans, Tibetans see their world quite differently. Rather than perceiving material things to be of ultimate importance, the spiritual realm has far greater significance. The need to appease the fearsome spirit world and gain merit for a better reincarnation are primary concerns for the average person.

National Prayer Concerns

Obstacles to Ministry
Pray about these challenging circumstances:
• Profound Demonic Influences
Interaction with demons and deities is commonplace
• Cultural Self-Satisfaction
Popular assumption is that to be Tibetan is to be Buddhist; little interest in change
• Isolation of Certain People Groups
Exceptionally rugged landscape makes contact difficult
• Few Indigenous Believers
National evangelists and teachers do not exist

Spiritual Power Points
Pray over these influential locations:
• Mt. Kailas (Western Tibet)
Cosmic center of the earth to Hindus and Buddhists
• Jokhang Temple (Lhasa)
Holiest temple in Tibet; major pilgrimage site
• Tashilhunpo Monastery (Xigaze)
Major Tibetan monastery and seat of the Panchen Lama
• Potala Palace (Lhasa)
Major pilgrimage site; former home of the Dalai Lama and Tibetan theocratic rule

Festivals and Pilgrimages
Pray during these spiritual events:
• Losar & Monlam Chenmo (February/March)
New Year and Great Prayer Festival; dances & feasting
• Sakadawa (May)
Temple ceremonies celebrate enlightenment of Buddha
• Festival of Lights (November)
Honors death of Buddhist leader with butter lamps
• Circumambulation of Mt. Kailas (All Year)
Thousands complete difficult journey to insure salvation

Tunisia

The small Tunisian peninsula is the northernmost point in Africa. It is only 140 miles from Italy, and has been a strategic Mediterranean stronghold for over two thousand years. This same coastline that once sheltered the mighty empire of ancient Carthage is now the playground of European tourists who come to share in Tunisia's warm climate and equally warm Arab hospitality. On this superficial level Tunisia seems to be a modern, forward looking young state, a comparatively pro-Western island of stability in the troubled North African Arab sea.

However, on a deeper level Tunisia is suffering an identity crisis. Alongside a modern, developed coast, complete with topless tourist beaches, lays an undeveloped interior whose soil favors the seeds of political discontent. Tunis, the modern high-rise capital, projects a contemporary air more representative of Europe than the Arab world. Somewhat ironically, the success of its modern educational system has produced an army of young fundamentalist intellectuals, not the Europeanized democrats that might have been expected, if not hoped for. As Tunisians ask themselves who they are, the answer is increasingly coming from the young: "We are Arab, we are Muslim, and we want an Islamic revival."

Basic Facts

Location:
North Africa

Neighboring Countries:
Algeria, Libya

Population:
9,019,000

Capital City:
Tunis

Major Cities:
Sfax, Aryanah, Bizerta, Djerba, Gabes

Government:
Republic

Leader:
President General Zine al Abidne Ben Ali

Major Religions:
Islam

Historical Background

Tunisia's pre-Islamic history can be counted from the Carthaginian Empire, which was founded by Phoenicians from Tyre in the 9th century BC Carthage was Rome's bitter, long-time enemy and is best known for the military campaign of its famous general Hannibal, who crossed the Alps with his elephants. It was obliterated by the Roman invasion of 140 BC, but the fertile valley of Majardah soon became known as the breadbasket of the Roman Empire.

Tunisia as we now know it came into its own in 909 AD, upon the founding of the Islamic Fatimid Dynasty. The Fatimids were a branch of Shiite Muslims who practiced a kind of communism and organized themselves around small cell groups. Allying themselves with the discontented native Berber population, the Fatimid's founder was quickly able to overthrow the Sunni Arabs who were then ruling North Africa. Their original base was Tunis, but wanting to control as much area as possible, the Fatimids moved their headquarters to Egypt. Once there, they founded the city of Cairo and Al Azar university, Islam's oldest and most prestigious school. Like the rest of North Africa, Tunisia eventually came under Ottoman Turkish rule, and then passed to the French. Tunisia gained its independence in 1956.

Unreached Peoples

The urban young of Tunisia are one of the most potent forces in the country today. They face an uncertain future in the face of Tunisia's collapsing economy, and are agitating for radical change, even the establishment of an Islamic state. Led by a highly educated cadre of Muslim fundamentalists, the young malcontents have espoused democracy and freedom of expression, insisting that this would be consistent with their Islamic ideals. This community has many connections to the outside world, especially in France. There is evidence that Iranian sponsored "revolutionary evangelists" actively reach out to these dissatisfied future leaders of Tunisia when they work and study abroad. The fact that the church has not made an equal effort is a clue to the reason why this group remains unreached by the gospel.

Tunisia's 180,000 Berbers live in several villages in the south of the country, and on Djerba Island, off the southeastern coast. The Berbers were the native peoples of North Africa before the Islamic conquest. Since the arrival of Islam in the late 600s, the Berbers have slowly been assimilated by the Arabic language and culture.

Spiritual Competition

T unisia's most powerful spiritual force is embod-ied in the young Hizb Nahda (Renaissance Party) which came to inter-national attention in the mid 1980s. Although banned from political activity, Hizb Nahda fielded independent candidates in the hastily arranged 1989 parliamentary elections. The balloting clearly showed that they were the government's primary opposition, but the winner-take-all constitution prevented them from gaining any parliamentary power.

Although Tunisia's Arabs have been Sunni Muslims for centuries, the strong histor-ical links with the Shiite Fatimids still has an impact. Much of the inspiration for the surging fundamentalist movement has come from Shiite Iran, as well as the theological center of Al Azar in Egypt, and it may be more than coincidental that Al Azar was founded by Tunisia's Shiite ancestors. Furthermore, Hizb Nahda openly admires the Iranian revolution. However, contrary to Iran's dictatorial regime, the Hizb Nahda has made sweeping statements about its democratic, egalitarian ideals and sentiments.

This new trend of an educated, fundamentalist Islamic youth corps is indeed a potent force, and as spiritual competition goes, may be the wave of the future in the Mideast. These disaffected but idealistic young people are a surging tide that merits serious attention from pro-active mission strategists, and Tunisia is perhaps the best case study.

Noteworthy Trends

T unisia has been considered a moderate Islamic state. Often supportive of pursuing peace with Israel, and generally westward looking, it came as a surprise to many when Tunisia refused to back the Gulf War coalition against Saddam Hussein. This change in policy is reflective of a general tilt toward the reactionary side of the Arab world, and seems to stem from widespread rioting in 1983-1984. The riots were has-tened by the removal of government food subsidies, but clearly the Islamic fundamentalists used Tunisia's economic crisis to stir up a spiritual revolution.

The government's anti-Western approach seems to be an attempt to satisfy the expanding Islamic fervor of its people. However, their hard line on the Gulf War resulted in the curtailing of U.S. aid. Kuwait also pulled the plug on desperately needed investment money. Meanwhile, the threat of Algeria's Islamic revolution has caused Tunisia to crack down hard on the Hizb Nahda for fear that Muslim successes in Algeria would spread across the border. Analysts are fearful of a "domino theory" in the Mideast. If Algeria falls to the rad-icals, as it seems likely to do, Tunisia may not be far behind, followed by Egypt and perhaps Jordan. The mostly youthful make-up of Hizb Nahda's hot-blooded constituents does not bode well for Tunisia's peaceful transition in the years to come.

National Prayer Concerns

Obstacles to Ministry
Pray about these challenging circumstances:
- Growing Islamic Fundamentalist Movement
  Influences from Egypt and Algeria
- Lack of Christian Workers
  Tiny national church meets in homes; few expatriates
- Evangelistic Apathy of Christian Population
  Due largely to historic unresponsiveness
- Repercussions for Muslim Converts
  Ostracism from family makes conversion difficult

Spiritual Power Points
Pray over these influential locations:
- Sidi Bou Said
  Traditional Islamic city and pilgrimage site
- City of Kairouan
  Most sacred Islamic city in North Africa
- Grand Mosque (Kairouan)
  Oldest and most famous mosque in Tunisia
- Bir Barouta (Kairouan)
  Well whose waters are said to be connected to Mecca

Festivals and Pilgrimages
Pray during these spiritual events:
- Ramadan & Eid al-Fitr (Varies: '96 = Jan/Feb)
  Month of fasting and prayer followed by two day feast
- Mawlid an-Nabi (Varies: '96 = July)
  Celebrations honoring Muhammad's birthday
- Ulysses Festival in Houmt Souk
  Islamic folklore celebrations on the island of Djerba
- Pilgrimage to Kairouan
  For believers, seven visits here equal a visit to Mecca

Turkey

For the soul seeking a land of exotic contrasts, Turkey is hard to beat. Among her waiting marvels are whirling Sufi dervishes, cave-like churches hewn out of ghostly mountain spires, and ancient Anatolian villages where people chirp like birds. Beckoning from every city are labyrinthine bazaars capable of consuming the most intrepid visitor.

For students of the Bible, however, Turkey is not quite such a mystery. After all, its ancient soil once bore the footsteps of Old Testament patriarchs like Noah, Abraham and Jacob. In later years, its cities provided the backdrop to Paul's missionary journey's and the first Christian churches outside of the Holy Land.

In fact, Turkey's strategic location astride the continents of Europe and Asia has allowed it to play host to many of the great movements of history. From the conquests of the Mongol Hordes and Alexander the Great through the subsequent Crusades and Islamic invasions, Turkey's expansive plains have attracted visionaries and tyrants from every direction.

While it remains a major East-West crossroads, the modern Turkish Republic is also contemplating its proper place within a 21st century world. Today, her teeming cities are filled not only with the scents and tumult of her famed bazaars, but with a pulsing self-confidence. The national target, according to former President Turgut Ozal, "is to be numbered among the first-class states of the world within five years." Turkey's success in reaching this objective will depend in part upon the willingness of her citizens to reject the advances of Islamic fundamentalism, pagan idolatry and ethnic intolerance.

Basic Facts

Location:
Middle East

Neighboring Countries:
Iran, Iraq, Syria, Armenia, Georgia, Greece, Bulgaria, Cyprus

Population:
61,151,000

Capital City:
Ankara

Major Cities:
Istanbul, Konya, Izmir, Adana, Bursa

Government:
Republic

Leader:
President Suleyman Demirel,
Prime Minister Mrs. Tansu Ciller

Major Religions:
Islam

Historical Background

While it is generally accepted that human history originated in Mesopotamia, the book of Genesis suggests that it may have restarted in Turkey when Noah's Ark landed on the "Mountains of Ararat." Unfortunately, it did not take long before pagan influences once again spread their hearty roots.

Some of ancient Anatolia's oldest settlements—Catal Huyuk, for example—were among the world's most influential proponents of the Mother Goddess cult—a spiritual bondage that subsequently impacted two great religions, Islam and Roman (Byzantine) Christianity. Another time-worn city, Haran, served as a cult center for the Babylonian moon goddess, Sin. As history reveals, the Sin cult also had a distinct influence on the development of Islam. As they conquered and absorbed the native peoples who populated Asia Minor, the Turks integrated many pagan beliefs and practices along the way. The resulting religious culture was a blend of Islamic creed and animistic practice now commonly known as folk Islam.

Other important spiritual markers in Turkish history include the Islamic sacking of Christian Constantinople (Istanbul) by Mehmet II, and the brutal massacre of millions of Armenians in the early 1900s.

Unreached Peoples

Most of the indigenous peoples engaged by the Turks as they entered Asia Minor have since been assimilated into the Turkish culture. Of the remaining non-Turkish minorities, the Kurds are by far the largest, accounting for 20% of the entire population. The Kurdish homeland is located beyond the Euphrates River in the far eastern reaches of Anatolia. Many live in the valleys and on the slopes of the rugged Taurus and Zagros mountain ranges. Referred to in Scripture as the Medes, these independent and largely inaccessible people went for many years without any significant attempt to reach them with the gospel. Described by other Middle Easterners as "the least Muslim of Muslims," however, the Kurds have recently begun to hear and respond to the good news of Jesus Christ.

Among the country's other non-Turkish groups, the conservative Anatolian Arabs of the eastern Siirt and Urfa provinces—numbering about one million—are still waiting for the gospel. Other unreached minorities include Kazakhs, Uzbeks, Tatars and Turkmen. And while a small number of Gypsies have recently encountered Christ in Izmir, the nation's estimated 400 to 800 converts from Muslim background ranks Turkey as one of the most unreached nations on earth.

Spiritual Competition

Spiritual competition in Turkey is hardly novel. Paul clearly encountered it in Ephesus, and in the Book of Revelation, Pergamos is mentioned as being a place where "Satan dwelleth." In modern Turkey, the Enemy is still present, albeit wearing a different cloak.

Undoubtedly the biggest challenge facing Christian ambassadors in Turkey today is Islam. Although the nation is officially presented as a secular republic, reality seems to smile wryly at this label. For engraved into the ethnic identity of every citizen is the notion that to be a Turk is to be a Muslim. In the minds of most Turks, a change of religion is considered a kind of treason; a betrayal of one's God-given identity. In cities such as Konya (Biblical Iconium) and Istanbul, Islamic fundamentalism is also becoming a force to be reckoned with.

Islam, however, is not the nation's only spiritual binding cord. No less compelling are the ubiquitous superstitions which linger on from the nation's pagan past. Even in Muslim homes, incantations and charms are routinely offered to ward off evil spiritual influences. Power-seeking pilgrimages to the tombs of holy men and other sacred sites—such as Istanbul's Eyup Mosque—are also commonplace.

Noteworthy Trends

Turkey's desire to modernize and become a "Western power" has produced several positive byproducts for those interested in carrying the gospel to her people. Not the least of these is the fact that the New Testament is legally available, and a certain degree of evangelical activity is tolerated. On the other hand, while the recent Gulf War did serve to strengthen Turkey's westward tilt, resultant political openness in Eastern Anatolia is now being tested by renewed conflicts with Kurdish separatists.

Turkey is also feverishly endeavoring to assume the regional leadership role thrust upon it following the collapse of the Soviet Union. According to many analysts, Turkey now stands as a potent force not only in the newly independent Muslim republics of the CIS, but in the entire Black Sea region as well. Public debate is now focused on the question of whether Turkey's democratic or Islamic values should predominate.

One encouraging note is that Turkey has lately seen a rising tide of Christian missionaries and national converts. Though the nation's Evangelical population remains small (0.001%), it can lay claim to a legacy that includes some of the finest chapters in the history of Christian missions.

National Prayer Concerns

Obstacles to Ministry

Pray about these challenging circumstances:

• Muslim Perception of Christianity
In the minds of many Turks, Christianity is still associated with the Crusades

• Prevalence of Spiritual Superstition
The use of charms, curses and spells is widespread in the country

• Repercussions for Muslim Converts
Ostracism from family makes conversion difficult

• Small National Church
While the church is growing, indigenous believers are still few in number

Spiritual Power Points

Pray over these influential locations:

• Catal Huyuk (Anatolia)
Site of ancient goddess worshiping society

• City of Konya (Iconium)
Islamic stronghold; center of Sufi dervishes

• Nemrud Dag
Ancient folk shrine consisting of giant head statues

• Blue Mosque/Topkapi Palace (Istanbul)
Contain holy relics of Islam which have both political and religious significance

Festivals and Pilgrimages

Pray during these spiritual events:

• Haci Bektash Festival
Celebrations of the heterodox Bektashsect

• Ramadan & Eid al-Fitr (Varies: '96 = Jan/Feb)
Month of fasting and prayer followed by two day feast

• Festival of Mevlana (December)
Nine day event with mystical ritual dances of Sufi dervishes

• Pilgrimage to Eyup Mosque (All Year)
Largest pilgrimage site in Turkey

Turkmenistan

Turkmenistan is a unique and hidden land of black sand dunes, wandering camels, and rare oriental carpets. A former Soviet republic, it occupies the area between the western Turkish world of the Mediterranean and the eastern Turks of Central Asia. Only one percent of the country is cropland; the vast interior is an inhospitable desert - cold in the winter and hot in the summer. Most of the population live in narrow, irrigated strips of land near the rivers in the north and south, or along the shoreline of the Caspian Sea.

The Turkmen people are best known in recent history as the fierce warrior inhabitants of the Black Sand Desert, a vast wasteland stretching east from the Caspian. This is a reputation which they cultivate, for the Turkmen (and women) pride themselves on their toughness and independence. Largely a rural nation, Turkmenistan is a collection of tribes whose clannish allegiances overshadow national concerns. Few would have considered the country ready for national independence, which was unwittingly thrust upon them with the collapse of the USSR.

Since they have had little choice but to continue down the road of national destiny, they have not shrunk back from the formidable task of building a nation. Despite their tribal ways, the Turkmen have always seen themselves as a distinct group, and while under Soviet rule they clung to their own identity. Turkmenistan was the Central Asian nation that held out the longest against the southward Russian expansion in the late 1800s. Although now the poorest of the new republics of the former union, the Turkmen hope to take advantage of their natural resources and harness the tenacious spirit of their people to succeed as the first Turkmen generation to join the family of nations.

Basic Facts

Location:
Central Asia

Neighboring Countries:
Uzbekistan, Kazakhstan, Afghanistan, Iran

Population:
4,039,000

Capital City:
Ashkhabad

Major Cities:
Chardzhou, Mary, Nebit Dag, Krasnovodsk

Government:
Republic

Leader:
President Saparmurad Niyazov

Major Religions:
Islam, shamanism

Historical Background

The area now called Turkmenistan was populated in ancient times by Indo-Iranian peoples who later migrated to the south, forming the current populations of India and Iran. Their beliefs are preserved in the earliest Hindu scripture, the Rig Veda, which is illustrative of the early religious life of this region.

The current inhabitants of Turkmenistan are descendants of the Turks who migrated from the Altai Mountain region bordering China and Mongolia. The southwestern branch of the Turks, the Oguz, are the ancestors of today's Azerbaijanis, Turks, and Turkmen. Seljuk, an Oguz tribal chief, converted to Islam in 960, and as a result was able to expand his power base rapidly. By 1040 the Seljuk Empire was the greatest kingdom on earth.

Upon the collapse of the Seljuk Empire, the northeast frontier of the Muslim world experienced a period of instability, and order was maintained by local tribal chieftains. Situated at a prime location along the famous Silk Road route, they prospered by controlling trade and engaging in occasional extortion and pillage, legitimized as "customs." It was in this environment that the Turkmen ethos began to form. In the 19th century the Czar's armies expanded the Russian empire south into the Muslim lands, finally conquering Turkmenistan in 1881.

Unreached Peoples

The Turkmen nation is a tribal confederation comprising seven major tribes and twenty-four smaller tribes. Of the smaller groups, four serve as "holy tribes," providing religious leadership for the Turkmen nation as a whole. As mentioned, the Turkmen identity is strongly independent, a trait encouraged by a sense of superiority and a significant measure of pride. The traditional aspects of Turkmen tribal culture include restricting marriage to the clan (a subset of the tribe), polygamy and marriage by abduction. Karshilik, or mixed marriages are also a part of these traditions. In a mixed marriage, the brother and sister of one family would marry a sister and brother of another. Traditional tribal distinctions among the Turkmen have survived Moscow's rule more intact than in any other Central Asian nation. The archaic division of master, slave and middle classes also survived the Soviet period.

Turkmenistan's location on the trade routes, coupled with its long history, has left minorities of other peoples. Russians, Ukrainians and Armenians make up about 10% of the population. There are also substantial numbers of people from the other Central Asian republics, as well as Iran.

Spiritual Competition

Although Muslim since the Seljuk era, many ancient spiritual influences are preserved in the beliefs and practices of the modern day Turkmen. A recent survey showed that most Turkmen believe that the mystical Sufi holy men of Turkmenistan do indeed possess supernatural powers. These spiritual guides are provided by the four holy tribes as a hereditary right. Spiritual pilgrimage sites and shrines are found in abundance across the country. Many of these shrines predate Islam, and in places like Divan-Burkh they still carry the names of ancient Indo-Iranian gods.

There is every indication that Soviet efforts to eradicate orthodox Islamic practice contributed to the increase of alternate mystical forms of Islam. In Turkmenistan this has often meant purely shamanistic beliefs disguised under a thin veneer of Islamic terminology. Mystical Islamic and shamanistic rites would include out-of-body travel, exorcism, metaphysical healing, prophecy, tongues, ecstatic trances and channeling of spirits. Since the term "Turkmen" is often used as a synonym for "Muslim," it is clear that these ancient ways are perceived as part of the Muslim experience. Turkmenistan is largely unevangelized; however, the New Testament has just been released in the Turkmen language, and in principle there is freedom of religion in the country.

Noteworthy Trends

Turkmenistan's transition from Soviet republic to independent nation has been relatively smooth. The tribal hierarchy that dominated the Communist Party under the Soviets has remained firmly in place, and is still the source of order in the republic. Democratization does not seem to be a priority. The government has an uphill battle ahead to rescue the country's economy, although there are considerable oil and gas reserves. To do so it is looking primarily to Iran and Turkey for guidance.

Turkey's natural ethnic and linguistic connection with Turkmenistan has made it a natural partner. Economic agreements with Iran aimed at exploiting Turkmenistan's mineral resources were rapidly completed after independence, but the construction of the rail system needed to make those agreements work has been bogged down ever since. Moreover, like Turkey, Turkmenistan's Muslims are of the Sunni sect, and there is some resistance to Iran's aggressive and suspect form of Shiite Islam.

Turkmenistan is wide open for aid, trade and investment, and health care is an urgent priority. A group of Western evangelicals have formed a consortium of tentmakers to meet these needs. Prayer is needed to support such strategic Christian enterprises throughout Central Asia before radical Islam slams the doors shut.

National Prayer Concerns

Obstacles to Ministry
Pray about these challenging circumstances:
- Strong Sufi Muslim Traditions

Sufi pilgrimages are more popular than ever
- Severe Economic Problems

Turkmen are poorest of Central Asia's new republics
- Lack of Christian Workers

Tiny national church meets in homes; few expatriates
- Growing Iranian Influence

Broadcasts, literature and new economic ties

Spiritual Power Points
Pray over these influential locations:
- Behaists' Mosque (Ashkabad)

Restored mosque and Islamic center
- Tomb of Sultan Vais Baba

Reputed burial site of Yemeni saint
- Tomb of Chopan Ata

Sufi saint and ancestor of the Shikh tribe
- Sultan Sandjara Mausoleum (Merv)

Ancient and sacred ruins of revered leader

Festivals and Pilgrimages
Pray during these spiritual events:
- Ramadan & Eid al-Fitr (Varies: '96 = Jan/Feb)

Month of fasting and prayer followed by two day feast
- Qurban Bayram (Varies: '96 = April)

Feast of Sacrifice; coincides with culmination of Hadj
- Pilgrimage to Abu Seid Meikheni Mausoleum

Disciple of Junaidi, famous Sufi Sheik
- Pilgrimage to Shrine of Kurban Murat (All Year)

Ancestral leader of the Akhal Tekke tribe

United Arab Emirates

A surprising mosaic of nationalities, the United Arab Emirates (UAE) has progressed from a group of seven backward and dusty Arab sheikdoms to a fast-paced modern federation of wealthy oil states, all in less than 25 years. A thin strip of desert on the eastern shore of the Arabian Peninsula, the UAE is ruled by conservative Muslim emirs (tribal chiefs) who have close ties with Saudi Arabia. The contrast between today's abundance of gleaming new bank buildings and the nomadic Bedouin heritage of the previous generation is illustrated by the story of the former Emir Shakhboot, who was said to have kept his substantial oil fortune stashed away in an old trunk, where the cash was nibbled away by mice.

The development of the Emirates on such short order required two commodities—oil and foreign labor. About 70% of the population of the UAE is of foreign origin, including about 50,000 Westerners who live in the country. It has often been alleged that some of the foreign workers, particularly young Asian women, are held in virtual slavery by wealthy Arabs, who use them as domestic help and unwilling mistresses.

Westerners tend to see the Emirates as a quintessential oil kingdom of modern folklore, a place of intrigue, adventure and rich Arabs in flowing robes motoring through the desert in air-conditioned Cadillacs and Mercedes. This image is somewhat exaggerated as well as a prejudicial stereotype, but it certainly does have some basis in fact. Two of the Emirates, Sharjah and Dubai, are best known for smuggling, or "re-exporting," which does not discourage the perception of these Gulf states as corrupt realms of excess.

Basic Facts

Location:
Middle East

Neighboring Countries:
Qatar, Saudi Arabia, Oman, Iran

Population:
2,176,000

Capital City:
Abu Dhabi

Major Cities:
Dubai, Sharjah, Ras al-Khaimah

Government:
Federation of Emirates

Leader:
President Zayid bin Sultan al-Nahayan

Major Religions:
Islam

Historical Background

The individual sheikdoms of the UAE were submerged in the broader histories of the Arabs, Persians and Turks until this century. For these people life revolved around a simple code of honor designed to preserve life and order in a nomadic desert society. Religion in old Arabia varied widely from animism and moon worship in the earliest period, to the acceptance of variations of Christianity and Zoroastrianism by the middle ages. Islam was born out of this cosmopolitan environment in the 7th century and quickly swept through not only Arabia but most of the Mediterranean area.

The coastal region of the Arabian Gulf only became a matter of interest to the West after the Portuguese began using it to service their ocean trade with India. By 1820 Britain imposed its sovereignty over the "Trucial States," as they were called, ending the endemic piracy that had plagued the route. They remained under British protection until 1971 when the UAE was formed. Since the building of the Suez canal and the discovery of oil, the shipping route passing through the Strait of Hormuz off the country's coast has become the most vital and strategic waterway in the world.

Unreached Peoples

The majority of people in the UAE are Arabs, most of whom are not native to the Emirates, but foreign-born workers who live in the country. Among the nations represented in the Emirates there are many Palestinians and Egyptians. These Arabs are Sunni Muslims, as opposed to the more radical Shiites in Iran, who are regarded with some fear and suspicion by the conservative Sunnis on the Arabian Peninsula. The Muslim Arabs in the Emirates essentially have no religious freedom, and are insulated from the gospel by tight government control over Christian activities and strong traditional ties to their religion, as well as tight-knit family structures and codes of honor.

Women living in Gulf Arab societies are particularly isolated, as they suffer under the prohibitions and injustices of a somewhat reactionary traditional Islamic culture. Often confined to their homes, it is very difficult for the gospel to reach them. There are also a large number of Iranian men working in the Emirates, who have the opportunity to meet Christian co-workers from other developing countries. Other groups in the UAE include the Pathan and the Baluch from south Asia, as well as a number of Somalis and other Muslims, Hindus and Buddhists from India and Sri Lanka.

Spiritual Competition

The mix of nationalities and cultures that form the expatriate majority living in the country is mirrored in the religious profile of the federation. The strongest force is of course overwhelmingly Islamic, but this is tempered in some measure by the number of Christians currently residing there as guest workers. Among the Muslims, most are Sunni, with a 20% Shiite minority. Egyptian influence in the UAE is strong, especially in Abu Dhabi, where Egyptians are not only employed as teachers but also make up a large proportion of the judges and spiritual leaders.

Conservatism among young students, many of whom study in Western countries, is an emerging trend. This is partly explained by the access the students have to fundamentalist missionaries who are active among Arab students in the West. However, the real spiritual competition comes in the form of virulent anti-Christian propaganda churned out by the Saudis across the border. Because the UAE is more tolerant of the activities of foreigners, the Saudi secret police, known as the mutawa, are active in the Emirates. Muslim Arab converts have been killed for their faith in the past.

Noteworthy Trends

Like other Gulf states, the UAE has been forced to come to terms with dwindling oil supplies. Belt-tightening has been thrust upon the Emirates in recent years, as the nation's per capita income of $28,000, once the highest in the world, plunged to less than $15,000 in 1988. Economic factors inevitably influence the spiritual character of a nation, and the precipitous changes inherent in this oil-based economy may make the UAE vulnerable to unexpected spiritual change as well.

During the Iran-Iraq war, the UAE maintained neutrality, always conscious of staying on favorable terms with their unpredictable neighbor, Iran. After the Iraqi invasion of Kuwait, this position was reinforced. Whatever pan-Arab sentiments may have been embraced by the Emirates before the Gulf War, they are now somewhat lessened and Iran is grudgingly viewed as an integral part of the region. The Gulf War had little effect on the state of Christianity in the UAE, and in general there is a more positive attitude toward Westerners and more contact between Emiratis and Christians. There are plenty of tent making opportunities available, as the UAE is quite open to the West because of its robust capitalist ways.

National Prayer Concerns

Obstacles to Ministry
Pray about these challenging circumstances:
• Islamic Fundamentalism
Sharia law is rigorously applied in some of the emirates
• Prevalence of Materialism
Oil wealth has prompted many to seek comforts of life
• Few Indigenous Believers
Only churches in the country are for expatriates
• Lack of Privacy
Little goes on in the tiny state without police knowledge

Spiritual Power Points
Pray over these influential locations:
• New Bazaar Mosque (Abu Dhabi)
Major Islamic worship center
• Umm Al-Nar (Abu Dhabi)
Island with sacred ancient burial grounds
• Al Hajar Mountains
Home of cave-dwelling, animist Shihuh people
• Dubayy and Sharjah
Former pirate states; now banking and smuggling centers

Festivals and Pilgrimages
Pray during these spiritual events:
• Ramadan & Eid al-Fitr (Varies: '96 = Jan/Feb)
Month of fasting and prayer followed by two day feast
• Eid al-Adha (Varies: '96 = April)
Feast of Sacrifice; coincides with culmination of Hadj
• Ashura (Varies: '96 = May)
Shiite passion play celebrating Hussein's martyrdom
• Mawlid an-Nabi (Varies: '96 = July)
Celebrations honoring Muhammad's birthday

Uzbekistan

$\mathcal{U}$zbekistan is perhaps the most important and influential of the predominantly Muslim nations that declared independence following the collapse of the Soviet Union. The birthplace of algebra and modern astronomy, its territory encompasses all of the great centers of classical Central Asian culture and history. Bukhara, Samarkand and Khiva are cities that resound with the fame of Genghis Khan and Tamerlane. This new nation, born perhaps prematurely by a dying Soviet empire, is now struggling for life and the hope of a stable future.

Considering the vast linguistic and cultural differences that existed among its peoples early in this century, it is remarkable that Uzbekistan emerged from the USSR with a national identity at all. History knows no Uzbekistan, just the names of local emirates and occasional foreign appellations like Transoxiana and Turkestan. A perennial target for invaders, the heart of the great Silk Road has seen a tide of peoples and armies pass by, leaving the residents of Uzbekistan with a rich and complex heritage.

However, after years as a Soviet vassal state, Uzbekistan is a land on the ropes. Social breakdown has resulted from the erosion of clan and family ties under Moscow's rule, and the country's women have been particularly hard hit, caught between the old ways of male dominance and the need to work to survive; Uzbek women have a high suicide rate. Environmental damage has also been severe, making a weak economy even weaker. The lack of medical facilities is bad even by post-Soviet standards, and toxic runoff from agricultural chemicals has polluted the water supply, causing chronic disease. As a result, Uzbekistan, is now wide open for Western technical and medical help.

Basic Facts

Location:
Central Asia

Capital City:
Tashkent

Leader:
President Islam A. Karimov

Neighboring Countries:
Kazakhstan, Kyrgyzstan, Tajikistan, Afghanistan, Turkmenistan

Major Cities:
Samarkand, Bukhara, Fergana

Major Religions:
Sunni Islam, shamanism

Population:
23,377,000

Government:
Republic

Historical Background

The earliest inhabitants of Uzbekistan were the parents of the modern Iranian and Indian nations. These primitive nomads possessed a complex religion, the heart of which is preserved to this day in Hinduism. As the native Indo-Iranians migrated to the south, they were replaced by Turks from the Mongolian steppes who brought the widespread practice of shamanism with them.

The Turkish shamanists relied on priestly intermediaries who could contact the spirit world and bring forth prophecy and effect healing for the common people. This intuitive spiritism was no substitute for structured religion, however. Uzbekistan's location at the crossroads of world trade allowed the Turks to sample each of the world's civilized religions; by the middle ages Buddhism, Christianity and Zoroastrianism were widely followed throughout the region, and there was even a tribe of Jewish Turks.

The Arab Islamic conquests in 673 AD introduced Islam to the mix, and over the following centuries Muhammad's creed won out as the religion of choice for the peoples of Central Asia. Neither the anti-Islamic period of Mongol rule in the 1200's nor the 20th century religion of Communism could break Islam's control over the region.

Unreached Peoples

Seventy percent of Uzbekistan's total population is considered Uzbek. Although the name is derived from an earlier tribal group, the modern Uzbeks are really a consolidation of at least three separate historical strains. The Uzbek culture is typically Central Asian and is rich in folklore, but isolation and frequent conflict with ethnic Christians have conspired to keep the gospel beyond this noble people's reach for centuries. The tight knit clan and family structure is a strong feature of Uzbek society and is the first line of defense against Christian teaching. However, it could serve just as strongly to strengthen and spread the gospel when it finally breaks through.

The large number of Tajiks in Uzbekistan is a legacy from the pre-Soviet era. Many Tajiks claim that their numbers by far exceed the official estimates, and that many of their people have been falsely listed as Uzbeks. Before the Soviet era there was little distinction made between these bilingual urban cultures. The Tajiks are the oldest group in Central Asia, descended from the original Indo-Iranian peoples. They are related to other Persian groups in Iran and Afghanistan.

Spiritual Competition

Lo call Uzbekistan the spiritual capital of Central Asia would not be an overstatement. Over the ages its cities have hosted the rulers of many different religious counterfeits. From Samarkhand's days as the center of Manicheism, an ancient form of Gnosticism, to Tashkent's administrative capacity as the headquarters of official Islam, Uzbekistan's cities have played the leading role in the organized spiritual life of Central Asia.

Scholars generally credit Islam's staying power during both the Mongol and Communist periods to a powerful network of Sufi brotherhoods. Uzbekistan was the birthplace of the largest such order, called the Naqshbandi. This form of mysticism combines many pre-Islamic shamanistic practices with an Islamic creed. The powerful devotional ties between the brotherhood's adherents and their spiritual masters lend the movement strength and durability. Many Sufi rituals revolve around pilgrimage sites called mazars, which are dedicated to Sufi leaders from the past. The most important mazars are those of Ali in the Fergana Valley and Naqshband (founder of the order) in Bukhara. The "place of the living lord," the Shahi Zenda shrine in Samarkand is also highly regarded.

Noteworthy Trends

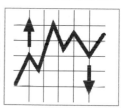

Stalin once called Uzbekistan the "Beacon for the East" and indeed it is still the most important among the Muslim Central Asian republics. The course it takes over then next few years is critical to the entire region. Questions of democracy, ethnic identity and economic reform are all at critical levels. One of the greatest influences on Uzbekistan at present is Turkey, because it is a nation with a similar language, history, and religious culture. Many in Uzbekistan view it as an ideal model for a modern Islamic society. Not everyone agrees however, and a great deal of money has been poured into Uzbekistan from Iran and Saudi Arabia expressly for the propagation of their respective forms of Islam throughout Central Asia. The removal of communist restraints has resulted in an Islamic revival that may yet become a disruptive factor in Uzbek politics. Although the opening of the borders to western aid has allowed the first Christian witness to the Uzbeks, this has not gone unopposed. The traditional role of the Sufi brotherhoods in protecting the Muslim community from outside "attacks" is definitely still very much intact. It is not clear what affect they and the traditional community structure will have on the evolution of the country's government.

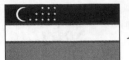

National Prayer Concerns

Obstacles to Ministry
Pray about these challenging circumstances:
• Neo-Communist Government
New regime has allowed few democratic reforms
• Influx of Cults
Many have committed significant resources to country
• Islamic Revival
Substantial encouragement coming from Saudi Arabia
• High Unemployment Rate
Leading to economic and social instability

Spiritual Power Points
Pray over these influential locations:
• Ali Mazar (Fergana Valley)
Most famous of all holy places in Central Asia; Sufi pilgramage site
• Naqshband Mazar (Bukhara)
Pilgrimage site dedicated to founder of largest Sufi brotherhood in Central Asia
• Shahi Zenda Shrine (Samarkand)
The "place of the living lord", a highly regarded Sufi pilgrimage site
• Muslim Board for Central Asia & Kazakhstan
Islamic headquarters in Tashkent serves entire region

Festivals and Pilgrimages
Pray during these spiritual events:
• Ramadan & Eid al-Fitr (Varies: '96 = Jan/Feb)
Month of fasting and prayer followed by two day feast
• Mawlid an-Nabi (Varies: '96 = July)
Celebrations honoring Muhammad's birthday
• Pilgrimage to Ali Mazar (All Year)
Main Islamic shrine in Central Asia
• Pilgrimage to Shahi Zenda Shrine (All Year)
The tomb of Islamic saint, Queam Ibn Abbas

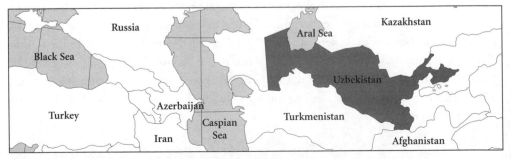

Vietnam

Vietnam is one of the most beautiful countries in Asia, stretching over 1,000 miles from the misty mountains along the Chinese border to the flat Mekong Delta. It is roughly divided into two geographic regions: the mountains running north-south along the western border and the lowlands along the coast. These two regions also separate the two major ethnic divisions in the country, the hill tribes and the lowland Vietnamese.

Beneath the veneer of tropical beauty lies a nation that is traumatized, despairing and fearful. Few other nations have suffered as much in the last 50 years as Vietnam, and this is principally due to a series of devastating and brutal wars. While Vietnam is chiefly remembered because of the disastrous U.S. involvement there, it was actually at war almost continuously from 1941-1985, first in World War II, then in a war of liberation from the French, followed by the protracted civil war that ended with the fall of Saigon in 1975. After that, fighting with Cambodia and China continued to devastate the population and the economy, resulting in a stream of desperate refugees fleeing their homeland in flimsy boats. Many are economic refugees, as the average yearly wage is about $190 - 1% of that in the United States.

The devastated economy left by the wars, strict socialist policies and world isolation have made for slow recovery. However, with the collapse of communist governments in other parts of the world, economic survival has become more of an imperative than ideological purity. Vietnam has been opening gradually for tourism and foreign investment.

Basic Facts

Location:
Southeast Asia

Neighboring Countries:
China, Laos, Cambodia

Population:
75,030,000

Capital City:
Hanoi

Major Cities:
Ho Chi Minh (Saigon), Hai Phong, Da Nang, Hue

Government:
Communist (socialist republic)

Leader:
General Secretary Do Muoi

Major Religions:
Buddhism, animism, Roman Catholicism

Historical Background

Vietnamese history goes back as far as 3,000 years and is fairly well documented, due mainly to almost one thousand years of Chinese rule. The earliest inhabitants practiced various forms of spirit worship. Ancestor worship may also have been involved and was certainly reinforced, if not introduced, during the years of Chinese occupation. During this time Buddhism, Confucianism, and Taoism also began to grow in the country, and while Buddhism later became the common religion, it is a diluted form, influenced by spiritism, magic and ancestor worship.

Christianity entered Vietnam in the 16th century when Roman Catholic missionaries from Spain, France, and Portugal first arrived. Despite official opposition and persecution from the emperors, the Catholic faith was established and flourished under the French, when it received preferential status. Between eight to ten percent of all Vietnamese now consider themselves Catholic, a higher percentage than any other country in Indochina. Protestant missions began in 1911 and attracted a significant number of followers. All missionaries were forced to leave the country in 1975 after the victory of the communists in the south.

Unreached Peoples

The hill tribes have changed very little through the centuries and best embody the original culture of Vietnam. Traditionally they have been nomadic, moving easily back and forth through the mountains between Vietnam, Cambodia, Laos, and Thailand. There are shamans and sorcerers among all of the highlanders, and witchcraft is found in some groups. There are a number of believers among them, but large numbers of tribesmen have yet to hear the gospel, particularly in the north. The lowland Vietnamese majority are predominantly Buddhist and non-religious/atheist. Despite these general labels, spirit and ancestor worship still are at the core of most people's beliefs.

The ethnic minorities of the north have been off limits to missionaries since before World War II and are believed to be completely unreached. The largest of these groups are the Thai-Dai and the Miao-Yao. The Hung, May, and Nguon in the central highlands are also unevangelized. Perhaps the most strategic unreached people group in Vietnam are the many communist government officials. They may be quite receptive to the gospel at this time, since the socialist ideals for which they fought and sacrificed for so long have not brought the expected result - the nation continues to flounder and suffer, and many are depressed and disillusioned.

Spiritual Competition

The Communist Party has severely repressed Christianity in Vietnam, with both Catholics and Protestants suffering greatly. Persecution, surveillance, and arrests continue. Christian literature, especially that which is in tribal languages, is outlawed. Because the mountain tribes have long been hated and despised, the suffering of Christians among these people has been particularly severe.

While Buddhism may be the professed religion of most people, spirit and ancestor worship is the reality behind Vietnamese spiritual life. Being the oldest known forms of religion in the country, these animistic practices are merely overlaid with Buddhist or Taoist ritual and practice. These ancient spiritual patterns have resulted in strong demonic bondage, which may very well be the cause of Vietnam's continuing agony.

Throughout the highlands ritual offerings and animal sacrifices were common, particularly before the ascendancy of the communists in 1975. Invocations were made to specific deities, accompanied by offerings of food and a jar of alcohol. An animal was normally sacrificed, and depending on the type of ritual, it may have been a chicken, goat, pig, buffalo, or occasionally a dog. Gongs and drums were played when the animals were slaughtered as well as during feasting, which took place afterward.

Noteworthy Trends

Despite harsh, continued opposition to Christianity in Vietnam, the church continues to grow. Since 1975, the number of Christians has more than doubled. However, this has not been without great cost. The communist government, alienated from China, viewed the collapse of the Soviet Union with great alarm. As a result, the hard line leaders have stepped up security against perceived enemies of the state. The church is viewed as a primary threat, and the registered (officially sanctioned) church is strictly controlled; the unregistered house churches are infiltrated and the leaders jailed. While there is an increase in interest in the gospel, the Vietnamese church is in dire need of prayer for strength and deliverance from the hand of the oppressors.

The collapse of the Communist Bloc and its internal trade agreements has forced Vietnam to open to the outside world to survive economically. Foreign trade, investment and tourism are being welcomed, which all provide avenues for the spread of the gospel; there is also a tremendous desire to learn English. European, Australian and American businesses are now investing in Vietnam, which hopefully will lead to better economic times and a loosening of the government's paranoid and repressive policies.

National Prayer Concerns

Obstacles to Ministry
Pray about these challenging circumstances:
• Severe Ministry Restrictions
Christianity must be practiced inside the walls of the church
• Prevalence of Animistic Buddhism
Philosophy is deeply ingrained into Vietnamese culture
• Ban on Foreign Missionaries
Many of those forced out after the war have not been allowed to return
• Lack of Resources
Church is poor and Christian literature is in short supply

Spiritual Power Points
Pray over these influential locations:
• Marble Mountain (Danang)
Major Buddhist pilgrimage site
• Thien Mu & Ling Mu Pagodas, Khai Din Tomb
Monuments of the Nguyen Dynasty
• Van-Hanh University (Saigon)
Prominent Buddhist intellectual center
• Village of Phram Rang
Home of indigenous Indian-Islamic Cham people

Festivals and Pilgrimages
Pray during these spiritual events:
• Tet Festival (January/February)
Seven day New Year celebrations with sacrifices for the dead
• Buddha's Birth, Enlightenment, and Death (May)
Temples and pagodas crowded
• Thanh Minh (April)
Spirits of dead relatives are invoked through offerings of food, flowers, and joss sticks
• Doan Ngo (June)
Summer solstice day; offerings made to spirits and ghosts of ancestors

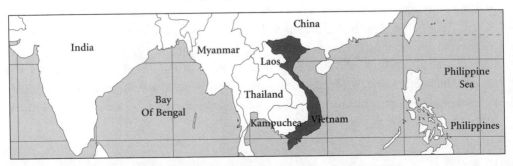

Western Sahara

The Western Sahara is Africa's last colony and most remote outpost. For centuries, the Western Sahara has had a reputation for being one of the most forsaken areas on the planet. In fact, it is so forsaken that only a small number of hardy travelers and lonely map makers even know where it is. In the 1980s, it was not even recognized as a country by the UN.

Why rocket all the way to the moon if you can sail to Western Sahara? Upon arrival in either place, you'll find about the same conditions. One traveler has called the landscape, "eerily silent, apparently lifeless in its vastness." The Western Sahara is a land characterized by climactic extremes. Temperatures on the Atlantic coast often reach 100 degrees, and 135+ in the interior is common, while winter temperatures plummet to below freezing. With annual rainfall of less than two inches a year, there is little hope for agriculture.

But surely there are beautiful oases, little gardens blooming in the midst of the baking desert? Sorry, they don't have those either. In fact, there are only 17 acres of palm trees in the entire country. The economy is captive to the lack of surface water and the harsh climate, and the populace is largely dependent on migrant grazing, fishing and mining.

Although the Western Sahara suffers from a desert climate and a bleak landscape, it is at least blessed with some variety of mineral resources, which support a mining industry.

Basic Facts

Location:
North Africa

Neighboring Countries:
Morocco, Mauritania, Algeria

Population:
194,000

Capital City:
La'Youn

Major Cities:
El Aaium, Cabo Bojador, Villa Cisneros

Government:
Constitutional Monarchy (administered by Morocco)

Leader:
King Hassan II of Morocco (not recognized by Polisario Front)

Major Religions:
Islam

Historical
Background

Prior to the twentieth century, the Western Sahara remained largely outside of any central authority. During these dim centuries life in the Western Sahara revolved around nomads and camels, and the nomads' lives were characterized by frequent tribal feuding for grazing and water resources. Piracy, the world's second-oldest profession, was an important source of livelihood, as the locals raided camel caravans traveling between Marrakech and Mali.

A new and quite different chapter in the Western Sahara's history began in the late 19th century when Spain colonized the region. When the last Spanish troops left in 1976, Morocco immediately laid claim to all the territory of Spanish Sahara. At the same time, the Polisario Front, a political party comprised of indigenous Saharans, proclaimed the birth of a new state, the Saharan Arab Democratic Republic (SADR). This Western Saharan national movement, armed by Algeria and Libya, fought a war on two fronts against Mauritania and Morocco. The Polisario were successful in their guerrilla war against Mauritania, leaving them with one focus, independence from Morocco. This costly war has forced tens of thousands of Saharans into refugee camps and is estimated to have cost Morocco one to two million dollars per day, and is now essentially stalemated.

Unreached
Peoples

The indigenous people of the Western Sahara are called Saharawis and are a unique mixture of Arab and African Muslim peoples. In the north the Tekna tribe are descendants of Berbers who migrated from North Africa during the Roman era. They were the nomadic raiders who preyed on caravans, engaged in robbery and extortion, and feuded with rival tribes.

The Ulad Delim of the southern coastal region are the descendants of Arabs who immigrated first to Egypt and then to North Africa. Between the 14th and 17th centuries the Ulad Delim settled in Western Sahara and gradually blended into the Berber population through tribal alliances and intermarriage. Hassaniyya Arabic, the language of the Ulad Delim, finally replaced Berber, and the conversion to Islam accelerated.

The Reguibat, a large Bedouin tribe of Arab ancestry, comprise another major component of the Western Saharan population. The members of this tribe are distinguished by their fierce fighting qualities, remarkable tracking abilities and pride in their own traditions. All the nomadic people of the Western Sahara are Muslim. Their harsh living conditions have further instilled in these peoples a sense of pride, aggressiveness and self-righteousness, which makes them quite resistant to the gospel message.

Spiritual Competition

$\mathcal{I}$slam has a virtual stranglehold on the Western Sahara, with 99 percent of the population within the Muslim fold. Almost all Saharawis belong to the Sunni branch of Islam. The first traces of Christianity were found in the area around the second century, but were eventually erased by the advancing tide of Islam.

There is no known Christian witness in the Western Sahara, nor has there been any coordinated effort to evangelize them. Missionaries are excluded from the region and constant turmoil caused by the war between the Polisario and Morocco also make it difficult to place tentmakers in the area. However, the country is not completely closed. There may be a significant opportunity for Moroccan national Christians who settle in the Western Sahara to establish a witness. Unfortunately, intimidation of Christian seekers takes many forms: lengthy police interrogations, expulsion from employment, family harassment and occasional imprisonment. Another possible avenue for the gospel has been opened through the witness of fishermen who work in the Western Sahara's waters, off the Atlantic coast. The region also receives TV broadcasts from the nearby Canary Islands. The scriptures have been translated into Hassaniyya Arabic, which is spoken by the majority of Saharawis.

Noteworthy Trends

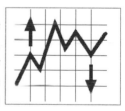

$\mathcal{T}$he nomadic way of life has almost become extinct. Most remaining nomads are in Polisario camps in Algeria, while those remaining were forcibly relocated in small towns by Moroccan forces and encouraged to build fixed homes there. Since Mauritania withdrew and made peace with the Polisario, Morocco has seized the entire country, up to the southern border with Mauritania.

Morocco's King Hassan has not been able to extricate himself honorably from the Western Sahara conflict, which is steadily draining his government's coffers. The high stakes in this dubious war were recently reiterated by an intransigent Hassan, who declared on Moroccan TV that "We will not renounce a single grain of this Moroccan Sahara, for which so many of us have sacrificed blood, and which has cost us so much money."

Hundreds of Saharawi refugees have settled in the Canary Islands off the coast of Africa. In this European vacation resort they seem to be more open to the gospel than in their own restricted country. It would appear that this is a divine door of opportunity that has been opened. Pray that the fiercely proud and stubborn spirit of these hard-bitten nomads would be soft and receptive for the gospel of abiding peace and permanence that these wandering people unknowingly seek.

National Prayer Concerns

Obstacles to Ministry

Pray about these challenging circumstances:
• No Known Indigenous Christians
There is not even an expatriate church in the country
• Continuing Conflict Between Polisario Resistance and Morocco
Morocco claims to rule; many native Saharawis object
• Isolation of Certain People Groups
Nomadism, war and inhospitable desert terrain
• Lack of Evangelistic Initiatives
Few mission agencies have any interest in the country

Spiritual Power Points

Pray over these influential locations:
• Koubba of Sidi Lemsid
Shrine of ancestral saint of the Tidrahin people
• Algerian border Area (Tindouf)
Stronghold of the Marxist Polisario guerrillas
• Sidi Mohammed Lagdal Mosque (Tan Tan)
Islamic center; former base of the 1975 Green March
• Oasis of Daoura
Community center of the Izarguin tribe

Festivals and Pilgrimages

Pray during these spiritual events:
• Ramadan & Eid al-Fitr (Varies: '96 = Jan/Feb)
Month of fasting and prayer followed by two day feast
• Yennair Festival (Varies: '96 = May)
Islamic New Year commemorating the hegira
• Mawlid an-Nabi (Varies: '96 = July)
Celebrations honoring Muhammad's birthday
• Boujloud Festival
Pagan celebrations commemorating sacrifice

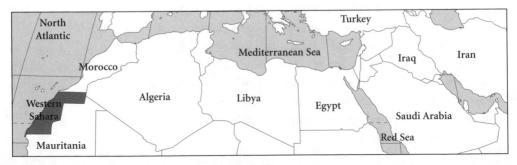

Yemen

For years Yemen was divided into two countries, North and South Yemen; the North was a traditional Arabian Muslim society, but the South was a Marxist state until its benefactor, the Soviet Union, collapsed. After unification in 1990, the president and vice president began to feud, resulting in a bloody civil war in the summer of 1994. The northern forces led by the president finally prevailed, but not without some lasting physical and psychological scars.

Located across from the Horn of Africa in southwest Arabia, Yemen is the traditional site of the Kingdom of Sheba and an early center of near eastern civilization. Yemen controls the Bab el Mandeb passage on the Red Sea, one of the world's narrowest and most active shipping lanes; all ships going through the Suez Canal must pass through Yemeni waters.

A hot semi-desert terrain and mountainous interior separate Yemen's western and southern coastlines. As a result of its topographical extremes, a variety of crops are produced, including khat, a narcotic leaf that is chewed by 90% of the population on a daily basis. The people are predominantly Arab, though black African peoples do exist in the southern part of the country.

The Yemen of antiquity was known for its great wealth, which was derived from the incense trade and the control of commerce between Asia and the Mediterranean. It also boasted a sophisticated agricultural system based on an elaborate array of irrigation works that effectively made up for the lack of major rivers in the region. Sadly, the upheavals of the past several decades have left the country poverty-stricken and greatly underdeveloped.

Basic Facts

Location:
Middle East

Neighboring Countries:
Saudi Arabia, Oman, Djibouti

Population:
16,102,000

Capital City:
Sana'a

Major Cities:
Aden, Taiz, Hodeida, Mukalla

Government:
Republic

Leader:
President Ali Abdullah Saleh

Major Religions:
Islam

Historical Background

$\mathcal{A}$ British colony until 1967, Yemen was formerly home to one of Arabia's most ancient civilizations. Even before the time of Christ, during the reigns of Persia, Greece, and Rome, the Sabean people of southern Arabia were a power in their own right. Sustained by the flourishing trade route between Yemen and India, the Sabeans also colonized East Africa, and were the first to make the goods of Asia available to the Romans. But in the sixth century an avalanche of misfortune struck the region. The fall of the Roman Empire, several large dam breakages, an Ethiopian invasion, and an economic depression, all during the sixth century, hurt the Yemeni Arabs considerably.

At that time, Yemen was largely Christian, but a short time later Islam emerged in Arabia. Even before the death of Muhammad, his son-in-law Ali had already converted some of the Yemeni tribal confederations of Hamdan. They have maintained close links with Muhammad's descendants ever since, keeping the country Muslim. Yemen was also a moon god cult center prior to the introduction of Islam. Since the 7th century, the country has been continuously Muslim. Although it is split along Sunni and Shiite lines, this is the result of foreign invasions and security arrangements as much as theological conviction.

Unreached Peoples

$\mathcal{Y}$emen for the most part is made up of Arab peoples, of which about 53% are Sunni and 47% are Shiite. Among these groups, numerous tribal distinctions can be observed. The Sunnis break down into over 1300 tribes or clans, while the Shiites are divided among some 400 different tribes. Other minorities and non-Semitic peoples may also be found within this number, including an ancient band of about 2,000 Jews.

The Socotri, who are completely unreached, are indigenous to a small island which is part of Yemen, although it lies just off the Horn of Africa. The Mahri and Bedouin nomads dwell together in the central and eastern section of the republic and remain totally out of reach of any modern evangelistic effort. They number more than one-quarter million and were being forcibly settled by the former Marxist government of South Yemen. Some Indians, Pakistanis and Somalis also live and work in the country. If democratic reforms continue now that the civil war is over and foreign investment increases, the accessibility of the people of Yemen to the outside world should increase, allowing them to be more available to the gospel than in the past.

Spiritual Competition

$\mathcal{A}$s in many places around the Arab world, a definite swing toward a more fundamentalist version of Islam is taking place in Yemen. According to one observer, about 100,000 Yemenis took part in a rally in December 1992 calling for the government to introduce the conservative Quranic Sharia Law code. This popular movement seems to be the result of growing dissatisfaction over the state of the economy and the current government, the same conditions that have fueled other Islamic movements. Included in this law is a ban on the building and repair of churches. While it has recently been reported that the government may allow the reopening of a particular Anglican church building in the south, the threat of this radical Islamic party should not be underestimated. Economic factors were critical in Yemen's early conversion to Islam and may yet again become the motivating force toward fundamentalism.

Another very real spiritual bondage that exists within Yemeni culture is the use of the narcotic khat. It is a stimulating addictive leaf, easily grown in Yemen's climate, and is also exported to Africa. An amazingly large percentage of the population chews this leaf, which produces effects similar to that of amphetamines or opium.

Noteworthy Trends

$\mathcal{S}$ince reunification of the north and south in 1990, the country has been dominated by political tension, violence and economic crisis. This probably was inevitable, as the merger was an unstable alliance between the Marxist south and the conservative tribesmen of the north. However, chaos and bloodshed is no stranger to the southern Arabian coast, which has been plagued with tribal clashes, wars, and conquests over the centuries. Yemen also backed the wrong horse by siding with Iraq in the Gulf War, which has isolated them economically on the Arabian Peninsula.

Democratic elections, which were the price agreed to by the north for reunification with the south, took place in April 1993, but could not head off the brutal civil war that erupted a year later. Nonetheless, the election was a big step for Yemen in that it allowed women to run for office and vote. It is important to note that the Saudi-supported Islamic fundamentalist party, Islah, captured a surprisingly low 20% of the vote; a much higher level of support had been anticipated. At any rate, since the 1994 war the country's future has been placed on hold; it is still too soon to predict when the country will heal and stabilize.

National Prayer Concerns

Obstacles to Ministry

Pray about these challenging circumstances:

• Strict Prohibitions on Muslim Evangelism
Police are on alert for evidence of violations
• Cultural Suspicions
Yemenis are not generally open to outsiders
• Weak and Isolated National Church
The few believers are poorly trained and persecuted
• Widespread Use of Khat
Populace hooked on this chewable narcotic stimulant

Spiritual Power Points

Pray over these influential locations:

• Al Mohdar (Tarim)
Most prominent of the city's 300-plus mosques
• City of Shabwah
Restricted Muslim city and former Arabian power center
• Al-Jami 'Al-Kabir (San'a)
Significant mosque and center of Islamic learning
• Al-Janad Mosque
Yemen's oldest; major pilgrimage site

Festivals and Pilgrimages

Pray during these spiritual events:

• Ramadan & Eid al-Fitr (Varies: '96 = Jan/Feb)
Month of fasting and prayer followed by two day feast
• Eid al-Adha (Varies: '96 = April)
Feast of Sacrifice; coincides with culmination of Hadj
• Ashura (Varies: '96 = May)
Shiite passion play celebrating Hussein's martyrdom
• Pilgrimage to Hatim bin Ibrahim Tomb (All Year)
Burial site of Ismaili saint

Glossary

Animism: Derived from the Latin anima, meaning soul or spirit, as well as from the English word animate, animism is the attribution of conscious life to nature, especially such things as rocks, trees, wind, and sometimes animals. It frequently involves an attempt to control or influence spirits through rituals, pacts, or sacrifices. It is common in primitive religions worldwide as well as Hinduism, Buddhism and Islam. Chinese folk religion and Japanese Shinto are good examples of sophisticated cultures that are in bondage to animism.

Fetish/Fetishism: An object such as an idol, implement, or work of art that is believed to have magical or curative powers. Fetishism is common in superstitious tribal religions, especially in Africa.

Folk Islam: Sometimes called the "soft underbelly of Islam," folk Islam is a syncretistic combination of orthodox Islamic tenets with folk religion or animism. This type of Islam is especially strong in Indonesia, south Asia and Africa. Occult rites and spells such as the "evil eye" are common in folk Islam.

Hadj (Hajj): The annual pilgrimage to Mecca, which all devout Muslims are obligated to make at least once in their lifetime. A person who has fulfilled this obligation is called a hadji.

Jihad: Usually translated as "holy war" (against the enemies of Islam), it can also have a less militant meaning, such as "struggle for Islam," which is Yassir Arafat's preferred translation since the signing of the Mideast peace accord.

Marabout: An Islamic holy man who uses occult powers; common in Africa.

Shaman/Shamanism: A worldwide pattern of healing that has been known since the beginning of history. It is a religion, but it is also a medical system. Shamanism is thought to be the prototype of unrevealed human religion, the lowest common denominator to which mankind invariably sinks when left without divine revelation. The shaman, or holy man is a "nature-guru," who uses natural potions and spells to heal, and frequently travels out of the body to commune with spirits. Shamans, who are sometimes called witch doctors, are often demonically possessed and have great supernatural powers.

Sharia Law: A legal system based upon the teachings of the Koran. In countries where it is the law of the land, such as Saudi Arabia, apostates can be executed and thieves sometimes have their hands severed. As Islamic fundamentalist movements gain more power, there is growing pressure to adopt Sharia law in many Muslim nations, such as Pakistan.

Shiite Islam: The minority branch of Islam, they trace their lineage to Ali, the first cousin and son-in-law of Muhammad. Muhammad had no sons, so after his death in 632 there was a dispute over who would succeed him. Ali's followers felt that he was the logical successor, but he was killed by his rivals, insuring a permanent split. The Shiites have traditionally represented the underclass and the disenfranchised in Islam. Today this movement is centered in Iran, and political violence and terrorism are increasingly associated with Shiism.

Sufi, Sufism: The Sufis constitute the mystical wing of Islam, skirting the line between heresy and orthodoxy. While culturally Muslim, their beliefs are sometimes closer to Hinduism or Buddhism, often with a belief in reincarnation and a pantheistic worldview.

Sunni Islam: The majority of the world's Muslims are Sunni. After Muhammad's death the Umayyad caliphs killed their rival Ali (see Shiite Islam, above) and gained political control of Mecca and Medina, the holy cities of Islam, which they still rule today. The split between the Shiites and the Sunnis is in some ways comparable to the Protestant/Catholic rift in Christianity.

Syncretism: The belief and practice of fusing together two or more religions. Folk Islam, a blending of traditional animistic beliefs and orthodox Islam is one example; Christianity also has the same problem in Africa, Asia and Latin America, where occult superstitions from native religions are blended with Christian liturgy and doctrine. On a more sophisticated level, syncretism refers to the philosophical attempt to blend all religions together into one all-embracing faith, denying absolute truth to any one religion. In the universities of the West, this worldview is sometimes called phenomenology.

Photo Credits

Afghanistan ....UNHCR/Boccon-Gibod Sipa
Albania...Phyllis Berry
Algeria...Arab World Ministries
Azerbaijan
Bahrain ....George K. Otis, Jr.
Bangladesh ....Adam Buchanan/World Concern
Benin...SIM USA
Bhutan ....George K. Otis, Jr.
Brunei ....George K. Otis, Jr.
Burkina Faso ....World Concern
Cambodia...World Concern
Chad...John Warren/World Concern
China (PRC).......................................Charlie Sturges
China (Taiwan) ROC........................Assemblies of God, Division of Foreign Missions
Djibouti
Egypt...George K. Otis, Jr
Eritrea ....World Concern
Ethiopia ....John Warren/World Concern
Gambia ....Joanna Pinneo/Foreign Mission Board, SBC
Guinea ....SIM USA
Guinea-Bissau ....Gerald Jackson/AoG, Division of Foreign Missions
India
Indonesia...Assemblies of God, Division of Foreign Missions
Iran ....Assemblies of God, Division of Foreign Missions
Iraq...News Network International / W. Nicolai
Israel ....George K. Otis, Jr.
Japan ....George K. Otis, Jr.
Jordan ....George K. Otis, Jr.
Kazakhstan ....Rolling Hills Covenant Church
Korea, North......................................Cornerstone Ministries
Kuwait...Elaine Keith/Women's Aglow
Kyrgyzstan
Laos..Assemblies of God, Division of Foreign Missions
Lebanon...George K. Otis, Jr.
Libya ....Bob Sjogren
Malaysia..Don Rutledge/Foreign Mission Board, SBC
Maldives..ADS
Mali...Assemblies of God, Division of Foreign Missions
Mauritania
Mongolia ....Peter Iliyn
Morocco...George K. Otis, Jr.

Myanmar	Assemblies of God, Division of Foreign Missions
Nepal	George K. Otis, Jr.
Niger	John Warren/World Concern
Nigeria	SIM USA
Oman	George K. Otis, Jr.
Pakistan	Assemblies of God, Division of Foreign Missions
Qatar	
Saudi Arabia	
Senegal	John Warren/World Concern
Somalia	John Warren/World Concern
Sri Lanka	Assemblies of God, Division of Foreign Missions
Sudan	Across/Pip Land
Syria	George K. Otis, Jr.
Tajikistan	Paul & Mary Filidis
Thailand	Assemblies of God, Division of Foreign Missions
Tibet	Charlie Sturges
Tunisia	Arab World Ministries
Turkey	George K. Otis, Jr.
Turkmenistan	Paul & Mary Filidis
United Arab Emirates	Aramco World
Uzbekistan	Issachar
Vietnam	Open Doors
Western Sahara	Jacqueline Brown
Yemen	

Additional Resources Available From The Sentinel Group

The Sentinel Group offers a variety of unique programs and products for serious intercessors and those interested in missions. The foremost of these is the 20/20 Program which is designed to provide up-to-date information and analysis on countries within the 10/40 Window.

• **20/20 Program**
A monthly Target Update of analysis and prayer points, quarterly audio tapes called "The World in Twenty" and special discounts on Sentinel products are all part of the 20/20 Program. This exclusive membership package asks participants to pray 20 minutes each week and give $20 each month to advance ministry breakthroughs in the world's most spiritually impoverished nations.

• **The Last of the Giants,** by George Otis, Jr. (272 pages)
A well documented analysis of the global challenges that lie ahead for the Church. It explains how demonic powers have deceived millions by supernaturally animating human systems.

• **Spiritual Mapping Field Guide,** by George Otis, Jr. (110 pages)
The only tool available that walks you through an entire spiritual mapping project from beginning to end, covering organization, implementation, selection and development of teams, and data collection and analysis. Contains a total of 220 specific research questions, divided into six specific categories. A must for all local research projects.

For information on these or other products and services, please contact:

> **The Sentinel Group**
> PO Box 6334
> Lynnwood, WA 98036
> Phone: 206-672-2989
> Fax: 206-672-3028